# THE
# MILLIONAIRE'S
# INEXPERIENCED
# LOVE-SLAVE

# THE MILLIONAIRE'S INEXPERIENCED LOVE-SLAVE

BY

MIRANDA LEE

MILLS & BOON®

*Pure reading pleasure*™

First published in Great Britain 2008
Large Print edition 2008
Harlequin Mills & Boon Limited,
Eton House, 18-24 Paradise Road,
Richmond, Surrey TW9 1SR

© Miranda Lee 2008

ISBN: 978 0 263 20083 6

Set in Times Roman 17½ on 21 pt.
16-1008-40412

Printed and bound in Great Britain
by Antony Rowe Ltd, Chippenham, Wiltshire

# CHAPTER ONE

SHARNI was about to have lunch in a very trendy Sydney café when her dead husband walked in!

Her hands shook as they gripped the menu, her heart racing as she stared at Ray with shocked eyes.

Common sense finally kicked in, steadying her thudding heartbeat and whirling head.

Of course it wasn't Ray. Just some man who looked like him.

No, that was an understatement. A huge one. This man didn't just *look* like Ray, he was the spitting image of him. If she hadn't personally identified her husband's lifeless body five years ago, Sharni might have imagined he'd somehow not been on that horrible train that fateful day.

My God, he even walked like Ray!

Sharni's stunned gaze slavishly followed the man as he was shown to a table by the window, not all that far from her own. She kept trying to find something different, something out of sync with her mental memory of the husband she'd loved, and lost.

There was nothing.

Maybe this man was a little taller. And dressed a little better. That rusty brown suede jacket he was wearing looked very expensive. So did his cream silk shirt and smart fawn trousers.

Other than that, everything was the same. The same body shape. The same face. The same hair, both in colour and style.

Ray had had the loveliest hair: thick and wavy, a rich brown with a hint of red. He'd worn it longish, well down onto his shirt collar. She'd loved running her hands through his hair. He'd loved it, too.

Ray's double had exactly the same hair.

Sharni's mouth dried as she waited for him to sit down, waited to see if he would scoop his hair back from his forehead the way Ray had done every time he sat down.

When he did, Sharni only just stopped herself from crying out.

What cruel trick of fate was this?

She'd been doing so well lately, finally feeling capable of moving on with her life. She was working again. Okay, only part-time, but it was better than sitting at home all day.

This trip to Sydney had been another huge step for her. When her sister had given her a weekend package holiday in Sydney for her thirtieth birthday a couple of months ago, Sharni had initially shrunk from the idea.

'I can't leave Mozart for a whole weekend,

Janice,' she'd said straight away, even though she knew this was just an excuse.

Admittedly, Mozart was not the easiest of dogs to mind. He still pined for Ray and could become snappy with other people. John, however—a local vet and Sharni's employer—had a way with the sad little terrier, and would happily mind him for Sharni.

Janice had seen through her excuse and worked on her quite relentlessly. So had Sharni's psychologist, a very kind lady who'd been treating her since she was diagnosed with post-traumatic stress a year ago.

Finally, Sharni agreed to go.

Getting on that damned train yesterday had been difficult, but she'd managed, though she'd grabbed for her mobile the moment the train had moved away from the station, fearing a panic attack coming on. Janice had calmed her down with some sympathetic but sensible talking, and by the time the train had arrived in Sydney Sharni had felt a little like her old confident self. Confident enough, anyway, to have her hair done first thing this morning in the hotel beauty salon before hitting the shops to buy some new clothes. Just casual ones, but more expensive than what she usually bought.

Money wasn't a problem, Sharni hardly having touched the three-million-dollar compensation payment she'd received eighteen months ago.

When she'd walked into this café shortly after one, dressed in one of her new outfits, her spirit had been much more optimistic, and her stomach free from anxiety.

Now, suddenly, her whole world had tipped out of kilter again.

She couldn't stop staring at the handsome stranger with his heartbreakingly familiar features.

Sharni had read somewhere that everyone

had a double in this world, but this was way beyond being a double. If she hadn't known better, she would have said this man was Ray's twin brother.

Her mouth fell open at this last thought. Maybe he *was!* Ray, after all, had been adopted, and had never found out the circumstances behind his birth, saying he didn't want to know.

It wasn't unheard of for twins to be separated at birth and adopted out to different families. Could that be the solution to the startling evidence before her eyes?

She had to find out.

*Had* to.

# CHAPTER TWO

ADRIAN had spotted the attractive brunette through the glass front of the café before coming inside. Despite his having a penchant for attractive brunettes, her presence had nothing to do with his entering. Since moving into his luxury apartment in Bortelli Tower a month ago, Adrian had become a regular at the ground-floor café, partly because of its convenience but mostly because the food was great.

The brunette had looked up when he'd walked in. Looked up and looked right at him. Hard.

At another time, Adrian might have encouraged her by returning solid eye contact, instead of averting his own gaze and pretending he hadn't noticed her interest.

Today, however, he was not in the mood for female company. He was still smarting over what Felicity had said to him last night.

'You should never have a real girlfriend,' she'd thrown at him after he'd been appallingly late for a dinner date. 'What you need is a mistress! Someone on tap who's just there for the sex. Someone you don't have to seriously care about, or consider. What *I* need is a man to love me with his whole heart and soul. The only thing you love, Adrian Palmer, is yourself, and your bloody buildings. I'm sick to death of waiting for you to ring me, or to show up. A good friend warned me about your reputation as a womanising workaholic, but I stupidly thought I could change you. I see now that I can't. So I'm out of here. Maybe one day you'll meet some girl who'll break *your* heart. I sure hope so.'

Being told he had a reputation as a womanising workaholic had shocked Adrian. So had the realisation that he'd hurt Felicity, whom he'd always thought was as career-orientated as he was. Obviously, she'd been more emotionally involved with him than he'd ever been with her.

He should have noticed, he supposed. But he hadn't.

He'd spent a sobering few hours last night, vowing to change his self-centred ways. Which was why he continued to ignore the brunette, despite his male ego being seriously stroked by the way her eyes followed him all the way across the room.

But when he sat down and scooped his hair back out of his own eyes, he caught a glimpse of her reflection in the window.

Wow, she wasn't just attractive. She was *very* attractive, with long glossy black hair framing a pretty face and big brown eyes, which remained flatteringly glued to him.

When he picked up the menu, Adrian couldn't help slanting a quick glance her way. Her eyes immediately dropped away, but not before he saw embarrassment in them.

Thank goodness she wasn't the bold type, he thought, otherwise he might be tempted to go over to her table and ask her to join him for lunch. Which didn't say much for his resolve to mend his womanising ways.

The brunette's action of getting up from her table and approaching his totally surprised Adrian.

'Um…excuse me,' she said, rather hesitantly.

He glanced up from where he'd been pretending to read the menu.

She was even prettier up close, with a heart-shaped face, clear skin, a sweet little turned-up nose and a very kissable mouth. Her figure wasn't half bad, either, shown to advantage in superbly tailored black trousers and a fitted pink jumper, which emphasised her full breasts and tiny waist.

'I'm sorry,' she went on, 'but I have a question which I simply must ask you. You'll probably think it very rude of me, but I...I need to know.'

'Know what?'

'Are you adopted, by any chance?'

Adrian blinked up at her. As a pick-up line, this was a highly original one and very effective. Far better than the old 'Have we met somewhere before?'

Maybe he'd misread her earlier. Maybe she *was* bold. But with enough womanly wiles to be subtle in pursuit of what she wanted.

That was one of the reasons he was drawn to brunettes. He'd always found them interesting. And more of a challenge.

Adrian was a man who liked a challenge.

'No, I'm definitely not,' he replied, and wondered what she'd do now.

She frowned, her expression bewildered.

'Are you absolutely sure? I mean...I don't

want to cause trouble, but some parents don't tell their children they're adopted. Is there any chance at all that you could be?'

Adrian finally appreciated that she wasn't trying to pick him up. Her question was genuine, evidenced by the distress in her quite lovely brown eyes.

'I assure you that I am my parents' biological child, and I have photos to prove it. Besides,' he added, 'my father would never have kept something as important as that from me. He was a real stickler for honesty.'

'That's incredible, then,' she said. 'Truly incredible.'

'What is?' he asked, curious now.

She shook her head. 'No matter,' she muttered rather dispiritedly. 'I'm sorry for bothering you.'

'No, don't go,' he said when she began to turn away. There was a mystery here to solve.

Adrian loved mysteries almost as much as challenges.

'You can't leave me up in the air like this. I need to know why you thought I was adopted. Sit down and tell me.'

She glanced worriedly back at her table where she'd left her handbag, along with several shopping bags.

'Why don't you get your things and join me for lunch?' he suggested.

She stared back at him for a long moment. 'I'm sorry. I…I don't think I can do that.'

'Why not?'

Her eyes grew agitated, as did her hands, their wringing action bringing his attention to her wedding and engagement rings.

The realisation that she was married disappointed Adrian more than anything had in a long time.

'Because your husband wouldn't like it?' he said, nodding towards her left hand.

Mentioning her husband seemed to agitate her more.

'I…I don't have a husband any more,' she blurted out. 'I'm a widow.'

Adrian found it hard to hide his satisfaction at this news.

'I'm sorry,' he said, and tried to sound sincere.

'He was killed in an accident. I…I identified his body. I…Oh, God, I…I have to sit down.'

She slumped into the chair opposite him, her pale skin having gone a pasty grey colour.

Adrian hastened to pour her a glass of chilled water from the carafe on the table. She gulped it down, after which she shook her head again.

'You must think me mad. It's just that you…you look so much like him.'

'Like who?' he said just before the penny dropped.

'Ray.'

'Your dead husband.'

'Yes. The resemblance is uncanny. You… you could be twins.'

'I see,' Adrian said. 'So that's why you wanted to know if I was adopted.'

'It…it seemed the only solution.'

'They say everyone has a double, you know.'

'Yes, yes, so I've heard. That must be the case here. But it was still a shock.'

'I can imagine.'

'Actually, now that I see you up close, your features are not exactly the same as Ray's. Some things are a bit different. I'm just not sure what…' Her head tipped to one side as she studied his face.

'How long ago was your husband killed?' he asked, thinking it had to be recent.

'Five years.' ·

Adrian frowned. Five years! And she was grieving still. She must have loved him a lot. Still, it was high time she moved on. She was still young, and very lovely. Very, very lovely, he thought with a familiar prickling in his loins.

'Ray was killed in a train derailment in the Blue Mountains,' she explained sadly. 'Several people died that day.'

'I remember that. It was very tragic. And preventable, if I recall rightly.'

'Yes. The train was going too fast for the conditions of the track.'

'I'm very sorry for your loss. Did you and your husband have any children?' She looked old enough to have had children. In her late twenties, or maybe thirty.

'What? No,' she said a bit brusquely. 'No, we didn't. Look, I…I think I'd better get back to my own table. I'm sorry to have bothered you. Thank you for the water.'

Adrian extended his right hand over the table towards her before she could escape.

'My name is Adrian Palmer,' he introduced himself. 'I'm an only child, son of Dr Arthur Palmer, general practitioner, now deceased, and Mrs May Palmer, one-time nurse, long retired. I'm thirty-six years old, unmarried and a successful architect. I designed this building.'

She stared at his outstretched hand, then up at his face. 'Why are you telling me all this?'

'So that I won't be a stranger. That is why you refused to have lunch with me, isn't it?'

# CHAPTER THREE

SHARNI didn't know what to say. Because her refusal to have lunch with Adrian had nothing to do with his being a stranger.

'Oh, I see,' he said knowingly, his hand dropping back to the table. 'It's because I remind you too much of your husband.'

'Yes,' she choked out. And it wasn't just his looks. She still could not forget the way he'd swept his hair back from his forehead. Not to mention the way he walked, with long, loose-limbed strides.

Just like Ray.

'Is that such a bad thing?' he asked gently.

'Well, no, I guess not…'

'Now that you're over the shock of our physical similarities, I'm sure you can see lots of differences.'

His voice was certainly different. Ray had had a rather strong Australian accent. This man—this Adrian Palmer—spoke with a voice that betrayed a private-school education. Not plumy, but cultured and refined.

He also had a confident air about him that Ray had never possessed. Her husband had been a quiet, shy man whose emotional neediness had appealed to Sharni's nurturing nature.

It was ironic, however, that his double was an architect, the profession Ray had always aspired to but which he'd never felt he had the ability to enter. Instead, he'd become a draughtsman.

'Please don't say no,' his double said, and smiled a smile that was totally unlike Ray. It was a seductive smile, showing dazzlingly white teeth and an almost irresistible charm.

Sharni was surprised to find herself wavering. Maybe because, suddenly, he didn't remind her of Ray at all.

'It's only lunch,' he added, blue eyes twinkling up at her.

Ray's eyes had rarely twinkled, she recalled. They'd been quiet pools whilst this man's resembled a sparkling sea.

'All right,' she agreed before she could think better of it.

He was up out of his chair in a flash, getting her things before she could hardly draw breath.

'Been clothes shopping, have we?' he said breezily as he placed her carrier bags on the spare chair next to her.

'What? Oh, yes. I...I still have some more to do this afternoon.'

'Right.'

When he sat back down, he swept his hair back with his hand again, leaving Sharni speechless once more.

He smiled at her across the table. 'You'd better introduce yourself.'

'What?' she said blankly.

'Your name. Or do you want to remain a mystery woman?'

Sharni gave herself a mental shake. 'There's not much mystery about me,' she said with a small laugh. 'It's Sharni. Sharni Johnson.'

'Sharni,' he repeated. 'That's a most unusual name. But it suits you. Ah, here's the waiter for our order. Do you know what you want, Sharni, or would you like to take a risk and let me order for you? It's not too much of a risk, as I've eaten here several times before, haven't I, Roland?'

'Indeed, you have, Mr Palmer,' Roland answered.

'Very well,' she said, thinking to herself that Adrian Palmer's confidence bordered on arrogance.

'You like seafood?' he asked as he studied the menu.

'Yes.'

'What about wine? Do you like white wine?'

'Yes.'

'In that case, Roland, we'll have the steamed bream fillets with side salad, followed by the almond and plum tart. With cream. But first, bring us a bottle of that white I had the other day. You know the one. It's a Sauvignon Blanc from Margaret River.'

'Right away, Mr Palmer.'

Sharni had to admire his *savoir-faire*. It had been a long time since a man had ordered a meal for her with such panache. Ray had been a bit of a waffler when it came to deciding what to order in a restaurant. Making decisions had not been her husband's forte. That had been her domain.

Or it had once. Sharni's decision-making capabilities had disintegrated shortly after she'd won the compensation case. It was as though she'd stayed strong whilst she'd sought justice. But the moment the verdict had come down in her favour, she'd gone to mush.

Winning three million dollars compensation had proved to be a hollow victory, because all the money in the world would never make up for the loss of her husband and her beautiful little baby.

Still, life did go on, as Janice kept telling her.

Her sister would have been proud of her for not running away just now. Though she might be suspicious of Sharni's motives for agreeing to having lunch with Ray's double. Janice might think she was pretending Ray were still alive, and nothing had changed at all.

That was not the case. This man might look like Ray, but he was nothing like him in personality. The only time she could ever pretend he was Ray was if he didn't speak. Or if he was asleep.

'You really designed this building?' she asked once the waiter departed.

'I certainly did. Do you like it?'

'To be honest, I haven't had a proper look at it. I was walking past on this side of the street, smelt food, realised it was lunch-time and came in for something to eat.'

'After lunch, I'll give you the royal tour. I live on one of the upper floors.'

Lord, she thought. What a fast worker!

'I don't think so, Mr Palmer.'

'Adrian,' he corrected with another of those seductive smiles of his.

Sharni had to confess that she found his attention flattering. She also found him very attractive. Which was only logical. Ray's looks had been the first thing to attract her. Physically, he'd stood out in a crowd. It wasn't till she'd talked to him that she'd realised how shy he was.

That had appealed to her at the time. Nowadays, however, she would probably go for a more confident, outgoing kind of man, the kind who would look after her, not the other way around.

But she wasn't ready yet to leap back into the dating world, especially not with the dead spit of her dead husband. And *certainly* not with such an accomplished ladies' man.

Sharni knew a womaniser when she met one.

'I don't think so, Adrian,' she said quite coolly. 'Lunch is all I agreed to. Take it or leave it.'

He sighed. But it didn't sound like a defeated sigh. Sharni suspected he was already thinking of another tack to take.

The wine's arrival brought that confident smile back to his handsome face, reminding her not to drink too much. She'd gone through a stage a year or so back when she'd drunk far too much. Nowadays, she limited her alcoholic intake, having been advised that alcohol was not good for depression, which she fell into every time her thoughts dwelled on all that she had lost.

It had been too much to bear. First her husband, and then their baby. Oh, God…

'Penny for your thoughts.'

Sharni gritted her teeth as she glanced up, then reached for her glass of wine. To hell with being sensible, she thought, I need this drink today.

Adrian watched her sweep the glass up to her lips and take a deep swallow.

'They're worth a lot more than that,' she replied. Somewhat bitterly, he thought.

'I'm not sure what you mean there.'

She took another gulp of wine before answering. 'I was thinking about the compensation I received from the Rail Authority.'

'I hope they gave you a decent amount.'

Her laugh was very definitely bitter. 'They weren't going to. So I got myself a lawyer and sued them.'

'Good for you.'

'I was very lucky. My lawyer was brilliant. A woman. She was so incensed by my case that she gave me her services, *pro bono*.'

'That doesn't happen too often.'

'Jordan was wonderfully kind to me.'

Adrian's eyebrows arched in surprise. 'Jordan as in Jordan Gray of Stedley & Parkinsons?'

Sharni's wineglass stopped in mid-air. 'Why, yes. Do you know Jordan?'

'She's married to Gino Bortelli, the Italian businessman who commissioned me to design this building. It's called the Bortelli Tower.'

'Good heavens! When did all this happen? Jordan wasn't married when she represented me.'

'About a year or so back. It seems Jordan and Gino knew each other years before and ran into each other again by accident when Gino was up here on business. Just in time, since Jordan was about to become engaged to another man. Anyway, to cut a long story short, true love won out. They've not long returned from an extended honeymoon in Italy. But they don't live in Sydney. Their home is in Melbourne.'

'What a shame. I would have loved to catch up with Jordan.'

'I can give you their home phone number, if you like.'

'Oh, no. No, I wouldn't impose like that. I was just a client after all, not a close friend. But I'm glad to hear Jordan's happily married. I presume she is happy?'

'Very. She and Gino have a baby already. A boy. They called him Joe.'

'How lovely,' she said, her eyes going all misty for a moment. 'I'm so glad for her.'

'How much compensation did she get you?' Adrian asked. 'Or is that a rude question?'

'Three million.'

He whistled. 'That's a nice tidy sum. I hope you've invested it wisely.'

'It's safe.' Safe, sitting in a bank account that paid a reasonable rate of interest and had absolutely no risk at all.

'Do you still live in the Blue Mountains?' he asked her.

'Yes. On the outskirts of Katoomba.'

'So you're just down here in Sydney today to shop?'

'Not exactly. My sister thought I needed a little holiday. She gave me a weekend package at one of Sydney's boutique hotels as a birthday present.'

'You mean it's your birthday today?' What a perfect excuse to take her out this evening. If he could persuade her to go, of course!

'No. My birthday was quite a few weeks ago.'

'And you were?'

She slanted him a sharp glance. 'Now that

*is* a rude question. You should never ask a woman her age.'

He smiled. 'I thought that only applied when they reached forty.'

'Not in my book.'

'Fair enough. So what do you do? Or don't you work any more?'

'I'm a veterinary assistant. But I'm only working part-time these days.'

Why was that? he wondered. Because she didn't need the money, or because she was still traumatised by the tragedy of her husband's death, or perhaps the subsequent trial?

There was something in her eyes when she mentioned the compensation that told him the trial had been just that. A trial. Adrian was well aware of how stressful it was to go to court over anything. He himself had had to sue a client once, and it hadn't been pleasant. How much worse when it involved the tragic death of a loved one.

Her air of sadness touched him. But so did her Madonna-like beauty. It was damned intriguing, the effect Sharni was having on him. He could not recall ever feeling quite like this. She brought out the gallant in him. More than anything he wanted to make her smile. Wanted to give her pleasure.

More like give yourself pleasure, a sarcastic inner voice piped up. You want to get her into bed. That's the bottom line. That's always the bottom line with you, Adrian.

Adrian frowned. Normally, he would agree. But not this time. This time, something was different. He didn't want to seduce Sharni so much as have the opportunity to spend more time with her. He wanted to get to know her. *Really* know her, not just in bed.

'I wanted to become a vet,' she went on, 'but my marks at school weren't good enough. I never was one to study. I'm a practical, hands-on kind of person.'

'I don't think it matters what you do in life, as long as you enjoy what you're doing.'

'You obviously enjoy being an architect,' she said, and he smiled.

'Does it show?'

'You seem a happy man.'

'I love my work,' he said. 'Too much, some people would say.'

Even his own mother thought he was way too obsessive.

But that was his nature. Adrian could never do things by half. When something interested him, he became consumed, body and soul.

This woman interested him, in ways no woman ever had before.

This in itself was intriguing. What was it about her that made her so interesting to him? Yes, she was very pretty, but he met lots of pretty girls. She wasn't super-clever, or super sophisticated, or super sexy, as Felicity had been.

Aside from being a brunette, Sharni was different from every woman he'd ever dated. They'd all been highly educated career girls whom he'd met through his work. Felicity had been a top interior designer. Before that, there'd been a female architect or two, a corporate lawyer, a computer expert and one super-smart marketing manager.

There'd not been one veterinary assistant who lived in the bush and blushed when caught in the act of looking at a man.

'You're staring at me,' she said in a low voice.

Adrian smiled. 'Well, that makes us even. You've stared at me a good deal today.'

His counter-attack clearly flustered her. 'Yes, but you know why.'

'Are you saying you only find me attractive because I remind you of your husband?'

She blinked her surprise at his directness. 'Who said I find you attractive?'

'Your eyes told me. The same way my eyes are telling you I find you attractive.'

Her cheeks went pink. 'Please don't flirt with me, Adrian.'

'Why not?'

'Because I…I can't handle it.'

'Are you saying I'm the first man to pay you this kind of attention since your husband died?'

'I haven't been with another man since Ray, if that's what you're asking. I don't go out. And I don't date.'

Her admission stunned Adrian. Five years of living by herself. Five years without male company, or sex of any kind. It wasn't natural. Or healthy.

'I find that terribly sad, Sharni.'

'Life is sad,' she said, and took another sip of wine.

'You are coming out with me tonight,' he stated firmly.

Her eyes widened before meeting his over the rim of her glass.

'Am I?'

There was enough wavering in those two words, and in her eyes, to satisfy Adrian.

'Absolutely,' he said, just as their meals arrived.

# CHAPTER FOUR

'COFFEE or tea?' Adrian asked.

Sharni looked up from where she'd been devouring the last bite of the simply delicious almond and plum tart.

Roland was standing by their table, patiently waiting for her decision.

'Coffee, please,' she said after dabbing her mouth with the white linen serviette. 'Cappuccino.'

'I'll have a short black,' Adrian told the waiter who swiftly departed to do their bidding.

Sharni could see why Adrian came here often. Not only was the food great, but the service was very quick.

'So where would you like me to take you tonight?' he asked.

Sharni sighed. She should have known he'd come back to that sooner or later. He'd very cleverly lulled her into a false sense of security over their meal by stopping the flirtatious talk and steering any conversation onto more impersonal topics such as food, politics and the weather.

Now, his eyes were back on hers again, their focus disturbingly intense. But oh-so-flattering.

He was right. She did find him attractive. How could she not? But Adrian's charm for her was not just physical. It was the way he made her feel, as if he found her the most fascinating female in the world.

There was no use pretending she didn't want to go out with him tonight. But the prospect was accompanied by a measure of fear. What if he tried to seduce her? What if he succeeded?

For the last five years Sharni had lived a

sexless existence, that part of her body having totally shut down. She hadn't had a period since she'd lost her baby, various doctors suggesting her lack of hormonal activity was caused by shock and grief. To be honest, she hadn't given sex a second thought in ages.

Now, suddenly, she was very definitely thinking about it.

Was the wine over lunch to blame, or this man's amazing resemblance to Ray?

She'd been sexually attracted to Ray from the moment. But they'd dated for several weeks before they'd slept together. Even then, it had been left up to her to make the first move, Ray having been chronically shy in the bedroom department.

Not so this man, she thought as she glanced across the table. He would know all the right moves.

If only he didn't look so much like Ray…

'We could have an early dinner then go to a

show afterwards,' he said, breaking into her ongoing silence. 'Or a show first and supper afterwards, if you'd prefer. Have you seen *The Phantom of the Opera*? The musical, not the movie. They say this latest revival is better than all previous productions.'

Sharni had always loved the story of the phantom. She thought it highly romantic. Andrew Lloyd Webber's music was marvellous too, echoing the uncontrollable passions that consumed the main character.

'No, I haven't,' she admitted. 'But—'

'No buts, Sharni,' he broke in. 'Your sister gave you this weekend in Sydney so that you could enjoy yourself. It's not much fun sitting in a hotel room by yourself, especially on a Saturday night. If you're still worried about my being a stranger, then I'll ring Jordan right now so that she can vouch for me.' To show he meant it, Adrian pulled a silver mobile phone from his jacket pocket and flipped it open.

'No, no, you don't have to do that,' she said hurriedly. 'I can see you're not some kind of creep.'

His handsome face showed shock. 'I should hope not.'

'I suppose it wouldn't be much fun sitting in the hotel room tonight all by myself.'

'So you'll come?'

'You've talked me into it.'

'Fantastic,' he said, smiling.

Her heart fluttered. So did her stomach. He really was utterly gorgeous when he smiled like that.

'What about *The Phantom*?' he asked. 'Is that a goer, or would you prefer a different show? A play, perhaps.'

'No, no, I love musicals.'

'Would you like me to book dinner before or supper afterwards?'

'I think supper afterwards.'

'That's great,' he said with a satisfied glint

in his bright blue eyes. 'Now, after we finish our coffee, I'm going to take you across the street to a spot where you can have a proper look at my pride and joy. Then, after you've been suitably impressed with my brilliance at designing the outsides of the building, I'll give you a quick tour of the inside.'

'It'll have to be very quick,' she told him. 'I'll need some time before the shops close to buy a suitable outfit to wear tonight. I only bought casual clothes this morning.'

'I could come shopping with you, if you like?'

Sharni could see he was very much a takeover type of person. 'Don't you have something else you should be doing this afternoon?'

'Not really,' he said. 'I finished my latest plan to my satisfaction late yesterday. I always give myself a complete break between projects.'

'For how long?'

'At least a day,' he said, laughing. 'So what do you say? I have good taste in women's clothes.'

'I hate taking anyone clothes shopping with me,' she said quite truthfully. 'I prefer to trust my own taste.'

'And an excellent taste it is, too,' he complimented, his gaze admiring as he looked her up and down.

Sharni could not help smiling. 'I think you are an incorrigible charmer.'

'And I think you could do with a bit of charming. Ah, our coffee's coming.'

'Just as well. I need sobering up. I think I'm a little tipsy.' It wasn't like her to feel this light-hearted. Or this happy.

Once they'd finished their coffee, Adrian saw to the bill whilst Sharni picked up her shopping bags and stood up.

Oh, dear, she thought when her head whirled alarmingly. There was no doubt about it. She'd had *way* too much to drink!

# CHAPTER FIVE

'OH, MY!' Sharni exclaimed. 'That is one magnificent building.'

They were standing together on the pavement across the street, Adrian holding her shopping bags whilst Sharni shielded her eyes from the sun's rays and gazed up at Bortelli Tower.

'I never imagined anything this big, or this beautiful!' she said with ego-stroking awe in her voice. 'I love the grey colour of the glass you've used.'

'The manufacturer calls it smokescreen. Naturally no UV rays can get through. Or heat, or cold.'

'It's gorgeous. And the hexagonal shape is just so unusual.'

'I like it.'

She smiled up at him. 'I dare say you do, since *you* designed it. How many floors are there?'

'Twenty-five. The first ten are devoted to office space. There's a health club and heated pool on the eleventh floor. After that, it's all privately owned apartments, with lots of balconies to take advantage of the views.'

'I bet they're very expensive.'

'They are. But Gino sold every one of them off the plan.'

'Wow! That's incredible. So what floor do you live on?'

'The twenty-fifth.'

'The twenty-fifth.' She frowned momentarily before gaping up at him. 'You live in the *penthouse*?'

Adrian loved her sweet surprise. 'It was part

of the contract I made with Gino when he commissioned my services.'

'But a penthouse right in the middle of Sydney has to be worth millions! I didn't realise architects got paid that much.'

'Some of us do,' he replied, thinking of the seven-figure fee he usually commanded for this type of job. 'But Gino asked me to oversee the construction of the building as well, so the penthouse came as a bonus.'

'Do you do that kind of job often?'

'Sometimes. It's great watching my designs take shape. But projects of this scale take a special sort of commitment. That's why I was able to negotiate such a good deal with this one. Come on, let's go back over the road and I'll take you up onto the rooftop. The view from up there is incomparable on a clear winter's day.'

'Will that take long?' she asked. 'It's getting on for two-thirty.'

'I could have you up there in five minutes,'

he said. 'And back down here shopping in fifteen, tops. All the lifts are the latest high-speed design.'

She still hesitated.

Adrian understood why. Sharni was a nice girl. And nice girls didn't swan up to a man's apartment within a couple of hours of meeting him. Not even if that apartment was a penthouse worth millions.

'I promise I won't make a pass, if that's what you're thinking,' he reassured her. 'I just want to show you the view.'

This was only partly true. What he actually wanted, more than anything, was the opportunity to spend a little more time with her. She delighted him as no woman had ever delighted him. It was a serious shame that she wouldn't let him go shopping with her. He would have loved helping her choose the right outfit for tonight. A sexy little black dress, perhaps. With long tight sleeves, a short, bottom-hugging skirt and a low-cut neckline. Very low. The kind of neckline that needed a decent bust to show it off. Like the one Sharni had.

Adrian gave himself a mental shake when his train of thought began transferring messages to his body. Highly arousing messages.

Thank goodness it was winter and he was wearing a jacket.

His sudden upsurge in testosterone, however, urged him to take more control of this situation.

'Come on,' he said firmly, cupping his free hand around her elbow and steering her back towards the pedestrian crossing at the corner.

She didn't protest, he noted, going along with what he wanted. As a woman sometimes did when a man took the helm.

'This way,' he said once they reached the kerb, and led her along the street frontage towards the main entrance of the building. On the way, they had to pass two shops, one of which was a very exclusive ladies' fashion boutique.

As luck would have it, there, on a mannequin in the window, was an outfit that was absolutely perfect for going to the theatre. It wasn't totally black. Only the skirt, which fell in floaty folds to mid-calf length. The top was purple, and beaded, with three-quarter sleeves and a deep, crossover neckline, which was subtly sexy.

Not so subtle were the black five-inch heels that the window-dresser had put on the model's feet.

'Oh!' Sharni exclaimed, and ground to an admiring halt in front of the window.

'You'd look good in that,' Adrian said straight away.

More than good, but he didn't want to gush. Women didn't like men who gushed.

'You really think so?'

'I really think so,' he said coolly. 'Let's go inside and you can try it on.'

# CHAPTER SIX

SHARNI looked at herself in the dressing-room mirror and thought, Wow, I really do look good, just like Adrian said I would.

Not just good, Sharni amended as she turned this way and that, setting the black chiffon skirt swinging around her legs. I look sexy.

And I *feel* sexy.

Was it the wine she'd drunk over lunch? Or because the salesgirl had suggested she take off her bra?

Sharni's curves rarely went without support, despite their not being saggy in any way. She'd never been inclined to show off her breasts in public, Ray having always liked her conservative way of dressing.

What would he think if he saw you in this top? Sharni wondered as she stared at her exposed cleavage.

He'd be shocked, she knew. Shocked and disapproving.

She felt shocked, too. Not by the way she looked, but by the way she felt.

Unbearably excited.

A tap on the dressing-cubicle door sent a nervous gasp punching from her lips. 'Yes?'

'Your husband wants you to come out and show him what you look like,' the salesgirl called through the door.

Sharni should have denied he was her husband. But she didn't.

Instead, she swallowed, then opened the door.

'Oh, no,' the salesgirl said, glancing down at her stockinged feet. 'You can't go out there like that. I'll get you some shoes. What size are you?'

'Seven.'

'In that case the ones on the model should fit you. Wait here. I'll go get them.'

The shoes were produced, with Sharni having to sit down to put them on. They were cripplingly high and sinfully sexy, each having a narrow strap across the front, with two more straps attached at the back which wound round her ankles and tied in a bow. She'd never in her life worn anything like them.

Sharni teetered at first when she stood up, having to keep her steps small as she made her way very slowly out to where Adrian was waiting, leaning against a counter in the middle of the boutique.

He straightened on seeing her, his blue eyes narrowing as they raked over her from top to toe.

Never had any man looked at her in quite that way before, not even Ray. The intensity of his gaze overwhelmed her, making her knees go to jelly.

'Walk up and down a few times,' Adrian commanded in that masterful way that made Sharni's stomach flutter wildly.

Not a totally unknown state for her these days. But her nervous tummy was usually due to anxiety, not excitement.

Once she found her balance, her hips surprised her by developing a decidedly sexy sway. The effect on her psyche was amazing. Suddenly, she was a *femme fatale*; a temptress who commanded all male eyes be upon her.

But there was only one male Sharni wanted looking at her at that moment. And he very definitely was, with glittering blue eyes that evoked a heat in her that felt both shameful and shameless.

'I told you you'd look great in that,' he said, his voice low and sexy.

Sharni's heart quickened its beat.

'She'll take it,' he told the salesgirl before Sharni had a chance to come to a decision.

'The shoes as well?' the girl asked Adrian.

'Absolutely,' came his crisp reply.

'You…you do realise I'll probably never ever wear these shoes again,' she said, even as she admired them.

'Of course you will,' he countered. 'Every time you wear that fantastic outfit. Now go get changed, like a good girl, while I fix up the bill.'

Sharni flushed with the weirdest mixture of pleasure and embarrassment. 'I can't possibly let you pay for my clothes, Adrian,' she protested. 'It's not right.'

'What's not right about it? I can well afford a few hundred dollars.'

'That's not the point!'

He smiled, then reached out to stroke a tender fingertip down her nose. 'All right, sweet Sharni,' he said, his eyes soft on hers.

'You can pay for your own clothes. But this is the last time you get to pay for anything when you're with me. Off you go and change now. But don't be too long. Now that you have something suitable to wear tonight, you don't have to waste the afternoon shopping. We can spend it together, doing something more interesting.'

He was like a steamroller, Sharni thought as she changed back into her trousers and jumper.

But it was exciting, being swept along like this.

What did he have in mind for this afternoon? she wondered momentarily before deciding she wouldn't wonder. Or worry. About anything. Not even what it was about her that interested him.

After all, a man like Adrian would have no shortage of women—more beautiful than herself—throwing themselves at him.

This last thought did give Sharni something

to worry about. Surely Adrian must have a girlfriend. Surely!

Should she ask him and risk bringing an abrupt ending to their time together today? Or avoid the question altogether?

Sharni was still dithering over this dilemma when she emerged from the dressing room.

Adrian's satisfaction at the way things were going was temporarily derailed when he saw the expression on Sharni's face.

He didn't like whatever was going on in her mind, but didn't say a word whilst she paid for her purchases. Experience had taught him never to tamper with a woman's mind. They were minefields that could blow up in your face when least expected.

'Let me take a couple of those,' she said when they left the shop with him carrying all her parcels.

'If you insist,' he returned, thinking he would need a hand free to extract his key-card for the lifts.

'I insist,' she said, and took the two bags from the boutique.

They walked in silence over to the main entrance to the tower.

'This way,' Adrian said, the automatic doors opening when he stepped forward onto the entry mat.

Their reflection in the glass, however, showed that Sharni had ground to a halt behind him, that worried look still on her face.

Gritting his teeth against a flash of irritation, he turned and rejoined her on the pavement. 'What is it?' he asked. 'What's wrong?'

'I…I have to ask you something.'

'What?'

'Is there anyone in your life who would be upset with you taking me out tonight?'

'A girlfriend, you mean.'

'Yes,' she said, her eyes fixed unswervingly on his.

Man, but she would be a difficult person to lie to. Not that he had to, thank God. Felicity was definitely no longer his girlfriend.

'Absolutely not.'

If anything, her frown increased with his answer. 'I…I do find that hard to believe.'

Adrian's frustration was tempered by the flattery within her statement. 'There was someone till recently,' he said, but refrained from saying how recently. 'Let me assure you that there's no one who could object to my taking you out tonight.'

Her sigh showed genuine relief. 'That's good, then.'

'And if I'd said there *was* someone?' he couldn't resist asking.

Adrian empathised with the flash of indecision that crossed her face, because it echoed his feelings for her. Never in his life had he felt this strongly about a woman within hours of meeting her. He'd been attracted at first sight in the past. But this was more than that.

If there'd been some new man in Sharni's life, he would still have pursued her.

'No need to answer that,' he went on before she could put her obviously muddled thoughts into words. 'It was a silly question. Come on. I want to get you upstairs while the sun's still shining.'

# CHAPTER SEVEN

SHARNI TRIED to relax during the ride up to the twenty-fifth floor, but it was impossible. Something had taken possession of her when she'd paraded herself in front of Adrian in that sexy outfit, something that she'd pushed to one side when she'd changed back into her less sexy clothes, but which had emerged with a vengeance once she discovered Adrian didn't have a girlfriend.

That something was desire. The desire to be kissed, and touched, and made love to.

Not since Ray had she met a man who'd made her feel remotely like this. Of course, Adrian did look exactly like Ray, which could explain the heat washing through her. Her body could be reacting to old tapes.

But somehow, Sharni wasn't convinced. The sexual hunger consuming her body at this moment was much more intense than anything she'd felt with Ray. When Adrian asked her what she would have done if he'd said he did have a girlfriend, Sharni had been shocked by the realisation that she would still have come up here with him.

He'd promised not to make a pass. Yet she wanted him to. Quite desperately.

The lift whizzed to a halt on the twenty-fifth floor in no time at all, Sharni having no space to come to terms with the shockingly aroused state she was in.

When the lifts doors opened an extremely tense Sharni followed Adrian into an elegant, marble-floored foyer, which had a domed ceiling and a spectacularly modern chandelier hanging from it. Straight ahead were double

French doors through which she could see a huge and equally elegant living area.

'Put your parcels down here,' Adrian suggested, placing the ones he was carrying beneath a glass-topped hall table on their right.

She did so, then immediately asked him where the bathroom was.

Suddenly, she needed to go. Quite badly.

'That's the guest powder room,' he said, indicating a door on her left. 'When you're finished go on through into the lounge room and make yourself comfortable. I'll join you shortly,' he said, turning away and leaving her through the French doors.

The powder room had everything a multi-million-dollar penthouse would have: marble floors and walls, stylish firings and gold taps.

After she'd washed her hands, Sharni spent a couple of extra minutes combing her hair and refreshing her pink lipstick, all the while struggling to find some composure.

'I *look* the same as the girl who left the beauty salon this morning,' she said agitatedly to the reflection in the mirror. 'But I don't *feel* the same.'

Meeting Adrian had changed her. In ways she had yet to appreciate, or understand.

All Sharni knew was that she wanted Adrian as she had never wanted Ray.

This admission brought a wave of guilt. Because she'd had a good sex life with her husband, who'd been a gentle and considerate lover. On top of that, she'd loved him very much.

She didn't love Adrian. She didn't even know him. Not really.

You didn't get to know anyone properly in a couple of hours.

No doubt he'd been presenting his best face to her so far today, impressing her with his decisiveness, his charm, and yes, the evidence of his material success. What girl wouldn't be bowled over by a millionaire's penthouse in the middle of Sydney?

But did all that explain the sexual cravings that were currently consuming her?

Sharni shivered as she stared into her too bright eyes and flushed cheeks.

'What's happening to you?' she whispered.

Adrian waited impatiently in the living room for the powder-room door to open. In the end, he took off his jacket—the apartment was centrally heated—and draped it over the back of a chair, after which he started pacing around the room.

She was certainly taking long enough, he thought, his gaze continually darting her way. Finally, the door did open, but she was slow to emerge, moving over to place her handbag on the hall table before turning and walking even more slowly through the open French doors.

When her eyes met his across the room,

Adrian immediately regretted his earlier promise not to make a pass.

Damn it all. Why had he chosen today of all days to play the gentleman? He never had before, not when he saw that look in a woman's eyes.

Sharni was just as attracted to him as he was to her, he was sure of it. Given the situation, there was nothing to stop either of them acting upon the chemistry sizzling between them. They were both adults, after all. Both free to do what they liked, in bed and out.

Such thinking fuelled the passion that was already simmering just below the surface of Adrian's cool façade. If only he hadn't made that rash promise.

As she came towards him her hip-swinging walk stirred his hormones further. His belly contracted as he struggled to get a handle on his increasing desire, Adrian reminding himself that at least he hadn't made any promises about tonight. He only had to wait a few hours and he'd be able to pull her into his arms and kiss her senseless without feeling like a total heel.

'You have a very beautiful place,' she said, finally dragging her eyes away from his to glance around. 'You must have had it professionally decorated.'

'A decorator came with the deal,' he said. By the name of Felicity—that was how they'd met.

Frankly, he wasn't that thrilled by what Felicity had done. Her colour palette had been on the bland side: mostly pale, neutral shades with only the occasional touches of green and yellow.

He'd given her a totally free hand, because he'd already been preoccupied with his next project at the time the penthouse was being decorated. Now, he had to live with the results.

'It's lovely,' Sharni said.

'It'll do,' came his indifferent reply. 'Come

on. Come out onto the terrace.' Before I forget all my noble intentions and pounce!

Adrian slid back the nearest glass door, stepped slightly to one side and waved her through.

She glanced up at him from under long lashes as she hurried past, her expression a tantalising mixture of femininity and fear.

Adrian's flesh reacted excitedly to both. Which rather shocked him. Why should her fear arouse him? Unless, of course, it wasn't *him* she was afraid of. What if she was afraid of herself? What if she, too, was being besieged with almost uncontrollable desire?

He followed her out onto the terrace, his mind in turmoil as his frustrated body began to create havoc with his conscience.

'Oh my!' she said breathlessly as she gazed, first at the rooftop pool and spa, then out at the view.

Adrian already knew it was a magnificent

view, the penthouse's enviable position pro-
viding a wide panorama of the city, with
Sydney's famous icons clearly visible: the
Harbour Bridge, the Opera house and the
Botanical Gardens, all of them bathed at that
moment in the soft afternoon sunshine.

But none of them drew his eyes. Only her.

It was no use. His desire was too strong to
deny. To hell with his promise not to make a
pass. To hell with everything!

When he moved up behind her and cupped
his hands possessively over her shoulders, her
head jerked around to stare up at him with
widening eyes.

'I'm sorry,' he said thickly. 'But I have to do
this.'

Sharni froze as he turned her into his arms.

The surety that he was going to kiss her
brought panic. Because she knew, if he did,
she would be lost.

Her eyes pleaded for mercy but he ignored them, his left hand lifting to slide around her neck under her hair, his right hand cupping her chin, holding her face solidly captive in readiness for his descending mouth.

Her lips parted in a belated effort to voice a protest. But all that accomplished was to leave her mouth more vulnerable to his advances.

His kiss was far from gentle, in no way resembling Ray's kisses. Adrian's lips ground against hers, his kiss a branding on her mouth and *inside* her mouth. The forays of his tongue were aggressive and deeply sensual. Soon her head was spinning, her heart thudding loudly behind her ribs.

One kiss dissolved into another, then another, his hands dropping from her face to wrap around her back, crushing her against him. Her own arms responded by looping around his neck, her fingers entwining together, then pressing down to stop his head from lifting.

She didn't want him to stop kissing her. Not ever!

He didn't stop. He somehow managed to keep kissing her, even after he scooped her up off the terrace and carried her inside. By the time he lowered her to her feet—in the master bedroom, she was to discover later—Sharni's desire had moved beyond the need for just kisses. By then her body was sending messages to her brain for more intimate contact than mouth to mouth. She needed him inside her. And she needed him *now*.

Her mouth wrenched away from his, her desire-glazed eyes dropping to the black leather belt around his waist. It didn't seem shameless to undo that belt, just necessary.

Her fingers were clumsy with their speed. His, too. Together they stripped each other from the waist down, their carnal urgency having no patience with undressing any further than necessary.

Neither of them stopped to think once enough clothes had been removed. They fell onto the middle of the bed; he was on top of her. Sharni cried out at his rough penetration, a cry that echoed her desperate need. She didn't care that he wasn't gentle or considerate; she wanted him to pound into her. Wanted him to fill her to the utmost, over and over.

Which he did. Madly. Mercilessly.

It was wild and totally without thought. A raw, primal mating. An expression, not of love, but of the most primitive lust.

They came together, an experience that Sharni had never had before.

For an amazing length of time, her body was buffeted by twin pleasures: that of her own flesh spasming in helpless ecstasy, and the feel of his explosive, almost violent release.

The sensations were stunningly satisfying. Mind-blowing, in fact. Sharni was in seventh heaven.

Till Adrian muttered a four letter crudity.

All of a sudden, reality returned with a soul-shattering thud. Because what he'd just said was exactly what they'd just done.

Her eyes flew open to look almost despairingly up at him.

'Sorry,' he grated out.

Shame made her grimace, her head turning away as a distressed sound punched from her lips.

'Don't do that,' he bit out. 'What we just did, Sharni. It wasn't wrong. Foolhardy perhaps, since I didn't use a condom. But not wrong.'

Shock sent her head whipping back to face him. His not using a condom simply hadn't occurred to her. But now that it had…

'Oh, God,' she sobbed, and stuffed a white-knuckled fist against her mouth.

'I promise you,' he reassured her hurriedly. 'that I do usually practise safe sex. God knows what happened just now, because it's never happened before. Things got out of hand. But I don't regret it. And neither should you. You needed that, Sharni. It's not healthy, going without sex for five years. The only problem I can see is if there's a risk you might fall pregnant. Is there?'

She couldn't speak. Just shook her head from side to side in the negative.

'Are you sure about that?' he asked, a frown in his voice. 'You said you hadn't had sex in five years, so you wouldn't be on the pill. Unless you are for medical reasons. Are you?'

Again, she shook her head.

'How long since your last period, then?'

'F…five years,' she choked out.

His eyes flared wide. 'Five *years*?'

Sharni groaned. Now she would have to explain herself and she didn't want to do that. But she supposed she had to, under the circumstances.

But not whilst he was still inside her.

'I…I need to go to the bathroom,' she stammered, and wriggled her bottom in an attempt to eject him.

'Liar,' he said, the weight of his body keeping her solidly captive beneath him. 'You just went ten minutes ago. What you need is to stay exactly where you are till I'm ready to make love to you again. For longer then thirty seconds next time.'

Sharni blinked up at him. Next time? He actually thought there would be a *next* time?

'But first, I want to hear about your not having a period for five years,' he stated firmly. 'Given the time frame, I presume it's connected to your husband's tragic death. So what is it? A post-traumatic condition?'

Sharni was stunned by his intuitive conclusion, even though it was only half her story. Not having to go into a lengthy explanation of her barrenness was a huge relief.

'Something like that,' she agreed.

'What do the doctors say? Will you get better?'

'Hopefully. Eventually.'

He frowned. 'That's really sad, Sharni. Which is probably what your problem is. You've been sad for far too long. What you need is to inject some fun in your life. You've made a good start, resuming your sex life. But you need a whole lot more where that came from,' he added with a wicked twinkle in his eyes. 'Come on. Let's get naked.'

Sharni could not believe it when he lifted up her jumper and peeled it up over her head.

'Mmmm,' he said when his gaze dropped to her white bra, which was comfortable but not the sexiest of undergarments. 'This will definitely have to go. In future, please buy front-fastening bras,' he went on when he discovered hers didn't have one. 'Or better still, stop wearing one altogether. You undo it, will you?'

It was a defining moment, his asking her to undo her own bra.

If she complied, it would mean she accepted his view of this situation: that having sex with him wasn't wrong. Plus, it was something that could be good for her.

The decision was taken out of her hands when he made an impatient face, slid his hands under her back and unhooked the clasp.

Sharni sucked in sharply as he drew the bra away from her breasts. How swollen they felt, with nipples that, she knew without glancing down at them, were fiercely erect.

'Oh, yes,' he murmured, and tossed the bra aside. 'No bra for you in future, beautiful Sharni.'

His hot gaze on her bared breasts sent a wave of heat flooding through her. She wanted him to touch them with the same kind of desperation she'd wanted him to be inside her earlier.

Which he still was, she remembered with a startled gasp when he grabbed her hips, pulling her hard against him as he sat back on his haunches.

'Wrap your legs around my waist,' he ordered her.

Another defining moment.

Impossible to turn her back on the pleasure that she knew awaited her with this man.

Her heart quickened when she obeyed him, her head spinning at the thought of her naked body spread before him like a virgin sacrifice on an altar.

She was helpless, his sex anchored deep inside hers, his hands free to caress her at will.

Dear heaven, but she was shameless with him. Utterly, completely shameless.

She lay there, hopelessly excited, whilst he undid the buttons on his shirt, then stripped it back off his shoulders. He had the same mat of dark curls in the middle of his chest that

Ray had had, she noted. But Adrian was slightly larger all over and much fitter-looking, with well-defined muscles in his stomach and arms.

He was a bit larger everywhere, it seemed.

She'd only had a quick glimpse of Adrian's erection when she'd undressed him, but there'd been enough time to see that he was circumcised, another physical difference.

She found his differences oddly comforting. Not so his being totally naked in front of her. Her eyes travelled excitedly down the length of his torso, fixing onto where their bodies blended into one. His own gaze was riveted to *her* body, his eyelids heavy with desire.

'I've so been wanting to do this,' he said throatily as he reached forward to stroke his hand back and forth across the tips of her breasts.

Sharni bit her bottom lip in an effort not to

cry out. How could such a simple thing tie her up in so many knots? Her nipples immediately felt twice as long, and twice as hard.

'Come here, you sexy thing,' he growled and scooped her up off the bed, leaning her back over his arms whilst his head bent to her chest.

She did cry out when he started licking a nipple, a strangled sound that was half moan, half whimper.

Oh, Lord…

When he sucked her nipple into his mouth, the muscles inside her contracted fiercely.

His head jerked up, his eyes dark and smouldering.

'No more of that,' he ground out, and lowered her back to the bed before shooting her a thoughtful look. Then he started touching her down there.

Her mouth fell open as her nerve-endings became electrified by his knowing caresses. Soon all she could think about was the burning pleasure of his touch, and the build-up of delicious tension in her body.

His stopping brought an agonised groan to her lips, her dilated eyes flaring wide as they lifted to his in frustrated bewilderment.

'I've decided you should wait a while,' came his coolly delivered explanation. 'Why rush things? We have all afternoon. Come on,' he said, and scooped her up off the bed. 'Let's go have a lovely hot shower together.'

# CHAPTER EIGHT

JANICE glanced at the clock on her kitchen wall.

Ten past six.

She glared at the phone, which had been ominously silent all day.

'I'm going to kill that sister of mine,' she grumbled out loud as she attacked the onions on the chopping board. 'Ungrateful wretch!'

'I hope you're not talking about me,' her husband said drily as he came through the back door.

'You'd think she'd at least call, wouldn't you?'

Pete sighed. 'I presume you're talking about Sharni.'

'Who else?'

'You worry about her too much.'

'I know. I can't help it.'

Pete came over and rubbed his wife's very tense shoulders. 'Have you tried her mobile?'

'Several times. It just goes straight to her message service.'

'What about the hotel?'

'They say she's out.'

'Then she must be enjoying herself.'

'That'll be the day.'

'You never know, love.'

Janice sighed. 'I hope you're right.'

The phone ringing made her heart jump.

'That's probably her now,' Pete said.

'I certainly hope so.' Janice dropped the knife and hurried over to the kitchen extension.

'Hello?' she said as she swept the receiver to her ear.

'Hi. It's me. Sharni.'

'Sharni!' she exclaimed, throwing a relieved glance at her husband who smiled and walked off into the living room.

'I was just saying dreadful things about you to Pete,' she went on, but laughingly. 'For not ringing me, that is.'

'Oh. I'm sorry. I…oh, Janice! You've got no idea what happened today.'

Janice couldn't quite make out the tone in her sister's voice. Was she excited, or shocked?

Maybe a bit of both.

'Obviously not,' she said. 'Why don't you tell me?'

'I…I've just spent all afternoon in bed with a man,' Sharni blurted out.

The deafening silence that greeted Sharni echoed her own bewilderment at her highly uncharacteristic behaviour.

Sharni had always confided in her big sister, so Janice already knew that she was not a girl to jump into bed lightly. She'd only had one serious boyfriend before Ray and none since. It simply wasn't in Sharni's nature to sleep with a man unless she thought she was in love.

Or it hadn't been, up till now…

'Really?' Janice said at last, surprising Sharni by not sounding too shocked. 'Well, I did tell you to enjoy yourself in Sydney. Still, I have to admit I wasn't expecting that. So who is this Casanova? And how did you meet him?'

Sharni sighed with relief that her sister was taking her news so well. 'His name is Adrian Palmer,' she said. 'He's an architect and a friend of Jordan. You remember Jordan, my lawyer?'

'Of course. So you'd met this Adrian before, had you?'

Sharni winced. If only she had…

'Well…no. No, I hadn't, actually. I…oh, golly, it's just so hard to explain.'

'Try.'

'I was in this restaurant, having lunch, when he walked in.'

*'And?'* Janice prompted when Sharni started

waffling over whether she should tell Janice that Adrian was Ray's double. Or not.

'He…he asked me to join him for lunch.'

'He picked you up, you mean.'

Lord, but this was difficult. 'Well…sort of. But he did introduce himself properly first. And he did offer to ring Jordan and have her vouch for his character.'

'Mmm. Smart move. So how much wine did you drink over lunch?'

Sharni bit her bottom lip. 'About two thirds of a bottle.'

'That's quite a bit for a girl who's been on the wagon.'

'I don't think it was the wine, Janice. It was the man.'

'Wow! He must be really something to seduce *you* that quickly. So after lunch he took you where? Back to your hotel room?'

'No. We went to his place. But not straight away,' she hastened to add, hoping that made things sound a little less sluttish. 'We went shopping first. For a dress for me to wear out tonight. He…he's taking me to the theatre. To see *The Phantom of The Opera*.'

'Brother! He's a fast worker all right. And after the shopping?'

'We…um…we went up to the top of this building he designed. It's called the Bortelli Tower. Adrian lives in the penthouse.'

'The penthouse, no less! This is getting better and better.'

Sharni's eyebrows lifted. Janice didn't sound as if she was disgusted at all. In fact, she sounded almost…approving.

'I presume he's handsome as well as successful,' Janice rattled on in a bright and breezy voice.

'Well…yes. Very.'

'Then what on earth are you sounding so worried about?'

'There's something I haven't told you yet.

Janice, he's the spitting image of Ray. I mean, the *spitting image*!'

Janice groaned a deeply disappointed groan. There she'd been, thinking Sharni had finally moved on with her life.

She should have known better.

'Please don't tell me you only went to bed with this man so you could pretend he was Ray.'

'No!' Sharni denied. 'No! It wasn't like that at all. Yes, he does look like Ray. Startlingly so. But in personality, he's as different as chalk is from cheese. What Adrian made me feel when he kissed me, Janice…it's nothing like what I felt when I was with Ray. To tell you the truth, I think I'm still in shock. The things I did with him, Janice. I'm blushing just thinking about them.'

Janice had to smile. The poor sweet love.

Ray had been a nice man, but very shy and lacking in confidence.

Clearly, Ray's double had all the confidence in the world.

'So where are you now?' Janice asked her sister.

'I'm back at my hotel. I...I made the excuse that I needed at least two hours to get ready for our date tonight. But the real reason was I wanted time to think. And to ring you.'

'I'm glad you did.'

'You know, I thought you'd be disgusted with me.'

'Not at all. A little surprised, maybe.'

'Not as surprised as I was. I still don't know what happened. I couldn't seem to control myself. I wanted him like crazy. I still do. What's happening to me, Janice?'

'Maybe you're falling in love again.'

'No, no, it's not love. It's wild and wicked.

I'm not myself with Adrian. I'm someone else: a sex-mad stranger.'

'Not sex-mad, Sharni. A normal healthy young woman of thirty who's been alone too long.'

'That's what Adrian said.'

'Did you tell him about Ray?'

'Yes. Yes, I did. If you must know I was so shocked when I first saw Adrian walk into the restaurant that I went over to his table and asked him if he was adopted.'

'Adopted!'

'I had this crazy idea he had to be Ray's twin brother.'

'Oh, yes, that's right. Ray was adopted, wasn't he?'

'Yes.'

'I presume this Adrian wasn't.'

'No.'

'Still, he must look a hell of a lot like Ray to make you think that,' Janice said, even more convinced now that this was why Sharni had ended up in bed with him.

'There are some slight physical differences. And he's nothing like Ray in the way he acts. He's much more…um…'

'Confident?' Janice finished for her.

Sharni laughed. Not a sound Janice had heard often on her sister's lips during the past few years. 'I was thinking more of arrogant… and masterful.'

'Especially in bed.'

'Yes…'

'Sounds like exactly what the doctor ordered.'

'That's what Adrian said, too.'

'Mmm. You've told him quite a bit about yourself, haven't you?'

'Not everything…'

Janice knew what her sister was referring to. The baby. Sharni could never bring herself to talk about the baby. Not without crying…

'No need to tell him about that,' she said

quickly. 'Let's face it, Sharni, love, this is probably only going to be a weekend fling, so there's no need to spill your entire heart out to the man.'

'You're probably right.'

'You sound unsure. Do you think he's serious about you?'

'I can't see why he would be. A man like him. He could have anyone.'

'Don't you dare put yourself down like that. You are a very beautiful girl, with the kindest nature and a good brain. Any man would be lucky to have a girlfriend like you.'

'You're biased.'

'Too bloody right I am!'

When Sharni laughed again, tears pricked at Janice's eyes. There'd been a time when she'd thought she'd never hear that sound again.

'Look,' Janice said after swallowing the great big lump in her throat. 'Why don't you stop worrying and just lie back and enjoy the experience? There's nothing wrong with having a wild and wicked weekend with a man, provided he's nice to you. He is nice to you, isn't he?'

'*Very* nice.'

'Then go out tonight, have fun and whatever comes, comes. Off you go now and keep me posted.'

Sharni suppressed a moan as she hung up the phone.

She knew what would come tonight.

Being with Adrian *had* turned her sex mad.

Sharni still could not believe she'd allowed him such liberties with her body. There wasn't an inch that he hadn't explored, either with his hands or his mouth.

Her mouth went dry as an image flashed into her mind. That of herself in the shower with Adrian, her hands braced against the tiled wall, him behind her.

Shameless, she'd been, utterly shameless.

Yet she'd enjoyed every moment, hadn't she? No use being a hypocrite and pretending that she hadn't.

Sharni took some comfort from her sister's reaction. Janice didn't seem to think what she was doing was wrong.

Janice also didn't expect the affair to last beyond this weekend.

Which was only logical, Sharni supposed, even if it was a depressing thought.

If she was brutally honest, she didn't want her affair with Adrian to end. Not tomorrow. Not ever!

Because whilst she was in his arms, there were no painful memories. There was nothing but the heat of the moment and the most incredible pleasure.

Sharni shivered, then glanced at the bedside clock. Six twenty-seven. In just over an hour she would be with him again.

An hour to make herself as beautiful as she could possibly be.

An hour to think about what her lover might do to her later that night.

The longest hour of her life.

# CHAPTER NINE

ADRIAN found himself whistling as he walked the two blocks to the boutique hotel Sharni was staying at, a four-star establishment down near the Rocks.

He could not recall when he'd felt this carefree. Or this light-hearted. Certainly not over the last few years.

He'd mistakenly thought he was happy with his life and his career. But it had become obvious to Adrian today that his rise to fame as one of Sydney's wealthiest, most sought-after architects had come at a price. He'd lurched from one project to the next, never going on a holiday, never committing himself to anything that would take too much of his precious time.

Which was why his relationships never lasted.

Felicity had been so right to call him a womanising workaholic, because that was exactly what he'd become, bedding one brunette after another during the miserably small blocks of time he'd allotted for dating.

But architecture had been the last thing on his mind since meeting Sharni. His focus had been all on her, especially once he got her into bed. He could not seem to stop making love to her, especially once he realised how inexperienced she was. He'd wanted to show her everything, wanted to *do* everything.

And she'd been with him all the way. Delightfully, deliciously.

Okay, so she'd been a bit shocked a couple of times, and slightly hesitant once or twice. But not for long.

He'd kept her in bed as long as he could, only

letting her go because he'd temporarily run out of steam. He was a man, after all, not a machine.

But the moment she'd gone, he'd missed her. Missed her warm presence, her soft voice, her sweet smile.

He'd showered, shaved and dressed with considerable speed, and now he was heading for her hotel, due to arrive a good fifteen minutes before the time they'd agreed upon.

But what the heck? He just had to see her again, had to kiss her again.

Probably not a good idea to kiss her too much, though. Hell, even *thinking* about kissing her was not a good idea.

Suddenly, Adrian didn't feel so carefree any more. Hot blood charged through his veins. Within seconds, he was as hard as the Rock of Gibraltar.

The thought of sitting in the theatre all evening like this was almost unbearable.

Adrian's teeth clenched hard in his jaw. Think about something else, you dummy!

Ah, there was the hotel, a three-storey, cement-rendered structure of no particular style, which would normally have offended his architectural eye. But not tonight. Tonight, architecture could go take a flying leap!

He took the front steps two at a time, telling the rather portly doorman that he would require a taxi shortly. No problem, he was told. They came by all the time on a Saturday night.

'Excuse me, sir,' the middle-aged dragon behind the reception desk called out sharply when Adrian strode swiftly through the foyer. 'Are you visiting a guest? If so, I need to know who, and if you're expected.'

'Sharni Johnson,' he replied without stopping. 'In room nineteen. And, yes, I'm expected.'

Sharni was in the bathroom, titivating, when she heard the knock on her hotel-room door, the sound sending a shot of adrenaline racing through her already aroused body.

He was early!

Heart racing and head whirling, she hurried to the door, all the while trying to find some much-needed composure.

Whatever she was planning to say died on her tongue when she opened the door, Adrian's stunning likeness to Ray striking her once more.

Not that Ray had ever owned a pale grey suit like the one Adrian was wearing. It shouted designer wear, as did his mauve silk shirt and vibrantly purple tie.

Not many men could carry off such colours without looking gay.

But Adrian could.

'I'm almost ready,' she said at last. 'You're early.'

He didn't say a word, just stared at her for a long moment, then pulled her into his arms and kissed her with a passion that made the earth move beneath her feet.

By the time his head lifted they were somehow inside the room with the door shut behind them.

'Sorry,' he ground out. 'Didn't mean to do that. It's all your fault, you know. You do dreadful things to me.'

'You do even more dreadful things to me,' she countered, the provocative words tumbling from her still-tingling lips.

'I'd certainly like to,' he growled. 'I have to have you, Sharni. Right now. We have several minutes before we have to go. Would you mind terribly?'

*Mind?* She would die if he didn't!

When she blushed furiously, he groaned.

'You must think me very crass. I haven't even said how beautiful you look. Which you do,' he added, taking her arms and holding them wide whilst his eyes travelled slowly over her.

But then he groaned again. 'Hell, Sharni, I don't have time for gallantry. I'm like a rock. Here, feel me,' he bit out and pressed her hand against his erection. 'I can't possibly wait till later tonight. I promise I won't mess up your hair or anything. We'll do it like we did in the shower. Remember?'

She nodded, her mouth drying at the memory.

'This will do,' he said, and pulled her over to the writing desk in the corner.

'Hold onto this,' he commanded, and curled her hands over the back of the upright chair. 'Lean forward slightly.'

Her pulse rate galloped as she obeyed, her heart lurching to a stop when he flipped up her skirt, then yanked her pantihose down just far enough to expose her bare bottom.

'So beautiful,' he muttered as he slid his hands over her tensely held buttocks.

Sharni's hands tightened on the chair.

Adrian had a penchant for talking during

sex, mixing orders with compliments, both of which drove her crazy with desire.

'No, don't,' he bit out when she tried to move her legs apart. 'Leave them together.'

She moaned when he eased into her. She wanted to push back against him, forcing him in deeper. But he held her hips captive with an iron grip whilst he rocked back and forth just inside her.

Gradually, he moved in deeper, then deeper still.

'Not yet, sweet Sharni,' he whispered when her thighs started to tremble. 'Wait. Wait.'

She could not wait. Could not think. She was out of control again, a helpless victim to the heat of the moment. And to him. She came with a rush, and so did he, his hot seed flooding her womb for ages.

When their bodies finally calmed, he pulled her upright, groaning as he slipped his hands inside her top to cup her throbbing breasts.

'We don't have to go to the theatre,' he suggested in a raspy voice. 'We could stay here. Order room service.'

The temptation to agree was intense. But at a crucial moment, Sharni glimpsed their reflection in the glass of the window behind the desk.

'I…I think we should go to the theatre,' she said, shaken by the decadence of their image.

'If you insist,' he replied thickly, but he made no move to release her.

Sharni swallowed. 'I…I need to go to the bathroom, Adrian,' she pleaded. 'Please let me go.'

When he did as she asked without further argument, Sharni bolted for the bathroom.

Ten minutes later, she emerged with her clothes in place and new lipstick on. But she still felt like a woman who'd been ravished too much in one day.

'You're not angry with me, are you?' he asked as they made their way down the hotel stairs.

'Why should I be? I could have said no.'

But of course, that wasn't true. She couldn't seem to say no to him, not once he started making love to her.

Uncontrollable passion was not a situation Sharni had ever had to deal with before. Sex with Ray had never been all that urgent. To be spun out of her head all the time evoked total confusion.

'I know what's bothering you,' he said as they reached the bottom of the stairs.

'What makes you think something's bothering me?'

His laugh was dry. 'Come now, Sharni. Your face is an open book. But trust me when I say I'm not just using you for the sex.'

Sharni ground to a halt and stared at him. That thought hadn't really occurred to her. She'd been too busy, worrying about her own rather shocking behaviour.

When he reached out to lightly caress her cheek, her heart flipped right over.

'From the moment we met, I knew you were going to be something special in my life.'

A wave of relief flooded Sharni. A wave of sweet pleasure, too. Janice had been wrong. He didn't want just a weekend romp with her. It sounded like he wanted a real relationship.

The prospect was as thrilling as it was un-expected.

'I could say more,' he said, planting a tender kiss on her cheek. 'But if we don't get going, we'll be late. Come on, my darling,' he said, and took her hand in his. 'The Phantom awaits.'

# CHAPTER TEN

HE REALLY cares about me, Sharni kept thinking as the taxi wove its way through the city streets.

What had been a big problem in her head—the uncontrollable passion and raunchy sex—suddenly seemed all right. Adrian's hand in hers brought a warm fuzzy feeling to her stomach. His side pressed against hers felt protective, rather than provocative.

She didn't speak, just leant her head against his shoulder.

They arrived at the theatre just in time, the curtain going up within seconds of being seated, leaving Sharni no time to ask Adrian how he'd managed to secure a booking at the last minute. Then, once the show started, she was so captivated, so enthralled, that nothing existed for her but what was being played out on that stage.

It soon became obvious why *The Phantom* was such a popular musical all over the world. The combination of a bitter-sweet romance with magnificent melodies and sets of visual splendour were a sure fire recipe for success. The touches of humour were great, too. Sharni laughed several times.

The intermission annoyed her, however. She didn't want the story to stop. She wanted to see it through to the end in one sitting.

But she had no choice once the curtain dropped and the lights came on. Only then did she realise how great their seats were, right in the middle of the front row of the dress circle. Yet Adrian had only asked her to go at lunch-time.

'How on earth did you get such wonderful seats?' she asked. 'Were you just lucky?'

'Contacts, my darling,' he said, thrilling her again with this new term of endearment. 'I was the architect in charge of the refurbishment of this theatre. The owner was so delighted with the result that he granted me permanent access to his reserved seats whenever he didn't need them. He's overseas at the moment, so I suppose there was an element of luck in our being here. Though they say one's luck improves with hard work. It was a damned difficult job turning what was a dump of an old movie house into what you see tonight.'

'It's lovely,' she said, glancing around at the classy decor. 'Best of all are these seats. I love the black leather. Most theatres have simply dreadful seats.'

'Yes, I know,' Adrian said drily. 'I've suffered in them. I had a friend design these with comfort in mind and had them specially made. The leather is the softest available.'

'That must have cost a small fortune.'

'The owner will recoup the cost with people coming back time and time again. I also made sure there was a decent bar area where people can be served quickly during the intermission instead of having to line up ten deep, then spill everything as they try to weave a hazardous path through the crowd. Come on, I'll show you, and get us both some champagne at the same time.'

Adrian was right. The bar area was huge and extremely user-friendly, with plenty of staff serving the drinks. Eye-friendly too, with no glitzy mirrors or gaudy bits. The carpet underfoot was the same dark red that covered the theatre floor, the walls and ceiling painted black with recessed lights. Again, the same as inside. The effect was rich and relaxing.

'What did I tell you?' Adrian said as he handed

over her glass of champagne. 'Quick as a flash. It's quality wine, too. Not cheap rubbish.'

Sharni smiled. 'I probably wouldn't know the difference.'

'You would, once you got a headache. Which is something we don't want you to get tonight.'

Their eyes met, with Sharni trying not to blush. But failing miserably.

He leant close and kissed her on her flushed cheek. 'I love it when you do that,' he whispered.

'Well, well, well!'

Adrian froze at the sarcastically delivered words.

Damn and blast. Felicity!

His stomach churned as he straightened, then slowly turned around. Because he already knew this wasn't going to be pleasant.

She stood there, her grey-blue eyes cold as ice as they flicked over Sharni.

'That's fast, even for you, lover,' she said in

a droll tone. 'Or was she the reason you were so late for our date last night? I can see you're already shagging her, so don't deny it. He is shagging you, isn't he, sweetie?' she directed at a stunned-looking Sharni. 'Yes, of course he is. And doing it very well, by the look of things. Of course, Adrian does do sex well. When he has the time, that is.'

Adrian suppressed a groan. Of all the theatres in Sydney, she had to come to this one. Tonight. To a show that was booked out for months ahead.

This puzzling mystery seemed partially solved when a good-looking but middle-aged man approached Felicity with two drinks in his hands and a frown on his face.

'I think you're the one who had someone in the wings, sweetheart,' Adrian countered. 'And he's right behind you.'

Felicity didn't even blink. 'You don't honestly think I was staying home pining for you all the nights you stood me up, did you? Kevin's been in love with me for years. Something you know nothing about.'

'Felicity, darling,' Kevin said from a short distance behind her.

'Coming,' she tossed back before throwing a sneering look at Sharni. 'You should know before you get in too deep that Adrian has this thing for brunettes. So if you're thinking you're special, then think again. You'll go the way the rest of us have gone. Do yourself a favour, sweetie, and find yourself a man who loves you, not this self-obsessed bastard.'

It was a brilliant exit line, if this were a play and not real life, Adrian thought wretchedly as Felicity whirled and stalked off, taking the hapless Kevin with her. Adrian might have taken some comfort from discovering that Felicity was not exactly heartbroken over their failed relationship, if it hadn't been for the way Sharni was now looking at him. As if she'd been hit by a truck.

'Sharni,' he began earnestly. 'Darling…'

'Don't,' she said, her voice breaking. 'Don't call me that.'

'Let me explain.'

'There's nothing to explain. I'm not stupid, you know. I got the picture.'

'What you got is a twisted picture. Felicity's a bitch.'

'Is she? Okay, then answer these simple questions. Did you have a date with her last night?'

'Yes. But—'

'Yes will do,' Sharni interrupted sharply. 'She dumped you, didn't she? When you were late.'

Adrian sighed. 'Yes. But—'

'So when you told me there wasn't any woman who would get upset by your taking me out tonight, you lied.'

'I didn't think she'd be all that upset. It was over between us. Well and truly. During the last couple of months we'd only been out three, maybe four times. I hadn't been to bed with her for at least two weeks.'

'Oh my! Two whole weeks. An eternity. *Do* you have this thing for brunettes?' she snapped.

Adrian didn't like the feeling of being cornered. Why wouldn't she let him explain, instead of shooting off all these loaded questions, then never letting him elaborate properly on his answers?

'Look, we all have a physical type which attract us. You said yourself how much I look like your husband. It's the way things work with male-female chemistry. Just because you're brunette doesn't mean you're not special to me. Don't let Felicity's spite ruin things for us, Sharni.'

She began shaking her head at him, as though he didn't have a clue what he was talking about.

When the call came for them to return to the

theatre, she handed him her glass. 'It was never going to work, anyway. I was a fool to think it could. Best we finish it right now.'

'No!' he exclaimed fiercely, bringing several startled glances from passers-by.

'Yes,' she said quite firmly. 'It's over, Adrian. Please don't make a scene.'

'Come back inside and watch the second half of the show,' he urged, desperate to persuade her to stay. All he needed was time and he'd make her see things differently.

'You really don't get it, do you?' she said. 'Your ex-girlfriend was right. You are a self-obsessed bastard, Adrian Palmer. Now get out of my way. I'm going back to the hotel. By myself. Don't try to follow me. Don't try to contact me. I'm sure you've had several brunettes say this to you over the years. But I'm adding my bit for good measure. I don't want to see you ever, ever, *ever* again!'

# CHAPTER ELEVEN

'CALM down, Sharni.'

'I can't calm down,' she sobbed into the phone. 'I'd like to kill him.'

'What you'd like,' her sister said, 'is to *not* have run into his ex-girlfriend tonight. Then you'd still be at the theatre, having a lovely time. Ignorance is bliss, especially with men like your Adrian.'

'You knew he was a womaniser, didn't you?'

'I knew he was a fast worker. That usually goes hand in hand with womanisers.'

Sharni groaned. 'He said I was special.'

'You *are* special.'

'He called me darling,' she wailed.

'You *are* a darling.'

'I thought he really cared. Oh, Janice! I don't think I'm ever going to forget him.'

'He was that good, eh?'

'What?'

'In bed.'

In bed *and* out, she thought despairingly, her fingers tightening around the receiver when she glanced over at the chair at the writing desk.

Shame curled around her heart as she realised just how easy she'd been with him. He must have thought all his Christmases had come at once. No wonder he hadn't wanted to let her go tonight. He'd probably been looking forward to another night of shenanigans.

'It's not the end of the world, love,' her sister said gently. 'Once you get over your indignation, you'll see that he was actually good for you.'

'Good for me! How can you say that?'

'Easy. Not only did he give you some great sex, he made you laugh, which is something you haven't done in a long time.'

'He made me cry, too.'

'Tears of temper more than true hurt.'

'You really think so?'

'He made you feel a fool,' Janice said. 'No woman likes that.'

Yes, he had, Sharni admitted. But he'd also made her feel beautiful and sexy and special and loved.

That had been his worst betrayal of all. She could have coped with his having had a girl-friend the day before he'd met her, if he'd just kept their weekend together strictly sexual.

But, no, he'd had to feed her a line of bull, hadn't he? Had to make her believe they might have a future together. That had been cruel and unnecessary.

It finally sank home that she was terribly

naïve when it came to men of the world. Naïve and stupid.

Her involvement with Adrian reminded her of another salutary lesson she'd learned during the last five years: you could not rely on people to be just, or decent, or honest. The world was unfair and life was unfair.

But it went on, regardless.

The sun would come up tomorrow and she would somehow have to find the courage to go on. And the courage to go home. Which she had to do, first thing in the morning.

Because she could not stay here, in Sydney. What if Adrian contacted her tomorrow? What if he showed up at this very door?

She wouldn't put it past him. He was not the kind of man to take rejection lightly. He'd followed her outside the theatre when she'd stormed off, watching her closely as she'd jumped into a taxi. When she'd glared at him through the back window, he'd glared right back, his expression more frustrated than defeated. He probably thought he could still talk her round, once she'd calmed down.

Sharni could not trust herself with him.

'Would you feel terribly offended if I cut my weekend short and went home tomorrow?' Sharni asked her sister.

Janice sighed. 'I suppose not. But I don't want you moping around all by yourself.'

'I promise I won't mope. The house needs a good clean. I'll do that.'

'Why don't you catch a train up here instead of going home? Stay a couple of days.'

'I can't. I'll pick up Mozart tomorrow. I know he'll be fretting already.'

'Poor little dog. You know, he might benefit from a change of scene. We could take him. The boys have always wanted a dog.'

'No, I couldn't do that, Janice. He's all I've got left of Ray.'

'Mmm. Do you have an appointment with Dr Flynn this week?'

'No. I'm down to once every three weeks now. Look, I'm not about to do anything stupid, if that's what you think. I've used up all my stupidity for this week.'

'Don't be like that.'

'Like what?'

'Defensive. Can't you see I'm worried about you?'

'No need. I'm fine.'

A weary sigh came down the line, making Sharni feel guilty. She had a habit of saying she was fine when she was anything but.

'I'll ring you tomorrow night,' she promised.

'You'd better.'

'Love you.'

'Love you, too.'

Sharni hung up, lay down on the bed and stared up at the ceiling.

Twenty-four hours ago she'd been dreading this getaway.

Now she dreaded going home, dreaded looking at the photographs of Ray dotted around the house, and thinking, not of him, but of his double.

Part of her felt guilty over what she'd done, as if she'd betrayed her husband's memory. But her overriding emotion was despair that she would never feel again what she'd felt when Adrian had been making love to her.

With a strangled sob, Sharni rolled over and started to weep.

# CHAPTER TWELVE

THE train ride home the following morning did not produce an anxiety attack. Crying for most of the night had left Sharni too tired for anything except just sitting there, staring blankly through the window.

She looked dreadful, she knew, with puffy lids and dark rings under her eyes. But who cared? There was no one she knew in the carriage, which was almost empty.

Rain started to fall halfway up the mountains, a bleak steady drizzle. Sharni grimaced as she realised the house was going to be freezing. Even if she lit the wood heaters as soon as she got there, it would be at least an hour before the air inside reached a comfortable temperature.

She really should sell and move. Regardless of how little she got for the place—small, weatherboard cottages on the outskirts of Katoomba were not in great demand—she had enough money to buy a house closer to her sister's home in Swansea.

Apart from the benefit of nearby family, the weather was better on the coast. And there was the beach. She liked the beach, had grown up near one.

Janice had suggested this move to her several times over the past eighteen months, but she'd always rejected it, saying she couldn't bear to leave the home she and Ray had made together. Now Sharni saw that that had just been a pathetic excuse. The truth was she'd been too depressed to make *any* decisions, let alone a mammoth one such as selling and moving.

Suddenly, she couldn't wait.

She sat up straight in the seat, invigorated by the idea that cleaning the house today would have a purpose. *She* would have a purpose, a goal.

As though on cue, the train pulled into her station. Sharni grabbed her two bags and jumped off, eager to get home and get started.

Thankfully, her car hadn't been stolen from the station car park. Not an uncommon occurrence during the week, with people leaving cars there all day whilst they caught the train to work down in Sydney. It was a long commute—two hours—but more reliable than driving, especially in the winter. The roads were often slick with sleet, making driving hazardous and slow.

It took her five minutes to drive the two kilometres from the station to her home, which was situated at the end of a narrow, poorly tarred road.

Sharni frowned as she turned into the driveway.

Maybe it was just the rain, but the house looked terrible. As if no one had lived there for years.

'And no one has,' she muttered as she gazed with shocked eyes at all the evidence of her neglect.

There were weeds growing out of the gutters. The outside walls needed painting. The garden beds were overgrown and the browned-off, straggly lawn hadn't been mown in months.

It hadn't been like that when Ray had been alive. The place had been beautiful, like something out of a romantic movie, with a white picket fence and roses trailing over the iron archway that framed the front steps. Now the fence was a mouldy grey, with several loose palings. As for the climbing rose bushes…

They'd died, because she'd forgotten to water them.

Ray would have been devastated to see it like this, Sharni conceded sadly.

'Oh, Ray, I'm so sorry. About everything. I've let you down.'

But instead of succumbing to another bout of useless weeping, Sharni vowed to do something about it. She could paint, couldn't she? And mow lawns and pull out weeds. Maybe not today, since it was raining. But that didn't stop her from attacking the inside, which she suspected was almost as neglected as the outside.

If nothing else, all this activity would distract her from thinking about a certain person.

With house keys in hand, Sharni jumped out of the car and raced through the rain towards the front veranda.

'About bloody time,' Adrian muttered when he finally reached Katoomba shortly after three in the afternoon.

As drives went, that one was a doozy. The

combination of continuous rain and curving roads meant his concentration couldn't flag for a moment, or his extremely expensive yellow Corvette would have gone over a cliff, or up the back of a truck.

It was a relief that Sharni had taken the train home, the only information he'd been able to get out of that dragon at the hotel.

'I'm sorry, sir,' she'd said with a sniff when he'd asked for Sharni's address or phone number. 'But the lady said I wasn't to give out her personal details to anyone.'

Adrian had been seriously frustrated, till he remembered that Sharni had been Jordan's client.

Jordan had finally supplied Sharni's address and home phone number, which thankfully had been still in her computerised files. But only after she'd quizzed him on why he wanted them.

He'd explained how he'd met Sharni, mentioning his likeness to her dead husband. He hadn't told Jordan about the sex, claiming instead that they'd exchanged life stories over a lovely lunch, but that Sharni had left afterwards to go shopping without giving him her phone number and address. He'd added—quite truthfully—that he simply hadn't been able to forget her and wanted to see her again.

When Jordan had warned him to go gently with Sharni, he'd promised that he would.

*If* Sharni let him, he thought as he drove slowly through Katoomba.

Adrian could not ignore the fact that Sharni wasn't going to be pleased to see him, especially since he hadn't rung to warn her that he was coming. He'd anticipated that she would have hung up without giving him a hearing. It wouldn't surprise him if she slammed the front door in his face as well. She'd been seriously angry with him last night. More angry, even, than Felicity.

When the taxi had sped off with her glowering at him through the back window, he'd been in two minds whether to go after her straight away, or not. In the end, he'd decided to let her calm down first.

He'd spent a wretched night, tossing and turning, upset that he'd hurt Sharni, when all he'd wanted to do was make her happy.

When he'd hurried to the hotel first thing this morning, Adrian had still been reasonably confident that he'd be able to talk Sharni round.

The news that she'd checked out had floored him. His inability to secure her phone number and address had infuriated him.

He'd brooded all the way home before a light had gone on in his head. She'd been *afraid* to stay, the same way she'd been afraid the day before.

He still wasn't sure if she was afraid of him, or herself. But either way, he wasn't going to let her get away. Because what he'd told

Jordan was correct. He could not forget her. She'd got under his skin as no woman ever had before.

Adrian slowed the car even further once he left the centre of Katoomba, peering through the rain in search of the street on the left down which he had to turn to reach Sharni's house. He'd done a search of her address on the internet and printed off the relevant map, studying it before he left home. The trouble was distances looked different in reality than they did in maps.

The houses thinned. He crawled past a motel and a garage, wondering if he'd missed the sign.

No, there it was!

He swung the wheel left and drove slowly down the street, travelling a good way before turning into Gully Creek Road, which looked little more than a bush track. It had a narrow strip of tar down the middle and far too many potholes for Adrian's liking. Not too many houses, either.

The first one to have a readable number on the postbox was number eight.

Sharni's number was thirty-four.

He finally found it, right at the end of the road. There was a tidy white sedan parked in the driveway. But that was the only thing neat about the place.

Adrian's architectural eye found some pleasing aspects in the design of the house. He'd always liked colonial cottages with pitched iron roofs and verandas all around.

But they could look like dumps if they weren't well maintained.

Sharni's home looked like a dump. A deserted dump! He would not have thought anyone lived there if it hadn't been for the puffs of smoke coming out of the chimney.

As Adrian's shocked gaze took in the condition of the place and its surrounds he tried to work out why a woman who'd received three million dollars in compensation would live like this.

He found the answer with his own mother's behaviour when his father died a few years back. After the funeral, she'd gone into a serious decline, letting everything go. Her home, her garden, herself. Bills had not been paid and phone calls not answered. Friends had been turned away from the door. She'd spent most days in her dressing gown, sitting in an armchair and staring into space.

Her doctor had explained to her worried son that she was suffering from depression. He'd prescribed antidepressants and counselling but she'd refused both. This had gone on for over a year, at which point Adrian had stepped in and bought her a ticket on a world cruise. He'd virtually packed for her, put her on the boat and just left her there.

It had done the trick, her melancholy lifting

after she met a charming gentleman on the ship who had shown her that there was still life to be lived, even at the age of sixty-eight. Their ship-board romance had not survived once the cruise was over. He lived in England and wasn't prepared to leave his roots. But Adrian's mother had come home a different woman, full of energy and ideas.

It occurred to Adrian that maybe that was why Sharni's sister had given her a holiday in Sydney. To snap her out of her depression.

And it had been working, too. Till fate—and Felicity—had ruined everything.

The rain suddenly stopped, Adrian taking that as a good sign. He'd always been a positive thinker, having a cup-is-half-full rather than half-empty attitude.

He felt certain that Sharni had really liked him, the same way he'd really liked her. It was not just the sex, despite the chemistry between them being very powerful. If it were just the sex she would not have reacted to Felicity the way she had. That level of indignation and anger came from the beginnings of an emotional involvement. His own distress over Felicity's unfortunate appearance confirmed what he'd already suspected about himself: that he was on the verge of falling in love for the first time in his life!

Which was why he was here, determined not to return to Sydney till Sharni saw sense.

Climbing out of his Corvette, Adrian locked it, then strode through the open gate and up the weed-filled front path. He had to duck to pass under an archway that was covered in some kind of thorny bramble. Three stone steps brought him up onto the veranda. The front door had a tarnished brass knocker in its middle, which he lifted and banged against a brass plate.

The sound of someone knocking at Sharni's door brought a sigh of exasperation. Because at the time she was down on her hands and knees, scrubbing the kitchen floor. Also because she knew exactly who it would be.

Louise, from next door.

Louise was the only neighbour of Sharni's whom she would label a busybody. Most people who lived in the more remote areas of the Blue Mountains tended to keep to themselves, having chosen to live up here for the peace and quiet, the cooler air and the proximity to some of Australia's best bush walks.

When Ray had been alive, he'd given the woman short shrift. After his death, Sharni had welcomed Louise's seemingly kind visits for a while. But she'd soon come to realise that Louise's only interest in life was sticking her nose into other people's lives.

Unfortunately, by then, the infernal woman had been in the habit of dropping by at all hours of the day and night.

Fortunately, Mozart had upped and bitten her one day. Which had made her visits much less frequent thereafter. She also always came to the front door now, instead of just walking in the back door, unannounced.

Sharni suspected Louise had binoculars trained on her house most of the time. Because she always seemed to show up after Sharni had done something out of her usual routine. She would have noticed that Sharni had been away over the weekend. Also that Mozart wasn't at home. And she'd have spotted the smoke from the chimney, signalling her return.

The only surprise, Sharni thought as she rose to her feet and threw the scrubbing brush in the sink, was that Louise hadn't come over earlier.

Sharni sighed as she made her way along the central hallway to the front door, not bothering to remove the scarf that she'd tied around her hair. Louise wouldn't care what she looked like. All Louise wanted was to satisfy her curiosity over where Sharni had gone and what she'd been doing.

As she reached for the door knob a small smile crossed Sharni's face. The old duck would die of shock if she told her what she'd been up to down in Sydney.

'Hi, Lou…'

The greeting died in Sharni's throat when she saw who was standing on her front doorstep. Adrian, looking dead sexy in blue jeans and a black leather jacket with a white polo-necked jumper under it.

For a split second, a wild thrill shot through her.

But it wasn't long before her overriding emotion was anger. Or was it embarrassment that he'd caught her looking such a fright?

'How did you find out where I lived?' she threw at him whilst she yanked the scarf from her hair. 'I told the hotel not to give out my address to anyone. Especially you.'

'Jordan told me.'

Sharni groaned. She'd forgotten they had a mutual acquaintance.

Still, never in her wildest dream had she expected Adrian to follow her up here. It was easy to walk over to a hotel a couple of blocks away from where you live, quite another to drive all this way on a cold, rainy Sunday.

She glanced over his shoulder to see a bright yellow sports car parked outside her house, sparkling with raindrops.

It annoyed her, for some reason, perhaps because it looked so incongruous, parked next to her tumbledown house.

More angry red spots heated her cheeks.

'What is it that you want, Adrian?' she asked, arms folding in front of her. 'If you've come for more sex, then you've come to the wrong house.'

* * *

Pity, he thought. Because he'd never wanted her more.

Her feistiness turned him on no end.

'I've come to apologise,' he said.

'For what? Lying to me, then shagging me senseless?'

Wow. This was a Sharni he hadn't met before. But he liked her even more than the sweet, vulnerable creature he'd met yesterday.

He should not have smiled. It was a tactical mistake.

'You listen to me, you egotistical bastard,' she said, unfolding her arms and jabbing the middle of his chest with a furious finger. 'If you think you can just show up here and I'll fall into your arms again, then you're very much mistaken. I admit you're good in bed. No doubt you've had a lot of practice. With any number of brunettes whose names you probably can't remember. But I don't aim to be your next playmate. Now get back in your fancy car and go back to your fancy penthouse, because you're not wanted here.'

'Really,' he said, all his good intentions flying out of the window in the face of her insults and that poking finger.

He grabbed her wrist and pulled her inside the hallway, swinging her round so that her back slammed flat against the wall. He ignored the alarm in her eyes, grabbing her other wrist and pinning her arms against the wall above her head.

'Let's see about that,' he growled just before his mouth crashed down on hers.

# CHAPTER THIRTEEN

SHARNI'S lips betrayed her. They should have stayed firmly shut. Instead, they flowered open, welcoming the savage invasion of Adrian's tongue.

He pressed his body against her, squashing her breasts flat, his legs spread wide so that his hips were at the same height as hers. She felt his erection dig into the soft curves of her stomach, felt her outrage disintegrate as desire took over. She moaned softly into his mouth, the sound one of abject surrender.

His letting her go was as unexpected as it was by then unwanted.

Her arms dropped limply to her sides as she stared up at him.

'Don't you ever tell me again that you don't want me,' he ground out, his expression tight and angry. 'I could have you right here and now. The only reason I'm stopping is to show you that I'm not here just for the sex. I care about you, damn it. And I'm not leaving this house till you believe me,' he pronounced, stunning her further by moving over to fling the front door shut.

'I don't care how long it takes,' he added, turning to face her once more with implacable blue eyes. 'But right now, I need to go to the bathroom. Then I could do with a cup of coffee. It's been a long hard drive.'

When she didn't answer him, or move, Adrian took matters into his own hands, striding off down the hallway in search of the bathroom.

The open doorway on his left revealed a living room, the one on the right a bedroom.

The next door on the right was shut, Adrian presuming this had to be the bathroom. But when he went to open it, Sharni screamed out, 'No!' and came charging down the hallway after him, snatching his hand from the door knob and slamming the door shut again.

'That's not the bathroom,' she said sharply. 'It's in here,' she added, moving along to throw open the next door on the right. 'When you're finished, the kitchen is at the end of the hallway. I'll go make you that coffee.'

Adrian frowned as she hurried off, his curiosity sparked as to what lay behind that other shut door. In a cottage this size, it could only be another bedroom. What could it possibly contain that she didn't want him to see?

He couldn't think of a single thing.

It was probably just a mess, he decided during his visit to the old-fashioned bathroom. The way the outside of the house was a mess.

The kitchen wasn't a mess. It was a large,

country-style room that smelt of recent cleaning. The cupboards were pine, the counter tops painted a dark green. A round table and four chairs sat in the middle of the cork-tiled floor, a wood-burning heater occupying the hearth in one corner. A small flat-screen television—not turned on—sat on top of the surprisingly small fridge. A wide rectangular window stretched over the sink, which looked out over a covered veranda and a tree-covered valley beyond.

Sharni was standing in front of that window with her back to him, her slender shoulders hunched and tense. She turned when she heard him, her eyes angry.

'Why did you have to come?' she snapped. 'Why couldn't you have left me alone?'

'I've already told you why,' he said as he came forward and pulled out a chair at the table.

She shook her head. 'I don't believe you,' she pronounced, then turned to finish making the coffee. 'How do you have your coffee?' she threw over her shoulder. 'I can't remember.'

'Black. No sugar.'

'Aren't you having any?' Adrian asked when she placed the steaming white mug in front of him.

'No,' she said coldly, and crossed her arms again.

'Sit down, then. You make me nervous, standing there like that.'

Her laugh was dry. 'You? Nervous? That'll be the day.'

But she did sit down, opposite him, with the chair pushed well back from the table, her arms still crossed.

'What can I say to make you believe me?' he asked after he'd taken a few sips of the scalding-hot coffee.

'Absolutely nothing. I judge a man by his actions, not his words. You're a confirmed womaniser, Adrian Palmer, and I don't want anything further to do with you. Now, please, drink up your coffee and leave. I have to go out.'

'What for?'

'To buy fresh milk and to collect my dog.'

'Where's your dog?'

'He spent the weekend in a kennel and won't be too happy if I leave him there much longer.'

Adrian was surprised to find that she had a dog. He would have thought she was more a cat person. 'What kind of dog?'

'A Jack Russell terrier.'

'No kidding. I had a Jack Russell terrier when I was a boy. Lovely little dogs, so full of life.'

Sharni sighed. 'Usually. But Mozart hasn't been the same since Ray died. He was Ray's dog, really, not mine.'

Adrian frowned. 'Ray called his dog Mozart?'

'Yes. Why?'

'He's my favourite composer.'

'Mozart is a lot of people's favourite composer. Now, have you finished your coffee?'

Adrian drank it down, then set the empty mug on the table.

'I told you, Sharni, I'm not leaving.'

She stood up and glowered down at him. 'If you don't go, I'll call the police.'

'Don't be ridiculous. Come on,' he said and stood up also. 'I'll go with you whilst you get your dog.'

'You can't!'

'Why not?'

'Because everyone there is going to stare at you.'

'Why?'

'They'll think you're Ray, come back from the dead.'

Adrian frowned. 'I look *that* much like him?'

'Yes.'

'Show me a photo of him, then. Let me see for myself.'

She didn't want to, he could see. Which made Adrian all the more determined.

Suddenly, he wanted to know what was behind that shut door, too. He didn't want to leave a stone unturned in the mystery that was Sharni Johnson.

Because nothing she said and did made sense to him. She'd kissed him back at the front door, with a passion that was mind-blowing. So why was she trying to send him away without giving him the slightest chance to prove his sincerity? Even if she wasn't convinced that he cared about her, why not have some more of the great sex they'd shared?

It wasn't logical for a woman to deny herself male company, certainly not one as lonely as Sharni obviously was.

'I can't show you any photos of Ray,' she said stubbornly. 'I packed them all away earlier today.'

'Why would you do that?'

'Because I've decided to sell and move.'

'Good idea.' With a bit of luck he might persuade her to move to Sydney. 'So where are you planning on moving to?'

'That's none of your business.'

'Fine,' he said, whilst privately thinking that he aimed to make it his business. 'I still want to see a photo of Ray. I think I have a right to see exactly how much I resemble him.'

She hesitated for a few seconds, but then seemed to make up her mind. 'Very well,' she said. 'There's one on the piano in the living room which should do. I haven't packed in there yet.'

He followed her down the hallway into the living room, which was a lot chillier than the kitchen. The furniture was country comfort, in warm autumnal colours: a large squashy lounge suite grouped around the unlit hearth, no television set in sight, just several book-cases, crammed with books, along with an upright piano in one corner.

'So who's the piano player?' he asked as he followed her across the room.

'Ray was,' she said.

Adrian frowned. Just another coincidence, he supposed. But he'd always wanted to learn the piano. But his attending an all-boys, mad-about-sport school had stopped him from taking lessons. The few boys there who'd learned the piano had been considered pansies.

'I took that a few weeks before he died,' Sharni said, and nodded towards a silver-framed photo sitting on top of the piano.

Adrian picked up the photo and stared at the man who'd been Sharni's husband.

'Bloody hell,' he muttered under his breath as his shocked gaze studied every feature of the dead man.

'I'm not just like him, am I?' he said, turning to stare at Sharni. 'I could *be* him. Even our hair's the same style!'

'You walk the same as well,' she added for good measure.

For the first time since he'd kissed her at the door, Adrian's confidence over this woman wanting him wavered.

'So *was* it me who made love to you yesterday, Sharni? Or Ray?'

The temptation to lie to him was acute. It would solve all her problems. Or the ones he created in her whirling mind and treacherously weak body.

But something in his voice, and in his eyes, touched her heart.

Adrian was not a man she would have ever thought of as vulnerable. But, suddenly, he was. Maybe it would only be his ego that would be hurt if she lied, but she still could not do it.

'You asked me that yesterday,' she hedged.

'And?'

Her sigh carried reluctance, and resignation.

'I didn't lie to you. I wasn't pretending you were Ray. Not once.'

'How could you *not* be thinking of him? I'm the dead spit of the man, in every way.'

'You might look like Ray, Adrian, but you're two very different people. My husband was…well, he was a very gentle, rather introverted man.'

'Who had a Jack Russell Terrier and played the piano,' Adrian said thoughtfully as he stared down at Ray's photo one more time. 'And read lots of books.'

'Yes.'

He'd gone through a stage a few years ago when he'd read lots of books, becoming quite addicted to legal thrillers. Not so many now. Still…

Adrian walked over to the bookcases to see up close what kind of books his double liked.

The subjects they covered were wide, from romantic sagas to biographies to lots of self-help books. Adrian was thinking he wasn't into that much, when his eyes narrowed on a large book lying flat on one of the bottom shelves. It was entitled *Great Buildings of the World*.

He glanced up at Sharni, who was hovering nearby, looking anxious. 'What did your husband do for a living?'

'He was a draughtsman.'

Adrian's eyebrows rose.

'Yes, I know what you're thinking,' Sharni said. 'Ray told me when we first met that he actually wanted to be an architect.'

'And I always wanted to play the piano.'

They stared at each other for a long time before Adrian shook his head.

'This is crazy. It can't be. I'm not adopted. I know that for a fact. I'm my mother's biological child. There are photos of her pregnant with me in the family album. And photos of me, having my first bath.'

'Could she have had twins? And adopted one out?'

'Mum would never have given away a child. She was a wonderful mother. She always said she would have loved more babies, but something went wrong after I was born and she couldn't have any more.'

'So all these things… They're just coincidences?'

'They must be. They say fact is stranger than fiction.'

'I suppose so,' Sharni murmured. But it was hard to accept. She could see Adrian was finding it hard to accept too, now that he'd seen Ray's photo.

'There are some small differences,' she said. 'In your face. Not from the side so much, but front on. Other people probably wouldn't notice but I did, once we were face to face in that restaurant. You've also got a bigger body frame. And there's…um…

something else,' she finished up somewhat awkwardly.

'What?'

'You're circumcised. Ray wasn't.'

Adrian heaved a huge sigh of relief as he placed the photo back on top of the piano. He'd honestly begun to think that his parents had been involved in some ghastly deception.

'That seals it, then. If, by some miracle, Ray and I were twins, we would both have been circumcised at the same time.'

'I guess so,' Sharni said. 'I didn't think of that.'

Adrian smiled. 'Perhaps because you were thinking of something else at the time you noticed that little detail.'

Adrian took comfort from her blush. How could he have forgotten her delightful responses to him yesterday? There'd been nothing false in them, the extent of her pleasure clearly surprising herself. She'd been a woman discovering true passion for the first time. With him.

Even in hindsight there'd been nothing to indicate that she'd been pretending he was someone else.

Adrian would have liked to pull her into his arms and remind her of the chemistry that had sizzled between them from the moment they'd met. But he wasn't going to risk spoiling what he wanted with Sharni. Which was a real relationship, not just a sexual fling.

'Come on,' he said, and took her hand. 'Let's go get your dog.'

# CHAPTER FOURTEEN

HE WAS doing it again, Sharni thought with panic in her heart but excitement fizzing along her veins. Taking over.

'You'll have to stay in the car,' she said as firmly as she could manage. 'I don't want people looking at you and thinking they're seeing a ghost.'

Adrian's sigh sounded exasperated. 'That's ridiculous, Sharni. I'm planning on becoming a fixture in your life, so the sooner your friends get to know what I look like, the better.'

More panic. 'A fixture? What kind of fixture?'

'Friend. Lover. Boyfriend. I'll answer to any of those.'

'Don't I have any say in the matter?'

'You had your say when you kissed me back at the door.'

'After which I asked you to leave.'

His smile was somewhat smug. 'You're the one who said actions speak louder than words. You can tell me to leave till the cows come home but your lips don't lie when they're under mine.'

'You're an arrogant bastard.'

'Who knows what he wants. And that's you, Sharni Johnson.'

His impassioned words made her head swim. So did the look in his eyes.

'Please don't,' she choked out when he lifted her hand to his mouth.

He lowered her hand and nodded, his expression rueful. 'Thank you.'

Sharni blinked. 'For what?'

'For stopping me. I vowed to myself that I would not make love to you today. I was going to show you that my feelings for you encompassed far more than just the physical. But I find being alone with you in this house is a highly corrupting environment. Collecting your dog might be a good thing.'

'Mozart's been known to bite,' Sharni warned. 'Maybe you'd better just leave altogether.'

Adrian smiled at her with his eyes. 'Good bluff, darlin'. Stop thinking up excuses and let's go.'

*He* was the corrupting environment, she thought as she drove towards the veterinary clinic. No matter where he was.

The man was sex on legs. When he'd kissed her hand back then every pore in her body had begun to dissolve. If his intention was to stay the night—and it seemed unlikely that he would drive back to Sydney at this late hour—then they were sure to end up in bed together, regardless of his so-called resolution not to make love to her today.

The thought of sleeping with Adrian in the same bed that she'd shared with Ray brought waves of guilt.

'You can't stay the night at my place, Adrian,' she said at last.

'I don't intend to. I'm going to book into that motel we just passed. Hey, watch the road!'

Sharni's hands gripped the steering wheel more tightly.

'I won't join you there, if that's what you're thinking.'

'I wasn't.'

That surprised and disappointed her at the same time. Oh, Sharni, Sharni, Sharni, you are a foolish woman.

'So what are you going to do tomorrow?' she asked him.

'Go to work.'

'Oh.' So much for her equally foolish thought that he was going to stay and take her out somewhere. 'The traffic's awfully bad on the highway on a Monday morning,' she advised in flat tones. 'You wouldn't want to get on the road too late.'

'The only road I'll be getting on is the road to Katoomba. I'm going to hit the shops first thing for some suitable clothes, and then I'm coming to your place and I'll start fixing it up.'

When shock sent her eyes jerking away from the road, Adrian grabbed the wheel. 'If you're going to keep driving like that, then I suggest you let me take over.'

Wasn't that what he was already doing?

'You fancy yourself as a handyman, do you?' she said with a touch of irritation. But she suspected the irritation was more with herself than with him. She hated being such a pushover.

He smiled over at her. 'Amongst other things.'

'You are truly incorrigible. But be my guest. The house could do with some work.'

'I did notice.'

His remark wasn't sarcastic, but it still stung.

'I know this will sound pathetic, but I didn't. Notice, that is. Not till I came home yesterday. I think being away opened my eyes to a lot of things.'

'Having a holiday can do that.'

She glanced over at him, surprised by this insightful remark.

'Eyes on the road, madam.'

'It's all right,' she said, turning from the highway into the clinic car park, which was starkly empty at this hour on a Sunday afternoon. 'We're here now.'

'But this is a veterinary hospital,' Adrian said. 'Is your dog sick?'

'No. Though he does come here when he is sick. This is where I work. As a veterinary assistant. Remember? John…That's my boss. He said Mozart could stay here for the weekend. I don't like to leave him with strangers.'

'I see. It looks a nice clean place. But that building's crap. He should have employed a better architect.'

Sharni had to laugh. 'I won't tell John that. Wait here and try to behave yourself.'

He didn't argue with her. Thank heavens. Just rolled his eyes and stayed put. 'Try not to be too long,' he said. 'Patience is not one of my virtues.'

'You mean you have some?'

He smiled a droll smile. 'What happened to that sweet girl I met yesterday?'

'She found out that her prince charming was really a big bad wolf!' she quipped as she climbed out, slammed the car door and marched off.

John was where he always was on a Sunday afternoon. At the hospital, in the section behind the consultation rooms where he kept his recovering patients. He was an extremely devoted vet and the kindest man Sharni had ever met. Most other vets would have been retired at seventy two, but not John. Healing sick animals was his life.

'Hush up,' she said when she walked in and one of the dogs started barking like a lunatic. 'It's only me.'

John glanced up from where he was tending a large ginger cat.

'Is that Sharni Johnson, actually smiling?'

'Am I?' She hadn't realised. She didn't particularly feel happy, but could not deny that her verbal sparring with Adrian had given her a buzz.

'You certainly are. Looks like that weekend in Sydney has done you the world of good, even if you have come back a day early.'

'I don't know about that. I spent a lot of money on clothes I'll probably never wear.'

'Then maybe it's time you started going places to wear them,' he advised. 'You're not getting any younger, you know. One day you'll wake up and forty will be just around the corner. Then fifty. Then sixty. Then seventy.'

'Thank you for that cheery advice. How's Mozart been?'

John pulled a face. 'He wouldn't eat. Bess took him into the house and gave him what we were having. That always works with our dogs. But he refused to be tempted. He's out in the back yard, lying under the big pine.'

'Oh, dear! What am I going to do with him, John?'

John shrugged. 'Some dogs are one man dogs and there's nothing you can do about it.'

'I'll take him home and see if I can get him to eat something. Thanks for looking after him.'

'No trouble, love. I'm glad to see that one of you is looking happy. Would you mind if I don't come out with you? I think I should stay with Marmalade.'

'She's not going to die, is she?' That was the one thing Sharni found hard about her job now. Animals dying. Death of any kind could spiral her into a depression within minutes. She no longer watched the news on television for fear of what it might contain.

'Not if I can help it. Off you go now and don't worry too much about Mozart. He'll survive.'

Sharni forced a smile, said goodbye, and left.

But was surviving enough? she wondered as she walked across the back yard towards the big pine. Sometimes surviving was worse than death.

Mozart stood up when she approached, but he didn't wag his tail, or bark excitedly. Still, he let her pick him up, which was something he didn't let many people do. Any attempt at patting him these days usually brought a snap or a snarl. Louise knew to keep her distance from him. And so did the postman.

It hadn't occurred to Sharni when Adrian came with her that his being in the car would present a problem once they were joined by

Mozart. This lack of forethought annoyed her. Because it was typical of her thought processes around Adrian. He made her lose her head.

She also hadn't anticipated Adrian climbing out of the car as she approached with the dog in her arms. She certainly hadn't anticipated Mozart's reaction. He wriggled like mad, burst out of her hold, dropped to the ground then raced to Adrian, going up on his short hind legs and doing three hundred and sixty degree twirls, the way Ray had taught him when he was a little puppy.

'What a clever dog you are,' Adrian said, getting down on his haunches and chucking Mozart under his chin.

Mozart responded by leaping onto his lap, putting his front paws on Adrian's chest, then reaching up to cover Adrian's chin with slurpy licks.

Adrian rose, laughing, and taking Mozart with him. 'And you said he bites, you naughty girl,' he said as he tucked Mozart under one arm. The dog immediately quietened, as if he knew who was the boss once more. But his small dark eyes were alive with happiness, his upwards glances at Adrian the same adoring glances he'd once given Ray.

Sharni swallowed the huge lump in her throat. 'He's not usually like this,' she said. 'Especially with strangers.'

'Maybe he's just glad to be out of there,' Adrian said, nodding towards the clinic. 'Must be like being in jail, being in a kennel. Come on, let's take him home. I'll bet he didn't eat a thing in there all weekend. He feels awfully thin.'

'He hasn't eaten well since Ray died,' Sharni informed him, then added with a frown, 'Or been this happy. I hate to say this, but I…I think he thinks you're Ray.'

Even as she made that statement, Sharni knew it didn't ring true. Dogs didn't recognise people by what they looked like. It was more a matter of scent and voice and mannerisms. You could not fool a dog.

Yet Mozart was obviously fooled. Sharni supposed there was an exception to every rule. Adrian had almost fooled her, for a few seconds. Now, he just made her act foolishly.

'No kidding,' Adrian said, obviously not fazed by the notion. 'Well, I don't mind if you don't mind. Do you mind? What harm is there, if he's happy? You're happy, aren't you, little fella?' he said, and tickled the dog's ribs.

Mozart answered by trying to slobber all over him again.

Adrian laughed. 'See? He's happy. Come on, Mum, get me home, he's telling you. I'm hungry.'

Sharni's stomach contracted at Adrian calling her Mum, even though she knew he didn't mean anything by it. But it reminded her of the near miss she'd had today when

Adrian had almost gone into the nursery. If he was going to work around the house for any length of time, then she would have to tell him about the baby she'd lost. If she didn't, someone else might, like big-mouth Louise from next door.

Better it came from her.

She looked over at him as she climbed in behind the steering wheel. What would he think when she told him? Would he put two and two together and know that that shut door hid a nursery? Would he want to see it?

He wasn't a totally insensitive man. Yesterday, he'd had moments of kindness, and tenderness. He was, however, a bachelor. How could a bachelor understand the grief of losing a child the terrible way she had?

He'd think she was crazy, keeping the nursery as it was all these years. He wouldn't appreciate that it had given her a place to grieve at first. Or that later, she'd been too depressed to follow Janice's suggestion and give everything away to charity.

In truth, she hadn't been in there for ages.

Still, if she was serious about selling and moving—and she was!—then she would have to find the courage to follow her sister's suggestion.

Maybe Adrian would help her do it. With him around, she would have to keep it together. She'd couldn't cry all the time. Or try to hang onto anything.

'You're very quiet,' Adrian said.

Sharni came back to the present, surprised to find that she was almost home. Yet she couldn't even remember starting up the car, let alone the drive back along the highway.

'I was off in another world,' she admitted.

'Thinking good thoughts, I hope.'

'Actually, I was thinking that my next-door neighbour is going to have a fit when she spots you. That car of yours is a gossip magnet, and dear old Louise is a busybody of the first order. She's sure to find an excuse to come over sooner or later. I can only imagine the rain has kept her away so far. That's her house there,' she said as she drove past a small red brick cottage.

'No point in worrying about things you can't control, Sharni. We'll cross the bridge of dear old Louise when we come to it.'

Sharni actually liked that philosophy of life. She'd been brought up in a house where worrying about the future was not the norm. Ray, however, had been a worrier. His adoptive mother had been an anxious, over-protective woman, he'd told her. Not the kind of upbringing to produce an outgoing, confident man.

'You forgot the milk,' Adrian said as she turned into her driveway.

'It's all right. I can do without. I'll do a proper food shop tomorrow.'

'You're sure? I can go get you some if you

like? I know where the garage is. They always have stuff like milk and bread in garages.'

'No, no, Mozart would be most unhappy if you left right now. Come inside and we'll get him something to eat.'

It was a delight to see Mozart gobble up his food for once, but also a worry. What would happen to the dog when Adrian went back to Sydney? Which he would, eventually.

Sharni was under no illusions about Adrian. He found her a challenge at the moment. The fish who'd got away. That was why he was here, she had finally realised. Not *just* for more sex. He was probably telling the truth about that. Because, let's face it, a man like him could get sex anywhere, with more beautiful and much sexier women than herself.

No, he was here to win.

She'd read about personalities like him in some of the many books on the human psyche that Ray had bought in an attempt to work out why he was the way *he* was. She'd read quite a few of them over the last year, trying to heal herself.

'Man, that was one hungry dog,' Adrian said. 'Should I take him out for a walk now? After all, what goes in one end has to come out the other.'

'No need. He has his own special exit,' she said, showing Adrian the one Ray had made in the back door. Immediately, Mozart pushed through the swinging gate and ran out into the back yard. 'He can come and go as he pleases. I do lock it last thing at night, though. To stop the possums getting in.'

'What about bad guys?'

'No, you wouldn't fit.'

Adrian shot her a twisted smile.

'Very funny,' he said. 'So is that how you still think of me? As one of the bad guys?'

'Let's just say the jury's still out,' Sharni retorted.

His eyes were not at all amused. 'If I were really a bad guy, madam, I would already have exploited the one thing you definitely *do* like about me. I could reduce you to begging if I wanted to,' he ground out. 'In fact, you will have to beg me for it, before I touch you again.'

'Never!' she retorted.

His smile was the smile of the devil. 'Never say never, darlin'. You might have to eat your words.'

Sharni's face flamed at the image his words evoked.

So why did just the thought of what Adrian had said bring heat, not just to her cheeks, but to the rest of her body? Why had her mouth gone as dry as the Sahara? Why was her heart racing behind her ribs as if she'd just done a marathon?

His eyes narrowed on hers before he suddenly pushed her away, turned round and strode off towards the hallway.

She wanted to run after him, but she managed not to humiliate herself further.

'I'll be back tomorrow morning,' he called back from the front door. 'Don't forget to keep the home fires burning.'

Sharni groaned at this remark, because of course he was talking about herself. She was the home fire, burning for him. And she did. Quite literally.

And he knew it.

'Oh, God,' she cried, and sank down into a chair at the kitchen table.

Simultaneous with the sound of Adrian's car roaring off up the street, Mozart shot into the kitchen through his trapdoor. His first action was to glance around the room, then up at her with bright, expectant eyes.

'He's gone, Mozart,' she told the dog.

Mozart dashed off up the hallway. Sharni knew what he was doing. He was checking each room as he'd done so many times during the days after Ray had died.

This time, however, when he came back to the kitchen, he didn't curl up in a corner, whimpering. He jumped up onto the chair that Adrian had occupied and settled down.

He was waiting, Sharni realised. Waiting for his master to return.

Like me, Sharni thought with a telling tightening of her belly.

Would he touch her tomorrow? Kiss her? Make love to her?

No use pretending she didn't want him to any more.

But what if he didn't? What if he made her wait even longer?

She'd die if he did that.

She should have been nicer to him. Shouldn't have called him a bad guy. Even if he was.

Well, not seriously bad. But he was a serial

womaniser with no concept of true commitment or caring.

The phone ringing gave Sharni a fright. Who could it be? Maybe Janice. Or John, perhaps?

Before she had time to stand up and answer it, the ringing stopped.

Sharni sighed and sank back into the chair. Probably a wrong number. Still, the phone ringing reminded her that she'd promised to call Janice tonight. When she did, no way was she going to tell her anything about Adrian following her up here. She didn't want her sister to know what was going on. She certainly didn't want to hear all her dire warnings.

Sharni already knew Adrian wasn't in love with her. And, heaven help her, she wasn't in love with him. Love was a warmer, kinder emotion than what was raging through her at this moment. She'd experienced love. With Ray. And this was not love. This was something else entirely. She'd sensed that from the start.

What was consuming her had many names. Sexual attraction; chemistry; desire; passion; lust.

Lust, Sharni decided, came closest to describing what she felt for Adrian.

Lust was one of the seven deadly sins. For good reason, she agonised.

Lust banished your conscience, and your common sense. It made you a slave to your senses, and to your desires, which seemed to become darker and stronger by the moment.

She wanted to go to that motel and throw herself at Adrian's feet. She craved his arms around her and his mouth on hers.

Only her pride stopped her.

But for how long? How long before she begged him to touch her; before she did every wicked thing that was running through her head?

'Oh, God,' she cried, and buried her face in her hands.

# CHAPTER FIFTEEN

NEARLY noon, and Adrian still hadn't come.

Sharni was getting agitated. So was Mozart, who was pacing up and down the front veranda. Or he had been, last time she'd looked.

The possibility that Adrian had decided to forget about her and go back to Sydney was a constant torment in her mind. Although to do that seemed terribly cruel. Was Adrian cruel? She hadn't thought so. But what did she know?

He'd said he was going into the shopping centre this morning to buy some work clothes. Sharni had estimated that would probably take him a couple of hours. She'd dashed along to the closest shopping centre to grab some food first thing this morning, leaving herself plenty of time after coming home for some female titivation before Adrian's estimated time of arrival at around eleven.

That ETA had come and gone an hour ago.

For the umpteenth time, Sharni joined Mozart on the front veranda.

The sight of Louise waddling across the street towards her front gate brought a frustrated groan to her lips.

But it was inevitable, she supposed.

'Hello,' Louise called out. 'Nice day, isn't it?'

'Very,' Sharni returned.

'You've been away,' she said, stopping at the front gate when Mozart gave a low growl.

Good dog, Sharni thought.

'Yes. I visited my sister in Swansea,' she lied.

'How nice. I have the most dreadful cold so I won't come too close. I've been in bed all weekend.'

That was good news. Louise's bedroom

was at the back of her house, which meant she probably hadn't seen Adrian yesterday, or his car.

But she was going to any second, Sharni thought with a mixture of delight and dismay when she spotted the bright yellow sports car coming down the street.

Louise turned at the sound of the engine, which had a deeper throb than most cars.

'Are you expecting someone?' the older woman asked when Adrian's car did a U-turn at the end of the road and pulled up outside Sharni's house.

Sharni had to think quickly on her feet. 'Yes, I've hired a renovation company to do the place up a bit. I've decided to sell. That's the owner now.'

Sharni was about to add that he looked amazingly like Ray when the words died in her throat.

Because the man who climbed out from behind the wheel didn't look like Ray at all.

He didn't look much like Adrian, either. But it *was* Adrian, with very short hair, dark stubble all over his lower face, and a pair of wraparound sunglasses that totally hid his gorgeous blue eyes. He strode round the front of the car, very workmanlike in blue jeans, brown boots, a red checked shirt and a brown bomber jacket, with lambswool trim.

'Mornin, ma'am,' he greeted Louise, who quickly moved out of his way.

'Mornin', Mrs Johnson,' he added with a sneaky wink as he strode up the front path. 'Sorry I'm a bit late. Hi there, little fella,' he directed at Mozart, who quivered with pleasure when Adrian bent to pat him.

'Watch it,' Louise warned. 'He bites.'

'Not me, ma'am. Dogs just love me,' Adrian said as he scooped Mozart up into his arms. 'Now, if you'll excuse us, I need to have a little chat with Mrs Johnson about what needs to be done around here.'

With that, he used his free hand to take Sharni's elbow and shepherd her inside the house, well away from a bug-eyed Louise.

'Did I do well?' he asked once they made it safely into the kitchen.

'You did very well,' she complimented. 'You know, I didn't recognise you when you first got out of the car.'

'Really.' He dropped Mozart gently onto his feet, then swept off his sunglasses and slipped them in his shirt pocket.

Sharni stared up into his ruggedly handsome face, which no longer reminded her so much of Ray. Though his eyes were still the same. 'You look different with your hair like that,' she said. 'And this…' Without thinking, she reached up and ran her hand slowly over his stubbly chin.

Adrian froze under her touch.

Shortly after leaving yesterday, he'd gone

through a weak moment when he'd rung Sharni's home number with the intention of apologising for his no-sex-until-she-begged-him threat.

Fortunately, he'd changed his mind before she'd answered. Because he really wanted her to beg him; wanted her to face the depth of her desire for him. *Him*, not her dead husband.

His dramatically changing his appearance this morning had not been done to fool her friends and neighbours. It was a test, one which she seemed to be passing if the look in her eyes was anything to go by.

She still desired him, he realised with a rush of relief.

Unfortunately, he desired her more.

It was agony ignoring the urge to crush her to him. But it had to be done. Because if he gave in and started making love to her, she would never believe that his feelings for her went beyond desire. She would continue to think of him as the big bad wolf; as one of the bad guys.

No. He had to wait. And make her wait, till she couldn't stand waiting any longer. It would be worth it to hear her put her desire into words; to force her to make the first pass.

Adrian replaced his sunglasses, then took a step backwards, so that her hand fell from his face.

'Time for me to get to work,' he said abruptly. 'Where do you keep your lawn-mower and garden tools? I'll attack the grounds today. Tomorrow I'll do some general repairs. Then on Wednesday, I'll get started on the painting.'

She frowned up at him. 'Don't you have to get back to your own work in Sydney?'

'No. Like I told you. I'm between projects at the moment.' Not strictly true as of today. He had planned to start on a revolutionary new design for a retirement village, one he was going to enter into a competition, with the winner awarded a multimillion-dollar contract.

But that would just have to go on the back-burner for a week or two. His priorities in life had changed.

'The lawnmower and tools?' he repeated with arched brows.

She shrugged, then led him through the back door, down into the back yard where there was a garden shed in the far corner. In there was everything he needed, including a half-full petrol can and a surprisingly wide range of DIY tools, all hanging in a highly or-ganised fashion on a huge board. Adrian liked things to be organised, not being able to stand a messy desk, or messy drawers.

'Can I help?' she asked as he busied himself, filling the mower.

'I'd rather do this by myself,' he replied, not wanting her around him all the time. If he kept her at a distance he just might make it through the day without jumping her very beautiful bones. Adrian was an observant man and it hadn't escaped his notice that Sharni had gone to considerable trouble with her appearance today. Her hair was faultless, falling in smooth bangs around her beautifully made up face. She was only casually dressed, but flatteringly so, in tight black jeans and a cream ribbed jumper that moulded over her breasts and hugged her slender waist. She smelled good, too, her perfume a musky scent, which made him think of sex.

Adrian suspected that subconsciously—or even consciously—she was trying to seduce him.

As he glanced up at her Adrian steeled himself to resist her womanly wiles. 'If you're serious about selling, then there must be things for you to do inside. Give the place a thorough spring-clean, then throw out everything you haven't used or worn in the past two years. That way, when you move, you won't need too big a truck.'

'Yes, yes, I suppose I could do that,' she said in a not very convincing manner.

He straightened and looked hard at her. 'You are serious about selling and moving, aren't you?'

Her arms folded defensively. 'I don't usually say things I don't mean.'

'That's good. You'll have plenty to occupy your mind, then, won't you? Now, if you'll excuse me, I want to get on with this.'

I *am* serious about selling and moving, Sharni lectured herself as she trailed somewhat reluctantly back inside.

Janice had been over the moon when she'd told her about her decision last night. So there was no going back now, even if inside just the thought of such a massive life change made her feel sick.

She didn't start cleaning, or sorting out her clothes as per Adrian's suggestion. Instead, she stood at the sink, staring through the window, watching Adrian mow the back lawn.

He's even sexier with his hair cut short, she thought.

She liked the stubble on his chin, too.

An erotic image popped into her head of his lying between her naked legs, as he had more than once last Saturday afternoon. She shuddered as she relived the feel of his tongue licking her most sensitive spot. Shuddered a second time as she imagined how it would feel with his roughened cheeks rubbing against the soft flesh of her inner thighs at the same time.

Oh, God. She wanted him to do that to her. Wanted to do it to him as well. Use her mouth on him.

The intensity of her desire was perturbing, but merciless, forcing her to make the most humiliating decision of her life. She would go to him tonight. And she would beg him to take her to bed.

It seemed perverse, Sharni was to think when she called him in for lunch an hour later, that, having come to such a pride-crushing decision, she could behave around him with amazing composure. She coolly served him a very nice lunch, making polite conversation during the fifteen minutes it took him to eat it.

After lunch, she did make a move on cleaning the house, giving the living room a proper going-over, even taking down the curtains and popping them in the washing machine, though she wasn't able to hang them out till Adrian moved from the back yard to the front.

When he refused afternoon tea, saying he wanted to work till the sun went down, Sharni decided to do what Adrian had suggested earlier and go through her wardrobe. It came as no surprise that most of her clothes were over five years old, some of them even older. Lots were hopelessly out of fashion. She quickly filled two garbage bags with things to be given to charity, including several pairs of shoes and a couple of old handbags that had seen better days.

During this rather ruthless throwaway, Sharni kept ignoring the large plastic shopping bag that she'd thrown down in the bottom of her wardrobe after returning from Sydney on Saturday. It contained the outfit she'd worn to *The Phantom* and which she'd never wanted to look at ever again.

Even now, she remained hesitant, till, in a burst of self-irritation, she grabbed the shopping bag and spilled its contents onto the bed.

The beaded top sparkled up at her, its neckline not as low cut as she'd thought. Sharni picked up the skirt, pleased to see that it hadn't creased one bit. She laid out the whole outfit on top of the patchwork quilt, placing the shoes on the floor under the hem of the skirt.

It didn't look anything special like that. It needed a woman's body in it.

Her heartbeat quickened as she quickly stripped off down to her panties and pulled the clothes on before she could think better of it. She didn't bother with pantihose this time. After all, she wasn't going anywhere. She just wanted to see what she'd looked like last Saturday night.

The shoes took her a while, her fingers clumsy with the bows at her ankles. Finally, she stood up, astonished at the height of the heels and how sexy they made her feel.

It only took her five steps to cross the bedroom to where there was a cheval mirror in one corner. But they were enough to transform her once again into the turned-on creature who'd let Adrian have sex with her bending over a chair.

Sharni stared when she saw her reflection.

Who was that girl with the wide dilated eyes and the panting parted lips?

'Going somewhere?'

She whirled at Adrian's voice, embarrassment making her face flame. 'How dare you sneak up on me like that?'

'I didn't sneak. I knocked on the back door to tell you that I'd finished for the day, but you didn't answer. It still looks great on you, by the way. But not exactly the right outfit for cleaning. Unless, of course, you've something else in mind…'

He levered himself away from where he'd been leaning on the doorframe, his blue eyes glittering as they raked over her.

She didn't say a word. Couldn't. Till he took a step into the room.

'Don't come in here!' she cried out.

He halted, his eyes clouding over with frustration. 'Why not? You want me to. You know you do.'

'Not in here,' she choked out.

His eyes narrowed as he glanced around the room. 'Oh, I see. Not in here, in Ray's bedroom. Or in Ray's house. Very well. I'll try to be sensitive to your feelings, though for pity's sake the man's been dead for five years. Somehow I don't think he would mind.'

'*I'd* mind!'

'Very well. Come to my motel room. Tonight. At ten.'

'*That* late?' The moment those two telling words left her mouth Sharni knew there was no going back.

'Take it or leave it,' he bit out. 'It's room eighteen. The place isn't full so there's plenty of parking spaces nearby.'

She hated him at that moment. Hated him and wanted him at the same time. So much for her earlier composure. Her pride was once again in tatters, lust reigning supreme with all its primal power.

'I will take your silence for agreement.'

She gritted her teeth and glowered at him.

'By the way, don't wear that,' he snapped. 'That's far too many clothes for what I have in mind. The shoes can stay, but nothing else. Absolutely nothing else.'

Shock sent her mouth gaping wide. 'I can't come to your door, stark naked!'

'Then wear a coat. But I want you totally naked underneath.'

'That's disgusting.'

'No. That's what you'll have to do to get what you want. I am what you want, aren't I, Sharni? Or is just sex with any man now? Tell me so that I can be sure of where I stand.'

'You *are* cruel,' she threw at him.

'A cruel man would not have stopped at this door,' he refuted. 'Now tell me what I want to hear, Sharni. Or. God help me, I'm going to go get in my car and I'm never coming back.'

For a split second, she almost let him go.

But the devil wouldn't allow it. He whispered in her ear, promising wicked pleasures that only Adrian could give her. All for the price of a few simple words.

'I don't want sex with any other man,' she blurted out. 'Only you.'

'And you'll do what I asked?'

'Yes,' she said, trembling at the thought.

'Don't be late,' he growled. And was gone.

# CHAPTER SIXTEEN

ADRIAN found the next five hours almost un-bearable. He managed to force some dinner down. And he drank way too much, searching for some mental peace.

But nothing could ease the emotional torment that had consumed him back in that bedroom, once he'd realised that Sharni would never love him. Because she was still in love with her husband.

The pain of this pride-shattering discovery had made him cruel, as she'd said.

But she was cruel, too.

Agreeing to his outrageous demands had shown him better than any words that she didn't want his love, or his caring. Just his body.

Adrian had no doubt that she would show up right on time, wearing nothing but her birthday suit and those shag-me shoes. And when she did, there would be nothing left for him but to do exactly that, till she begged him to stop.

Sharni could not believe that she was doing this. Driving to a motel for an assignation with Adrian with nothing on but a trench-coat and a pair of high heels.

What would happen if she had a car accident? What would the ambulance officers think?

That you're a whore, came back the soul-destroying answer.

So why didn't her soul feel destroyed? Why were her only feelings those of anticipation and excitement?

Maybe I've sold my soul to the devil. Maybe I'm possessed.

The sight of the motel sign on the right sent her stomach into uncontrollable flutters. Nearly there.

'You can still drive past,' she urged herself out loud. 'Still go home.'

She didn't do either. She turned the car into the motel's concrete driveway, her heart pounding behind her ribs.

The drive past Reception brought another burst of anxiety that someone might stop the car and ask her what she was doing here. No one did, but by the time she parked next to Adrian's yellow car Sharni felt faint with nervous tension.

No one else was arriving or leaving, she noted with relief as she climbed out of her car, closed the door, then locked it.

'Oh, Lord,' she said with a shaky sigh, then turned and made her way very unsteadily to the door of unit number eighteen, which was thankfully on the ground floor of the two storeyed building.

Scooping in a deep breath, Sharni gripped her car keys with one hand whilst she knocked with the other.

No answer.

She knocked again.

Still no answer.

Her head whirled when it occurred to her that Adrian might not be going to answer.

Suddenly, the door was wrenched open and there he stood, dripping wet with a white towel slung low around his hips.

'Sorry,' he muttered, lifting his hand to sweep back hair that was no longer there. 'I was in the shower, and didn't hear you knock.'

'You…you said ten o'clock.'

'I lost track of time.'

She blinked. How could he have lost track of time? She'd been counting down every second, dying for the moment when they would be together again.

'I'm sorry too,' she choked out. 'Look, I don't think I can do this, Adrian. Not now…'

'What in hell are you talking about?'

'Your asking me to come here dressed like this was some kind of payback, wasn't it? You wanted to humiliate me. You don't care about me at all. Not really.'

His face filled with too many mixed emotions for her to fathom.

He shook his head, his arms rising and falling from his sides in an attitude of total exasperation. 'Hell, Sharni, I'm just a man, not a saint. Yes, I confess there was an element of revenge in my demands. But that was because I thought *you* didn't care.'

'Oh…'

*Did* she care about him?

Sharni wasn't sure. All she could be sure of was that the sight of him standing there in nothing but a towel made her heart race and her insides go to mush. All she could think about was his being inside her again.

Maybe she was a whore after all. Or she was, with him.

'For pity's sake, don't just stand there, looking guilty,' he ground out, pulling her into the room and shutting the door behind her. 'Like I told you last Saturday, there's nothing wrong with enjoying yourself in the sack. It also isn't mandatory that you fall in love with every lover you have in your life. But it would be nice not to be thought of as just a piece of meat.'

'But I don't think that!'

'Don't you?'

'No!'

'Then how do you think of me? Be honest now.'

'I'm not sure what I think, or feel. You've confused me from the start.'

'Because I look like Ray. No, don't bother to keep denying it. It's written all over your face. At least I know where I stand now, and I won't go imagining tonight means more than it means. Now take that damn coat off and let me look at you.'

She stared at him, astonished at how such an angrily delivered request could turn her on with all the speed and power of a lightning bolt. Her nipples tightened against the silk lining of the coat, her stomach flipping over in anticipation of what was to come.

'Don't make me take it off you,' he went on, his blue eyes glittering.

Her hands trembled as they lifted to the top button, her head dizzy with instant desire. Suddenly, she could not wait to stand naked before him. To have those cold, sexy eyes on her.

She'd taken ages earlier this evening preparing herself for this moment. She'd bathed at length, she'd rubbed scented moisturiser into her denuded skin, then painted her nails a deep scarlet, her mouth glossed to match.

And now she was about to show him all that she had done.

The coat dropped off her shoulders and she stood there, frozen.

'You shouldn't have, you know,' he muttered as his heavy-lidded gaze raked over her. 'I won't have any mercy on you now. But then you haven't come here for mercy, have you?' he said as he stripped off the towel and walked slowly towards her.

Sharni's mouth dropped open at the sight of him. He was so huge, and so hard.

She swallowed. Then swallowed again.

He smiled the devil's smile, then pulled her roughly to him.

'I'm not going to kiss you,' he grated out when she turned her face expectantly up to his. 'Not this first time.'

Sharni gasped when he took her up into his arms and literally threw her on the bed. His hands were brutal as they pried her legs wide apart, his penetration just as savage. Her raw groan echoed the mad mixture of pleasure and pain that ricocheted through her as he grabbed her hips and drove in even deeper.

The swiftness of his orgasm shocked Sharni, her strangled cry of protest bringing a wry laugh to his lips.

'Looks like I won,' he said.

'You really are a bastard,' she returned with a flash of true venom.

He levered himself up onto his elbows, then smiled down at her. 'And you, my love, are beautiful beyond compare.'

Sharni groaned. Why, oh, why, did he have to throw in that kind of compliment when she wanted to hate him?

'I think a hot shower is in order,' he said. 'Then back to bed for some serious sex.'

Adrian lay stretched out on the bed next to her, his hands behind his head, his eyes on the ceiling. Sharni was sleeping, her back to him, her breathing deep and even, the sleep of a thoroughly satisfied woman.

For a man who'd had several whiskeys before she'd arrived, he'd acquitted himself extremely well. Never before had he made love to a woman so many times in succession.

What on earth were you trying to prove, Adrian? he asked himself. That you're the greatest lover in the world? Do you honestly think giving her multiple orgasms would make her fall in love with you?

Adrian sighed and turned his head towards the bedside clock, the red numbers showing one seventeen.

He should try to sleep, he supposed. But sleep didn't seem important any more. He had to find a way to win this woman's heart.

It wasn't going to be through sex, he finally accepted. And it probably wasn't going to be because he helped her fix up her house.

There was something about him that didn't fulfil her. Something that her husband had, and that he obviously didn't.

Adrian wasn't used to not getting what he wanted in life. Wasn't used to being considered second best.

This time, however, things seemed to be out of his control.

Felicity would be pleased to know, he realised with considerable irony, that she would probably get her wish.

A woman was going to break his heart.

And her name was Sharni Johnson.

# CHAPTER SEVENTEEN

'So what's this I hear about some handsome hunk doing up your place?'

Sharni's head shot up from where she was helping John operate on a kelpie who'd had a run-in with a car.

'How on earth…?'

'Louise came in yesterday with her cat for me to worm,' John explained, without lifting his head from what he was doing.

An exasperated sigh punched through Sharni's lips. 'That woman!'

Her Nosy Parker neighbour had taken every opportunity during the last few days to drop over. Unfortunately, Mozart had stopped snapping and snarling at her, Adrian's presence having changed the dog's personality back into the engaging little terrier he'd been when Ray had been alive.

'That's not an answer to my question,' John pointed out.

'Which is?'

'Who is this hunk and where does he come from? He's not a local because I also heard he's staying at the motel down the road. Been there all week.'

Sharni's mouth dropped open. 'How on earth do you know *that*?'

'When a man drives a bright yellow Corvette, he's going to be noticed.'

At last John raised his head, having completed the stitches.

'So tell me about him.'

Sharni couldn't possibly tell him the truth. She'd be way too embarrassed, especially how she'd spent every evening this week.

'He's just a friend of a friend from Sydney,' she said. 'He's helping me do up the house with a view to selling.'

'A friend of a friend? Don't take me for a fool, Sharni. He's more than that.'

'Very well…yes,' she admitted, blushing. 'Yes, he is.'

'That's good, then. It's high time you started to live again. And it's good that you've decided to sell. That place has far too many bad memories for you. So tell me a bit more about him?' he finished up, his eyes dropping back to his patient.

Sharni hesitated, then decided it might be a relief to talk to someone who was both sympathetic and objective. She'd been tempted a couple of times to ring Janice and tell her about her ongoing affair with Adrian, but was worried about her sister's reaction.

She still wasn't about to confess all to John.

218 THE MILLIONAIRE'S INEXPERIENCED LOVE-SLAVE

There were some details that would simply have to remain her own dark little secret.

'He *is* a friend of a friend, actually,' she said, hoping this made the speed of her affair not seem so sluttish. 'I…um…I ran into him when I was down in Sydney last weekend.'

'What does he do for a living? Something tells me he's not a house painter, not driving a car like that.'

'He's an architect. A very good one.'

'Mmm. He'd be quite a catch, then.'

'I have no intention of ever marrying him!' This was the kind of comment she would have expected from Janice.

John glanced up again. 'Why not? The man must be mad about you to spend every day working like a dog out in this weather.'

It had been bitterly cold all week, with today just a little bit warmer.

It bothered her somewhat, the thought that Adrian might be in love with her. She didn't want him to be in love with her.

'I've only known him a week,' she said.

'I only knew my Bess for two days before I decided to marry her.'

'Adrian's not into marriage.'

'What's he into, then?'

Sharni was glad John's eyes were on the dog and not her reddening cheeks.

'Brunettes,' she said a bit sharply.

John looked up and laughed. 'Sydney is full of brunettes, love. He doesn't have to come to Katoomba to find one.'

'I think I was the one who got away.'

'Ah. I see. You became a challenge.'

Not as much as she would have liked to be, she thought as she recalled the way she'd presented herself to him last Monday night.

Adrian seemed to like making her do things that were potentially humiliating. He'd vowed to make her beg. And she had, this past week, more than once. She'd done a lot of other things, too.

Thank God she was at work today and didn't have to endure the frustration of being around the house, watching him and wanting him.

He never touched her there. Or kissed her. But he would look at her occasionally and she would literally burn for him. It was no wonder that by the time each evening came she was beyond shame. Beyond everything but doing whatever he wanted her to do.

'What are you afraid of with this man, Sharni?'

John's question startled her.

'Ray wouldn't mind, you know,' he went on before she could answer. 'He would want you to be happy. If this man loves you, then give him a chance.'

She shook her head. 'You don't understand.'

'I understand more than you think. You're different this week, Sharni. You've come to life again. Now all you have to do is decide to love again.'

'Love is not a decision, John. It just happens.'

'Then let it happen. Don't shut this man out. I'll bet you haven't told him about the baby you lost, have you?'

Sharni stiffened. 'No.'

'Then you should.'

But she didn't want to. Didn't want to do or say anything that would prevent her going to his motel room tonight.

She knew what she was living was just a fantasy. Knew it would end one day. But she wasn't going to end it. That would have to come from Adrian.

Till then…

'How's Mozart?' John asked, obviously changing the subject.

'He's fine.'

'Louise said he's a changed dog since your helper arrived.'

Sharni gritted her teeth. Louise again! But she refused to bite. Pity Mozart had given up the habit. 'He does seem to be enjoying having a man around the house.'

'Dogs are sensitive creatures. Maybe he knows something that you don't know.'

'Like what?'

John shrugged. 'Who knows? If I was Dr Dolittle, I could ask Mozart for you.'

Sharni was late leaving the clinic that Friday afternoon, an emergency coming in at the last moment. She usually knocked off at four, but by the time she arrived home her watch showed after five, and the sun had just set.

Adrian, however, was still painting the newly mended front fence with the paint spray-gun he'd hired the previous day. Mozart was keeping a safe distance from the spray, running to greet Sharni when she arrived.

'What you know,' she told the dog as she bent to stroke his head, 'is where you're best off.'

Adrian lifted the protective glasses from his

paint-spattered face at that moment, and smiled over at her. 'Just five more minutes and it'll be done. What do you think?'

She gazed with true admiration at all he'd achieved in five short days. John was right. He had worked like a mad dog, especially today. When she'd left this morning, the house had only been half painted. Now it shone a brilliant white under the fading light.

'It looks great,' she said. 'But you must be exhausted.'

His smile turned wicked. 'Not that exhausted. But I'll need some time to clean up and get a few things ready before you come.'

Sharni froze. 'What kind of things?' she asked, unable to keep the worry out of her voice.

Last night, he'd introduced her to some mild bondage, securing her wrists behind her back with the sash of his bathrobe, telling her to pretend that she was a love-slave who'd been sold to an evil prince who could do what he liked to her. He, of course, was the evil prince. He'd turned her on with the erotic verbal pictures he painted of her being kept naked for his pleasure; of being shackled to his bed every night; of being made to kneel before him on command, and take him into her mouth.

Which she had.

But she didn't want things to go any further than that.

Worry crinkled her forehead.

'Not those kind of things,' he told her brusquely. 'Shall we say eight? No, that's a bit early. Make it eight-thirty.'

Eight-thirty! That was eons away. Last night it had been seven-thirty.

'Wear what you wore when I first saw you in Sydney,' he commanded, then returned to doing what he was doing.

She just stared at him, her heart thudding behind her ribs. But he didn't look up at her again. He wouldn't, she knew. This was what he always did at the end of each day. Gave his orders for the evening ahead, then ignored her.

It always turned her on. Always. But more so, each time.

Shaken, she let herself into the house and ran to her bedroom where she threw herself onto the bed and burst into tears. What she was crying about she had no idea. This was what she wanted with Adrian, wasn't it? A strictly sexual affair.

Yes, of course it was, she told herself, and began punching the pillows. I don't want to love him. Or for him to love me. I don't!

But the tears kept coming and so, finally, did acceptance of the hidden truth.

John had been so right. She *was* afraid. Afraid of giving her heart and having it broken once more. Afraid of loving and losing.

But what she was doing with Adrian no longer made her feel good about herself. If she kept going, she would end up turning into a conscienceless sex-addict.

It had to stop. And it had to stop tonight!

# CHAPTER EIGHTEEN

SHARNI had worked herself up into a right state by the time she arrived at Adrian's motel-room door that night.

It wasn't going to be easy, telling him that she didn't want to do this any more; that she wanted a real relationship.

She should not have worn the clothes he'd commanded her to wear, she realised as she lifted her hand to knock. It didn't set the right tone. She should have come in old jeans and the most unattractive jumper she owned. Or a daggy track-suit. She certainly should not have taken so much time over her hair and make-up. She very definitely should have put on a bra under her pink jumper.

Erect nipples poking out were going to give him the wrong message.

'Oh!' she exclaimed when Adrian swept open the door. Not because he was naked, as he had been the previous night. But because the room was filled with candles of varying shapes and sizes, all lit and glowing in the darkness.

'You like?' He smiled as he took her hand and drew her inside.

'It's…lovely.'

'I thought I'd do romance tonight, complete with champagne.'

He shut the door, then walked over to the coffee-table where there was an ice bucket hiding in the middle of the candles, along with two tall wineglasses. Some soft music was playing in the background, probably from the radio.

Sharni watched, torn, whilst he popped the

cork and filled the glasses. How could she tell him that she didn't want to do *this*? This was sweet and, yes, romantic. Nothing like their erotically charged rendezvous last night. *He* was different too. He was dressed, for starters, in stylish grey trousers and an open-necked royal blue silk shirt. He looked very handsome and elegant. He'd shaved as well, she noticed.

'When on earth did you find time to do all this?'

'Yours is not to reason why, beautiful. And you certainly are that tonight,' he added as he handed her a glass.

'Thank you,' she said, struggling with the temptation not to say anything now.

He eyed her closely when she didn't drink. 'Is there something wrong? Have I made a mistake with the candles and champagne?'

'No, no, I love them. It's just…'

'Just what?'

'Nothing,' she said, and took a quick swallow of the champagne. 'Nothing.'

Adrian gripped his glass so hard he was surprised it didn't snap.

Nothing was going to work with this woman.

It was perfectly obvious she was disappointed. She didn't want romance. She wanted sex. Rough sex, loveless sex.

She liked him talking dirty to her. Liked being tied up and ravaged. Liked playing at being his love-slave.

He'd mistakenly thought that she'd get bored with nothing but sex. That she'd eventually want something more.

He'd been a fool!

Tonight would definitely be his swansong. The house was in pretty good order. She could sell it now without losing too much money. As for him…he was out of here. Or he would be in the morning.

Tonight, however, was going to be just for him. He was going to have her every which way, without giving a hoot if she enjoyed it or not!

His cell phone ringing snapped him out of his increasingly vengeful thoughts.

'Excuse me,' he said abruptly, and moved over to where he'd put his phone on the bedside table.

'Adrian Palmer,' he answered.

'Adrian. It's your mother.'

'Mum! It's not like you to ring me on my mobile.'

'I did try to ring you at your home number but I keep getting your answering machine. I've left several messages for you to ring me back, but you haven't.'

'Sorry. I'm away at the moment.'

'Not on holidays, surely. You never go on holidays. Or visit your mother,' she added snippily.

He had to smile. 'You're right again, Mum. I've been working. So what's up?'

'Does something have to be up for me to ring you?'

Not really. She rang him on a regular basis. But it seemed she'd been pretty desperate to contact him this time.

'I wanted to see if you'd like to fly up and visit me this weekend.'

'Is there any particular reason?'

'Just that I haven't seen you since Easter. Of course, if you're working…'

'I'd love to come,' he said immediately.

'That's wonderful. When can I expect you?'

'Just one sec.'

He put the phone on temporary hold and looked straight at Sharni, thinking this was sure to be the final nail in the coffin of his non-relationship with her.

'My mother has asked me to fly up this

weekend for a visit,' he said. 'Would you like to come with me?'

Her eager smile was so unexpected that he nearly dropped the phone. 'I'd love to,' she said. 'But…'

'But what?'

'What about Mozart?'

'We'll take him with us.'

'Could we?'

'Why not?'

'He doesn't settle too well in strange places. I tell you what. We could take him to my sister's place at Swansea, then fly the rest of the way from Newcastle airport.'

'Or we could drive,' he counter suggested. 'We could stop at a motel midway tomorrow night, then go the rest of the way on Sunday morning.'

She seemed pleased with that idea. 'I'd like that. I'm not all that keen on flying.'

Adrian's elation came through in his voice as

he reconnected with his mother. 'Mum, would you mind if I brought someone with me?'

'What, you mean a girl?' No missing the shock in his mother's voice.

'Yes.'

'I can't believe it. Are you serious?'

'Yes,' he said, and glanced over at Sharni. 'Very.'

'I was beginning to think you might be gay.'

Adrian had to laugh. 'Sorry. No such luck.'

'Oh, Adrian, I'm so pleased.'

'Wait till you meet her. Look, I'm going to drive up, so we won't get to your place till lunch-time on the Sunday. Of course, I won't come unless you cook my favourite dinner,' he added teasingly.

'Baked leg of lamb.'

'Right in one.'

His mother chuckled. 'You always did love your baked lamb.'

'With apple pie and ice cream for afters.'

'I'm glad to see you're still a simple boy at

heart. So what's she called, this girl?' his mother asked.

'Sharni,' he said, and looked over at her with adoring eyes.

Sharni felt the impact of his loving glance right down to her toes.

Never before had Adrian looked at her that way. It shattered any lingering doubt that he might only have wanted her for sex, making her feel both wonderful and ashamed at the same time.

She didn't catch the rest of his conversation with his mother, already planning in her mind what she would say to him when he came off the phone.

He turned to her after hanging up, his expression somewhat guarded. 'I have to admit you've surprised me,' he said. 'I was sure you'd say no.'

Her smile was soft. 'I might have, even as

recently as yesterday. But I realised today that I was acting like a fool. I'm sorry I've let you think that all I wanted from you was sex, Adrian. That's not true. I want more than just an affair with you.'

'How much more?'

'I don't know yet. But I'd like the opportunity to find out.'

He frowned at her. 'Does that mean you don't want any sex tonight?'

She looked at him, at the candles, at the bed.

To lie didn't seem the best way to begin a relationship.

'I don't want sex. No.'

He could not hide his disappointment.

'I want you to make love to me,' she added, and walked into his waiting arms.

# CHAPTER NINETEEN

'I'M STILL totally gobsmacked,' Janice said, shaking her head as she glanced over at Sharni.

The two sisters were sitting under the covered pergola at the back of Janice's house. Pete was busy cooking steak and sausages on the nearby barbecue whilst Adrian stood next to him with a light beer in his hands. Janice's two boys were haring around the back yard, playing army games, with Mozart chasing after them, having the time of his life.

'You mean about how much Adrian looks like Ray?' Sharni returned.

'Well, yes, that too. It's no wonder you

thought he could have been Ray's twin brother. But I was thinking more of the change in you. You're positively glowing.'

Sharni smiled. 'I'm very happy,' she said.

Last night had been wonderful, Adrian showing her he could be a tender as well as a dominating lover. Then today, during the car ride here, they'd finally started talking in a deep and meaningful way. She knew all about his childhood, which sounded pretty perfect. His parents had obviously doted on him.

Adrian knew a lot more about her background, too, including the tragic death of her mother when Sharni had been only thirteen, plus her poor father's succumbing to alcoholism afterwards, resulting in his death from liver failure a few years back.

One thing he still didn't yet know, however, was about the baby she'd lost. She couldn't seem to find the right moment to bring the subject up.

'He loves you,' her sister pronounced.

'Yes,' Sharni agreed, despite his never having said so much in words.

But she had seen his love last night. And felt it, over and over.

Janice frowned. 'Don't you love him back, Sharni?'

'I do,' she said. 'He's a wonderful man, and a marvellous lover.'

'But?' her sister prompted.

Sharni sighed. Trust Janice to pick up on the one lingering doubt she had about her own feelings. 'It doesn't feel the same as what I had with Ray. Don't get me wrong. It's great, what we have together. But there's something missing.'

Janice said nothing for a minute or two, just sat there, with a thoughtful expression on her face. 'I know what's missing,' she said at last.

'What?'

'Need.'

'What do you mean? Need?'

'Sharni, as a kid, you were always bringing home stray cats and birds with broken wings. You loved looking after wounded animals. That was what Ray was, another wounded animal. His needy nature fulfilled your nurturing nature. I'll bet that, down deep, you don't think Adrian needs you. You believe he'd survive without you.'

'Well, he would. Just look at him, Janice. He has everything a man could have. Looks, brains, success, charm, confidence. He could get any woman he wants.'

'But he only wants *you*, dear sister. Can't you see that?'

She could. And she still wasn't sure why.

'Have you told him about the baby?' Janice asked gently.

'Not yet,' she admitted. 'But I will. Soon.'

Sharni could feel her sister frowning at her.

'I've only known him a week, Janice,' she said swiftly. Although it had felt like a lifetime.

'Don't let him get away, Sharni.'

Sharni was still thinking about her sister's words of advice when they resumed their trip North shortly after two.

'I've booked us into a motel at Nambucca Heads,' Adrian told her as the powerful car began to eat up the miles along the Pacific Highway. 'That's a bit more than halfway to our destination.'

'Great,' she said, and settled right back into the leather seat.

Adrian slanted her a warm smile. 'Comfy?'

Sharni's smile carried appreciation. 'This is a gorgeous car to ride in. So smooth.'

'Like they say in the classics, you only get what you pay for.'

'Mmm.'

'Mozart didn't seem to mind our leaving him behind,' he remarked.

'He's a different dog since you came along. Doesn't even snap at Louise any more. Which is a shame,' Sharni added drily.

Adrian laughed. 'She's not that bad.'

'You don't have to live next to her.'

'True. Care for some music? Or do you want to talk some more?'

Now was her chance to tell him about the baby. But once again, she shied away from the subject.

'Some music would be nice,' she said. 'Janice talked non-stop and I'm feeling a little tired.'

'Why don't you try to have a nap?'

Adrian turned on the radio and she closed her eyes.

Sleep came surprisingly quickly, possibly because she hadn't had much rest during the past week, or possibly because she'd had a couple of glasses of red wine with her barbecue lunch.

When Sharni resurfaced, she was startled to

find that the sun had set and they were turning off the main highway.

'Feeling refreshed, Sleeping Beauty?' Adrian asked.

'Much. Where are we?'

'Nearly there.'

'You must be tired of driving.'

'A little. We might eat in tonight. Would Chinese do?'

'Sounds good to me.'

'Do you know you are the most accommodating woman?'

'I come from a long line of accommodating women.'

Adrian laughed. 'You could be right. Your sister's great. And so is her husband. I won't mind having them for in-laws.'

Sharni sucked in sharply. 'What did you say?'

'You heard me.'

'Are you asking me to marry you?' Sharni could not keep the shock from her voice.

'Damn. I meant to do it right, down on one knee with a huge diamond in my hand. And so I will. When I get the chance.'

'But…but…you haven't even said that you love me.'

'Really? I thought I did. Last night.'

'No, you didn't.'

'Damn. Another boo boo.' He pulled over to the side of the road, skidding a little in some gravel before stopping abruptly and turning to face her.

'Then let me remedy that mistake immediately,' he said, cupping her face and kissing her startled lips. 'I love you, Sharni Johnson. I love you so much that I refuse to live the rest of my life without you as my wife.'

'Marriage is a big step, Adrian.'

'Yes, I know.'

'But I…I might not be able to have…um… children.' She'd almost said *more* children.

'We'll cross that bridge when we come to it. Together.'

That touched her. Terribly.

But he was also doing it again. Taking over. Much too fast this time.

'You're rushing me,' she said.

'Life is short, Sharni.'

'I need more time.'

'Not too long. I'm not a patient man.'

Her smile was wry. 'I've gathered that.'

'But you do love me, don't you?' he said, kissing her again. More hungrily this time.

By the time his mouth lifted, her head was swimming and her heart was pounding.

'Yes,' she said. 'Yes, I love you.'

He smiled the smile of a satisfied man.

Adrian was smiling that same smile into the bathroom mirror the following morning when Sharni came in to tell him their breakfast had arrived.

She'd become used to the small differences between him and Ray—especially around his face. So the unexpected sight of Ray's features looking back at her from that mirror shocked Sharni rigid.

But then he turned around and she thought she must be going mad. Because face to face, the differences were all there again.

'What's wrong?' he said.

'What? Oh, nothing. Nothing. Breakfast's ready.'

'Good, because we have to be on the road soon if we're going to make it to Mum's place by lunch-time.'

His mother lived at Kingscliff, a seaside town not far south of the border between New South Wales and Queensland. They reached it just before noon, Sharni tensing a little at the prospect of meeting Adrian's mum. But she tried not to show it.

Kingscliff was a truly lovely spot, the beach long and white and inviting. His mother's house was lovely too, a long, two-storeyed blond-brick place, perched on the top of a hill, perfectly positioned for a splendid view of the Pacific Ocean. Distance-wise, it was probably only two hundred metres to the beach, and even less to the main road, which had plenty of shops and restaurants.

'This used to be our holiday house,' Adrian explained as they climbed out of the car. 'Dad's practice was in Brisbane, but we spent every Easter and Christmas down here. When he retired, he told me he wanted to live here, permanently. But the house was only half the size then. He asked me to draw up some plans for a more substantial but traditional home, and, voilà, you have what you see today.'

'You are obviously a brilliant architect,' Sharni said, and was being given an affectionate hug when the front door opened and a lady who looked nothing like Adrian emerged.

She was very short, with silvery grey hair, dark brown eyes and a large nose, which he hadn't inherited.

Her rather plain face broke into a wide smile as she hurried down the sloping path.

'You're earlier than I expected,' she said. 'I hope you didn't speed, you bad boy.'

Adrian laughed, and gave her a big hug. 'I tried, but Sharni told me she'd have my guts for garters.'

'Good girl,' Adrian's mother said warmly. 'He needs reining in, my boy. He think he's invulnerable.'

Sharni smiled. 'Yes, I have noticed that.'

'I can imagine,' his mother said drily, then came forward to give Sharni a hug as well. 'You've no idea how glad I am to meet you, my dear. Do you realise you are the first girl that Adrian has brought home since high school?'

'I'm hardly a girl, Mrs Palmer. I'm thirty.'

'You look like a girl to me. I'm seventy-six next birthday.'

'You don't look it.'

'Oh, she's a sweetie, this one,' she said,

linking her arms with Sharni. 'You can keep her, Adrian.'

'I intend to,' he said, shooting Sharni a possessive glance.

'By the way, call me May,' his mother said as she drew her up the steep driveway to the open front door.

The knot in her stomach finally unravelled, Sharni's tension soothed by the genuine warmth of the woman's welcome. It had worried her that Adrian's mother might think she wasn't good enough for her brilliant son.

The house was as well designed inside as outside, with the garages and guest and rumpus rooms downstairs and the master bedroom and living areas upstairs. It was furnished the way Sharni would have expected a seventy-six-year-old lady to furnish her home, with an eye to stylish comfort rather than any particular fashion.

She liked the furniture a lot, especially the pale-green-velvet-covered lounge suite with its huge armchairs and large squashy cushions.

After a brief visit to the bathroom, Sharni allowed herself to be settled on the lounge with a cream sherry served in a beautiful crystal glass. The smell of baking lamb permeated the air, whetting her appetite and making her feel even more at home.

'So what do you think of Mum?' Adrian whispered when his mother retreated to the kitchen to check on the progress of the meat.

Sharni didn't think she should say that his mother was nothing like him at all, except perhaps for her charm.

'She's very nice,' she said.

The woman herself bustled back into the lounge room and swept up her own sherry from one of the many side tables dotted around the room. 'Dinner won't be ready for another forty minutes,' she said as she sat down. 'Are you sure you won't have a drink, Adrian? There's some beer in the fridge, if you'd prefer.'

'I'll have some wine with dinner. Meanwhile, there's something I want to show Sharni.'

He stood up and moved across the room to a long oak sideboard, which had more framed photos sitting on it than Sharni had ever seen. Most of them were of Adrian, but some were of his parents. Even from a distance, Sharni could see that his father had been only marginally taller than his mother. So where had Adrian got his height from?

'Are the family photo albums still in here?' Adrian asked as he slid open one of the lower doors.

'Yes,' his mother replied. A little tensely, Sharni thought.

All those niggling doubts she'd had about Adrian's parentage came back with a rush, twisting her stomach back into a tight knot.

'Ah… Here's the one I want,' Adrian said.

'This entire album is devoted to yours truly,' he added after he sat back down next to her and opened the album across both their laps. 'There's Mum when she was preggers. About six months, weren't you, Mum?'

'About that,' his mother replied tautly.

The photo surprised Sharni, with his mother looking younger than the forty she must have been at the time, with short dark hair and dancing dark eyes that sparkled with happiness. She was standing in a park somewhere, leaning against a tree, her hands curled lovingly over her rounded stomach.

'And this is me having my first bath,' Adrian pointed out. 'And, yes, you don't have to say it. I was a bit scrawny back then. But I was born a month early. See? This is me at three months, all filled out.'

Sharni didn't look at the photo of Adrian at three months. She was still frowning down at the photo of him having his first bath, and at the woman holding him in that bath. His mother. May.

A man might not have noticed her hair. But Sharni did. Straight away.

It wasn't short as it had been in the photo of her when she was six months pregnant. It was long, longer than shoulder-length.

Hair didn't grow that long in a couple of months. It wasn't a wig, either. You didn't buy a wig with strands of grey in it.

My God, she thought with a quiver of true shock. He *was* adopted. All her suspicions hadn't been unfounded. Adrian was Ray's twin brother. He had to be!

'Would you believe Sharni thought I was adopted?' Adrian said laughingly, and glanced up at his mother.

Sharni looked up too, her stomach contracting when she glimpsed the flash of fear in the woman's eyes.

'Why on earth would she think that?' May replied.

'Sharni was married once before,' Adrian rattled on, apparently oblivious of his mother's alarm. 'Her husband was tragically killed in a train derailment a few years ago.'

'How awful. I'm so sorry, Sharni. But I still don't understand why you would think my son was adopted.'

'It's because I'm her husband's physical double,' Adrian explained. 'He was adopted, you see. I'm so much like him that Sharni thought we might have been twins, separated at birth and adopted out to two different families.'

Maybe if his mother hadn't spilled her sherry into her lap, Adrian might have remained unaware of the truth. Sharni certainly hadn't been about to tell him the truth.

His freezing next to her, rather than going to his mother's aid, told the story. It was left to Sharni to jump up and help the flustered woman, taking the half-empty glass from her shaking hands and putting it to one side.

'I'm such a clumsy fool these days,' May said in one last desperate attempt to cover things up.

But it was futile.

'I *am* adopted, aren't I?'

Adrian's sharp words sliced through the air from where he'd remained sitting on the lounge, with that damning photo album still open on his lap.

Sharni saw the despair in his mother's eyes as they lifted to look at her son. 'No, Adrian, you're not.'

'Don't lie to me!' he snapped.

'I'm not lying. Your father and I… We didn't adopt you,' she said, her shoulders sagging in defeat. 'We stole you.'

# CHAPTER TWENTY

ADRIAN STARED at his mother, then at Sharni, who was looking as shell-shocked as he was feeling.

'Stole me,' he repeated in a somewhat dazed tone. 'What do you mean you *stole* me?'

His mother slumped back down into her armchair, her head sinking down into her hands. 'I never thought you'd find out,' she cried. 'I can't believe this is happening.'

'Mum, for pity's sake, pull yourself together and tell me what you and Dad did.'

'Adrian, don't,' Sharni warned, and began stroking his mother gently around her shoulders. 'Can't you see she's upset?'

'*She's* upset!' he snapped, fury and confusion raging within him. 'What about me?'

Sharni's eyes were soft upon him. 'You're upset, too. But you're stronger than she is.'

'Am I?' He didn't feel strong at this moment. He felt shattered, the foundations of his life crumbling with his mother's stunning revelation.

'Yes,' Sharni said. 'You are.'

The conviction in her voice calmed him, as did the sympathy in her eyes.

'Mrs Palmer,' Sharni said gently, and knelt down beside his mother. 'You have to tell Adrian what happened. He needs to know the whole story.'

'He…he won't understand,' the woman sobbed.

'He will.'

Adrian wasn't sure that he would. But Sharni's belief in him was touching.

His eyes dropped back to the album still

open on his lap, his anger quickly on the rise again.

'This photo of you pregnant,' he said, jabbing at it with his finger. 'Was that just a sham? Is that a pillow stuffed under there?'

His mother lifted her tear-stained face. 'No. That's me, really pregnant. I'd already suffered three miscarriages, but, this time, everything seemed to be going well. I…I went into labour shortly after that photo was taken. The baby died a few hours after he was born,' she finished in a bereft voice. 'A boy.'

'Go on.'

'There were complications, and I…I couldn't have another baby after that. I became seriously depressed. Your father…he… he was very worried about me.'

'So he went out and stole a baby for you? I can't believe he'd do that. Not Dad. He was such a stickler for doing the right thing. Hell, he brought me up on honesty is the best policy!'

'I knew you wouldn't understand,' his mother wailed.

'Adrian, don't,' Sharni said with a reproving glance.

'Don't what?' He threw the album to one side and stood up, unable to sit still any longer.

'Don't be cruel,' Sharni chided, but gently.

'It's all right, dear,' May said. 'He has a right to be angry.'

Angry? He was more than bloody angry. Adrian stalked around behind the sofa where he ground to a halt, his hands gripping the back with white-knuckled intensity.

'So how did it happen?' he demanded to know. 'Where did you steal me from? A hospital?'

'No! It wasn't like that at all,' his mother choked out. 'It wasn't intentional!'

'I just landed in your lap one day, is that it?'

His mother's sigh was ragged. 'No, of course not.'

Sharni shot him an exasperated look.

'Adrian, why don't you shut up and let your mother explain?'

Adrian threw up his hands in disgust. 'Fine. Explain away. If you can.'

'Oh, God,' his mother cried.

Sharni patted her hand. 'Just tell the truth, May.'

Adrian had to admire Sharni's gentle touch with his mother. Not that she was his *real* mother, he thought bitterly!

'I'll try, dear,' she said, and glanced nervously over at Adrian. 'At the time, your father had a medical practice in Sydney. In Surrey Hills. Not the most salubrious of areas, but you know how your father liked helping those less fortunate than himself. I hadn't worked since my baby died three years earlier. I couldn't. I…I came in to the city to meet your father for dinner one Friday evening. His receptionist had just left and he was closing the surgery when this young woman burst in, obviously in labour. It was too late to ring an ambulance, the baby already coming. I helped your father deliver you, not knowing at the time that there was a second baby as well. It all happened so quickly. We were shocked when a second baby arrived on the scene. The girl admitted she hadn't been to a doctor during her whole pregnancy, and had no idea she was having twins. Had no idea who the father of her babies were, either. She was a runaway and had been squatting in some derelict building up at the Cross. Arthur was attending to her afterbirth when she complained of a fierce headache. Within seconds she was dead. An aneurism had burst on her brain, we found out later. Suddenly, we had these two newborn babies in our arms.'

'And you decided to steal one,' Adrian said drily.

His mother winced, making Adrian feel momentarily guilty.

'Arthur was against the idea but he could see I was determined. I wanted to take both babies, but he said we would never get away with that. He said I had to choose.'

'Why me? Why not my brother?'

'You were a bit bigger. And stronger. And you didn't cry. Your brother. He never stopped. Arthur said a crying baby would bring unwanted attention. I took you home in a taxi whilst Arthur rang the police and ambulance, not telling them the girl had had twins. I still had everything I'd bought in preparation for our own baby boy. I couldn't bear to throw anything away. I packed everything that night and drove with you to Brisbane the following morning. I had an aunt there. Aunt Charlotte. My only living relative. You probably don't remember her. She died when you were only little. Anyway, I told her the truth and she kindly let me stay with her till Arthur settled things in Sydney. We knew we had to get away and start a new life where we could pretend you were our real baby. Luckily, Arthur didn't have any close relatives here in Australia who would ask awkward questions. As you know, he migrated from England when he was in his thirties. When his father died, his mother married a man he couldn't stand. He didn't write and they'd lost touch with each other.'

'What about friends?' Adrian asked. 'Didn't you have any friends who'd wonder where you'd gone? And why?'

'We hadn't socialised much since our baby died, due to my depression. So, no, we didn't have any close friends.'

Adrian found it difficult to take everything in. Suddenly, the need to get away by himself was acute. He had to think, had to try to come to terms with everything.

'If that's all, then I'm going to go for a walk,' he said abruptly.

'Adrian, no,' Sharni said. 'Don't do that.'

'It's all right,' his mother said. 'It's what he always does when he's upset.'

It irked him that she knew him this well, this woman who wasn't really his mother.

'One thing before I go,' he said sharply. 'Did you ever find out anything about my real mother?'

Again, that grimace of hurt. And again, more guilt.

'Arthur did make enquiries. She came from a wealthy Sydney family. But her parents didn't want anything to do with their illegitimate grandson. They quite happily signed the papers to allow for his adoption.'

Adrian could not believe he could be hurt by a rejection from people he didn't even know. But he was.

'I see,' he bit out. 'They wouldn't have wanted me either, then, would they?'

'*I* wanted you,' May said with a fierce love

shining in her teary eyes. 'From the first moment I held you in my arms.'

Tears pricked at his own eyes, making him panic. He refused to cry in front of the woman he loved. Refused to let her see him as any less than the confident, self-assured man she'd fallen in love with.

But *had* she? came the sudden awful fear.

I am her husband's twin brother. Not just his double. I carry the same DNA. It fooled his dog. Has it fooled her, too? Is she mine for real, or have I just stepped into my brother's shoes?

The thought horrified him.

'If you'll excuse me, I need some time alone.'

# CHAPTER TWENTY-ONE

'HE HATES me,' May said brokenly after Adrian left the house.

'No, he doesn't,' Sharni denied. 'He's in shock. But you were right about one thing. He doesn't understand what drove you to steal him. But I do, May. Honestly, I do. I know what it's like to lose a much-loved baby.'

'You do?'

'Yes. I was expecting when my husband was killed. The shock put me into premature labour and the baby died. A little boy.'

'Oh, Sharni. You poor love. At least I had Arthur to comfort me.'

'It was a very hard time for me,' Sharni

admitted, surprised to find that she could talk about it now without dissolving into tears. She would never forget the pain of that time, but at last she was capable of moving on.

'What was he like?' May asked. 'Your husband, I mean. Adrian's brother.'

'He was a lovely man,' she said with fond memory. 'Very sweet, and gentle. But not all that confident in himself. Nothing like Adrian, except in looks. I think he might have been Adrian's mirror-image twin. You must know about that, being a nurse.'

'I've heard about it. Yes.'

'When I first saw Adrian I thought he was Ray's exact physical double. But after a while I could see little differences in his face. Then the other morning, I saw his reflection in the mirror and it was like Ray was looking straight at me.'

May shook her head. 'It's unbelievable that you should meet Adrian, don't you think? In a city with four million people, and you come across your husband's twin brother.'

'Maybe it was destiny. Or Ray up in heaven, directing me to the one man who could make me happy again.'

'And he has? Made you happy?'

'Very. Tell me, do you know where he might have gone?'

'He's sure to be down on the beach somewhere.'

'I'll go find him.'

May glanced down at her sherry-stained top. 'And I'll change, then see what I can do about keeping that dinner from spoiling.'

'Everything is going to be all right, May,' Sharni said with a reassuring smile. 'Adrian loves you very much. Nothing is ever going to change that.'

'I hope you're right, dear. It can't be easy, finding out something like this at his age. I could see it rocked him.'

'I know that, May. My husband, Ray…he never really came to terms with being adopted. He always suffered from a sense of abandonment.'

'But he wasn't abandoned!' she protested. 'His mother died. Wasn't he ever told that?'

'No. His adopted mother always told him he'd been given up because he wasn't wanted.'

'Oh, how dreadful!'

'She was a stupid, selfish woman. I never could take to her. After she died I encouraged Ray to find out the details of his adoption but he wouldn't. At least Adrian knows what really happened.'

'Yes, that's true.'

'I haven't told Adrian yet about the baby I lost. I think now is the right time. It might help him to understand why you did what you did.'

Tears glistened in May's eyes. 'And there I was, thinking how unlucky he was to meet you, of all people. But that's not true. My boy is very lucky to have you. You are just what he needs.'

*Just what he needs.*

May's words reverberated in Sharni's head as she walked down the road towards the beach.

Janice had been so right. That was what had been missing from her relationship with Adrian. The feeling of being needed.

She could not wait to go to him, to make him see that he would survive this, that nothing of value in his life had changed. His mother still loved him, and so did she. More than ever.

Adrian felt her presence before she sat down beside him on the sand. He didn't turn to look at her, just continued to stare out at the sea.

'Okay, so you were right and I was wrong,' he bit out. 'I am your dead husband's twin brother.'

'Yes,' she said quite calmly. 'You are.'

Now his head did whip round, his eyes

stabbing resentment at her. 'Doesn't that bother you at all?'

She blinked genuine surprise at him. 'No.'

'Well, it bothers me.'

'Why?'

'If you have to ask then you don't understand men at all.'

'Ray wouldn't mind, Adrian.'

'*I* mind. You're his wife. You loved *him* first. I come a poor second.'

'That's not true,' she said firmly. 'Yes. I did love Ray. But I love you just as much.'

He shook his head at her, still unconvinced. 'I don't want to live my life in another's man's shoes.'

'It's impossible for you to do that, Adrian. If you'd known Ray, you would see how different you are from him.'

'Well, I didn't know my brother, did I? I was denied that chance when my darling mother stole me. Not that she's my real mother.'

Adrian was startled by the outrage that zoomed into Sharni's eyes. 'Don't you dare say that! May is your real mother, just as your father was your real father. They gave you everything a child could hope for. Love, security, a good education and lots of self-esteem. Ray didn't have much of that, I can assure you.'

'He might have, if we'd been kept together,' he said stubbornly.

'Maybe. Maybe not. I suspect he might have always been in your shadow. You were the stronger twin, Adrian. But what's done is done and it can't be changed. We're all victims of circumstance, especially when we're children. But once we become adults, we have choices. You can choose to be bitter and resentful over a decision you had no part in thirty-six years ago. Or you can choose to be understanding and forgiving.'

'That's all very well for you to say, Sharni.

But how can I be understanding when I simply *don't* understand? Not every woman who loses a child goes around and steals someone else's.'

'No,' she said. 'But your mother hadn't just lost one child, Adrian. She'd already lost three. On top of that, she'd been given the news that she could never have another.'

'They could have adopted. Through the right channels,' he added caustically.

'They were too old to be considered.'

'Not if they'd gone overseas.'

'Thirty-six years ago? Come on, Adrian, no one did that back then.'

'You still don't steal a child.'

'She didn't plan to, Adrian. Fate stepped in and put a terrible temptation in your mother's path. She simply couldn't say no.'

'Dad should have said no.'

'He couldn't. Not if he loved her as much as he obviously did.'

Adrian nodded reluctantly. 'He adored her.'

'And they both adored you. That can't be a bad thing, can it?'

A rush of air escaped Adrian's lungs as he let go of some of the tension gripping his insides. 'No. They were wonderful parents,' he admitted. 'But it's just all so unbelievable.'

'You've had a big shock,' she said.

His smile was wan. 'That's putting it mildly.'

But she was right, Adrian conceded. About everything. He was being irrational and emotional. Still, it was hard not to be.

'You know that room in my house which I wouldn't let you go into? The one next to the bathroom.'

Adrian frowned at Sharni's abrupt change of subject. When he turned his head to look at her, she wasn't looking at him, her eyes straight ahead.

'Yes,' he replied somewhat hesitantly,

because there was something in her body language that worried him. 'What about it?'

'It's a nursery,' she told him.

'A nursery,' he repeated.

'Yes. A blue one.'

'A blue one.'

'It was never used,' she said. 'But it had everything. A cradle and a cot, with a mobile hanging over it, plus a change table and more clothes than any baby could ever wear.'

Only then did she turn to look at him, her chin quivering slightly. 'I was five and a half months pregnant when Ray died. The shock sent me into labour and my son wasn't old enough to live.'

Oh, God. The poor darling.

'I *know* the pain your mother felt, Adrian. It tears you apart then leaves you feeling dead inside. You brought her to life again. That was why she couldn't let you go. That was why she had to keep you. *I* was dead inside for five long years. But then you came along and brought me to life again in a way I never thought possible.'

She reached out and lay a soft hand against his cheek.

'You are not a substitute for Ray. You are you, Adrian Palmer, and I love you more than words can describe. You asked me to marry you on the way up here. If that offer is still open, then my answer is yes.'

As Adrian looked deep into her eyes all his emotional confusion fell away, replaced by the absolute certainty that she was telling him the truth. She loved him. Truly loved *him*.

What an incredible woman she was. After all she'd been through, she was still capable of facing life with courage and optimism. Still capable of loving.

He pulled her into his arms and held her tightly against him.

'You make me feel humble,' he said. 'I don't deserve you.'

A wonderful peace filled Sharni's soul as Adrian held her. It had been so good to finally tell him about the baby. Now, there were no secrets between them. Only love.

'I'll make you happy,' he promised her as he pressed his lips into her hair.

'You already have. Come on, let's go back and have that dinner your mother very kindly cooked us.'

'I hurt her, didn't I?' Adrian said as they walked, hand in hand, up the hill.

'Nothing that a big hug won't fix,' Sharni replied. 'Mothers are very forgiving people.'

'She's been a brilliant mother, really,' he admitted.

Talking of mothers brought his mind back to the child Sharni had lost. Clearly, having a baby would mean a lot to her.

I'll give you another baby, my darling, he vowed privately, his fingers squeezing hers. Or I'll die trying.

# CHAPTER TWENTY-TWO

ADRIAN could not sit at his desk any longer. His mind was not on his work, his ability to concentrate totally shot.

Pushing back his chair, he stood up and made his way from his study to the kitchen where he poured himself some coffee. A glance at his watch showed it had just gone noon. Sharni's appointment with the specialist had been for ten-thirty. Surely she would be finished by now. He'd asked her to call him as soon as she could, but his phone remained silent.

Five weeks had gone by since their memorable trip to Kingscliff, more than enough time for Adrian to buy Sharni an extremely expensive engagement ring, then start making plans for a wedding before the end of the year.

He hadn't convinced her to move in with him as yet, Sharni insisting that she stay in Katoomba till her place was sold. She did, however, come down every weekend, which she said was easier than his coming up to her.

Mozart had found a new home at her sister's place—he'd become very attached to Janice's two boys—so leaving him behind wasn't a problem any more.

Meanwhile, Adrian had set about getting his fiancée an appointment with the best fertility expert in Sydney, a task that had taken longer than he'd hoped. The infernal man had been overseas till recently.

The sound of the front door opening sent his heart racing and him hurrying towards the foyer.

It was Sharni, of course, looking her usual lovely self in his favourite black trousers and pink jumper. Her cheeks were pink as well, her dark eyes sparkling with what he hoped was good news.

'You naughty girl,' he said, bending to give her a peck on the cheek. 'Why didn't you ring? I've been like a cat on a hot tin roof this last half-hour.'

'Sorry. I didn't want to ring. I wanted to tell you what the doctor said personally.'

'You look happy, so I take it it isn't bad news.'

'It's wonderful news.'

'Your ovaries are working again?'

She smiled. 'It seems so.'

He frowned. 'But you still haven't had a period.'

'Funny that, isn't it?' she said, looking impossibly smug.

The penny dropped and his pulse rate took off.

'You're already pregnant,' he said breathlessly.

She squealed an excited, 'Yes,' then threw herself into his arms.

Adrian could hardly believe their luck.

'How far gone are you?' he asked.

'He said about six weeks.'

'That means…'

'Yes. I must have conceived the very first weekend we were together.'

'That's incredible.'

'No, I think it's perfectly credible. I told you you made me come alive again. You did, in the most marvellous way. Oh, but I love you, Adrian Palmer,' she said, and hugged him tightly once more, her head resting over his heart.

Adrian sighed with happiness. This was what he'd vowed to do, what he wanted most in the world. Because this was what *she* wanted, this beautiful, brave woman he loved.

Every time he started feeling down or upset about the circumstances of his birth— which happened more often than he'd antici- pated—he would think of Sharni, and all she'd had to endure.

Her wise advice would come back to him about making adult choices instead of indulging in negative emotions.

I choose not to be angry, he would tell himself. Or judgemental. I choose to go forward and make the best of my life.

Which was what he was doing.

And now he was going to be a father.

How lucky could he get!

'Maybe we should ring Janice,' Sharni said, her head lifting. 'And your mum. Tell them the good news.'

'I think they can wait a few minutes, don't you?' he said. 'I want to savour this moment with just you. Come on, let's go open a bottle of champagne.'

'Uh-uh,' she said, shaking her head. 'No alcohol for mums-to-be.'

He smiled. 'Coffee, then? I have some perking in the kitchen.'

'Sounds good.'

MIRANDA LEE

'You simply have to move in with me now,'

he said once they retreated to the terrace, mugs

in hand. 'I want to look after you. I'm also

going to have to design and build us a house.

Can't raise a family in this place. Tell you

what, there's no need to sell your place at all.

Let's just rent it out. That way you can move

in with me this week.'

'Okay,' she said, seeming happy with that idea.

'But you're not to pack. I'll hire a company to do all that.'

'If you insist.'

'I insist.'

She glanced at him over the rim of her mug. 'I can see that your son is going to be a real bossy-boots.'

'What makes you think it'll be a boy?' he said.

Sharni looked at the man she loved, and smiled. 'Intuition.'

She was right. Their first-born was a boy.

But he wasn't a bossy-boots at all. He was an easygoing child who loved animals and music.

He was named Raymond Arthur, but everyone called him Ray.

# MILLS & BOON PUBLISH EIGHT LARGE PRINT TITLES A MONTH. THESE ARE THE EIGHT TITLES FOR OCTOBER 2008.

———————— ✄ ————————

## THE SHEIKH'S BLACKMAILED MISTRESS
Penny Jordan

## THE MILLIONAIRE'S INEXPERIENCED LOVE-SLAVE
Miranda Lee

## BOUGHT: THE GREEK'S INNOCENT VIRGIN
Sarah Morgan

## BEDDED AT THE BILLIONAIRE'S CONVENIENCE
Cathy Williams

## THE PREGNANCY PROMISE
Barbara McMahon

## THE ITALIAN'S CINDERELLA BRIDE
Lucy Gordon

## SAYING YES TO THE MILLIONAIRE
Fiona Harper

## HER ROYAL WEDDING WISH
Cara Colter

MILLS & BOON®
*Pure reading pleasure*™

0908 Rom LP

**MILLS & BOON PUBLISH EIGHT LARGE PRINT TITLES A MONTH. THESE ARE THE EIGHT TITLES FOR NOVEMBER 2008.**

——————— ✄ ———————

BOUGHT FOR REVENGE, BEDDED
FOR PLEASURE
Emma Darcy

FORBIDDEN: THE BILLIONAIRE'S
VIRGIN PRINCESS
Lucy Monroe

THE GREEK TYCOON'S CONVENIENT WIFE
Sharon Kendrick

THE MARCIANO LOVE-CHILD
Melanie Milburne

PARENTS IN TRAINING
Barbara McMahon

NEWLYWEDS OF CONVENIENCE
Jessica Hart

THE DESERT PRINCE'S PROPOSAL
Nicola Marsh

ADOPTED: OUTBACK BABY
Barbara Hannay

◎™MILLS & BOON®
*Pure reading pleasure*™

# The Christmas Card

# Dilly Court

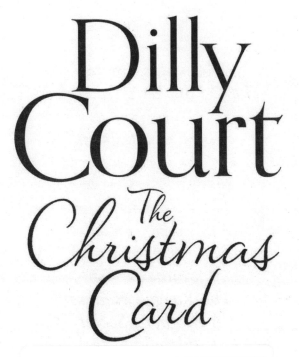

## The Christmas Card

HarperCollins*Publishers*

HarperCollins*Publishers*
The News Building,
1 London Bridge Street,
London SE1 9GF

www.harpercollins.co.uk

Published by HarperCollins*Publishers* 2016
1

A catalogue record for this book is available from the British Library

ISBN: 978-0-00-815193-5

Typeset in Sabon Lt Std by Palimpsest Book Production Ltd,
Falkirk, Stirlingshire

Printed and bound in Great Britain by Clays Ltd, St Ives plc

MIX
Paper from
responsible sources
FSC C007454

Find out more about HarperCollins and the environment at
**www.harpercollins.co.uk/green**

For Georgina Hawtrey-Woore.

# Chapter One

*Doughty Street, London, December 1862*

The grandfather clock wobbled dangerously, its pendulum swinging to and fro in a carillon of chimes as it toppled off the carter's wagon and hit the frosty cobblestones with a resounding crash. With her arm around her sobbing mother nineteen-year-old Alice stood on the pavement outside their home, watching helplessly as the bailiff's men picked up the splintered wood and hurled it on top of her late father's favourite armchair. For a moment it was as if Clement Radcliffe was still sitting there, his spectacles balanced on the tip of his nose as he studied the morning newspaper. With his nightcap slightly askew on his balding head and his moth-eaten red velvet robe wrapped tightly around his thin frame, he had always seemed oblivious to the world about

1

him. An academic by profession and inclination, Clement had rarely come down to earth, and when he did it was usually to ask for another lump of coal to be placed on the fire, or another candle to make reading easier. And now he was dead.

'Gracious heavens, that clock should have come to me.' Jane Radcliffe clicked her tongue against her teeth. 'Your father, God rest his soul, knew how much my dear husband wanted it, but Clement was his favourite, even though Robert was the elder son.' Her thin lips disappeared into a pencil-line of discontent below the tip of her nose, which was glowing red in the cold air. 'And now the disgrace of having the bailiffs come in and take every last stick of furniture is too much to bear.' She turned her head, focusing her attention on her sister-in-law. 'You married an extremely selfish man, Beth. Your husband spent most of his time with his head in a book instead of working to support his wife and child. My dear Robert always said his brother was a fool with money.'

Beth Radcliffe buried her face in her already sodden handkerchief, mumbling something unintelligible.

Alice contained her anger with difficulty. In their precarious situation it was not a good idea to antagonise Aunt Jane, who, despite her strong religious convictions, was notoriously judgemental and quick-tempered. Dressed in unrelieved black Jane seemed to tower over them like a dark cloud. Although it was six years since her husband had died from congestion of the lungs, Jane had clung stubbornly to the role of grieving widow. Her mourning clothes were old-fashioned and now tinged with green, but she wore them like a badge of honour. She shunned all forms of entertainment and spent more time in the church of St George the Martyr than she did in her own home. Jane Radcliffe was well known for her good works, but Alice suspected that her aunt's charity was handed out with as little warmth as the frozen River Thames during the famous frost fair.

'As usual it's left to me to pick up the pieces. My brother-in-law was a wastrel and it's my Christian duty to take you both into my home.' Jane folded her hands in front of her, raising her eyes to heaven as if she expected a divine being to acknowledge her good deed. 'I would have treasured that clock.'

'I'm sorry,' was all Alice could think of to say. It was just days until Christmas and her whole life was disintegrating before her eyes, although it was a shame to see the old clock smashed to bits it was the least of her worries. With a feeling close to despair she glanced up at the terraced house in Doughty Street where she had been born and raised. It was not a mansion, but there were two reasonable sized rooms on each of its three floors, plus the basement kitchen and scullery. It was a desirable residence with a pleasant view of Mecklenburgh Square at the front, and a small back garden with a scrap of lawn and an ancient apple tree. In spring-time it had showered pink and white petals onto the grass, and in summer she had sat beneath its shady branches reading or sketching. In autumn she had picked and eaten the juicy fruit but she had always been on her own. A shy girl and an only child, she had longed for the company of brothers and sisters, but her mother was delicate and suffered bouts of illness that laid her low for weeks if not months. With only the servants for company it had been a lonely life, but Alice had discovered early on that she had a talent for drawing and painting, and that had been her greatest pleasure.

She gave her mother a comforting hug. 'We'll be all right, Mama. I'll find work so that I can look after you.'

'Pull yourself together, Beth,' Aunt Jane said impatiently. 'Stop snivelling and pick up your valise. There's no point in loitering about here.' She started off along Doughty Street, heading for the gated entrance despite the bitter east wind that tugged at her widow's weeds. 'We'll walk to Queen Square. There's no need to waste money on a cab.'

Alice picked up the valise and portmanteau, which contained all that was left of their worldly possessions. Her mittened fingers were numbed with cold, but her concern was for her mother, whose pale cheeks were tinged with blue.

'Are you all right, Mama? It really isn't too far to Queen Square.'

'I can walk.' Beth mopped her eyes on a white cotton hanky that Alice had given her last Christmas, having spent hours embroidering it with tiny rose-buds and her mother's initials. 'I won't allow that woman to get the better of me.'

'I should say not.' Alice walked on, measuring her pace so that her mother could keep up with her, although Jane was striding on ahead brandishing her furled black umbrella, whacking any unwary pedestrian who got in her way.

Beth tried valiantly to keep up, but Alice was too burdened with the heavy luggage to help her mother and their progress was slow.

By the time they reached the house Jane was divesting herself of her cape and bonnet in the large, echoing entrance hall. She handed the garments to a young maidservant who could not have been more than ten or eleven years of age. The child's knees bowed beneath the weight of the merino cape and she seemed to disappear beneath the folds of the material.

'Hang them up, you stupid girl,' Jane said impatiently. 'Do I have to tell you how to do every single thing?' Ignoring the child's quivering lips and the tears that had sprung to her eyes, Jane turned on her sister-in-law. 'You managed to walk this far then? It just proves that you can do it if you try. Sloth is one of the seven deadly sins, Beth. You will not be allowed to idle away your time under my roof.'

'Mama is unwell,' Alice protested angrily. 'She has a delicate constitution.'

'Bah! Rubbish. There's nothing wrong with her

that cannot be cured by long walks, a plain diet and prayer.' Jane fixed Beth with a stern gaze. 'You will accompany me to church on Sunday, and we will read the Bible together every evening. You may reside here, but only if you adhere to my rules. Is that understood?'

'Yes, Jane,' Beth said meekly. 'It's very good of you to take us in.'

The sight of her mother being browbeaten by Aunt Jane was almost too much to bear, but Alice managed to bite back the sharp words that tingled on the tip of her tongue. Her mother had suffered enough recently and did not deserve such treatment. As for herself, she was young and strong and she would survive, but one look at her mother's ashen face was enough to convince her that this situation could only be temporary. There had to be another way, although she was at a loss to know where it lay.

'And you, girl,' Jane spun round to face her. 'I can see that you're going to be trouble, so you can take that look off your face. The devil finds work for idle hands, and I'll see that you are fully occupied from the time you rise in the morning until you retire to bed at night.'

Beth clutched her daughter's arm. 'Alice is a good girl. She took care of both of us during Clement's illness. She has been such a help and a comfort to me.'

'Enough of that trite sentimentality,' Jane said

severely. 'Snippet will show you to your rooms, and luncheon will be served in the dining room at noon.' She reached for a bell pull and tugged at it. 'Snippet. Where are you, girl?'

The sound of clattering footsteps preceded the child, who came running and skidded to a halt on the slippery floor. 'Yes, ma'am.'

'Show Mrs Radcliffe and Miss Alice to their rooms.' Jane stalked off, disappearing into a room on the far side of the hall.

Alice was curious. 'Is your name really Snippet?'

The girl hung her head. 'It's Clara, miss. Clara Snipe, but the missis chose to call me Snippet because I ain't very big.'

Beth reached out to lay her hand on Clara's arm. 'We will call you Clara.'

'She won't like it, ma'am. I'll get it in the neck if she thinks I've been blabbing to you.'

'Then we'll only call you Clara in private,' Alice said, smiling for the first time that morning. 'Now, if you'd care to show us to our rooms, Clara, we can unpack and be ready in time for luncheon.'

Clara pulled a face. 'Don't get too excited, miss. What her majesty calls luncheon wouldn't feed a sparrow. I knows that only too well.' She picked up the valise despite Beth's protests, and with a great deal of heaving and pulling she managed to get it to the foot of the stairs.

'Let me help.' Alice could not bear to see such a small girl struggling valiantly with a heavy case.

Clara held up her hand. 'I can do it, miss. Her majesty says it is lack of willpower if you can't do things for yourself. I got to practise me willpower.' She began to bump the case up the stairs and Alice picked up the valise, proffering her free arm to her mother. She shivered as an icy draught whistled past her head. Outside there was the promise of snow, but inside the Radcliffe domain the chill of previous cold winters lingered like a bad memory. The polished floorboards were bare of rugs and carpets, and the pristine expanse of whitewashed walls was unrelieved by the addition of pictures or mirrors. The sound of their footsteps echoed off the high ceilings as they made their way upstairs, and when they came to a halt the house reverberated with silence.

'I'm so sorry, Alice,' Beth whispered as Clara opened the door to a room on the second floor. 'To have brought you to this breaks my poor heart.'

Alice glanced at the Spartan interior, comparing it mentally to her cosy bedroom in Doughty Street with its floral curtains, matching coverlet and brightly coloured rag rugs. 'It's not so bad, Mama,' she said, forcing a smile.

'Yours is next door, and it ain't no better,' Clara said gloomily.

'I'm sure this will suit me very well.' Beth slumped down onto the bed. 'A few pictures on the walls will brighten is up.'

'The missis don't approve of anything what ain't

of a religious nature.' Clara folded her skinny arms around her body, shivering. 'There ain't much she does approve of, if you don't mind me saying so.'

'We don't, but you'd better not let her hear you talking like that,' Beth said gently. 'Anyway, this is better than being cast out on the streets. Misfortune brought us to this sorry pass, and we should be grateful to Jane for taking us in.'

Alice could not agree, but she was not going to make things worse by speaking her mind. 'I'll leave you to unpack, Mama. Where am I to sleep, Clara?'

Her room, she discovered, was identical, and as cheerless as a prison cell. She thanked Clara and sent her off with a smile, but when the door closed she sank down on the bed, which, as she had expected, was hard and lumpy. The four white walls seemed to close in on her, adding to the winter chill, and the only patch of colour in the room was the faded crimson and blue tapestry of her valise as it rested on the snowy Marseilles coverlet. An oak chest of drawers and a washstand with a white enamel bowl and jug were the other items of furniture, and a piece of drugget matting was the sole concession to comfort.

As she opened her case and started to unpack Alice could not help wondering whether this was her aunt's idea of a punishment. She had never bothered to hide her contempt for her sister-in-law, and Alice had not forgotten a conversation she had overheard when Jane scolded Pa, insisting that he had made a mistake by marrying for love instead of choosing a woman of property. Alice knew that her uncle had done well in the City, but it was common knowledge that the house had been part of Jane Hubble's dowry and she was inordinately proud of her family history. There had been a Hubble fighting the French at Agincourt, and somewhere along the line a Hubble ancestor had been elected to Parliament, and another had been a royal physician. Alice would not have been surprised if Aunt Jane had claimed that a Hubble had discovered the Americas. A wry smile curved her lips. Aunt Jane had been an only child, and her one surviving relative was a bachelor cousin, so it seemed that the name of Hubble was already consigned to history. That was a cross that Aunt Jane would have to bear.

Luncheon, as Clara had prophesied, was a simple meal. The dining room was huge, and might have been the refectory in a monastery for all the warmth and comfort it offered. Aunt Jane said grace, which went on for so long that Alice's stomach began to rumble, which earned her a warning glance from her aunt. The meal for which they had to be truly thankful was bread and cheese with water to drink, and an apple for dessert. Jane ate her piece of fruit until all that remained was a single stalk. She frowned at Beth when she left the core on her plate.

'We don't waste food in this house. There are people starving on the streets who would be grateful for an apple core, let alone an apple.'

Alice and her mother exchanged meaningful glances, saying nothing.

Jane finished her water and replaced the glass on the table. She cleared her throat. 'I've made arrangements for you to start work tomorrow morning, Alice.'

'Work?' Beth stared at her open-mouthed. 'What sort of work? Alice isn't trained for anything.'

'My point exactly. You and Clement brought her up to be neither use nor ornament, but I have contacts through the Church, and as a favour to me a wife of a respectable and prosperous owner of a printing works has agreed to take Alice on to teach her daughter to draw and paint. There will, of course, be other duties for her to perform, but she will find that out when she starts tomorrow morning at seven thirty.'

After spending less than a day in Aunt Jane's house, where the list of rules seemed endless and meals had to be earned by doing menial work, Alice decided that almost anything would be an improvement. Jane employed the minimum of servants needed to run the household. Cook and Clara lived in and there were a couple of daily women who came in to clean. Alice spent the afternoon polishing the silver cutlery and the brass cross and candlesticks from the small altar in Jane's boudoir. Beth was given the task of cutting up a sheet that had already been turned sides to middle, but was now

11

too worn to use on a bed. The resulting squares then had to be hemmed and the cloths used for cleaning and dusting. Jane was nothing if not frugal, although Alice knew that her aunt was a wealthy woman.

Supper that night was again taken in the cheerless dining room where a few lumps of coal smouldered feebly in the grate. 'You should dress according to the weather, sister-in-law,' Jane said sternly when she saw that Beth was shivering. 'A woollen shawl is all you need.' She glared at Alice who was about to pick up her spoon. 'We will say grace.'

The soup was cooling rapidly by the time Jane came to the end of what turned out to be a sermon on gratitude aimed, no doubt, at her reluctant guests. Alice was too hungry to care and she spooned the vegetable broth into her mouth, wiping the bowl with a chunk of dry bread. She waited eagerly for the next course, but it did not materialise. Jane folded her hands, murmuring a prayer before rising from the table. 'I spend my evenings studying the Good Book. You may do as you please, but bear in mind that candles cost money, and I don't approve of fires in the bedchambers. We rise early in this house; therefore you should retire at a reasonable hour. Do I make myself clear?'

'Yes, Jane,' Beth said meekly.

'Yes, Aunt Jane.' Alice sighed inwardly. She waited until her aunt had left the room. 'I don't think I can stand much more of this, Mama,' she whispered, glancing over her shoulder to make sure that Jane was not within earshot.

Beth rose wearily from the chair. 'We haven't much choice, my love. It's this or the workhouse, and I know which I prefer.' She leaned her hands on the table, taking deep breaths. 'It's all right, I'm quite well, just a bit stiff from sitting on a hard wooden seat. I think I might go to bed and rest. It's been a long and trying day.' She held her hand out to her daughter, a smile sketched on her thin features. 'You don't mind, do you?'

'Of course not, Mama. You must take care of yourself, and I'll try to be patient and deserving, but it isn't easy.'

'It's all strange and new,' Beth said softly. 'Jane is a worthy woman, and we must be grateful to her for putting a roof over our heads. It was good of her to think of finding you a suitable position. Teaching drawing is a ladylike occupation.'

'Yes, Mama.' Alice could see that her mother was having difficulty walking and she held out her hand. 'Let me help you upstairs.'

'Thank you, dear. It's these silly legs of mine. They're aching miserably this evening, but once I get going I'm quite all right.'

After seeing her mother settled for the night, although it was only seven o'clock, Alice did not fancy an evening of Bible study with Aunt Jane and she went to her room. She lit the single candle provided and went to draw the curtains, pausing for a moment to watch the large feathery snowflakes whirling and dancing as they fluttered slowly to the pavement and lay there like a white fleecy blanket. A man wearing a greatcoat with his collar pulled up to his ears trudged past the house, leaving a trail of stark black footprints in his wake. Alice sighed. The pristine beauty of the fallen snow was despoiled and ruined forever. She pulled the curtains together, shutting out the harsh reality of the world before going to sit on the bed. In her reticule was her most prized possession and she took it out carefully. The paper was yellowed with age and slightly dog-eared, but the picture on the Christmas card was of a family gathering at yuletide, and it had always seemed to her to be imbued with the true spirit of the season. It was the first such card to have been produced commercially, and her father had bought it in the year she had been born. He had kept it for her until she was old enough to appreciate the message of peace and goodwill that it contained. Sadly, so Pa had told her, the first cards had not been a huge success. In fact he had invested money in their production, losing heavily, as so often happened on the rare occasions when he had ventured into the business world.

Alice held the hand-coloured lithograph to her bosom with a whisper of a sigh. 'Poor Papa,' she said softly. 'I'm glad you're not here to see us in such a pickle, but I promise you I'll do everything I can to make things better for Mama. I won't let you down.' She rose to her feet and stowed the precious card out of sight of prying eyes in the chest of drawers.

At first when she opened her eyes to darkness she thought it was the middle of the night, but Aunt Jane was shaking her by the shoulder and she was fully dressed.

'Get up, you idle child. It's nearly six o'clock and you have to be at the Dearborns' establishment in Russell Square at half-past seven sharp.' She tugged the coverlet off the bed, leaving Alice curled up in a ball, shivering. 'I expect you to be washed, dressed and in the dining room in ten minutes.' Jane marched out of the room, slamming the door behind her as if to ensure that Alice remained wide awake.

Stiff and cold, with no inclination to remain in the uncomfortable bed any longer than necessary, Alice did not hesitate. She padded barefoot to the washstand only to find that the water in the jug had frozen. After some difficulty she managed to crack the ice and had a cat's lick of a wash before throwing on her clothes. Her numbed fingers made it difficult to do up the buttons on her bodice and even harder to tidy her mouse-brown hair into a chignon. Without the aid of a mirror it was impossible to see the end result and she tucked a stray strand behind her ear, hoping that Aunt Jane would not notice.

When she reached the dining room she found that Jane had already eaten and was sitting at the head of the table, sipping a cup of tea. The sight of steam rising was encouraging, but Alice experienced a feeling of acute disappointment when she realised that there was neither milk nor sugar to make the strong brew more palatable. Breakfast consisted of a slice of bread, thinly spread with butter, and that was all. There was an eerie silence as she ate her frugal meal, broken only by the sound of Jane's cup being replaced on its saucer.

Without bothering to see if Alice had finished, Jane rose to her feet. 'Come along. I'll take you to Russell Square as it's your first morning, but in future you will get yourself up and out in good time. I'm not going to pamper you as your mother has done since you were born. You're a child no longer, Alice. You are plain and penniless and you will have to get used to earning your keep.' She reached for her bonnet and rammed it on top of her lace cap. 'Hurry up, girl. We'll stop at the church on the way to ask God's blessing in the hope that he will save you from your profligate ways.'

There appeared to be no answer to this. Alice stuffed the last crust into her mouth, washing it down with a mouthful of tea. She followed her aunt from the room, stopping only to snatch her bonnet and cape from the hallstand as they left the house.

It was getting light as they made their way carefully along snow-covered pavements to the church on the west side of the square. Candles blazed on the altar and the smell of hot wax and musty hymnals filled the still air. Following Jane's example Alice dutifully went down on her knees beside her. Jane's lips moved in silent prayer, but Alice's mind was elsewhere. Her fingers were itching to draw the scene outside. The bare branches of the plane trees were dusted with snow, and the pools of yellow light created by the gas lamps sparkled with frost crystals. The piles of straw and horse dung on the cobble-stones were concealed beneath several inches of virgin snow, but as the day progressed and traffic began to move it would all vanish into a mess of slush. The outside world had a fleeting fairy-tale appearance too beautiful to ignore, but she would have to commit it to memory until, at some time in the future, she could replicate the scene in pen and ink or delicate watercolour.

She rose to her feet automatically when Jane finished her prayer, and followed her aunt as they set off once again with Jane in the lead, using her black umbrella as if she were a lancer at the head of a cavalry charge. Luckily it was not far to Russell Square and they arrived without any unwary passer-by sustaining a serious injury.

Jane marched up the steps to the front door and hammered on the knocker. Moments later a stern-faced butler answered the summons. He glared at Jane, eyebrows raised. 'Might I be of assistance, madam?'

Jane tapped the ground with the ferule of her umbrella. 'I wish to see Mrs Dearborn. Tell her that

Mrs Jane Radcliffe is here with her niece, Alice Radcliffe. Mrs Dearborn is expecting me.'

'I doubt if the mistress will be receiving this early in the morning, but if you'll wait a moment, I'll return.' He shut the door without giving Jane the chance to step over the threshold.

She bridled visibly. 'Such bad form. I'll report him to Mrs Dearborn, you see if I don't.' She kept prodding the step with her umbrella, tapping her foot to the same beat until the door opened once again. 'I should think so too.' She stepped inside without waiting to be invited. 'Come along, girl,' she snapped, beckoning to Alice.

'Mrs Dearborn is not ready to receive visitors.' The butler took a step backwards, eyeing Jane's umbrella nervously. 'But the housekeeper, Mrs Upton, will see you in the morning room. This way, please.'

He stalked off across the highly polished floor, which was as slippery as a frozen pond. Jane trod carefully and Alice had to curb a sudden childish desire to run and slide. Boughs of holly intertwined with fronds of ivy were strung from the banisters on the galleried landing, and bowls of hothouse flowers provided splashes of bright colour against the wainscoted walls. The air was warm and redolent with their scent.

'Mrs Upton will be with you shortly,' the butler said as he ushered them into the morning room.

Jane walked over to the fireplace, holding her

hands out to the blaze. 'Such extravagance. No wonder the world is in a parlous state.'

Alice did not offer an opinion. She moved as close as she dared to the fire, revelling in the luxury of warmth, and her spirits rose as she looked round the comfortably furnished room. The walls were lined with framed watercolours of flowers, birds and country scenes, and the mantelshelf was cluttered with ornaments, spill vases and a large gilt clock with a garniture of candelabra supported by smiling cherubs. Her feet sank into the thick pile of the carpet and she was tempted to take a seat in one of the velvet-upholstered, button-back armchairs, but did not dare take liberties. Jane, as expected, was unimpressed. She sniffed. 'Vulgar display. Ostentatious and decadent.' She spun round as the door opened to admit a small woman, dressed in black bombazine with a chatelaine hanging round her waist from which dangled a large bunch of keys.

'I was expecting to see Mrs Dearborn in person,' Jane said haughtily.

'At this hour of the day?' Mrs Upton looked Jane up and down with barely concealed disdain. 'I don't know what sort of establishment you run, madam, but ladies don't usually rise before ten o'clock at the earliest.'

Jane's mouth opened and shut, reminding Alice of a goldfish she had once owned, but her aunt made a quick recovery, drawing herself up to her full height so that she towered over the housekeeper. 'I was asked to bring my niece here at half-past seven.'

'And she will be set to work immediately.' Mrs Upton met Jane's hard stare with narrowed eyes. 'Mrs Dearborn will see her later in the day.' She beckoned to Alice. 'Come with me, girl. I'll find you something more suitable to wear.'

Summarily dismissed, Jane clutched her umbrella to her flat bosom. 'Well!' The word exploded from her lips. 'I'll have words to say to your mistress when I see her next in church.'

Mrs Upton opened the door. 'Good day to you, madam. Hoskins will see you out.' She marched off, leaving Alice little alternative but to follow in her wake.

Glancing over her shoulder Alice caught a glimpse of the butler ushering Jane out of the house, and she could tell by the affronted twitch of her aunt's shoulders that she was not very happy. Even so, Alice was puzzled. If she was supposed to be instructing a little girl in drawing and painting why was she here so early? And why did the housekeeper think it necessary to provide her with a change of clothes?

She caught up with Mrs Upton at the foot of the back stairs. 'Excuse me, ma'am, but I don't know exactly what is expected of me.'

Mrs Upton stopped to pick up an oil lamp and turned to faced her. 'Are you simple or something, girl?'

Alice recoiled at the sharp tone of Mrs Upton's

voice and the scornful look on her plump face. 'No, certainly not. I thought I was here to teach art to Mrs Dearborn's daughter.'

'That amongst other things.' Mrs Upton marched down a long, dark passage. She opened a door at the far end and held the lamp high as she examined shelves piled with gowns, caps and aprons. 'You're not very big,' she said, looking Alice up and down. 'Try this on for size.' She selected a black cotton garment.

'I don't understand.' Alice stared at the uniform, shaking her head. 'Surely what I have on is quite appropriate for a teacher or even a governess?'

'This will suit you much better, believe me, it will.' Mrs Upton thrust the gown into her hands. 'Try it on for size.'

'You want me to undress here?' Alice looked round nervously.

'Change your clothes in the cupboard if you're shy. I haven't got all day, girl.'

Alice hesitated, trying to decide whether to make a run for it and face Aunt Jane's wrath, or to do as the housekeeper said and put on the uniform. She stepped into the cupboard and took off her grey merino gown, replacing it with the black cotton frock and a starched white apron.

'Let me look at you.' Mrs Upton held the candle higher in order to get a better view.

'I want to know why I'm dressed like a servant.'

'Because that's what you are. Didn't Mrs High-and-Mighty tell you?'

'No, ma'am. She said I was to be a teacher.'

'Personally speaking I wouldn't take on someone without any previous experience or training, but because you come from a respectable home the mistress has decided to give you a chance.'

'For what exactly?' Alice demanded. 'I'm dressed as a servant and I want to know why.'

Mrs Upton raised an eyebrow. 'You'll find out soon enough. Follow me.'

# Chapter Two

Alice was too shocked to argue. If Aunt Jane had told her that she was going into service it might have given her time to prepare, but this sudden turn of events had caught her unawares. She hurried after Mrs Upton, who took the stairs with the ease of a mountaineer. Clearly she was used to such exercise, but by the time they reached the third floor Alice was out of breath and her legs were aching. The somewhat gaudy décor had ended on the second floor, and the third floor seemed to have been reserved for the nursery suite. Mrs Upton selected a key from the bunch hanging at her waist and unlocked the door.

'Stand back and don't let her slip past you. Miss Flora is as slippery as an eel.' She opened it and ushered Alice inside, quickly closing the door behind them as a small child hurtled towards her and tried to grab the handle. 'Now, Miss Flora, that's not the way to behave, is it?'

Flora Dearborn skidded to a halt, glaring at her through a mop of tousled blonde hair. She was barefoot and wearing a cambric nightgown. 'I want to see Mama. You shouldn't lock me in, you horrible person.'

'That's no way to speak to anyone, Miss Flora,' Mrs Upton said, bristling but obviously making a huge effort to control her temper. 'What will Miss Radcliffe think?'

Flora tossed her hair back from her face, staring at Alice with a hostile look in her china-blue eyes. 'Who the devil are you?'

'Language, Miss Flora.'

'Shut up, Upton. You're just a servant.' Flora stood, feet wide apart, arms akimbo. 'Cat got your tongue, Miss Radcliffe?'

Alice met Flora's unfriendly gaze with a steady look. She saw a disturbed and angry child and felt a sudden burst of fellow-feeling for the little girl, who could not have been more than nine or ten. The mere fact that Flora had been locked in her room all night, and possibly longer, was enough to make Alice feel outraged and arouse her sympathy. It brought back unhappy memories of her childhood when, during one of the long bouts of illness suffered by her mother, the woman who had been hired to look after Alice had proved to be a drunk and a bully. If it had not been for the sharp eyes of their maidservant the situation might have escalated, but she had discovered the tell-tale empty gin bottles and had reported the woman to Clement, who had sacked her on the spot. Alice had been six at the time, but she had never forgotten the feeling of isolation, and the frustration of being unable to communicate her fears with the adults who should have been there to protect her.

She held her hand out to Flora. 'How do you do, Miss Flora? My name is Alice.'

Flora clasped her hands behind her back, ignoring the friendly overture. 'What's she doing here, Upton? You know what I do to governesses, and I'm too old for a nanny.'

Mrs Upton slid her fingers around the door handle, her knuckles whitening. 'Miss Radcliffe is going to look after you. She is an artist,' she added, wrenching the door open. 'I leave her in your capable hands, Miss Radcliffe.' She shot out of the room, slamming the door behind her.

Alice waited for the rasp of the key in the lock and was relieved when nothing happened. The sound of Mrs Upton's retreating footsteps faded into the distance, and Alice stood facing Flora, whose sullen expression was not encouraging.

'Well,' she said slowly, 'you obviously don't want me here, Flora. Would you like to tell me why?'

A fleeting look of astonishment was replaced by a frown. 'What do you care? Who are you, anyway?' Flora threw herself down on her bed and pulled the counterpane over her head, peering at Alice from beneath its folds. 'You're just like the rest of them.'

Alice was quick to hear the note of desperation in Flora's childish voice. She stood perfectly still, as if facing a wild animal, clasping her hands in front of her. 'I don't even know why I'm here, Flora. Tell me about yourself.'

There was a moment of uncomfortable silence while Flora seemed to weigh this up in her mind. Then to Alice's surprise she leaped off the bed, flinging the counterpane onto the floor. 'I'm a bad child. They're always telling me so.' She glared up at Alice, teeth bared. 'I bite and I scratch.'

Alice stood her ground. 'If you bite or scratch me I'll do the same to you, Flora.'

'Lay a finger on me and I'll tell Papa. And it's Miss Flora to you, Radcliffe.'

'Miss Flora is a young lady. You are a spoiled brat.'

'I am not spoiled.' Flora lunged at Alice, grabbing her by the sleeve and tugging with all her might.

Alice felt the stitching give way at the shoulder seam and a searing pain where Flora's sharp finger-nails dug into the soft flesh of her forearm. Flora opened her mouth as if to bite but Alice was too quick for her. She raised her free hand and caught Alice a mighty clout round the side of her head, but at that moment the door opened and a maid entered carrying a breakfast tray. Flora uttered a loud wail, clutching her hand to her ear. 'You hit me. I'll tell Mama what you did.' She turned to the maid, who was standing in the doorway open-mouthed. 'You saw what she did, Nettie. She struck me.'

The maid recovered quickly. 'I'm sorry, Miss Flora. I never saw nothing.'

Alice rubbed her sore wrist where crescent-shaped nail marks had begun to bleed. She had always disapproved of corporal punishment, but Flora had been out of control. 'You will sit at the table and eat your breakfast, young lady,' she said firmly.

Nettie bustled over to the table and put the tray down, keeping a wary eye on Flora, who advanced on her with clenched fists. 'You're a liar,' she hissed. 'You saw what she did.'

'I'm sorry, Miss Flora. I dunno what you're talking about.' Nettie backed away. 'The porridge is just how you like it, miss. Nice and sweet with a dollop of honey.'

Moving swiftly, Flora snatched up the plate and hurled it, but Nettie was too quick for her and was out of the room in a flash of starched white petticoats. The bowl hit the door as it closed, spreading the thick, sticky oatmeal in a starburst on the floor. Alice watched it drip down the wall and her stomach rumbled. The waste of good food was appalling and she was hungry. She faced Flora, folding her arms across her chest. 'You will clear that up before you start your meal.'

Flora poked her tongue out as she took her seat at the table. 'It's your job, Radcliffe. You're the servant.'

Moving swiftly, Alice crossed the floor and lifted Flora bodily from the chair. 'You will do as I say, or we will not get on at all well. I've never seen

such disgraceful behaviour and it's quite unaccep-
table.'

'I knew you were like the others,' Flora said sulkily.
'They all hate me.'

Alice stood her ground. 'If this is how you behave
it's hardly surprising no one likes you.'

A look of uncertainly crossed Flora's small features
and she tossed back her unruly curls. 'They're paid
to like me. I'm Flora Dearborn. My pa is a rich man.'

'I don't care if your pa is an Indian nabob, you'll
clear up the mess you made.'

'What's a nabob?'

'Someone who is much wealthier than your pa,
and I don't suppose they boast about their riches.
It's not considered good manners.'

Flora's curious expression was replaced by a pout.
'I don't care about manners.'

Alice knew she was losing the battle of wills, but
was saved by the timely appearance of Nettie, who
entered the room with a bucket slung over her arm
and a scrubbing brush in her hand. 'I've come to
clear up the mess, Miss Radcliffe.'

'Thank you, Nettie, but Miss Flora has something
to say to you.' Alice sent a meaningful look in Flora's
direction. 'She wishes to apologise for her behaviour.'

Flora stared down at her bare feet. 'No, I don't.'

'I'll just do my work,' Nettie said hastily.

'No.' Alice moved to her side and took the bucket
from her grasp. 'Miss Flora created this mess and
she is going to clear it up.'

Nettie's lips worked silently as she stared wide-eyed at Flora.

Alice nodded her head. 'You may go, Nettie. This will be done, I assure you.' She waited until they were alone again. 'You and I have been thrust together, Flora. I didn't choose to work here and you didn't ask to have me, so we'll have to make the best of it.'

'I'll get rid of you like I got rid of all the others,' Flora muttered half to herself, but just loud enough for Alice to hear.

'We may have more in common than you think,' Alice said casually. 'I'll tell you my story and I'll be happy to listen to what you have to say. Maybe we can come to a truce, but first you will clear up the mess you made.'

'My boiled egg and soldiers are getting cold. I'm hungry.'

'Then you'd better hurry up or they'll be stone cold and I'll ring for Nettie to take the tray away.' Alice could smell the hot buttered toast and she was so hungry she could have gone down on her knees and lapped up the porridge like a cat, but she had her own feelings under control. She met Flora's rebellious gaze with a steady look. This was a battle she had to win.

'All right, but I'll make you suffer for this, Radcliffe.' Flora went down on her hands and knees and picked up the scrubbing brush.

Alice smothered a sigh of relief. Life was difficult

enough without a child dictating the odds. She stood in silence while Flora dabbed ineffectively at the glutinous mass, which was seeping into the cracks between the floorboards. In the end Alice went down on her knees beside her, taking the cloth from the bucket of rapidly cooling water and wringing it out. 'We'll do it quicker together.'

Flora said nothing and turned her head away, but not before Alice had seen tears glistening on the ends of her long eyelashes. She's just a child, Alice thought wearily; a lonely child in desperate need of companionship as well as a firm hand. She sat back on her haunches. 'I think we've done all we can, Flora. Eat your breakfast before it gets too cold.'

Flora scrambled to her feet, flinging the scrubbing brush into the bucket. 'I'll tell Mama of you, Radcliffe.'

'Do as you please, but I can play that game too. I don't suppose she would be too pleased to learn that you threw a plate at Nettie.'

Flora resumed her seat and ate in silence, while Alice tidied the room. It was simply furnished with a child's desk and chair at the far end and a larger desk, which presumably must have been used by Flora's governess, but was now littered with books and drawing materials. Sorting through them, Alice was encouraged to find that Flora had a talent for drawing, although most of the sketches had a dark, nightmarish quality that was disturbing. Another factor that seemed unnatural was the lack of playthings. There was not a doll in sight nor anything that might keep a nine-year-old amused during the long hours that Flora seemed to spend on her own. There was a bookcase but most of the shelves were empty, and there was not much reading material to occupy the mind of a lively child. There were a few framed prints on the walls, but these were mostly sombre lithographs of winter scenes, which were hardly cheering on a cold and snowy day. Alice sighed. This was not how she had foreseen her future, if she had ever thought about it at all, but at least she was attempting to put her time to good use. She put a shovelful of coal on the fire and sat down to wait for Flora to finish her meal.

Alice soon discovered that everything was a battle with young Flora Dearborn, from the frock she was to wear that day to the boots that went with it, and when Alice tried to run a comb through her young charge's tangled mop there were shrieks and tears.

'You're hurting me.' Flora cried petulantly. 'Leave me alone, you bitch.'

Alice held the tress of hair firmly in her hand so that Flora could not pull away. 'Mrs Upton said that we were to go down to the drawing room at half-past eleven to see your mama. I'm sure she wouldn't want to see you looking as though you've been dragged through a hedge backwards.'

Flora stopped struggling. 'Have you ever seen anyone who's been dragged through a hedge backwards?'

'It's just a manner of speaking, but you know very well what I mean.'

'You're tugging too hard. You're doing it to hurt me like Smithson used to.'

'Who is Smithson?'

'She was my nanny. She used to pull my hair and pinch me if I was naughty. She told me that Spring-heeled Jack would get me if I was bad. He'd jump up to my window and come in while I was asleep.'

'That's nonsense, Flora. Spring-heeled Jack is merely a tale told to frighten little girls. Now let's try and get the comb through the worst of the tangles so that your mama will be proud of you.'

'She's not my mama,' Flora said sulkily. 'I have to call her mama but she just wanted a little girl to show off to her friends.'

Alice paused with the comb poised over Flora's curly head. 'Is this a tale you're making up?'

'No.' Flora twisted round to look her in the face. 'That's why they lock me up at night. I keep trying to go home to my real mama, but they won't let me.'

Shocked and upset, Alice could hardly believe her ears. 'Where is your home then, Flora?'

'It's far away from here where the sun always shines. There are flowers all year round and tall trees with birds nesting in the branches. They took me from my real mama, but no one loves me here. I'm too horrible, like you said.'

'If what you say is true then it's quite appalling.'

'I'm not a liar.' Flora snatched the comb out of Alice's hand and started dragging it through her hair, tugging at the stubborn tangles with tears spurting from her eyes. Alice covered the small hand with hers, gently prising Flora's fingers apart and taking the comb from her.

'I believe you.'

'You do? No one else does. Mrs Upton says it's a wicked lie and the others laugh at me. I know they do.'

'How long have you been here, Flora?'

'I don't know. A long time.'

'Who told you that Mrs Dearborn is not your real mama?'

'Smithson did. She told me when she'd been drinking from the bottle she hid at the back of the cupboard. She said she'd been the midwife attending my real mama, and Mrs Dearborn gave her ten pounds to buy a baby girl.'

Alice stared at her, frowning. It was almost impossible to believe that a woman could sell her newborn baby, but Flora seemed certain that it was true. 'Perhaps she was lying. Sometimes people say stupid things when they've been drinking.'

'Rory says it's true.'

'Who is Rory?'

Flora smiled and her eyes lit up for a brief moment, but then the sullen look returned like a tragic mask. 'Rory is my uncle, or that's what I have to call him. He's Papa's younger brother.'

'I don't understand,' Alice said, frowning. 'Why would he say such a thing?'

'He came to visit and found me crying.' Flora's eyes filled with tears, making her look vulnerable and completely different from the wild child who had greeted Alice earlier that morning. 'It was after Smithson told me about my real mama. Rory said he'd find out if it was true, and if it was he promised that one day he'd take me to see my real mother.'

Alice ran the comb through Flora's tangle-free hair. 'There you are. Now you're presentable.' She glanced at the clock on the mantelshelf. 'We should go downstairs to see your mama.'

'Do you believe me?' Flora turned to face her. 'You think I'm lying, don't you? They all think I'm a liar.'

'No, I don't think you're making it up,' Alice said slowly. 'But I'd like to speak to your uncle. Does he come here often?'

'Not often enough. I love Uncle Rory. He makes me laugh.' She jumped to her feet. 'You won't tell Mama what I said, will you? She won't like it.'

'Of course not. It will be our secret.' Alice held out her hand. 'You'll have to show me where we will find Mrs Dearborn. I don't know where to go.'

The drawing room was a complete contrast to the nursery. It was furnished in the latest style and it did not take an expert to see that no expense had been spared. Alice would not have been surprised to see price tickets hanging from the opulent velvet upholstery of the chairs and sofa. The smell of the showroom still lingered, despite the bowls of potpourri placed on highly polished mahogany side tables, and the vases of hothouse chrysanthemums affordable only by the wealthiest in society. Alice felt her feet sinking into the thick pile of the Aubusson carpet, and each movement she made was reflected in one or more of the gilt-framed mirrors that adorned the walls.

Mrs Dearborn was handsome in an austere way, and elegantly dressed in the height of fashion. Pearl drops dangled from her ears and strands of pearls were hung around her slender neck. She was seated in a wingback chair by the fire with an embroidery hoop in her hand, although she did not seem to have progressed very far with the complicated pattern. She shot a wary glance at Flora. 'Sit down, child. Don't just stand there.' She turned her attention to Alice, looking her up and down with a critical gaze. 'So you are Mrs Radcliffe's niece?'

Alice inclined her head. 'Yes, ma'am.'

'They might have found you a better garment to wear.' Mrs Dearborn raised a lorgnette, peering at the ripped shoulder seam. 'You cannot go round looking like a ragbag, Radcliffe.'

'I'll see to it, Mrs Dearborn.' Inwardly seething, Alice made an effort to sound submissive.

'Stop fidgeting, Flora.' Mrs Dearborn put her embroidery aside, glaring at her daughter. 'Have you been behaving properly this morning? Radcliffe will tell me if you've been a naughty girl.'

'Miss Flora has been a model child,' Alice said quickly. 'I think we will do very well together.' The words tumbled from her lips before she had time to think, but she had taken an instant dislike to Mrs Dearborn, who might have been a beauty had it not been for her dissatisfied expression. Her thin lips hinted at a discontented nature, and this was borne out by the twin furrows on her forehead, which created a permanent frown.

Flora shot Alice a puzzled glance, as if amazed to think that an adult would stand up for her, and for once she seemed to have nothing to say.

'You surprise me,' Mrs Dearborn said, raising an eyebrow. 'Flora needs a firm hand. My husband spoils her and she thinks that she can do as she pleases, but the sooner she learns to behave properly the better.'

'May I ask you a question, Mrs Dearborn?' Alice moved closer, lowering her voice. 'Why was it thought necessary to lock Miss Flora in her room? Surely it's frightening for a young child to be treated so harshly?'

Mrs Dearborn leaned back in her chair, eyes narrowed. 'If you are to work for me you will not question my authority. Is that clear?'

The temptation to tell Mrs Dearborn that she would not be accepting the position in her household was almost too great, but one glance in Flora's direction was enough to convince her otherwise. Whether or not she was the daughter of the house was immaterial. Whether it was true or just a story made up by a lonely little girl, Alice could not simply walk away. She nodded. 'Perfectly clear, ma'am.' Even as she spoke she felt small fingers curling around her hand. She gave them an encouraging squeeze.

'You said we could have a Christmas tree, Mama,' Flora said slyly. 'I promise to be very good.'

'I'm not sure that you deserve anything at all for Christmas,' Mrs Dearborn said stiffly. 'Mrs Upton tells me that you attempted to leave the house again yesterday. Hoskins had to chase you round the square twice before he caught you.'

'I was going home.' Flora squared her small shoulders, meeting her mother's angry gaze with a toss of her head. 'You don't really want me. You only bring me down here to show me off when your friends are visiting.'

For a moment it seemed that Flora had gone too far. The look on Mrs Dearborn's face was a mixture of chagrin and rage. 'Take the child back to the nursery, Radcliffe. You have my permission to chastise her as you see fit.' She rose to her feet. 'And you, Flora Dearborn, will apologise or you will not have Christmas at all. There will be no tree and definitely no presents. I'll tell your father and he will agree with me, so don't think you can get round him.' She slumped down on her seat, mopping her brow with a lace handkerchief. 'Ring the bell on your way out, Radcliffe. I feel quite faint and in need of my smelling salts.'

Alice seized Flora by the hand and left the room, pausing to tug at the bell pull on the way out.

'Why did you say that, Flora? You can see that you've upset your mama.'

'She isn't my mama. I told you that, Radcliffe.' Flora stamped her foot and marched off towards the staircase.

Alice hurried after her. 'You and I need a serious talk if I'm to stay on here, Flora.'

'See if I care.' Flora took the stairs two at a time, reaching the third floor well ahead of Alice. She slammed the nursery door.

In no mood for childish tantrums, Alice followed her inside. 'Sit down, miss,' she said firmly. 'Stop behaving like that or you'll hurt yourself.'

'So what if I do?' Flora cried angrily. 'Nobody cares except Papa, and he's not here most of the time, and he doesn't always listen to me. He just pats me on the head and gives me whatever I ask for. The only one who does hear what I have to say is Uncle Rory.'

'I'd like to meet your uncle,' Alice said, choosing her words carefully. 'He sounds nice.'

Flora came to a halt, looking up at her with a sudden sparkle in her blue eyes. 'He is nice, and he's funny.' She threw herself down on the bed, beating the pillow with her small fists. 'Now I won't get any presents or a tree. Papa promised me a tree with candles on it and tinsel, like last year.' She began to sob, her whole body racked by intense emotion.

Alice sat on the edge of the bed, stroking Flora's wildly curling hair back from her damp forehead. 'I'm sure it was said in the heat of the moment. If you apologise to your mama it will all be forgotten.'

Flora raised a tear-stained face to look up at her. 'She won't forget. She's mean.'

'Wipe your eyes and I'll help you write a note to your mama. You could do a little drawing for her. I know you're good at that because I've seen some of your sketches.'

'I draw what I see in my nightmares.' Flora sat up, wiping her eyes on her sleeve. 'I'll draw her as a witch.'

'I don't think that's a good idea,' Alice said hastily. She rose to her feet and went to the washstand to dip a flannel in cold water. Having wrung it out she used it to wipe Flora's hot cheeks. 'It would be better to draw something to remind her that it's the season of peace and goodwill,' she said slowly. 'Perhaps some holly and ivy or mistletoe would be nice, and a little note from you saying you're very sorry.'

'But I'm not sorry,' Flora said crossly.

'It's your choice. You apologise and try to make amends or else you'll have a very miserable Christmas.'

Flora stared at her, head on one side. 'What sort of Christmas will you have, Radcliffe?'

'I think we should start by being on first-name terms. I want you to call me Alice and I'll drop the title Miss and simply call you Flora, at least when we're on our own.'

'All right,' Flora said, nodding. 'So will you be here with me on Christmas Day, Alice? Or will you go away like everyone else and have a jolly time with your family?'

'If you want me to be here, then I will. I told you how it is with me and my mama. There's little enough cheer in my aunt's house.'

Flora threw her arms around Alice, giving her a hearty hug. 'Then it's the same for you. I want you here, with me. You can bring your mama, if you like, and I'll tell Mrs Upton to give us a special luncheon.'

'Don't you ever take your meals with your parents, Flora?'

'Sometimes, but they have friends to dinner on Christmas Day. I just go downstairs when the ladies sit in the drawing room afterwards and they give me crystallised fruit. And sugared almonds – I like that.'

Alice rose to her feet, turning away so that Flora could not see the tears of sympathy that welled in her eyes. She went to the desk and searched for pen and paper. 'Come over here, Flora. You can write the words but I'll help you with the picture.'

After several false starts with ink blots flying in all directions, Flora finally managed to write a short note of apology, and she drew some spiky holly leaves with berries that varied in size and shape. It was a good effort, but she was not satisfied.

'Please draw some mistletoe, Alice. I remember Papa kissing Mama under the mistletoe last Christmas. She went red and giggled, but I think she liked it really.' She pushed the piece of paper towards Alice. 'Please. A lovely big bunch of mistletoe.'

Alice smiled. This was a different child from the brat who had greeted her first thing that morning. 'All right, I will, just this once.' She took the pen and began to draw. Flora leaned over her shoulder, making encouraging remarks and breathing heavily down Alice's neck.

'It's beautiful,' Flora said delightedly when Alice put the pen down. 'Let's go and give it to Mama now.'

'We'll wait until the ink dries or it will smudge, and then we'll go downstairs and you can give it to her.'

They were prevented from going straight away by the arrival of Nettie with a tray of food for their midday meal. Flora picked at hers but Alice was starving and she ate with relish. One thing in Mrs Dearborn's favour was her choice of cook. The chicken soup was rich and delicious, and the bread, hot from the oven, was liberally spread with butter. Followed by treacle tart and custard, it was the best meal that Alice had eaten in days and she finished off what Flora left for good measure.

'You'll get fat if you eat that much.' Flora shook her head, staring pointedly at the empty plates.

'There's little chance of that,' Alice said, wiping her lips on the starched white napkin. 'My aunt doesn't believe in overfeeding us. I just wish my mama could have had some of the chicken soup.'

'I'll tell Mrs Upton to prepare a basket for you,' Flora said grandly. 'Now, let's go downstairs and give the note to Mama. It's Christmas Eve tomorrow and it's getting very late to get a tree, or to buy presents.'

Flora ran ahead of Alice and burst into the drawing room without bothering to knock. Mrs Dearborn looked up from her embroidery, frowning ominously. 'What now, Flora? Where are your manners?'

'I'm sorry, Mama.' Flora ran to her side, thrusting the note into her hands. 'I made this for you.'

Mrs Dearborn scanned the paper. 'You did this unaided, Flora?'

'I had a bit of help from Radcliffe,' Flora said airily. 'I did most of it, but she did the mistletoe.'

'Mistletoe?' A male voice from the doorway made Alice turn with a start, but all she could see was a tangle of pine branches as a tall figure hefted a huge tree into the room.

'Uncle Rory.' Flora rushed to greet him. 'I hoped you'd come. There's someone I want you to meet.'

# Chapter Three

'I said that there was to be no tree this year.' Mrs Dearborn rose to her feet allowing Flora's note to drift to the floor. 'You spoil her, Rory. She doesn't deserve such attention.'

Alice stood aside, mindful of her lowly position in the household, but she was curious to see the uncle whom Flora seemed to worship. The tree reached almost to the ceiling and the scent of pine filled the room as Rory manoeuvred it with some difficulty towards the window. He leaned it against the wall and stood back, brushing spiky green needles off his well-cut pin-stripe jacket. He turned to his sister-in-law with a disarming smile.

'I'm sure you don't mean that, Lydia.' He bent down to lift Flora in his arms, placing a smacking kiss on her cheek before setting her back on her feet. 'Have you been a bad girl again, Floss?'

'No, of course not, Uncle Rory.' Flora gazed up at him adoringly.

He was, Alice thought, undeniably handsome, and he had smiling brown eyes. She could see why he must appear like a Greek god to a lonely little girl.

'Don't pander to her,' Lydia Dearborn said sharply. 'Anyway, you started this particular bout of bad behaviour by listening to the ranting of that drunken woman my husband was forced to dismiss. Now the child thinks she has another family living in Spitalfields, of all places.'

Flora grasped Rory's hand, holding it to her cheek. 'Tell her, Uncle Rory. You believe me, don't you?'

'It's time Miss Radcliffe took you back to the nursery, Flora.' Lydia sank down on her chair as if exhausted by the conversation. 'Run along now.'

'Miss Radcliffe?' Rory turned to Alice with an appraising look. 'You're new here.'

Alice inclined her head. 'Yes, sir.'

'She's my friend, Uncle Rory,' Alice said stoutly. 'I like her.'

'Do you indeed?' Rory met Alice's steady gaze with a smile. 'How do you do, Miss Radcliffe? It's a pleasure to meet any friend of Flora's.'

'How do you do, sir?' Alice felt her cheeks redden. The teasing look in his dark eyes made her feel ill at ease and she was not sure how she was supposed to respond. In the close confines of her home and subject to her father's strict upbringing she had had little contact with the outside world, let alone the opposite sex. But she was no longer Miss Radcliffe of Doughty Street, she was now a servant, and she was not sure what was expected of her. One look at her employer confirmed her suspicion that Flora's uncle had overstepped the boundary set by his sister-in-law. Mrs Dearborn was visibly bristling.

'Take Miss Flora back to the nursery, Radcliffe.' Lydia's voice was harsh and uncompromising.

'You'll come up and see me later, won't you, Uncle Rory?' Flora pleaded. 'Promise.'

He ruffled her hair. 'Of course I will, Floss.' He turned to Alice, holding out his hand. 'As I said, it's a pleasure to meet you, Miss Radcliffe.'

For a moment Alice was tempted to shake hands, but she could feel Lydia's eyes boring into her back and she bobbed a curtsey. 'Thank you, sir,' she said meekly.

'Her name is Alice,' Flora said impatiently. 'She doesn't like being called Miss Radcliffe.'

'That's enough, Flora. Little girls should be seen and not heard.' Lydia's frown deepened. 'Remember what I said would happen if you continued to misbehave.'

Flora shot a sideways glance at her mother. 'I will be good, Mama. Please let us keep the tree.'

Rory bent down to pick up Flora's note. 'This must be yours, Floss. I can tell by the blots.' He examined it closer. 'This is very good, but I don't think it's all your own work.' He held it out of reach as Flora tried to snatch it from his hand. 'Tell the truth now.'

'Miss Radcliffe did the mistletoe, but I did all the rest.'

'You're quite an artist, Miss Radcliffe,' he said, studying the drawing more closely. 'This shows talent.'

'Alice did most of it, sir. I only did the last little bit.'

'Well, we all need a little mistletoe in our lives, especially at Christmas.' He dropped a kiss on Flora's curls and handed her the note. 'I believe this belongs to your mama, Floss. Perhaps if you give it to her again she will relent.' He turned to his sister-in-law with a persuasive grin. 'It is the season of goodwill to all men, and that includes naughty children, don't you think, Lydia?'

She shrugged her shoulders. 'You are just like your brother. You give in too easily, Rory.' She reached out to take the piece of paper from Flora. 'All right, you may have the tree, but you will have to be very good if you want to receive a present.'

'Yes, Mama.' Flora ran to the door and opened it. 'Come along, Miss Radcliffe. I'm waiting.'

Rory kept his word and spent half an hour in the nursery before taking his leave, and Alice decided to leave them to enjoy each other's company. She went to find Mrs Upton, who directed her to the sewing room where she was able to take off her torn gown and repair the ripped seam. Rory had departed by the time Alice returned, but Flora was in high spirits and the rest of the day passed without any further incidents.

There did not seem to be any set hour when Alice was supposed to finish, but she waited until after supper when Flora was tucked up in her bed. She read her a story from a book that was so well used it was falling apart, and kissed her good night.

'Won't you stay, please?' Flora whispered. 'Smithson used to sleep in the next room, although it was no use calling out to her in the night because she wouldn't wake up.'

'I have to go home to see that my mother is all right,' Alice said softly. 'But I'll be here first thing in the morning. Perhaps we'll go outside and play snowballs, and roast chestnuts in the fire.'

Flora raised herself to lean on her elbow. 'Will we really?'

'I don't see why not. I'll make sure I have a stout pair of boots and warm clothes. It will be fun.' She could tell by Flora's baffled expression that the child had little idea of what constituted fun, but she would learn. 'And it will be Christmas Eve, so perhaps your mother will allow us to decorate the tree?'

Flora grabbed her hand and kissed it. 'You are my best present ever, Alice. I love you.'

Alice gave her a hug. 'You and I will do very well together, Flora Dearborn. Now I have to leave, but if you close your eyes and go to sleep it will soon be morning and I'll return. Good night, my dear.'

Snippet opened the door and Alice could tell by her expression that all was not well. She stamped her booted feet on the top step, shaking off the frozen lumps of snow before entering the house. 'What's the matter, Clara?'

'She likes her dinner on time, miss.' Clara glanced at the mahogany drop dial wall clock. 'She don't like to be kept waiting.'

Alice removed her bonnet and mantle, handing the snow-caked garments to Clara. The chill in the house struck her like a blow; it was, she thought, warmer outside than it was indoors. 'I didn't think they'd wait for me,' she said in a low voice.

Clara nodded sagely. 'She wouldn't have, miss. Not under normal circumstances, like, but he come to see her today, and Cook thinks there's more to it than meets the eye.' Clara winked and tapped the side of her nose. 'If you get my meaning, miss.'

'No, I'm afraid I don't. Who else is here?'

'Snippet. Get back to the kitchen and tell Mrs Jugg to serve dinner immediately.' Jane's strident tones reverberated around the entrance hall. Clara turned and ran, her small feet pitter-pattering on the bare boards as she headed for the green baize door.

'You're late, Alice. Punctuality is the politeness of princes.' Jane hovered in the dining-room doorway, putting Alice in mind of a bird of ill omen in her black dress with her shawl flapping in the draught like the wings of a carrion crow. 'Come and take your seat at table.'

To Alice's surprise the dining room looked almost festive, or at least it was a little less austere than the previous day. The table was laid with a white damask cloth and the best crystal glasses glistened in the candlelight. A bowl of holly added a festive touch and the fire had been banked up with extra coal, although it barely raised the temperature enough to prevent Alice's teeth from chattering. She experienced a feeling of relief when she saw her mother seated by the fire, but before she had a chance to speak to her she was accosted by her aunt. Jane grabbed her by the arm, twisting her round to face the fourth person in the room as he emerged from the shadows.

'Alice, I want you to meet my cousin, Horace Hubble.'

The resemblance between Jane and the gentleman who stepped forward was striking. He was taller than his cousin, and his dark hair was greying, as were his mutton chop whiskers and drooping walrus moustache. He held out his hand but the smile on his lips did not reach his eyes. 'I'm delighted to meet you at last, Miss Radcliffe. I've heard so much about you.'

'Really? I'm afraid I don't know anything about you, sir.' His handshake was limp and his palm moist. Alice withdrew hers quickly, hoping that he did not notice the shudder that ran through her at his touch.

'Cousin Jane,' he said, stretching his wide lips into a rictus grin, 'I thought better of you. You leave me at a disadvantage.'

'Stuff and nonsense.' Jane strode to the head of the table. 'Take your seats, everyone. We are very late dining.' She shot a reproachful glance in Alice's direction.

Horace moved swiftly to pull out Jane's chair. 'You really ought to employ more servants, Cousin.'

Jane sat down and rang the bell. 'Snippet does well enough. I don't approve of wasting money on underlings to eat my food and cost me money.'

Alice helped her mother to take her seat at the table. 'How are you feeling this evening, Mama?'

'Quite well, thank you, my darling. Jane has kept me fully employed today, which took my mind off my ailments, and the sorry position in which we find ourselves.'

'Self-pity is a waste of time,' Jane said severely. 'There's nothing wrong with you, Beth. It's all in your silly head.'

'Really, Aunt,' Alice protested. 'That's not fair. Mama has always been delicate.'

'Sit down, Alice. You too, Horace. I can't do with people hovering.' Jane rang the bell again. 'Where is that idle child?'

'Perhaps I ought to go and help?' Alice suggested tentatively. 'She's quite small to carry heavy dishes up from the kitchen.'

'People from her walk of life are born with the

50

strength of oxen,' Jane said dismissively. 'That's why they dig roads and plough the soil. We were put on earth to guide them and to help them control their base instincts. The child has to learn.'

The crash of breaking china was followed by a loud howl. Alice hurried to the door and opened it to find Clara on her knees amidst shards of broken crockery. She raised her to her feet. 'There, there, don't cry, Clara. It was an accident.'

'I've broke the best plates. I'll get a beating when Mrs Jugg finds out what I done.'

'No one will harm you; I'll see to that.' Alice patted her on the shoulder. 'Go and fetch a shovel and a brush and clear up the mess.'

'But the dinner, miss. I'm supposed to fetch it.'

'Leave that to me.' Alice stepped back into the dining room. 'Mr Hubble, would you care to assist me?'

His look of surprise was quickly replaced by a smug smile and he rose swiftly to his feet. 'Of course, Miss Radcliffe. Anything you say.' He was at her side in seconds, smiling down at her and exposing long, yellow teeth that put her in mind of a pony she had ridden as a child. It had not been a gentle animal and had taken every opportunity to give her a savage nip; it was not a pleasant memory.

'There has been a mishap,' she said, closing the door so that her aunt could not hear. 'I'm going below stairs to fetch the food and it would help to have someone like you to assist me.' She could see

51

that he was shocked by such a suggestion. 'You did say that Aunt Jane ought to employ more staff. Perhaps this will convince her.'

He fingered his cravat, clearing his throat nervously. 'This is highly irregular, Miss Radcliffe. Below stairs is the servants' domain.'

'And at present there is only the cook, and a young girl who is terrified that she will be beaten for her clumsiness. I think dinner will be delayed a lot longer if we simply sit and wait for it to arrive.' She walked off without waiting for his answer, and had just reached the baize door when he caught up with her.

'You're right, of course. You are a very wise young lady.' He held the door for her. 'And I look forward to furthering our acquaintance.'

'Yes, indeed,' she said vaguely as she hurried down the narrow staircase.

Cook stared at them in amazement. 'Oh my Lord, whatever next? The silly girl told me that she's dropped the plates, and she'll be punished severely.'

'It's all right, Mrs Jugg,' Alice said calmly. 'It was an accident and no one blames Clara. She is going to clear up the broken china and we will take the food upstairs.'

'Oh, no, miss. That's not right at all. And you, sir, what must you think of us?' Mrs Jugg glanced anxiously at Horace as if expecting the worst.

Alice picked up the soup tureen and passed it to

Horace. 'Mr Hubble is in complete agreement with me.'

His sickly smile was unconvincing, but he nodded his head. 'Just this once.'

Alice went to the dresser and selected four soup bowls. She picked up a basket of bread rolls. 'Tell Clara not to worry, Mrs Jugg. It could have happened to anyone.'

Cook's lips worked soundlessly as Clara rushed in from the scullery armed with a brush and coal shovel. 'I'm so sorry,' she breathed. 'Ever so sorry.'

Alice stood back to allow her to race on ahead. 'She's a good girl,' she said firmly. 'Nothing more will be said, Mrs Jugg. And the soup smells delicious.'

'There's roast beef to follow. The mistress always puts on a show for her cousin. He's her only living relative, apart from you, of course, Miss Alice.'

Alice knew that, but it did not explain the extravagance of the hospitality, or her aunt's desire for them to meet. She hurried after Horace and arrived in the dining room as he was about to place the tureen on the table.

Jane stared at them both, aghast. 'Horace, what do you think you're doing? And you, Alice, you should know better.'

'There was a slight mishap due to that clumsy young maidservant, but I could not bear to think of you waiting a moment longer for such an excellent repast,' Horace said, taking the credit for the idea even though he had been against it at the start. 'Miss Radcliffe was kind enough to assist me.'

'I've a good mind to send Snippet back to the workhouse. One takes these people in for the most Christian reasons and they invariably fail in their duties.'

Horace lifted the lid and was about to begin serving the soup when Jane held up her hand.

'We haven't yet said grace.' She launched into a much shortened version of the prayer. 'I don't know why I burden myself with these charity cases. They always let one down,' she added at the end.

'Your acts of generosity to the poor are well known, Cousin,' Horace said, ladling soup into a bowl and placing it in front of her. 'The world would be a happier place were there more people like you.'

Jane smile modestly. 'You're too kind, Horace. Do sit down and enjoy your meal.' She clicked her fingers at Alice. 'You may finish serving the soup, and after dinner you will go down to the kitchen and tell Snippet that unless she pulls herself together she will spend Christmas in the workhouse.'

'That seems a little harsh, sister-in-law,' Beth said timidly. 'The child is very young and she will learn.'

Alice filled a bowl with soup and passed it to her mother with a grateful smile. She knew how much courage it would have taken to enable her to speak up for Clara. 'I agree with Mama,' she said stoutly. 'Snippet is eager to improve.'

Jane's brows drew together in an ominous frown,

but Horace beamed at Alice. 'Well said, Miss Radcliffe.' He used his table napkin to mop up the soup as it dripped from his moustache. 'You have inherited my cousin's charitable nature.' He shot a sideways glance at Jane, who snatched up a bread roll and tore it into tiny pieces, popping one into her mouth and grinding it with her teeth.

Alice repressed a shudder as one of Flora's nightmare sketches flashed before her eyes. Jane was suddenly the wicked witch about to eat Hansel and Gretel. She blinked hard and found Horace staring at her with a bemused expression. She managed a weak smile. 'The soup is delicious.'

Jane curled her lip. 'This will be our festive repast. I spend Christmas Day attending church services. You would do well to come with me, Alice.'

'I would, of course,' Alice said quickly, 'but I'm afraid I have to work. Mrs Dearborn has not given me the day off.' It was not exactly a lie, nor was it the complete truth. In fact, nothing had been mentioned by the lady of the house, but Flora wanted her to be there, and even on such a short acquaintance her welfare had become important to Alice.

'Really?' Beth's eyes were moist with unshed tears. 'Must you, Alice? Surely everyone deserves to spend the day with their family?'

'You're invited too, Mama,' Alice said in desperation. 'Miss Flora will be glad of the company. The poor child spends most of her time alone in the nursery.'

'I'm proud to belong to such a caring family,' Horace said, clasping his hands as if in prayer. 'Although I was hoping that perhaps I might be invited to spend Christmas Day here with my only living relatives.'

Alice held her breath, praying that Aunt Jane would not weaken, and she could have cried with relief when her aunt shook her head. 'You have friends who will make you welcome, Horace. You're always telling me how popular you are.'

'Well, yes, indeed, but ...'

'No buts, Cousin. I'm sure you will find some-where to go, but it won't be here. I will be in church or helping the poor and needy, as is my wont.'

Horace mumbled something into his beard.

'What did you say, Cousin?'

He gave her a sheepish grin. 'I said you are a saint, Cousin Jane.'

She beamed at him. 'Oh, no. That I am not, but I'm glad that Alice is taking her work seriously, and Beth can spend the day in bed if she so chooses.' She pushed her plate away. 'Alice, you may ring the bell, and if that stupid child doesn't appear within minutes you will go below stairs and tell her to pack her bags.'

Snippet saved herself by arriving promptly, if a little dishevelled and out of breath, but she managed to clear the table without dropping anything and delivered the main course without further mishap. The roast beef was a bit tough, the potatoes not quite cooked through and the cabbage a little watery, but Horace ate ravenously and Jane cleared her plate. Alice had already eaten well that day and she only ate a small amount, and her mother, as usual, picked at her food, but there was apple pie to follow and that was delicious. The custard was thick and creamy and everyone did justice to the dessert, but the moment she had finished her meal Jane rose to her feet and announced that the evening must come to an end.

Horace stared at her. 'But it is early as yet, Cousin. Might we not sit for a while and allow our meal to digest?'

'There is nothing wrong with my digestion, Horace, and you have a long walk to your rooms in West Smithfield. Unless, of course, you intend to take a cab.'

'That costs money, my dear cousin, and as you know my finances leave much to be desired.'

'And that is because your father was a gambler and risked his fortune on unwise investments. My own dear Robert was a prudent man. He strived hard to provide for us in our old age.'

'And he worked himself to death, Cousin.' Horace's moustache quivered with suppressed emotion. Alice could not be sure whether it was grief or indignation, but he was obviously moved.

'Robert did not work himself to death. He caught lung fever when visiting the docks, and that was what took him to an early grave.' Jane produced a hanky and dabbed her eyes. 'I was widowed at the age of thirty-five and my heart is interred with my beloved husband.'

Horace rose to his feet. 'We all share your sorrow, Cousin.' He turned to Alice with a wolfish smile. 'Will you see me out, Miss Radcliffe? Or may I call you Alice?'

'I will see you out.' Jane stood up, brushing crumbs from her skirt. 'It's not proper for a young unmarried woman to be alone in the company of an eligible gentleman. You know that as well as I do, Horace.'

He bowed, clicking his heels together. 'You are right as always, Cousin Jane. Please forgive me for my boldness, but in the face of such youth and beauty I'm afraid it is difficult to remain aloof.'

Alice stared at him in horror. If Horace Hubble had any romantic ideas in his head he would do better to forget them. The mere sight of him revolted her and although they had only just met, her first impression of him had been far from favourable. For once she was grateful to her aunt for her rigid sense of propriety. Jane shooed Horace out of the room and Alice turned to her mother with a sigh of relief.

'Would you believe that, Mama? He seems to think a lot of himself.'

'I suspected that Jane had an ulterior motive in having him here tonight and treating us all to such a meal.'

'I can't think what that would be.'

'Nor I, but I've heard your papa speak about

Horace's father and it's true that he went through a fortune by playing the stock market. They lost everything and George Hubble blew his brains out, leaving Horace with virtually nothing. It seems that both our families have been unlucky.'

'Horace's misfortune has nothing to do with us, Mama.' Alice stared at her mother, eyebrows raised. 'Apart from losing Papa and Uncle Robert, what else is there?'

Twin spots of colour stained Beth's cheeks. 'All families have something they want to hide or are ashamed of, darling. Forget I said anything.'

'No, Mama. You can't leave it like that.' Her curiosity aroused Alice, moved to sit beside her mother.

'I don't suppose you remember your Aunt Viola, do you?'

Alice frowned. 'Papa's sister? I have a vague memory of her. She was young and pretty and she laughed a lot.'

'Viola was headstrong and spoiled. She was your father's half-sister, the child of your grandfather's second marriage. You were only seven or eight when she eloped with a man who was totally unsuitable. It was a terrible scandal.

'What happened to her, Mama? Where is she now?'

'I was told that she died of consumption.'

'Poor thing, how sad.'

'The family hushed up the details. It was very tragic.'

'What happened to her husband?'

'They weren't married. I don't know what happened to him, and it was all a long time ago.'

'How was Aunt Jane unlucky? What skeleton has she got hidden in her cupboard?'

'It's not a laughing matter, Alice.'

'I'm sorry, but I don't understand why Aunt Jane went to such a lot of expense entertaining her cousin.'

'Perhaps she has a generous side to her nature. From the little I know about Horace I believe he works in a counting office somewhere in the City and lives in rented rooms in a poor area. You might say he's come down in the world.'

'But why did Aunt Jane want us to meet him?'

'She once told me that she could not bear to think that the Hubble name would die out. Horace is the last in the line and hasn't shown any inclination towards marriage.'

'I doubt if there are many young women who would want him, unless they were desperate,' Alice said, chuckling.

'You shouldn't judge a person by their looks, my love. Poor Horace wasn't blessed with a handsome countenance, but I'm sure that deep down he's a kind man and would make someone a good husband.'

'You don't think that Aunt Jane means me to be the sacrificial lamb, do you? That would be too ridiculous.'

'Jane is a wealthy woman and Horace has few

prospects. Without a son and heir the Hubble line will come to an abrupt end. Jane doesn't want that to happen and I think she's desperate to find a bride for her cousin.'

'I pity the woman who is chosen, that's all I can say.'

'I was watching him closely and from the way he was acting and the attention he paid you, I think he sees a way out of his predicament.'

'No!' Alice stared at her mother in horror. 'I wouldn't marry Horace Hubble if he was the last man on earth.' She spun round at the sound of the door opening and saw her aunt standing on the threshold. Judging by the sour expression on her face she had heard everything. 'I – I mean it, Aunt Jane,' Alice said hastily. 'If you're thinking of encouraging me to marry your cousin, it won't work.'

Jane folded her arms across her chest. 'While you live under my roof you will do as I say. Horace might not be a young girl's dream of romance, but he is a respectable man of good family, and his wife will be assured of living in modest comfort for the rest of her life. I will see to that.'

'I'd sooner die than agree to such a marriage,' Alice cried passionately.

'People are expiring on the streets at this moment, and you have your mother to consider, Alice. How do you think she would survive in the workhouse? I advise you to think about it very carefully.'

'I'm sorry, Aunt Jane, but nothing you could do

or say would make any difference. I don't know Mr Hubble. He's a stranger to me, as I am to him. Surely he wouldn't consider marrying someone he didn't know?'

'My cousin will do as I think best. He knows that his future depends upon satisfying me that the Hubble name will live on. Our ancestors were here before the time of William the Conqueror and we once owned half of Kent. Marry Horace, give him a son, and then we will all be happy.'

'You might be,' Alice said indignantly, 'but I wouldn't.'

'It is asking a lot of her,' Beth said softly. 'Surely it would be better to allow them to get to know each other before making such demands, Jane?'

Jane turned on her in a fury. 'What do you know about anything? You had neither brains nor breeding and you didn't bring a dowry to the marriage. Clement could have done so much better.'

'We were happy.' Beth's voice broke on a sob. 'We loved each other. Doesn't that count for anything?'

Alice moved swiftly to her mother's side, placing her arm around Beth's trembling shoulders. 'Leave Mama out of this, Aunt Jane.'

Jane tossed her head. 'I have only this to say to you, Alice Radcliffe. Agree to marry my cousin or leave this house and make your own way in the world. It's your choice.'

# Chapter Four

Reluctantly, and only because of her mother's weakened state of health, Alice agreed to consider Horace's proposal should he pluck up the courage to make her an offer of marriage. She had no intention of accepting him, but until she could earn enough to support her mother and herself they would have to rely on Aunt Jane's charity. The future looked bleak, but Alice Radcliffe was not one to give in without a fight. She went to bed in the cold, cheerless room with the precious Christmas card tucked beneath her pillow. To anyone else it might be just a piece of paper, but to her it was a symbol of family, love and security. No one could take away what was in her heart, not even Aunt Jane.

The child who greeted Alice next morning was totally different from the angry little girl of yesterday. Flora was up and dressed and had even made an effort to drag a comb through her tousled mop of hair.

She gave Alice a wide smile. 'I was afraid you wouldn't come.'

'Why would you think that? I made a promise and I always keep my promises.'

'Most grown-up people don't,' Flora said darkly. 'They'll say anything to keep me quiet, and then they go away and forget about me.'

Alice took the comb from her hand and began teasing out the tangles. 'Well, I'm not like that, Flora.'

'And will we still go outside and play snowballs?'

'Yes, of course.'

'And decorate the tree?'

'Yes, if your mama permits.'

'She will or I'll have a tantrum and scream until I make myself ill, or else I'll hold my breath until I go blue in the face. That usually works.'

Alice shook her head. 'I think we might be able to persuade her without you endangering your own life. We'll try, shall we?'

'Oh, all right,' Flora said reluctantly. 'Do we have to wait until after breakfast? I'm not really hungry.'

'We don't want to upset Cook, especially as she'll be very busy with preparations for tomorrow. Can you imagine what it must be like to work in a hot kitchen?'

Flora put her head on one side, frowning. 'No. I'm not allowed below stairs.'

'Then perhaps we ought to visit the kitchens, and you can see how the servants have to live and work.'

'Mama wouldn't like it, but I would.' Flora snatched the comb from Alice's hand. 'Shall we go now?'

'Maybe later, but I think I hear Nettie coming with our breakfast. Don't forget to thank her.'

'Thank her? She's a servant. We don't thank them.'

'Well, we do now,' Alice said firmly. 'I'm a servant in this house and you thank me.'

'You're different. I like you.'

'And I like you too.' Alice heard the rattling of china as Nettie struggled outside the door and she moved quickly to open it for her. 'Good morning, Nettie,' she said cheerfully.

'Good morning, miss.' Nettie shuffled over to the table and put the tray down with a clatter, spilling some of the milk from the blue-and-white china jug.

'Thank you, Nettie,' Alice said, nodding to Flora.

'Thank you,' Flora echoed, although she did not sound very convincing.

Nettie shot her a sideways glance. 'I'm sorry I spilled the milk, but me chilblains are playing up this morning. You won't tell on me, will you, miss?'

Flora shrugged. 'I'll throw the jug across the room, if you like. They expect me to do things like that.'

Nettie's horrified expression made it hard for Alice to keep a straight face. She patted her on the shoulder. 'Miss Flora is teasing you.'

'Yes, miss.' Nettie backed towards the door, opened it and fled.

'Well done, Flora,' Alice said, smiling. 'You see, you can be nice when you put your mind to it. When Nettie gets over her shock she'll be really grateful.'

Later, after what to Alice was now a magnificent breakfast of porridge, toast and strawberry jam, they put on their outdoor clothes and were making their way downstairs when Mrs Upton waylaid them outside the drawing room.

'Where do you think you're going, Miss Radcliffe?'

Flora's small fingers tightened around Alice's hand. 'She's taking me to play snowballs in the square gardens.'

'Indeed she is not.' Mrs Upton stood arms akimbo, glaring at Alice. 'Miss Flora is not allowed outside unless accompanied by a responsible person.'

Alice drew herself up to her full height. 'Flora is in my charge and I'll see that she comes to no harm.'

'That isn't good enough. Miss Flora can be very persuasive when she wants to be and we've had incidences.' Mrs Upton seized Flora by the shoulders and propelled her towards the staircase. 'It's back to the nursery for you, miss. Your mama will send word when she wishes to see you.'

'But this is so unfair,' Alice protested angrily. 'I promised her that we could go out into the gardens and play snowballs. She's just a child, Mrs Upton. I'll keep an eye on her.'

Flora stamped her foot. 'It's always the same. They all hate me and want me to be miserable.' She threw herself down on the floor, drumming her feet and screaming.

'Now see what you've done.' Mrs Upton spoke through clenched teeth. 'She'll make herself ill and we'll have to send for the doctor.'

'Why?' Alice demanded, raising her voice to make herself heard above Flora's screeching. 'Why do you want to keep the child prisoner in her own home? Surely a breath of fresh air and some healthy exercise would do her more good than being shut up in the nursery?'

Mrs Upton drew her aside. 'She has tried to run away several times. Keeping her under strict supervision is the only way to protect her from herself.'

Ignoring her, Alice went down on her knees beside Flora. 'Stop this at once. This sort of conduct won't get you anywhere.'

Flora quietened for a moment, eyeing her warily. 'You're supposed to be my friend.'

'I am your friend, but if you continue like this you'll only make things worse for yourself.' Alice rose to her feet, holding her hand out to Flora. 'Get up.'

'Do as Miss Radcliffe says, Miss Flora.' Mrs Upton's voice shook with barely controlled anger. 'Your mama will hear about this.'

Flora's answer was to go into a fresh tantrum, sobbing and beating her fists on the floorboards.

'What is going on?' Lydia Dearborn leaned over the banister. Tendrils of fair hair escaped from beneath the goffered frill of her linen nightcap and she clutched her wrap around her. 'Why is Flora dressed for outdoors? I gave explicit instructions that she was not to be allowed out of the house, Mrs Upton.'

'It's not my fault, ma'am,' Mrs Upton said hastily. 'It was I who prevented them leaving.'

'Miss Radcliffe, I will have words with you later, but please stop the child making that dreadful noise.' Lydia retreated to her room, slamming the door.

Flora stopped howling, but her whole body shook with suppressed sobs. 'I – I hate you, Upton.'

'That's no way to speak to Mrs Upton,' Alice said severely. She pulled Flora to her feet. 'Say you're sorry.'

'But I'm not sorry. It's the truth. I hate you all.' Flora stamped her foot and genuine tears spurted from her eyes.

'The child is a she-devil.' Mrs Upton shook her head. 'She's past redemption. That's what you get when you take a brat from the slums into a decent home.'

Alice placed her arm around Flora's shoulders, holding her close. 'It's no wonder she misbehaves if that's what you think of her.'

'Mrs Dearborn will hear more of this and you will be replaced, Miss Radcliffe.' Mrs Upton turned on her heel and marched off with the keys on her chatelaine jingling, but it was not the happy sound of Christmas bells.

'Never mind, Flora,' Alice said, taking her by the hand. 'We'll go back to the nursery and I'll explain everything to your mama when she sends for me. I'm sure if she understands why we were going into the gardens then she'll change her mind.'

Flora wiped her eyes on her sleeve. 'Do you think so?'

'I do indeed. After all, it is almost Christmas, the season of peace on earth and goodwill to all men.' She chuckled. 'And women, including Mrs Upton.'

The summons to the morning room came two hours later. Mrs Dearborn was seated by the fire, hands folded in her lap with a judgemental look on her face that did not bode well.

'What did you think you were doing, Radcliffe? You know that Flora is easily upset and yet you decided to go against my wishes and take her out.'

'I only intended to take her into the gardens, Mrs Dearborn. I thought that she would enjoy playing snowballs and running around like any ordinary child.'

'I don't pay you to think, Radcliffe. You will know by now that a previous employee filled the child's head with nonsense about her natural mother. Flora is obsessed by the idea that she wants to find the woman.'

'Then it is true, ma'am?'

'Flora was adopted by my husband and me. She would never have known had it not been for the nursemaid who turned out to be a drunken slattern. Flora is unstable and given to bouts of temper tantrums that can only be controlled by large doses of laudanum. You were supposed to take care of her and prevent such outbursts.'

'No one told me what to expect, Mrs Dearborn. But I don't think that Flora is unstable, as you put it, and I decry the use of laudanum on such a young child.'

'You dare to tell me what to do?' Lydia stared at her, delicate eyebrows raised until they disappeared into her hairline. 'What gives you the right to question my authority?'

Angry and undaunted by her employer's indignation, Alice faced her squarely. 'I don't question your authority, ma'am. But from what I've seen of Flora she is a little girl who needs love and affection.'

'Flora has the best of everything. My husband spoils her and she wants for nothing.'

Alice could see that this was going nowhere. Lydia Dearborn did not seem to have any maternal feelings towards her adopted daughter, but arguing was not going to help. 'I can see that she is a lucky little girl to have come into such a comfortable home, but I was an only child and it's a lonely path to tread. Might I suggest that she be allowed a little more freedom? She is intelligent and talented, and if she were allowed out under my supervision I think I could help her.'

'I haven't decided yet whether or not to sack you, Radcliffe. If you are a bad influence on Flora then you must leave.'

Alice said nothing. She clasped her hands behind her back, feeling like a naughty schoolgirl standing in front of an irate headmistress, but there was little she could do other than wait for Mrs Dearborn to decide her fate. She could imagine Aunt Jane's smug expression if she were dismissed. It would give her added encouragement to see marriage as the only solution, but the thought of marrying Horace made Alice feel physically sick.

Lydia relaxed her hands with a sigh. 'I suppose I will have to allow you stay on for the time being, Radcliffe. Apart from upsetting Flora even further, it would be difficult to find a replacement at such short notice, and at this time of year.'

'I'll do my best to look after her, Mrs Dearborn.'

'You will indeed. There will be no more trips out unless you have my permission.'

'I understand.'

'You may go, but I expect you to work tomorrow, even though it's Christmas Day. I have guests coming and I don't want Flora to ruin my party.'

Alice nodded, biting back the sharp words that rose to her lips. This woman, she decided, was selfish to the core and she disliked her intensely.

'You may go.' Lydia dismissed her with a wave of her hand. 'Wait. On second thoughts you can make yourself useful. The wretched tree needs decorating and the servants are all fully occupied with preparations for tomorrow. I'm going out to luncheon and will be gone all afternoon, so you and my daughter may hang the baubles and tinsel. It will keep Flora occupied.'

Flora knew exactly where the decorations were stored. She led Alice to an attic room at the far end of the corridor where the servants slept. Cabin trunks and other items of luggage were piled from floor to sloping ceiling. Oddments of furniture, oil lamps and a couple of crinoline cages were littered about the room, together with tea chests spilling over with unwanted items.

With a cry of delight Flora pounced on a wooden box. 'There it is. I knew it was here.' She lifted the lid and pulled out a strand of tinsel, holding it so that the silver threads danced in rays of sunlight that filtered through the grime on the small window-panes. 'Isn't it beautiful?'

'Yes, it's lovely.' Alice glanced anxiously at the cobwebs that festooned the rafters, but to her relief there was no evidence of the creatures that had made them. She knew that for a grown woman to be afraid of spiders was irrational, but like Flora she had been at the mercy of a nanny who was addicted to drink and laudanum. The gruesome tales of giant arachnids that came in the night to punish naughty children had been told to subdue and scare her. The nightmares had ceased, but the fear remained. She closed the lid. 'Let's take them downstairs to the drawing room, Flora.'

'And I want to put the star on top of the tree.'

'I want doesn't get,' Alice said automatically, and for a moment she thought she was about to witness another tantrum, but Flora's angry look melted into a smile.

'May I put the star on top of the tree, please, Alice?'

'Of course you may.' Alice picked up the box. 'You see how easy it is to get along with people when you speak to them nicely?'

'I think I'm beginning to.' Flora held out her hand. 'Let me help you.'

Together they transported the heavy box to the drawing room and set about decorating the tree, stopping briefly at midday when Nettie summoned them to the morning room where, as a special treat, luncheon had been laid on a table in the window.

'I feel like a grown-up,' Flora said happily. 'I'm not usually allowed to have my meals anywhere but in the nursery.'

'We're very busy below stairs, Miss Flora.' Nettie placed a jug of gravy on the table next to the mutton pie with a glistening golden crust and a tempting aroma. 'Mrs Upton said it would be easier if you and Miss Radcliffe ate here.'

Alice took her seat at table opposite Flora. 'It looks and smells delicious, Nettie. Thank you.'

'There's boiled cabbage to come, miss. I'll fetch it now.'

'Ugh,' Flora said, pulling a face. 'I hate cabbage.'

'It's good for you.' Alice cut into the pie. 'But perhaps

on this occasion we'll just have the pie, Nettie. Miss Flora will forgo dessert and have an apple instead.'

Flora's eyes opened wide and her bottom lip trembled. 'No, it's all right. I'll eat my cabbage, but only if I can have pudding. What is it, Nettie?'

'Jam roly-poly, miss.'

'And custard?'

'Of course, miss. Cook wouldn't serve pudding without custard.' Nettie bobbed a curtsey and left the room, returning minutes later with a dish of boiled cabbage. Flora wrinkled her nose, but ate hers without further complaint. Alice smiled to herself and said nothing.

The pudding, as usual, was delicious and very filling. Flora ate all hers, scraping the dish with her spoon to get the last drop of custard, which made Alice laugh. 'I'm sure there's plenty more in the kitchen, if you're still hungry.'

Flora licked her lips. 'No, that would be greedy, and I'm full.' She sighed. 'But I would like to go outside and play snowballs. The sun's shining on the snow and it looks so pretty.'

Alice had also eaten her fill, mindful of the austerity she would face that evening, and she sympathised with Flora, but she did not dare go against Mrs Dearborn's wishes. She rose from the table. 'I think we'd better finish the tree, don't you? I'm sure it will please your mama to see it looking so lovely.'

*

Alice had to lift Flora up in an attempt to place the star on the topmost branch of the tree, but it was still out of reach and Flora was heavier than she looked. They tried again and toppled over, ending up in a giggling heap on the floor with a tangle of booted feet and frilled petticoats. Alice was struggling to rise when the door opened and Rory Dearborn strolled into the room. He came to a halt, staring at them in surprise, and a slow smile curved his lips.

'Well now, what happened? Has there been an earthquake?'

Flora leaped up and ran to give him a hug. 'You've come just in time, Uncle Rory. Alice was trying to lift me high enough to put the star on the tree.' She held it up for his inspection.

Alice rose to her feet with as much dignity as she could muster, and as she shook out her crumpled skirts she found herself wishing that she had something prettier to wear than the severe black cotton uniform provided by Mrs Upton. She adjusted her white cap, which had slipped over one eye in the fall. 'Good afternoon, sir.' She turned away, avoiding his amused gaze as she felt her cheeks redden with embarrassment.

'Let me help.' He lifted Flora as easily as if she were a toddler, and held her until she had fastened the slightly bent and battered star in place. 'That looks splendid, Flora. You and Miss Radcliffe have done an excellent job.'

Alice murmured an acknowledgement, but was still unable to look him in the face. For a gentleman to see a lady's unmentionables was shocking even to someone who considered herself to be a modern young woman. Flora, however, did not seem to be worry about such niceties and she clung to her uncle's hand.

'Have you brought me a present?'

'Need you ask?'

'What is it? May I see it now?'

He shook his head. 'You will have to wait until tomorrow, so there's no need for you to put on that sulky face, Flora.'

'But I want—' Flora broke off, shooting a sideways glance at Alice. 'I mean, I would like just to see it and feel it so that I can imagine what it might be. Please, Uncle Rory.'

He stood back, holding his hand to his heart with an exaggerated look of astonishment. 'Who is this polite child? What have you done with Flora, Miss Radcliffe? Where is my niece?'

His laugh was infectious and Alice forgot her moment of chagrin. 'Flora is standing beside you, sir. She is a reformed character.'

He bent down to ruffle Flora's curls. 'In that case I think I might allow her to fetch the present and put it under the tree.'

'Yes, please.' Flora tugged at his hand. 'Where is it?'

'I left it outside the door. Hoskins told me you were in here.' He watched her with a smile on his lips as she raced from the room. 'Such excitement,' he said, turning to Alice. 'I almost wish I were a child again at this time of the year.'

'You've made her very happy.' Alice folded her hands in front of her, not knowing quite how to behave in the presence of her employer's brother. It was hard to remember that she was a servant. Her father had always treated her as an equal, as had his intellectual friends and acquaintances, but her lowly situation put her at a distinct disadvantage.

'And you've wrought an astonishing change in her,' he said in an undertone as Flora returned, carrying a large package tied with red ribbon.

'It's quite heavy,' Flora said thoughtfully. 'Is it a book?'

He shook his head. 'I'm not giving you any clues. You'll have to be like everyone else and wait until the morning. I suggest you place it beneath the tree.'

Flora shook the package, holding it close to her ear. 'It rattles. Is it a box of coloured beads? You know I love necklaces.'

'Put it under the tree.' Rory turned to Alice with a wry smile. 'Perhaps the old Flora is still here, after all.'

'Flora,' Alice said sternly.

'Oh, all right.' Flora walked slowly towards the tree and went down on her knees to place her present under its spiky branches. She jumped up again, spinning round to face her uncle. 'Have you got a present for Alice, too?'

'No, of course not, Flora,' Alice said quickly. 'Servants don't get presents from their employers.'

'Perhaps they should.' Rory reached out to take Flora by the hand. 'I've just had a splendid idea; something that will take your mind off presents.'

'What is it? Tell me, please.'

'The sun is still shining and the snow is crisp and clean in the gardens. Would you like to go for a walk?'

'Yes, please. And we could make a snowman and snowballs.'

'Remember what your mama said, Flora.' Alice shook her head. 'I'm sorry, Mr Dearborn, but your sister-in-law specifically forbade us to go out and play in the snow.'

Rory angled his head, a mischievous smile curving his generous lips. 'Lydia is out and I'm reliably informed by Hoskins that she is not expected to return until four o'clock or even later.'

'Please, Alice,' Flora entreated. 'Just this once. It might never snow again and I'll die without having made a snowball.'

Alice looked from one eager face to the other and knew she was beaten. 'That would be a tragedy indeed,' she said softly.

Flora released her uncle's hand to throw her arms around Alice. 'I love you, Miss Radcliffe. May I call you Alice in front of Uncle Rory? He won't mind. He's a good sport. I heard my pa say so.'

'Come along, Flora.' Rory moved towards the

door. 'And you too, Alice. If Flora can call you that in private I claim that privilege too, and you must call me Rory.'

Alice hesitated. 'I don't think I ought to, sir.'

'What did I just say?' He paused in the doorway. 'If I'm allowed to use your Christian name then you must return the compliment, and I insist that you accompany us. If I'm to be bombarded with lumps of ice I refuse to undergo the humiliation alone.'

It was an invitation she knew she should forgo, but it was her duty to look after Flora, or so she told herself as she hurried upstairs to fetch their outdoor garments.

The paths were well-trodden by nannies pushing babies in their perambulators, and their older charges had shuffled through the icy carpet, churning it up so that it turned to slush, but the pristine whiteness of the snow-covered grass was smooth as icing on a cake. Flora uttered a cry of delight, running round in circles and leaving a trail of footprints. Alice hesitated, glancing over her shoulder to see if anyone was watching from the house, but common sense told her that the servants were far too busy to worry about the troublesome child who occupied the nursery. It seemed that Rory Dearborn was alone in regarding Flora as a person in her own right. He was watching her with an indulgent smile, which broadened as he turned to Alice.

'You've worked wonders. Flora is a different child.'

Alice shook her head. 'She's always been like this but she wasn't allowed to express herself. That's why she was so badly behaved.'

'Well, you've certainly brought out the best in her—' he broke off as a snowball hit him in the chest. 'Why, you little devil.' Laughing he bent down and made another, lobbing it at Flora, who dodged and counterattacked with yet another good shot.

Alice stood back, smiling at their antics until a snowball caught her a glancing blow on the cheek. Forgetting that she was supposed to be above such things, she joined in until they were all breathless with laughter. Flora's cheeks were flushed and her eyes sparkling as she danced over to Alice. 'Let's make a snowman.'

Rory brushed flakes of ice off his overcoat. 'You won that contest, I think, Flora.'

She grinned. 'Yes, I did. I won, Alice.'

Alice was about to congratulate her when she heard the rumble of carriage wheels and she looked round. 'Oh, my goodness,' she said, pointing at the vehicle. 'That looks like Mrs Dearborn. Your mama had returned, Flora.'

'What will we do, Uncle Rory?' Flora clutched his hand. 'Mama will send Alice away. Please do something.'

# Chapter Five

'Wait here,' Rory said firmly. 'I'll keep Lydia talking. Take Flora in by the servants' entrance, Alice, and go up the back stairs to the nursery.' He brushed Flora's cheek with the tip of his fingers. 'Don't look so scared, poppet. I'll take care of everything.' He nodded to Alice and set off, strolling out of the gardens and across the road to arrive just as Lydia stepped out of the carriage.

Under cover of the tall plane trees, Alice waited until they entered the house and as soon as the front door closed she took Flora by the hand and hurried her across the street. The wrought-iron gate opened noiselessly and they descended the steps to the basement area. Alice tapped on the door and after a minute or two it was opened by Nettie. She gaped at them open-mouthed.

'Lawks! What's going on, miss?'

'It's nothing to worry about,' Alice said, propelling Flora into the narrow passageway. 'We thought we'd come in this way so that Miss Flora could thank Cook and the kitchen maids for all their trouble.'

'Well, I never did. I never heard of such a thing.' Nettie backed away, turned and ran into the kitchen.

Flora glanced up at Alice, a frown creasing her brow, but Alice placed her finger to her lips. 'Just follow my lead.'

The kitchen was hot and steamy, filled with the savoury aroma of fried onions, herbs and roasting meat. Every surface was covered with baskets of fruit and vegetables and the ingredients for the festive meal. One of the daily cleaning women was at the sink in the scullery, plucking a large goose, and feathers floated to the ground like snowflakes. Cook was at the table whisking something light and frothy, while a small girl, even younger than Nettie, was attempting to peel the skin off blanched almonds.

Alice led her young charge across the slippery flagstones to the table. 'Miss Flora has something she would like to say to you and the kitchen staff, Cook.' She nudged Flora, who had been staring at the preparations, wide-eyed.

'Thank you for making such nice meals,' she said in a small voice.

Cook stared at her, gulped and swallowed. 'There's no need for thanks, Miss Flora. We're just doing what's expected of us.'

'Nevertheless, Miss Flora wanted you all to know

that she appreciates what you do. Merry Christmas to you all.'

'Yes,' Flora said, nodding. 'Merry Christmas.' She was about to take a mince pie from the table, but Alice hurried her towards the back stairs.

When they reached the nursery she saw to Flora first and then took off her sodden boots and hung her stockings from the mantelshelf to dry.

'Well, that was a near thing,' she said, pulling up a chair and resting her bare feet on the fender.

Flora sat on the floor, warming her hands in front of the fire. 'I don't care if I get into trouble, but I don't want Mama to send you away, Alice.'

'That won't happen, I promise you.' Rory's voice from the doorway made them both turn with a start.

Alice hastily covered her bare limbs with her damp skirts and rose to her feet. 'We were just getting warm.' She knew she was blushing and she was embarrassed to be caught barefoot and barelegged, but if Rory had noticed he gave no sign of it.

'That's very sensible of you. I came to reassure you that my sister-in-law suspects nothing.'

Flora gazed up at him. 'So Alice won't be sent away?'

'I think it's safe to say that Miss Radcliffe will stay for as long as she wants.'

'If Alice leaves then I'll go with her.' Flora jumped to her feet. 'Will I see you tomorrow, Uncle Rory? Are you coming to dinner?'

He nodded, smiling. 'I am indeed. My landlady is

the worst cook in London, and probably the worst cook in England, so I have to come here if I want a good meal.'

'I'm glad,' Flora said earnestly. 'I mean, I'm not glad that she's a bad cook, I'm just happy that you'll be here on Christmas Day. I only wish that I could see my real mother and give her a present.'

Forgetting everything other than the child's needs, Alice slipped her arm around Flora's shoulders. She met Rory's concerned look with a question in her eyes that she could not voice in Flora's presence.

He nodded, seeming to understand. 'I'm sure she was well compensated and now lives in a degree of comfort. She wanted the best for you, Flora.'

'Will you take me to see her, please?'

'Much as I'd love to make you happy, I'm not sure that would be the right thing to do. I can't go against your father's wishes.'

Flora stamped her foot. 'He's not my father. I want to know who my real father is, and I want to go and see my mother. If you don't take me I'll run away and I'll find Blossom Street. That's where she lives; Smithson said so.'

Alice laid her hand on Flora's shoulder. 'You can't do that, my dear. She might not be there now and you would be all alone in a part of London you know nothing about.' She turned to Rory. 'You shouldn't encourage her, sir.'

He nodded, frowning. 'Yes, you're right. What Miss Radcliffe says is true, Flora. But I'll see if I can find out exactly where she is living. I can't promise anything, but I might be able to arrange for us to visit her, if that would set your mind at rest.'

Flora's eyes shone with excitement and she jumped up and down. 'Yes, I want to see her more than anything in the world. I think it must be a lovely place where she lives with trees covered in pink blossom and the sun is always shining. Sometimes I see her in my dreams. She's beautiful, like a golden angel.'

'I think you're old enough to learn the truth about your family,' Rory said, frowning. 'I'll see what I can do, Floss, but I have to go now as I have an important business appointment. I'll see you tomorrow.'

Alice followed him to the door. 'You shouldn't tell her things just to make her happy. This could end badly.'

He met her searching gaze with a hint of a smile. 'I promise to do my best for everyone concerned. I wouldn't hurt Flora for the world.'

Flora was tired after playing in the snow and needed little persuasion to go to bed that evening after supper. Alice helped her to wash and put on her flannel nightgown, and when Flora was comfortably settled she read her a story, but Flora was asleep before the tale ended. Alice put the guard around the fire and blew out the candles before leaving the room, and as she made her way down-stairs she racked her brains in an attempt to think of a suitable present for Flora. She was still deep in thought when she reached the entrance hall where she met Rory, who was also about to leave the house.

'I wasn't expecting to see you, Mr Dearborn.'

'My meeting finished early and I had to come this way to give my brother some papers. Is Flora behaving herself?'

Alice suppressed a gurgle of laughter. 'She's being an angel.'

Hoskins opened the front door, staring at a point somewhere above their heads with an impassive expression.

'Good night, Hoskins,' Rory said easily. He prof-fered his arm to Alice. 'It's starting to snow again. We could share a cab.'

The steps were coated in ice and Alice accepted his help. 'Thank you, but I haven't far to go.'

'I believe you're residing in Queen Square. It's quite a long walk on a cold and wintry night.'

'Alice. There you are. I've been waiting for a good half-hour.'

To Alice's dismay Horace appeared as if from nowhere. Snowflakes sparkled on his top hat and the shoulders of his caped greatcoat.

'I didn't ask you to meet me,' she said angrily. 'I'm perfectly capable of finding my own way home.'

Horace uttered a whinnying snort. 'Now, now, my

dear, we're about to become engaged, so I am in some way responsible for your safety.'

Rory's expression gave nothing away as he released Alice's hand. 'May I be the first to congratulate you, sir?'

'And who may you be?' Horace demanded.

'This is ridiculous.' Alice looked from one to the other, shaking her head. 'We do not have an understanding, Horace. That was my aunt's idea and had nothing to do with me.' She could feel the cold seeping through the worn soles of her boots and she shivered. 'I thank both of you gentlemen, but I wish to be alone.' She marched off, leaving them standing on the pavement.

'Where is Horace?' Jane stood in the dining-room doorway, hands clasped together as if in prayer. 'He was told to meet you and bring you home.'

Angry words rose to her lips but Alice could see her mother standing behind Jane with an anxious look on her pale face. 'I don't need my hand held by him or anyone, and he seems to think that I've agreed to our engagement.'

'You have no choice,' Jane said coldly. 'You obey me in this or I wash my hands of the pair of you. Horace needs a wife and you and your mother need a home.'

'Have you no pity, Jane?' Beth's voice broke on a sob. 'How can you be so hard-hearted?'

Jane turned on her in a swirl of black silk. 'My

heart was broken when my dear Robert departed this world. How dare you question my judgement? You ruined my brother with your spendthrift ways, and your daughter seems to take after you. She would be a fool to turn down an offer from a man like Horace.' She pointed a shaking finger at Clara, who was standing by the open front door. 'Close the door, Snippet, you foolish child.'

'Yes, ma'am, but I think I see Mr Hubble walking through the snow.' Clara clapped her hand to her mouth to stifle a giggle. 'Oops. He's come a purler.'

Jane strode across the floor to push Clara out of the way. 'Horace Hubble, get up this instant and stop acting the fool.' She waited until he had limped into the hall before slamming the door. 'Just look at you, Horace. You're plastered in snow.'

Alice covered her mouth with her hand, trying hard not to laugh.

Horace shot her a baleful look. 'I suppose you think it's funny, but I could have broken a limb.'

'Well, you obviously didn't,' Jane said impatiently. 'I gave you explicit instructions to wait for Alice and see her safely home, instead of which you act the fool, sliding around in the snow like a five-year-old. I despair of you sometimes, Horace.' She turned on her heel and marched into the dining room. 'And don't think you can stay for dinner because you are not invited. Having two extra mouths to feed is an expense I could well do without, and you have an appetite like a horse.'

Alice felt almost sorry for Horace, who hung his head, looking sheepish. The tip of his nose had turned from red to blue and he was shivering convulsively. He clutched his top hat to his chest. 'That's rather harsh, Cousin. A drop of hot toddy would save me from catching a chill and it's a long walk to West Smithfield.'

'I do not hold with strong spirits, as you well know. A glass of sherry wine on special occasions is acceptable, as is communion wine, but strong drink is the work of the devil. Now go home and leave us to have our meal in peace.'

Horace made a move towards the door, ramming his slightly battered hat on his head. 'I suppose you'll pray for me when I'm dying of lung fever,' he grumbled.

Clara opened the door for him and he left the house still muttering.

'Bring the soup, Snippet,' Jane called from the dining room. 'We'll dine now.'

Alice nodded to Clara. 'I'll hang my things up. Better do as my aunt says.'

Clara skipped off, no doubt to relate the goings-on above stairs to an interested Mrs Jugg.

Having divested herself of her outdoor garments, Alice entered the dining room to find her mother already seated at table.

Beth looked up and smiled. 'How was it today, dear? Was the child better behaved?'

'Never mind that now.' Jane glared at Alice from

her place at the head of the table. 'I think you owe me an explanation as to your behaviour, young lady. Why did you refuse Horace's offer to walk you home? Are you going out of your way to be difficult?'

Alice took her seat at table. 'No, Aunt, but I've considered the matter carefully and I want nothing to do with Horace. I cannot stand the man and I'd rather live under a railway arch than tie myself to a creature like him.'

Beth gasped, staring at her sister-in-law wide-eyed. 'She doesn't mean it, Jane. Alice must be tired after a long day at the Dearborns' establishment.'

'That is no excuse for out-and-out rudeness. You will apologise, Alice.'

Alice could see that her outburst had upset her mother and she regretted her hasty words. 'I am sorry if I offended you, Aunt Jane. But I dislike Horace intensely and I cannot see myself married to him.'

'Whether you like or dislike your future husband is immaterial. You know my terms. You either accept them or you leave my house. Do you understand?'

After dinner, which as usual was badly cooked and meagre, Alice and her mother huddled by the fire in the dining room. Jane had gone to her room, warning them not to waste expensive candles by staying up late.

'I am sorry, Mama,' Alice said softly. 'I was angry but I shouldn't have spoken out against Horace like that.'

'He isn't the ideal husband,' Beth agreed, sighing. 'I'm sure he has many excellent qualities, but for a start he is much too old for you. I wouldn't want to see you married to someone like him, even if it meant that we were to live in luxury.'

'I can't do anything until after Christmas, but I'll start looking for a better-paid position so that we can find a room to rent, although I'll hate to leave Flora. She's a lonely little girl who pines for the mother she's never known.'

'That is sad, but if her mother gave her up willingly perhaps she is better off where she is.'

'It's hard being a servant, Mama. I keep forgetting that I'm supposed to be invisible and keep silent, especially when I see things going horribly wrong.'

'I'd like to meet Flora, and I'd like to give Mrs Dearborn a piece of my mind.'

Alice chuckled at the thought of her meek and mild mother taking on a termagant like Lydia Dearborn. 'I don't know about that, Mama, but you'll see Flora tomorrow. We'll spend Christmas Day trying to make her happy, but I wish I had a present to give her.'

Beth frowned thoughtfully. 'What would she like the most?'

'That's easy. She'd like to find her real mother.'

Next morning when Alice went to wake her mother she was alarmed to find her unwell and feverish.

'I must have caught a chill,' Beth said faintly. 'It's

so cold in this house, and Jane insisted that I polish the brass door knocker yesterday, even though it was snowing.'

Alice laid her hand on her mother's forehead. 'You are rather hot. You ought to stay in bed, but I don't want to leave you on your own.'

'I'll sleep most of the day, my darling. I would have loved to meet young Flora and see inside the Dearborns' mansion, but I'm better off where I am.'

'But it's Christmas Day and I have nothing to give you, Mama. I am so sorry it's come to this.'

Beth lifted a thin hand to touch her daughter's cheek. 'You are the greatest gift of all. What more could a mother want than a daughter who is kind as well as beautiful, and very talented?'

'Mama, you'll have me blushing if you say things like that.' Alice leaned over to drop a kiss on her mother's forehead. 'I'll ask Clara to keep an eye on you, and I'll come home as soon as I've finished work.' She was about to leave the room when her mother called her back.

'I want to give you something.' Beth's voice was hoarse and little more than a whisper. 'Look in my reticule. The only piece of jewellery that I have left is the silver butterfly brooch your father gave me when you were born. I want you to have it, my love.'

Alice hesitated; she knew how much her mother valued the delicate filigree brooch. 'Are you sure, Mama? You don't have to give me anything.'

'I'll have the pleasure of seeing you wear it, and

it's the only thing of value I managed to save from the bailiffs. Please take it, Alice.'

Not wanting to distress her mother, she reached for the reticule and took out the brooch, pinning it at the neck of her blouse. 'Thank you, Mama. I'll treasure it always.'

Beth's eyelids drooped. 'You mustn't be late or Mrs Dearborn might dismiss you, and I'm sleepy.'

Alice tucked her in and left the room quietly, closing the door behind her. Downstairs in the dining room she found a plate of cold porridge waiting for her but there was no sign of her aunt. Clara brought her a pot of tea, and as usual there was neither milk nor sugar to make it more palatable.

Alice stirred the thick glutinous oatmeal, wrinkling her nose. 'I can't eat this. Has my aunt left for church, Clara?'

'Yes, miss. She went out early and won't be back for hours. I'm sorry about the porridge, but she made me put it out even though you weren't here. She said something about being punctual for meals.' She eyed the plate, licking her lips. 'Mrs Jugg will tell her if you don't eat it, miss.'

'You can have it, Clara. If you don't mind eating a cold sticky mess—' She broke off as Clara seized the plate and proceeded to spoon the unappetising food into her mouth. 'Are you always this hungry?'

Clara swallowed a mouthful. 'I get my porridge watered down, miss. Cook says it goes further that way.'

'I suppose it does.' Alice finished her tea, ignoring the pangs of hunger that cramped her stomach. 'Will you look in on my mother later, Clara? She's unwell and I'd be grateful if you would take care of her for me. I'll get home as soon as I can.'

Clara gulped down the last morsel. 'I dare say there won't be much merriment below stairs today, miss. I don't think we'll be feasting on roast goose and plum pudding, but I'll keep an eye on the missis. She's been kind to me.'

'My mother is kind to everyone,' Alice said, smiling. 'I know I can rely on you, Clara. Merry Christmas, such as it is in this house.'

Alice arrived at the house in Russell Square to find the servants bustling about making ready for the guests to arrive. The kitchen was steamy and fragrant with delicious smells that made her mouth water when she collected Alice's breakfast tray. Nettie had been set to work churning ice cream for the elaborate bombe that Cook was endeavouring to recreate from one of Mrs Beeton's recipes. Mrs Upton was overseeing arrangements, marching around the kitchen like a sergeant major, and Hoskins had retired to his pantry to put the finishing touches to polishing the silver and the best crystal glasses. The Dearborns' Christmas feast was obviously going to be a very grand affair. Alice took the back stairs, carrying the heavy tray to the nursery with a growing feeling of admiration for Nettie, who in the normal course of things had to do this several times each day.

Flora was unexpectedly subdued and quiet. She picked at her breakfast, showing little enthusiasm for the food.

'What's the matter?' Alice asked anxiously. 'Are you unwell, Flora?'

'No. I'm quite well, thank you.'

'You've been so excited about Christmas, so what's wrong?'

'They don't want me here,' Flora said, her bottom lip trembling. 'And I want to be with my real mama.'

Alice moved swiftly to give her a comforting hug. 'I understand.'

'No,' Flora cried, burying her head in her hands. 'No one understands how I feel.'

Alice stroked her hair. 'Your uncle said he would try to help, and I think you should put your trust in him. I'm sure he'll do the right thing.' She turned with a start at the sound of someone outside the door, and was about to tell Nettie that Flora had not finished her breakfast when Rory entered the room.

'What's all this, Flora?' he said cheerfully. 'Why the long face? It's Christmas Day.'

She jumped to her feet and ran to him. 'Have you found out where my real mama lives? May we go and see her today?'

'I don't know about that, Flora. I'm in a difficult position.'

'But you promised, Uncle Rory. Alice told me you'd keep your word.'

He glanced at Alice, a wry smile curving his lips. 'Did she now?'

'Yes,' Alice said sharply. 'But it seems I was mistaken.'

'As it happens I've given it a lot of thought since yesterday, and I think Flora should be allowed to visit her mother. My brother and sister-in-law won't agree with me, but in this instance I'm prepared to risk their displeasure.'

Flora stared at him wide-eyed. 'You'll take me to see her?'

'I will, but only if Miss Radcliffe will accompany us.' He met Alice's startled gaze with a question in his eyes.

'Yes, of course I will. I think it's a splendid idea. Put your coat on, Flora, and your best bonnet.'

'You do realise that you could find yourself in serious trouble if we're found out.' Rory said in a low voice. 'I wouldn't ask it of you, but I think Flora will need you when she discovers that reality is sometimes hard to take.'

She nodded. 'Where are we going?'

'Blossom Street. It's in Spitalfields, off White Lion Street. I'm afraid it's not the most salubrious area in London.'

Rory had spoken the truth. Blossom Street sounded romantic and brought visions of trees in springtime decked with pink and white flowers, but nothing could be further from the truth. White Lion Street itself was lined on both sides with terraced Georgian townhouses, once owned by affluent silk weavers, but now fading into genteel poverty. Blossom Street was a mixture of warehouses, workshops and cheap lodging houses. The cabby had been reluctant to venture this far, but a large tip from Rory had persuaded him to wait for them on the corner.

The snow was knee-deep, giving Blossom Street a charm that it otherwise did not possess. Alice clutched Flora's hand as they made their way to the address where Rory hoped to find Molly Bishop, Flora's birth mother. He paused outside a red-brick house with green shutters that were hanging off their hinges, and a front door where the lower panels had either rotted or had been deliberately kicked in. Finding it unlocked, Rory opened it and stepped inside. Alice and Flora followed him, but the stench was suffocating and Alice covered her nose and mouth with her hand. Flora looked up at her, wrinkling her nose.

'That's disgusting,' she said loudly.

'Don't worry,' Rory said cheerfully. 'It's bound to get worse. If my information is correct Molly Bishop lives in the basement.' He opened a door beneath the staircase and they were engulfed in a waft of fetid air.

'Are you sure you want to do this?' Alice asked anxiously. 'We could leave now, Flora.'

'No,' Flora said in a small voice. 'I won't leave without seeing my mama.'

Rory patted her on the shoulder. 'All right, Floss, we've come this far.' He met Alice's gaze with a smile. 'I'll take her if you'd rather wait here.'

'No,' Alice said stoutly. 'We're in this together. Lead on.'

They descended into almost pitch-darkness where the evil-smelling air felt thick and cloying, like walking through a peasouper. The rancid odour of the tallow candle at the foot of the stairs added to the noxious vapours, and in its dim light there appeared to be just two rooms leading off a narrow hallway.

Rory motioned them to wait while he investigated the nearest, but he came out shaking his head. 'You don't want to go in there.' He disappeared into the room at the rear of the building and returned moments later. 'She's in there, but you can change your mind, Flora. You don't have to put yourself through this if it's too much for you.'

'Yes, Flora,' Alice said earnestly. 'We can leave some money for your mother and she'll understand. She made a huge sacrifice in giving you up.'

'I want to see her, and I want to ask her why she did it.'

Rory picked up the candle. 'I hope I've done the right thing by bringing you here.'

'It's a bit late to worry about that, isn't it?' Alice tightened her hold on Flora's small hand. 'I'm with you, dear.'

The appalling smell was made worse by the stench of unwashed bodies and human excrement. Even in the dim light of a single candle Alice could see fungus sprouting from the lichen-encrusted walls, and she was aware of hunched shapes, some lying on the floor as if dead to the world, while others propped themselves up against the bare brickwork. All of them were clad in filthy rags. The more fortunate adults wore boots, but the children appeared to be barefoot in the bone-chilling cold. A loud keening made Alice's blood curdle in her veins.

# Chapter Six

'What do you want, guv? If you're the landlord we ain't got no money for rent.' One of the shadowy shapes rose with difficulty, holding out stick-like arms. 'Have pity on a poor widow, sir.'

Rory took a step forward, keeping a wary eye on the other occupants of the cellar. 'Are you Molly Bishop?'

The woman shrank back into the darkness and another, bolder figure stepped forward. 'Who wants to know? If you're the law then I never done nothing wrong. It were Long Nell what bashed the cove over the head. I weren't even there at the time.'

'I'm not the law, madam,' Rory said hastily. 'If you are Molly Bishop speak up. There's someone who wants to meet you.' He held the candle closer to reveal a woman who, despite her dishevelled appearance, was better dressed and fractionally cleaner than the other occupants of the cellar.

'And if I am Molly Bishop, what would the likes of you want with me?'

'It was your child's Christmas wish to meet her mother.' Rory placed a protective hand on Flora's shoulder. 'This is your daughter, or so I've been led to believe.'

Molly clutched her bony hands to her breast. 'Is it really you, Fanny?'

'Flora,' Rory said sternly. 'Her name is Flora.'

'Of course it is. My mind wanders something terrible these days.'

'It's the laudanum, my duck.' The woman who had spoken first cackled with laughter. 'Got a penny piece so she can get some more, guv?'

'Shut up, you old troll.' Molly peered at Flora, twisting her lips into a parody of a smile. 'Come to your mama, darling.'

Flora's fingers curled around Alice's hand and she shook her head.

'You're frightening her, ma'am,' Alice said, drawing Flora closer.

'You are me long lost child.' Molly insisted. 'Me little daughter what was robbed from me by rich folk. I never wanted to give you up, me little angel.'

Rory stepped in between them. 'That's not quite true, is it, Molly?'

'As I said just now, I'm the child's mother.' She

inched towards Flora. 'I was tricked into giving you away, my baby girl.'

'As I heard it you were quite handsomely paid,' Rory said calmly. 'Where are your other children? You had seven of them, according to Smithson.' He held up his hand as Molly opened her mouth to protest. 'I know she's not the most reliable witness, but when I tracked her down yesterday she was reasonably sober and it was she who told me where to find you.'

'Well, I could lie to you, guv, but the sad truth is that they're all gone. The little 'uns is buried in paupers' graves and the older ones have run away, the ungrateful brats. They left their poor ma to survive on the streets. I ain't had a proper meal in days – weeks, even.'

'She lying, guv. It's her what owns the building. She's here to collect the rent from us poor devils.' The voice from the shadows spoke up again, accompanied by grunts of assent.

'Don't take no notice of her,' Molly said hastily. 'She's touched in the head – they all are. I'm poor like them and in need of help.'

'Have I got brothers and sisters?' Flora asked anxiously. 'Why did you give me away? Didn't you love me?'

Molly eyed her speculatively. 'Of course I did, me little flower. I loves you with all me heart, but they snatched you from me arms. I cried for a week after you'd gone.' She reached out to grab Flora by the arm. 'Now you've come back and you can look after your old ma. I got plans for you, darling.'

Flora pulled away, cowering against Alice. 'I don't want to live here. You're not the beautiful angel I see in my dreams.'

A ripple of grim laughter echoed round the room, and Molly turned on her companions with her hands balled into fists. 'Shut up, the lot of you.' She bent down so that her face was close to Flora's. 'You wouldn't leave poor Molly to rot, would you, sweetheart?'

'I think I'd like to go home,' Flora whispered.

'We've seen and heard enough.' Rory put his hand in his pocket and took out a small leather purse. 'This will keep you in laudanum or whatever takes your fancy for a few days, Molly. Merry Christmas.'

She snatched the money and slipped it down the neck of her blouse, glaring at him with narrowed eyes. 'So you're taking me baby away again, are you, guv? I deserve more compensation than that.'

'You surely don't expect the child to stay here, do you?' Rory moved closer to Alice and Flora as the other occupants of the basement room stirred, some of them rising to their feet and others slithering towards them on their backsides.

'You could take me with you, sir.' Molly eyed Flora with a sly smile. 'I could look after me girl. You needn't tell no one that we're mother and child. You could say I'm the new nursemaid.' She made a move towards Flora. 'You love your old ma, don't you, girl? Otherwise you wouldn't have come all this way to see me.'

Alice could stand no more. 'You are a mean, ungrateful woman, Molly. You don't deserve a lovely daughter like Flora. It was her dearest wish to find you and make sure you were all right, and this is how you treat her. Do you never think of anyone other than yourself?'

'I want to go now,' Flora whispered.

'That's right,' Molly pointed a bony finger at Flora. 'Run off with your rich friends and leave me here to rot. I'm the one what gave you life and this is how you treat me.'

Low growling sounds echoed off the walls as the other occupants advanced on them. Rory reached into his pocket once again and dropped a handful of coins in their midst. In the wild scramble that ensued he guided Alice and Flora out of the room and up the stairs. Screams and threats followed them even as they reached the street, but thankfully the cab was waiting for them on the corner, as instructed.

'It'll be double what I quoted you, guv,' the cabby said crossly.

'I won't argue with that.' Rory bundled Flora into the cab and Alice climbed in after her. 'Drive on, cabby.' Rory jumped in and slammed the door.

Flora sobbed all the way home and nothing that either Alice or Rory could say seemed to comfort her.

'This was a terrible mistake,' Alice said in a low

voice. 'We've only made things worse for the poor child.'

'She's upset now but maybe it's for the best. At least she knows what sort of woman her mother is.'

Alice was not convinced. She tightened her hold on Flora and they lapsed into silence until they reached Russell Square.

They were met in the entrance hall by Lydia, who had been issuing orders to Hoskins, but she broke off when she saw them.

'What's the meaning of this?' she demanded angrily. 'How dare you take Flora out without first consulting me?'

Rory handed his hat and coat to Hoskins, who backed away hastily. 'Merry Christmas, Lydia. I must say that the house looks very festive.'

'You can't get round me that way, Rory. I want an answer.'

Flora opened her mouth to speak, but Alice silenced her with a warning glance.

'I knew you would be busy preparing for your guests to arrive,' Rory said smoothly. 'So I took the liberty of asking Flora and Miss Radcliffe to accompany me to my office in Ludgate Circus, where I had a surprise for Flora.'

'What sort of surprise?' Lydia shook her head. 'Really, you are the most exasperating person, Rory.'

'It's a secret, Lydia.' Rory winked at Flora and patted his jacket pocket. 'One that must be put beneath the Christmas tree with the other presents.'

Lydia threw up her hands. 'You are talking nonsense, and you abused our trust by taking Flora from the house without my permission.' She turned to Alice, frowning. 'As for you, Miss Radcliffe, I'll deal with you later.'

'No, Mama.' Flora stamped her foot, scowling. 'You must not blame her. It was my doing and I threatened to have a tantrum if she didn't allow me to go with Uncle Rory.'

'Keep out of this, Flora. It's none of your business.'

'I'll scream and make myself sick if you don't promise to be nice to Alice.' Flora opened her mouth, closing her eyes and screwing up her face until tears oozed from beneath her eyelids.

'Stop that, you horrid child,' Lydia cried, holding her hand to her forehead. 'My guests will be arriving for luncheon at any moment. Stop it, I say.'

Flora opened one eye. 'Do you promise, Mama?'

'Yes, I suppose so.' She was shaking with barely suppressed anger as she spun round to face Alice. 'In the future if Mr Dearborn suggests an outing you must check with me first, Miss Radcliffe. Do you understand?'

Alice nodded and bobbed a curtsey. 'Yes, ma'am.'

'Come with me, Rory. I haven't finished with you.' Lydia marched off in the direction of the staircase, leaving Flora and Alice to make their way back to the nursery.

'Don't worry, poppet,' Rory said, winking at Flora.

'I'll see you later.' His expression changed subtly as he turned to Alice. 'All will be well, I promise,' he added in a low voice. 'Coming, Lydia.' He strolled off, following in his sister-in-law's wake.

Flora waited until they were back in the nursery. She grinned up at Alice. 'Uncle Rory is a good liar and I'm rather good at getting my own way.'

'Are you all right, my dear?' Alice asked anxiously. 'I know you were very upset by what we saw this morning. Your uncle meant well by taking you to see your mother.'

Flora sank down on the chair by the fire, holding her hands out to the blaze. 'I know that, and now I'm sorry I made such a fuss about finding her. Do you think that person was just pretending to be my mama? Maybe she wanted money. She didn't seem to have any or she wouldn't have been living in such a dreadful place.'

Alice sat down beside her. 'That could be a possibility.'

'But you don't think so?'

'To tell you the truth I don't know what to believe. There's one thing for certain, and that is your uncle really loves you and I'm sure that your father does too. Your mama might have an odd way of showing it, but she obviously cares about you or she wouldn't take so much trouble to keep you safe.'

Flora put her head on one side, a frown creasing her brow. 'I suppose so.'

'And you have a good home here, even if the rules

are very strict. I think what you need most is the company of other children.'

'I don't know how to play games. When Smithson used to take me for a walk in the square I used to see children playing together, but they never asked me to join in with them.'

Alice stared into the flames as they danced around the coals, creating glow fairies in the soot on the fireback. 'I know how you feel. I was an only child and it can be lonely, but you have me now.'

'And Uncle Rory. I wonder what's he's going to give me. There was that big present he put under the tree and now there's the little package he had in his pocket. I can't wait to find out.'

An hour later a flustered Nettie brought them their luncheon, complaining bitterly about the amount of work that guests created. She thumped the tray down on the table and stomped off, grumbling beneath her breath. Alice attacked her food with a keen appetite, but her thoughts were with her mother and she could only hope that Clara was keeping an eye on her. It had been a traumatic morning, but at least Flora seemed to have recovered from her meeting with Molly Bishop. She appeared to have convinced herself that the woman was lying and that her real mother was the angel she had imagined her to be. Alice did not try to persuade her otherwise. It seemed too cruel to make a nine-year-old face up to such a stark reality.

Shortly after Nettie had cleared the table and

taken the tray back to the kitchen, she returned breathless and red in the face to tell them they were summoned to the drawing room. 'Me legs will drop off if I have to climb them stairs again today,' she grumbled. 'Cook is in a flap because the jelly didn't set in time for luncheon and she had to serve the mince pies she was saving for dinner this evening. She threw a saucepan at Winnie what's come in to help with the serving up and covered her with custard. Luckily it was cold or she'd have been scalded and might have died.'

'I wish I'd seen it,' Flora said, giggling. 'I wonder if she licked it off. I love custard.'

Alice grabbed her by the hand. 'Yes, so do I, but I wouldn't like to wear it. Come along, Flora, we've been told to go downstairs. You want your presents, don't you?'

'You're lucky,' Nettie said gloomily. 'I won't get no presents. I'm off to Wapping to visit me mum and dad tomorrow, but I won't get nothing. Poor folk can't afford to give each other presents.'

'Do they live in a cellar, Nettie?' Flora asked eagerly. 'Is it cold and damp and smells nasty?'

'Certainly not, miss. They're respectable folks. Pa is a lighterman and Ma takes in washing, but there's twelve of us children and money is tight.' She made for the door and held it open with a dreamy smile on her face. 'One Christmas I had a poke of peppermint creams. I loves them more than anything, but I'm quite partial to toffee and barley sugar as well.'

She wandered off, still rhapsodising about the delights of sugary treats.

'I'll ask Uncle Rory to buy her some sweets,' Flora said in a whisper as she followed Alice downstairs. 'I've never thought about how poor people live before. It's not nice.'

'No,' Alice agreed. 'Poverty is dreadful.' A vision of Horace Hubble sprang to mind and she shuddered. Would such a marriage be preferable to living hand to mouth? She led the way to the drawing room, putting such thoughts aside, and was about to knock on the door when Flora pushed past her and barged into the room. She dropped a dramatic curtsey for the benefit of the visitors and smiling angelically she marched up to her parents.

'Merry Christmas, Mama and Papa, and everybody. May I have my presents now?'

A ripple of amusement greeted her theatrical entrance, and Lydia managed a tight little smile. Her husband leaned over to pick Flora up and he dandled her on his knee. 'Merry Christmas, my darling.' He kissed her on the cheek and set her back on the floor. 'You may open your gifts.'

Alice stood at the back of the room watching Flora's apparently carefree performance. She could only wonder at the resilience of children, and a quick glance in Rory's direction convinced her that he was thinking along the same lines. Flora was sitting on the floor unwrapping the large present he had given her, and he edged his way through the assembled guests to stand beside Alice. 'She's quite remarkable,' he said in a low voice. 'I was afraid she would be devastated.'

'Children are tougher than we imagine,' Alice answered in a whisper. 'She's convinced herself that Molly Bishop is not who she claims to be.'

He frowned, shaking his head. 'I was wrong to take her there. I should have known better.'

Alice was prevented from replying by a cry of delight from Flora as she opened a large wooden box and showed off its contents. 'It's a paint box,' she cried gleefully. 'With brushes so that I can make proper pictures. Maybe I could be an artist at your printing works, Uncle Rory.'

'An able apprentice, I'm sure. You're a lucky little girl, Flora.' A large man with a red velvet waistcoat straining at his corpulent belly slapped Rory on the back. 'That's a splendid gift.'

Flora closed the box, stroking the polished lid with the tips of her fingers. 'I want to be an artist like Alice.'

Heads turned to stare at her and Alice felt the blood rush to her cheeks. 'Thank you, Flora, but I'm sure you are more talented than I.'

'There is still our present, Flora,' Lydia said icily. 'Why not open it now?'

Flora reached beneath the tree and took out a much smaller gift, which she opened carefully. 'A Bible,' she said in a small voice. 'Thank you, Mama and Papa.'

'A leather-bound Bible,' Lydia said firmly. 'With

your initials embossed on it in gold leaf, Flora. Aren't you a lucky little girl?'

'It's very nice.' Flora laid it aside, peering under the tree. 'Where is the other present from Uncle Rory? He said he brought it especially for me.'

Once again heads turned to stare at Rory. 'Did I forget to put it under the tree?' he said loudly. 'My fault entirely, Floss.'

'You said you went to your office to fetch it,' Lydia said icily. 'Let us all see it, Rory.'

Flora jumped to her feet. 'I can't wait. I'm sure it's something very special.'

Rory leaned closer to Alice. 'It wasn't for her. I thought she might forget with all her other gifts to open.'

'You have to give her something,' Alice said in a whisper. 'You can't disappoint her now.'

'Well, Rory, we're waiting,' Frederick Dearborn rose from his seat. 'Don't tell me you've lost it.' He glanced round at the flushed faces of his guests. 'This is typical of my brother. He always was a scatter-brain. I could tell you stories of our childhood and the pranks he used to play. Our father beat him so often that at times he could hardly sit down.'

'Don't be vulgar, Frederick,' Lydia said primly. She glared at Rory. 'Well, where is it? We're waiting.'

Rory patted his pocket. 'I must have dropped it in the hallway. Perhaps Miss Radcliffe will be kind enough to help me look.' He held his hand up as Flora danced towards him. 'Wait there, poppet. This won't take a second.' He opened the door and stepped outside, followed by Alice.

'Did you have anything for her, or not?' she demanded angrily. 'You can see how disappointed she was by her parents' present.'

'That would be Lydia's doing. She's not over-generous when it comes to her daughter.'

'That's not an answer. Have you something for her or not?'

He shook his head. 'No, I'm afraid not. I just said the first thing that came into my head.'

'So what was in the little parcel?'

'It was a small gift for you, Alice.' He took the package from his pocket. 'I know it was a liberty, but I also knew that my sister-in-law would never think of giving you a present, even though you've done so much for Flora in such a short space of time. She's a different child.'

'I wasn't expecting anything. You must give it to Flora.'

'I can't.' He laid it in her hand. 'It's not suitable for a nine-year-old, and it's only a trinket, but you've been so kind to Flora, and I thought you'd like it.'

She opened it and found a gold ring with a single pearl in a claw setting. 'It's lovely.'

'I saw it in a jeweller's window and I thought of you.'

Alice shot him a sideways glance and realised that he was being serious. She knew she was blushing, but she was more concerned about Flora than she was for herself. Thinking quickly, she took off her precious butterfly brooch, which she had hidden beneath the stiff white collar of her uniform dress. She placed it in the paper and wrapped it, placing it in his hand. 'The ring is beautiful, but I can't accept it. Give this to Flora; she'll love it as I always have.'

'This obviously means a lot to you. I can't let you do this.'

'Flora means more to me. I can't bear to think of how she would feel if you let her down now. She's had enough disappointment today to last a lifetime.'

'I'd like you to accept the ring. It's a token of my respect and gratitude.'

She shook her head. 'Thank you, but it wouldn't be proper.'

A slow handclapping from inside the room and Flora's high-pitched voice urging them to hurry made it impossible to delay further. Rory placed the ring in his breast pocket. 'We'll talk about this later.' He leaned over and brushed her forehead with a kiss. 'Thank you, Alice. You're a very special person.' Opening the door, he stepped inside to a round of applause. 'I'm so sorry, poppet. We found it on the stairs. It must have leaped out of my pocket in an attempt to fly to you.' He pressed the hastily wrapped gift into her hand.

She tore off the paper with a squeal of delight.

'Do you like it?' Rory asked anxiously.

'It's the most beautiful thing I've ever seen.' She

jumped up and down, holding the silver butterfly up for all to see. 'Look, everyone. Isn't Uncle Rory wonderful? He knows how much I love butterflies and this one will be mine for ever.' She turned to Alice. 'Will you put it on for me, please?'

'Of course.' Alice pinned it to Flora's dress. Any regrets she might have felt were dispelled by Flora's happy expression. 'It looks lovely.'

To a chorus of, 'Let us see,' and, 'Come over here, dear,' Flora danced around the room showing off her butterfly brooch.

'Thank you, Alice,' Rory whispered. 'I'm forever in your debt.'

She glanced anxiously at Lydia. 'I don't think your sister-in-law approves.'

'She doesn't believe in spoiling children, as you'll have noticed. Freddie would have been much more generous.'

'Flora is happy, that's all that matters.' Alice smiled as she watched Flora being admired and petted by the guests.

Lydia, however, did not look pleased. 'I think it's time for Radcliffe to take you back to the nursery, Flora.'

Later, after they had eaten supper together and enjoyed the crystallised fruits and cake that Cook had taken it upon herself to add to the plain nursery fare insisted upon by Lydia, Flora leaped up from the table.

'May I do some painting, please, Alice? I want to use my new paint box.'

Alice was anxious about her mother, but she could not bring herself to disappoint Flora. She smiled and nodded. 'Of course you may.' She cleared the table, making room for Flora to lay out her paint box and paper. 'What do you want to paint?'

'I thought I'd make a picture of a butterfly to give to Uncle Rory. I haven't any money to buy him a present.'

'That's a lovely thought.' Alice gazed at the silver butterfly pinned to Flora's best dress, stifling a sigh of regret. She knew that her mother would understand her reasons for giving her treasured gift away. Even so, it had been a sacrifice, and now it was gone for ever. She sat back and watched Flora's attempts to capture the delicate shape on paper. 'Would you like me to do the outline for you?'

Flora pushed the paper towards her and Alice picked up the sliver of charcoal and began to draw. With deft strokes she outlined a butterfly and passed the sketch back to Flora, who concentrated on filling in the details. The clock on the mantelshelf ticked on and the minutes flew by, but Alice forced herself to sit patiently, offering help when asked and praise when necessary. Flora grew impatient and it was obvious that she was tiring. 'It's no good,' she cried, throwing the brush down. 'I'm not good at painting.'

'Of course you are,' Alice said softly. 'But it's a

matter of taking things slowly. The more you do the better you'll get.'

'Will you finish it off for me? I want to give it to Uncle Rory tonight, before he goes back to his horrid lodgings. He can pin it on the wall and think of summertime and sunshine.'

'I'm sure he'll love it just as it is.' The words had barely left Alice's lips when Rory burst into the room without bothering to knock.

Flora jumped to her feet and ran to give him a hug. 'You shouldn't barge into a lady's bedchamber without knocking,' she said severely. 'I might have been undressed and ready for bed.'

He picked her up and swung her round before setting her back on her feet. 'I'm sorry, young lady. I didn't realise that you had grown up so suddenly.'

Flora ran to the table and snatched up the painting. 'I did this for you. It's your Christmas present.'

He took it from her, studying it with an approving smile. 'I'll treasure it, Flora. It's beautiful.' He glanced at Alice. 'You have an apt pupil, Miss Radcliffe.'

'She did help me a bit,' Flora admitted grudgingly. 'But I did most of it, didn't I, Alice?'

'Indeed you did.' Alice rose from the table. 'It's getting late and I really should be going home. My mother was quite unwell when I left this morning.'

'Of course. We're being very selfish keeping Miss Radcliffe from her family on Christmas Day, Flora.' Rory laid the painting on the table. 'When this is dry I'll take it home with me, but I don't want to smudge the paint.'

'I suppose I have to go to bed now,' Flora said, yawning. 'I'm not tired.'

Rory bent down and kissed her on the cheek. 'I'll say good night then, Floss. I have to leave soon anyway so perhaps Miss Radcliffe will allow me to escort her home.' He laughed, holding up his hand. 'I know what you're going to say, Alice. You are perfectly capable of walking back to Queen Square on your own, but I would enjoy your company if you could bear with me.'

The mischievous twinkle in his eyes was impossible to resist. 'I'll see Flora comfortably settled first,' Alice said, smiling.

'Merry Christmas, Floss.' Rory left the room, shutting the door behind him.

Having put Flora to bed, Alice read her a story and made sure that she was warm and comfortable before kissing her good night. She left the room, closing the door quietly behind her, safe in the knowledge that Flora would soon fall asleep. She hurried down the back stairs to the entrance hall where Rory was waiting for her. Hoskins had either mellowed with seasonal good cheer or else he had been tippling in the butler's pantry and he managed a smile as he ushered them out into the bitter cold of the winter's night.

They walked slowly, treading carefully on the frozen surface of the fallen snow. 'I'm sorry I put you through such an unpleasant experience this morning,' Rory said with a rueful smile.

'It was Flora who suffered, not I.'

'I made a mistake and I only hope I haven't caused irreparable harm.'

'I think Flora needed to know the truth,' Alice said slowly. 'It will have hurt her, but she's very young and she'll get over it. It might be for the best.'

He came to a halt beneath one of the gas lamps at the corner of the square. 'You have been her salvation, Alice. I wish you would accept the present I bought for you as a token of my appreciation for what you've done.'

She shook her head. 'I can't. I'm sorry, but it wouldn't be right, and you owe me nothing.'

'Maybe one day I can repay you in some other way, but I wish you'd change your mind.'

They walked on in silence and parted outside the house in Queen Square. Alice watched him stride away with a mixed emotions. She realised that she was in danger of falling in love for the first time in her life, but she suspected that Rory Dearborn was well aware of his charm and used it to his own advantage. He was both good-looking and wealthy, and could look far higher for a prospective bride. It was probably just a mild flirtation as far as he was concerned, and she should be wary. She was about to mount the steps when she was seized from behind.

'I got a chiv and I'll use it if you scream.'

# Chapter Seven

A sharp pinprick in the small of her back bore witness to the truth spoken by a voice that brought back vivid memories of the cellar in Blossom Street, and the disgusting odour of an unwashed body made Alice feel physically sick.

'If you kill me, Molly Bishop, you won't get whatever it is you came for.'

'How do you know it's me?' Molly spun Alice round with surprising strength, holding the knife to her throat. 'Don't think I won't cut you, you stuck-up bitch.'

'Why? What have I done to you?'

'You was with him and you took my child away.'

'Yes, we did, and it was for her own good.' Alice brought her arm up with a swift movement, catching Molly off balance so that she tottered backwards, dropping the knife. Alice stamped on the handle.

'Don't try to pick it up or I'll scream so loudly that the whole street will turn out. You'll be caught and arrested.'

Molly cowered against the area railings. 'I'm a poor woman, not in the best of health, as you can see. I need my little girl to look after me in me old age.'

'We've no proof that you're Flora's mother. You couldn't even remember her name this morning.'

'It were a slip of the tongue, that's all. Flora is mine and I want her back.'

'If you had any feelings for her you wouldn't condemn her to a life like yours.'

Molly abandoned the subservient attitude for one of naked aggression. 'I want her back and you'll get her for me if you know what's good for you.'

'If you're really her mother why would you want to drag her down to your level? You should be glad that she's being brought up in a respectable family with a good future ahead of her.'

'I could make a fortune on the streets with a little peach like my Flora, or better still, the toffs would pay good money to get her back.' She narrowed her eyes, glaring at Alice. 'I got friends who'd be happy to slit your pretty throat as soon as look at you.'

'I'm not afraid of you. Say what you like, but I won't lift a finger to help you. Flora is beyond your reach.'

'I knows where she lives,' Molly snarled. 'I was waiting outside tonight, but you was with that toff what brought you to Blossom Street earlier. I followed you here so now I know where to find you. Be warned, because I ain't done with you yet.'

'If you bother me again I'll report you to the police. I know where you live too, so remember that, Molly Bishop.' Alice kicked the knife down through the iron railings at the top of the area and mounted the steps. She rapped on the door, but when she glanced over her shoulder there was no sign of Molly, who seemed to have vanished like a puff of smoke.

Clara opened the door. 'Come in out of the cold, miss. You look froze to death.'

It was only when she was inside the house that Alice realised she was trembling from head to foot. She had put on a brave face in front of Molly, but now the danger was past she knew that she had made an enemy, and she had no doubt that Molly would carry out her threats. Her hands were shaking so much that she could hardly undo the frogging on her mantle and Clara had to help her.

'You need a hot drink, miss. I'm afraid the fire's gone out in the dining room. I lit it before dinner but your mama wasn't feeling well enough to come downstairs, and the missis was invited to the parson's house after church. You'd best come down to the kitchen where it's nice and warm.'

'I – I need to see my mother first.'

'She was asleep when I looked in about ten minutes ago. If she sees you looking so pale and drawn it could set her back and make her worse.

Come with me, miss. I'm sure Mrs Jugg won't mind, just this once.'

If Mrs Jugg was surprised to see Alice in her kitchen she did not even raise an eyebrow. It was almost as if Alice was expected, and a cup of hot tea was thrust into her cold hands.

'Sit down by the range, and warm yourself, miss. It's no good for man nor beast outside tonight, Christmas or no Christmas.' Mrs Jugg slumped down on a chair, which she pulled as close as possible to the fire. 'There's some gruel on the hob, if you'd like to take it up to your poor ma. Clara says she's not at all well.'

Alice sipped her tea. 'Thank you, yes. I'll go up and see her as soon as I've drunk this.' She glanced round the kitchen at the bare surfaces of the work benches and the scrubbed pine table in the centre of the room. There was no sign of Christmas cheer in the Radcliffe establishment.

'The mistress doesn't believe in extravagance.' Mrs Jugg's mouth turned down at the corners in silent disapproval. 'We had boiled ox head for our Christmas dinner today. The broth will last the week out if I add more vegetables to the pot.'

'The meat was tasty, Cook,' Clara said hastily. 'I had two helpings, being as how it's the festive season, and then I had a mince pie.' She rubbed her tummy, smiling happily.

'Hush now, girl.' Mrs Jugg silenced her with a frown. 'I made the mincemeat myself, Miss Radcliffe.

It was our little treat and it didn't cost the mistress a penny.'

Alice was lost for words. She was not in a position to openly criticise her aunt's stinginess, nor could she do anything to improve the servants' lot. She finished the tea and laid the cup on the table. 'Thank you, that really has done the trick. I feel much better now.'

'Your teeth was chattering something chronic when you come in,' Clara said, grinning. 'You go on upstairs, miss. I'll fetch the gruel and a cup of weak tea for your ma, poor lady.'

'You're both very kind,' Alice said shyly. 'Thank you.' As she made her way up the back stairs to her mother's room she could not help wondering why Mrs Jugg and Clara chose to stay in her aunt's employ.

She found her mother awake and shivering. 'Mama, I'm sorry I've been away so long.'

'It's all right, my darling. I've been sleeping most of the day but I'm so c-cold.'

'You need more blankets and there should be a fire in here. I'll see what I can do.'

'Don't antagonise your aunt. We can't afford to get on the wrong side of her, Alice.'

'And I don't want you to die of lung fever, Mama.' In answer to a muffled knock Alice went to open the door. Clara edged in carrying a tray, which she put on a table by the window. 'You're awake, ma'am. Are you hungry?'

Beth shook her head. 'Not really, but thank you anyway, Clara.'

'This is ridiculous,' Alice said angrily. 'My mother is chilled to the marrow and this room feels like an ice cave. Where does my aunt keep the bedding?'

'There ain't no more blankets, miss. The mistress says that storing them to feed the moths is a waste of money.'

'Then where does she keep the coal? I'm going to light a fire in here.'

Clara's mouth dropped open. 'She won't allow it, miss.'

'I'm not going to ask her permission. Fetch me a bucket of coat, kindling and matches, please. I'll take full responsibility.'

Clara scuttled out of the room, her footsteps echoing on the bare boards. Alice lifted her mother to a semi-sitting position and plumped up the pillows. 'I'll hold the cup for you. Try to drink the tea and maybe you'll feel like taking a little sustenance.'

Beth drank thirstily, but only managed a few mouthfuls of the rapidly cooling gruel.

'Thank you, darling,' she said, falling back against the pillows. 'I feel a bit better now.'

Alice perched on the edge of the bed, taking her mother's hand in hers. 'You're still very cold, Mama. Clara should be back soon and I'll get a fire going.'

'Jane won't like it. We really shouldn't go against her wishes. It is her house, after all.'

'And we're her family. What would Papa say if he could see how she treats you?'

'They never got on, Alice. Clement was very fond of his brother and he tried to like Jane for Robert's sake, but she's not an easy person to get on with, as you've discovered.'

Alice was saved from replying by the sudden appearance of Clara, looking flushed and breathing heavily. 'I'm sorry, but the cellar is locked and Mrs Radcliffe has the only key. Cook said she's put the last of our daily allowance of coal on the range and there won't be any more until morning.'

Alice leaped to her feet. 'This is ridiculous. There must be ten or more bedrooms in this house, surely there are blankets hidden away somewhere?'

'The beds in those rooms aren't made up, miss,' Clara said, wringing her hands. 'I'm ever so sorry, but there's nothing more I can do.' She hesitated. 'There's the locked room, but I dunno what's in there. The cleaners aren't allowed in and ...'

'And I suppose my aunt has the key,' Alice said bitterly. 'Maybe she keeps my uncle prisoner in there and he isn't really dead after all.'

A hint of a smile lit Beth's blue eyes. 'Alice, that's a wicked thing to say.' She broke off, seized by a fit of coughing.

'If there is extra bedding in there I'll find it even if I have to break the door down.' Alice beckoned to Clara. 'I need you to show me where it is.'

'It's on the first floor, miss. But don't tell the mistress

I said so.' Reluctantly Clara led the way to a room on the second floor. 'This is it. May I go now, miss?'

Alice tried the door handle and found it locked. She hammered on the panels in frustration. 'Yes, go back to the warm kitchen, Clara. This is my problem, not yours.'

Clara raced off, coming to a sudden halt. 'I'm sorry, ma'am. It weren't my idea.'

Alice turned to see her aunt standing at the top of the staircase with a chamber candlestick in her hand. 'What is going on?'

'I never told her about the locked room,' Clara sobbed. 'It weren't me.'

'Be quiet, you silly child. Go back to the servants' quarters and don't venture above stairs unless I ring for you.'

Clara fled.

'I suppose this is your doing,' Jane said, advancing on her niece in the wavering light of the candle. 'Why are you prying into my business?'

'My mother is quite literally freezing to death in that icy room. I was looking for an extra blanket. Is it too much to ask?'

'Don't take that tone with me, young lady. Remember that you are beholden to me for everything since your father left you without a penny to your name.'

'What's in this room, Aunt? Have you some dark secret hidden away? All I want is a blanket or two so that Mama doesn't die from the cold.'

Jane selected a key from the chatelaine. She unlocked the door and thrust it open. 'There, see for yourself. This is just a bedroom. There's nothing sinister hidden from prying eyes.' She marched in, holding the candle high.

Alice stepped inside and found herself in a different world. A four-poster bed was hung with heavily embroidered damask curtains and a matching tester. The flower-patterned carpet was in soft muted shades that complemented the delicate patterns on the wall-paper and curtains. Despite the thick layer of dust that covered the rosewood dressing table and clothes press, and the festoons of cobwebs that hung like lace curtains from the crystal chandelier, it was a charming and very feminine room. The contrast between this quiet but faded opulence and the monastic austerity of the rest of the house could not have been more pronounced.

'Whose room was this?' Alice stared at her aunt in amazement. 'And why is it always locked?'

'It was my late husband's wish,' Jane said bitterly. 'I would have cleared everything away and be done with it, but he was devoted to his half-sister, even though she disgraced the family name.'

'Mama mentioned my Aunt Viola recently, but I've only a very hazy memory of her. I know that she died young.'

Jane pursed her lips. 'Viola was the baby of the family and her parents spoiled her, giving in to her every whim.' She paused, frowning. 'She came to live with us after they passed away within weeks of each other.'

'It must have been difficult for all of you,' Alice said tactfully.

'It was impossible. Viola wanted everything her own way, and then she formed an attachment to a totally unsuitable person. It was a very difficult time. She ran away from home, but my sainted Robert was convinced she would return. His dying wish was that I kept her room ready for her. It's all nonsense, of course. She was selfish and wayward and doesn't deserve to be remembered, but I've kept my promise and will do so until the day I die, even though I don't agree with it.'

'I'm so sorry,' Alice said with feeling. 'It must have been very hard for you to bear.'

'We put it about that she succumbed to lung fever,' Jane said with a casual shrug. 'She is dead to me anyway, so take what you need. The door will be locked again and I never want to hear Viola Radcliffe's name mentioned in my presence.'

Alice folded back the counterpane. There were two thick woollen blankets that were slightly moth-eaten and in need of airing, but would provide the warmth needed to give comfort to her sick mother. She looped them over her arm. 'Thank you, Aunt. I'm very grateful.'

Jane barred Alice's way as she was about to leave the room. 'What do I tell my cousin? Are you willing to accept his offer of marriage?'

'He hasn't proposed, Aunt.'

'Don't pretend to be more stupid than you are, Alice. You know very well what I mean.'

'I need more time to consider the matter,' Alice said evasively. 'Marriage is a big step and I don't want to make a terrible mistake.'

'You know my terms so don't play the innocent with me. My sister-in-law was led astray by foolish romantic notions, and I won't allow that to happen again. You have until New Year's Eve to make up your mind.'

'But that's no time at all, Aunt. This is a big decision for me.'

'You either begin the year as an affianced woman or I wash my hands of both you and your mother. I think you will see sense.'

'Yes, Aunt,' Alice said meekly. She hurried from the room, hugging the blankets to her. New Year's Eve seemed as far away as the moon, and all she could think of now was to get her mother through the night. She painted a smile on her lips as she entered the chilly room. 'Look what I found, Mama. You'll never guess where they came from.' She shook out the blankets and laid them on the bed. 'You'll soon be warm again, and tomorrow I'll ask Aunt Jane if you might have a fire in your room.'

'Don't get on the wrong side of her, Alice,' Beth said weakly. 'She's a stubborn woman and she has no liking for me, as you well know.'

'Never mind her now, Mama. I have something

interesting to tell you.' Alice perched on the edge of the bed, tucking the covers up to her mother's chin. 'There's a locked room in this house and it belonged to Aunt Viola. Apparently Uncle Robert's dying wish was that her room be kept ready for her when she returned home.'

'That can't be true, dear. Viola died from consumption.'

'Aunt Jane said that was a rumour put about to save the family the embarrassment of admitting that Viola had run off with a man they didn't like. I'd love to know the whole story.'

'Viola was spirited and could be quite difficult at times, but she was very pretty – like a china doll with golden hair and the bluest of blue eyes.'

'I envy her that. When I was little I used to wish that my mouse-brown locks would turn overnight into golden curls, and that my eyes were blue instead of grey.'

Beth reached out to hold her daughter's hand. 'Don't say such things, even in jest. You are a truly beautiful girl, far nicer than Viola, who only had her looks to commend her.'

Alice raised her mother's hand to her cheek. 'You're getting warm at last. A good night's sleep is what you need, Mama. I'll look in first thing tomorrow before I go to Russell Square.'

'Good night, my darling. Thank you for all your efforts on my behalf; I just wish I was able to look after you instead of being a burden.'

'That's nonsense, Mama.' Rising to her feet Alice tucked the covers up to her mother's chin. 'You're not a burden and I won't listen to such talk. We'll find a way to escape from Aunt Jane's cold charity, I promise you.'

The house in Russell Square was buzzing with activity when Alice arrived next morning. She had awakened early to check on her mother and found her sleeping soundly. Clara had promised to look after her, which was a relief as Alice knew she could trust the child, but that still left her with the problem of what to do about Molly Bishop. Her threat to take Flora away from the only home she had ever known had been real enough and Alice had experienced her tendency to violence first-hand.

She had toyed with the idea of warning Mr and Mrs Dearborn, but that would mean admitting that Rory had taken them to Blossom Street. Rory was the person to tell, but she had no way of knowing when he would call at the house. She thought about warning Hoskins that a strange woman was posing a threat to Flora, but she knew that he would go straight to his employer, as would Mrs Upton, who was marshalling the servants like a small general in an attempt to make everything ready for the next influx of guests.

She was at a loss to know what to do for the best, but it seemed the only thing she could do was to keep Flora close to her and remain indoors. She collected a tray of breakfast from the kitchen and took it upstairs to the nursery, where she found Flora still in her nightgown, seated at the desk with the paint box open and a brush in her hand.

'I'm making a picture for you, Alice,' she said, beaming. 'I was up very early. As soon as Nettie came in to light my fire I got out of bed and started drawing. She lit the lamp for me, too. I know I'm not allowed to play with matches.'

'That's very sensible of you.' Alice placed the tray on the table. 'Now stop that and eat your breakfast, and you can finish your painting when you're dressed.' She met Flora's rebellious look with a smile. 'May I see what you've done so far?'

Shielding the paper with her hands, Flora grinned. 'No. It's a surprise.' She angled her head. 'You look cold, Alice. Why don't you sit down and drink your tea while I finish my picture, and then I'll have my breakfast?'

Alice realised that she was being manipulated, but she resisted the temptation to exert her authority. 'Thank you, Flora. That's very thoughtful of you.' She pulled up a chair and sat down to drink the cup of tea she had added to the tray.

'Help yourself to toast,' Flora said graciously. 'Cook always gives me too much.'

'Thank you, Flora.' Alice sat quietly, sipping tea and enjoying the luxury of toast spread with a lavish amount of butter.

When Flora had finished she held her painting up

for inspection, and Alice swallowed hard, taking a deep breath before speaking. 'That's very interesting.'

'It's the cellar where we found my mother,' Flora said calmly. 'I dreamed about it last night so I had to put it on paper first thing while I could still see it in my head.'

'Your uncle didn't know it would be like that, Flora. He wouldn't have taken you there if he had had any idea that it would be so terrible.'

Flora nodded. 'I know he thought he was doing the right thing and I was upset, but I don't believe that person could be my mother. I think Smithson was lying.'

Alice repressed a shudder. The memory of Molly Bishop's threats was still fresh in her mind. 'You could be right, Flora.'

'I know I am,' Flora said confidently. She moved her paint box aside and reached for the bowl of porridge. 'We won't speak of her again.'

'No, indeed. What would you like to do today?'

'I'd like to go into the square and make a snowman.'

'We'll see.'

Flora paused with the spoon halfway to her lips. 'Why do grown-ups always say that when they really mean no?'

'I'm not saying we won't, but I think we have to wait and see if your uncle decides to pay us a visit. We can't go out unaccompanied. You know very well that your mama wouldn't hear of it.'

'Then I hope Uncle Rory comes today. I'll paint a picture for him, too.'

'What a good idea,' Alice said, hoping she sounded more enthusiastic than she was feeling. 'Perhaps something a little more festive and cheerful would be the thing.'

'I'm not a baby, Alice. I understand.'

It was late afternoon when Rory breezed into the nursery. Alice had almost given up hope of seeing him that day, but Flora had been convinced that he would visit. She leaped up from the chair where she had been sitting quietly while Alice read her the story of *The Little Mermaid*, and she threw her arms around her uncle.

'I knew you'd come, but Alice thought you'd forgotten about us.'

'That's not quite true, Flora,' Alice protested.

'I would have come upstairs earlier,' Rory said with an affectionate smile, 'but I was waylaid by one of my brother's clients. It took me an age to persuade him that this was not the most appropriate time and place to talk business.

'It will be dark soon,' Flora said, pouting. 'I want to make a snowman, Uncle Rory. Please take me into the square. I've painted a picture especially for you.'

Rory threw back his head and laughed. 'You make it hard to refuse, you bad child.'

'I know,' she said smugly. 'That's what I do best.'

'What do you think, Alice?' Rory sent her a sideways glance, his eyes twinkling. 'Shall we humour her?'

For a moment Alice was at a loss for words. It was such a simple thing to do and it would make Flora happy, but the child was in real danger. She had to warn Rory, but she could not say anything in front of Flora. 'Mrs Dearborn won't like it,' she said softly.

'My sister-in-law is fully occupied with her guests, and my brother is playing cards in the smoking room. Put your coat on, Flora, and wrap up warm because it's freezing outside.' He turned to Alice with a warm smile. 'You, too, Alice. I'm not doing this on my own.'

'I've waited all day for this,' Flora cried excitedly. She danced across the floor to snatch up the painting that she had completed earlier and handed it to him. 'This is for you.'

He studied it, nodding with approval. 'A snow scene. How cleverly you've used hints of colour and shade to represent snow on the white background. Did you do this all by yourself, Flora?'

'Yes – well, I did have some help from Alice, but I did most of it.'

'She's an apt pupil.' Alice held up Flora's coat, which had been hanging on the back of a chair since the morning in hope that Rory would make an appearance.

Rory waited while Alice put on her outdoor

garments, eyeing her thoughtfully. 'We could use talent like yours at the printing works. I'm trying to persuade Freddie to start producing Christmas cards. They're becoming very popular and we need to keep up with the times.'

'Really? I've a copy of the first one ever printed in this country.' Alice shrugged on her mantle. 'My father bought it to mark the year of my birth and it's my most treasured possession.'

'I don't think I've ever seen one. Maybe you'd let me have a look at it?'

'Would you really?' Alice stared at him in amazement.

'Most definitely. It would be of great interest to me.'

Flora tugged at his hand. 'Never mind that, may we go out now, please?'

A fitful sun the colour of a pale primrose slid behind a bank of clouds that threatened another downfall of snow, but there was enough light to enable Flora to set about building a snowman. She was engrossed in her task and Alice drew Rory aside.

'I didn't want to say anything in front Flora, but Molly Bishop knows where she lives.'

'What?' Rory's brows drew together in a frown. 'How did you find that out?'

'She followed me to Queen Square and accosted me on the front steps of my aunt's house.'

'Did she hurt you?'

'No, but she wants Flora, and I think she'll stop at nothing to get her. I don't believe she's the child's mother because the things she has planned for her are wicked and evil ...' Alice broke off, shuddering at the memory of Molly's vicious threats.

'I'm sorry, Alice,' Rory said humbly. 'I've brought this on you both. I should have realised that Smithson was lying and out for her own ends. I rewarded her handsomely for the information, which I regret bitterly, but I really thought I was doing something to help poor little Flora to find her real mother.'

Alice stiffened, staring into the gathering gloom. She grabbed his arm. 'Look – over there. I think someone is watching us.'

# Chapter Eight

Rory strode across the snow-covered grass, heading towards the shadowy area beneath the trees, and Alice moved closer to Flora, who was happily oblivious to anything other than the task in hand.

'I need two small bits of coal for his eyes, something for his nose, and a pipe to stick in his mouth and then he's finished,' she said excitedly. 'Isn't he splendid?'

'Yes, you've done well, but it's getting dark. I think we ought to go indoors.' Alice glanced over her shoulder and was relieved to see Rory hurrying towards them.

'Whoever it was has gone. I expect he saw me coming.'

'It might have been her,' Alice whispered. 'I only saw a vague shape.'

'What are you whispering about?' Flora demanded,

rubbing her hands together and blowing them. 'Tell me. I want to know.'

'Nothing to concern you, Floss.' Rory patted her on the shoulder. 'Let's go, before we all freeze and turn into snowmen.'

'I'm a snow girl,' Flora said, laughing. She skipped on ahead to open the gate.

'I really think we ought to warn her parents,' Alice said in a low voice. 'Molly made it quite clear that she intended to snatch Flora at the first opportunity, and that nothing would stop her.'

'Leave it with me. I'll speak to my brother, but it's best that Lydia knows nothing about it. I started this so it's up to me to make things right.'

That evening, as she left the Dearborns' establishment, Alice could see Horace loitering in the yellow light of a streetlamp. Her annoyance was tempered with relief that it was not Molly. He approached her with a sickly grin on his face and snatched off his top hat, bowing from the waist as if she were royalty.

'Good evening, Cousin Alice.'

'I'm not your cousin, Horace. We're only related by marriage.'

'Yes, quite.' He cleared his throat nervously. 'Might I escort you home? I happened to be passing.'

She knew he was lying, but her experience the previous evening had left her feeling vulnerable. 'Please don't go out of your way on my account.' She started walking in the direction of Queen Square.

'Jane has invited me to supper,' he said breathlessly as he lengthened his strides to keep up with her. 'I suspect it is to make up for missing my family on Christmas Day. I ate a meal of bread and cheese in my room, on my own.'

'We didn't celebrate in Queen Square, as you know, and I was at my place of employment so you missed nothing.' She quickened her pace, taking care to keep to the well-trodden path where the snow had turned to slush. Her boots leaked, but that was the least of her worries, and they continued in silence except for the sound of Horace's stertorous breathing.

Clara let them into the house. 'I got to tell you that the missis has been called away to help in the soup kitchen,' she said importantly. 'Your ma is still abed, Miss Alice, but she ain't took no worse. In fact I'd say she's a bit better, thanks to me. I been up and down them stairs all day, making sure she's all right.'

Alice took off her bonnet and mantle, handing them to Clara with a grateful smile. 'Thank you. I knew I could rely on you. I'll go up and see her right away.'

'What about me?' Horace demanded plaintively.

'Do as you will,' Alice said over her shoulder. She lit a candle from one on a nearby table and hurried upstairs without giving him a chance to argue.

Beth was awake and she struggled to sit up when Alice entered the room. 'How glad I am to see you, my love.'

'How are you feeling, Mama?' Alice placed the candlestick on the table by the bed. 'Has Clara been looking after you properly?'

'The poor child has done her best, and I feel such a burden to you all.'

'Nonsense, Mama. You mustn't think like that. All we want is to see you fit and well again.' She glanced at the empty grate. 'I suppose Aunt Jane refused to allow you the luxury of a fire.'

'I don't expect her to change the habits of a lifetime just for me. I'm quite warm beneath the blankets you found for me.'

'Do you feel well enough to come down to dinner?' Alice asked anxiously.

'Not tonight. I can't face the thought of anything other than soup or perhaps some gruel.' Beth scanned her daughter's face with a look of concern. 'Why, what's the matter?'

'It's nothing really, Mama. Aunt Jane has invited Horace to dine with us, but she's gone on one of her mercy missions, leaving me to cope with him on my own. You can imagine how awkward that will be.'

'Help me up, Alice.' Beth raised herself on her elbow. 'Jane must have planned it so that you were put in a compromising position. I cannot allow you to dine alone with a single gentleman. I'm coming downstairs if it's the last thing I ever do.'

If Horace was disappointed that Alice was being chaperoned he was too polite to let it show. In fact he spent most of the evening devoting his attention to Beth, who coped valiantly even though Alice could see that her mother was tiring. The meal of broth made from the ox head, followed by tough mutton chops and boiled turnips was finished off with a suet roly-poly pudding, which had it been worth its weight in gold would have made them all very rich indeed. Beth managed to eat a little and Alice toyed with the food, trying hard not to compare it with the delicacies served up in Russell Square, but Horace consumed everything on his plate with obvious relish.

'What a splendid meal,' he said, wiping his lips on the starched white table napkin. 'My aunt keeps a good table, just as I know you will when we're man and wife, Alice. I don't want to seem impatient, but I hope you'll give me your answer soon.'

'Since you haven't asked the question you can hardly expect me to know what to say, sir.' Ignoring her mother's warning look, Alice assumed an air of innocence. Horace Hubble seemed to have been born lacking a sense of humour, which was something she could not forgive in anyone, let alone the man she might be forced to marry. Sadly, the more she knew of him the more determined she was that such a match would never happen.

Horace ran his finger round the inside of his starched collar. 'I think you know what the question is, Cousin Alice.'

'As I told you earlier, I'm not your cousin. We aren't even friends. In fact, we barely know each other.'

Beth rose from her seat, grimacing with pain. 'I think perhaps we should say good night, Horace. I am very tired, but it's been a delightful evening and I'm sure you want to be on your way.'

He jumped to his feet, scattering breadcrumbs on the polished floorboards. 'I must not overstay my welcome. Perhaps Miss Alice would see me out?'

Alice reached for the bell and rang it. 'I believe that's what servants are for, sir.'

He stared at her nonplussed and then a slow smile creased his face into a grimace. 'I think you are teasing me, Miss Alice.'

'I was never more serious.' Alice moved to her mother's side, helping her to rise. 'I'll see you upstairs, Mama.'

Horace rushed to the door and opened it just as Clara appeared, flushed and with her mobcap slightly askew. 'I'm sorry, sir. I come as quick as I could but I fell up them stairs. The treads are so worn, missis. I could have broke a leg.'

Alice struggled to control a bubble of hysterical laughter that welled up inside her. 'Clara, will you please fetch Mr Hubble's hat and coat and see him out? He's leaving now.'

'Yes, miss.' Clara limped off to fetch Horace's outdoor garments.

'I really did want to talk to you in private,' Horace said in a low voice. 'Could we not have a moment alone, Alice?'

Beth took her daughter by the arm. 'That would

be entirely improper, Horace. Anyway, I need Alice to help me up to my room, so, again, I'll bid you good night.'

Seeing Horace looking abashed and sheepish, Alice felt a sudden wave of pity for him. He was, after all, a pawn in her aunt's game of succession to the historic Hubble name. She hesitated with her mother leaning heavily on her arm. 'Horace,' she said firmly, 'there is not the slightest possibility that I would agree to marry you. I'm telling you now to save you the embarrassment of proposing to me.'

His lips trembled and his moustache quivered. 'But Jane will be so angry.'

'I'm afraid she will,' Alice said calmly.

'Is there no chance you'll change your mind?' Horace sent a pleading look to Beth. 'Can't you make her see that it would benefit us all, Mrs Radcliffe?'

Beth shook her head. 'I'm afraid that once Alice has made up her mind there is nothing anyone can do.'

'But it would solve all our problems,' Horace insisted. 'I have my eye on a pretty little house in Islington where we three could live comfortably. Jane has promised to purchase it for me if I marry and she will give me a generous allowance into the bargain. One day I hope to be promoted to head clerk in the counting house. You could do worse, Alice.'

'That sounds more like a business proposition than a proposal, Horace.'

'I've never asked anyone to marry me before.' He bowed his head, but the calculating glance he gave her belied his humble words.

Alice had almost fallen into the trap, but she rallied in time. 'Then I've saved you the humiliation of receiving a rebuff. Be grateful for that, Horace.' She looked round to see Clara standing in the doorway clutching his overcoat and hat. 'Mr Hubble is leaving now.'

Having settled her mother in bed Alice made her way slowly downstairs, intending to make the most of the meagre fire in the dining room, but as she reached the foot of the stairs she came face to face with her aunt. Jane did not look pleased. She took off her bonnet and cloak, tossing them at Clara. 'I want a word with you, Alice.' She marched into the dining room and Alice had little option other than to follow her, but she was puzzled. Surely Horace had kept his humiliation to himself?

'I suppose you thought I wouldn't learn of your deceit,' Jane said, turning on her in a fury.

'Deceit, Aunt? I don't know what you mean.'

'Don't put on that innocent face, miss. Horace came to the soup kitchen, quite distraught. He had tears in his eyes when he told me of your cruelty, Alice. I don't like seeing a man brought to such straits by an ungrateful minx of a girl.'

'He's lying,' Alice said calmly. 'I was just being honest with him.'

'Wicked girl.' Jane cast her eyes heavenward. 'You

148

refused his offer of marriage in the most cutting way imaginable. Have you no heart?'

'I have a heart, but it does not belong to Horace, and it never will. I was being frank when I told him that there was no hope for us, and that I wanted to save him the humiliation of being spurned if he ever plucked up the courage to propose.'

'And that is your final answer?'

'It is.'

'Then you have no place in my house. From this moment on I'm severing the connection we have through my marriage to your father's brother. You and your sickly mother are no longer welcome in my home. You will leave tomorrow. Is that clear?'

It came as a shock even though Alice had known what the outcome would be. 'Surely you'll give me time to find alternative accommodation, Aunt? My mother is a sick woman.'

'You've had plenty of warning, and you've had time to think things over. I want you out of my house by noon tomorrow.'

'Have pity, Aunt Jane. At least allow me a day or two in which to find somewhere to live. I know you're disappointed in me and for that I'm sorry, but I wouldn't want to ruin a man's life by marrying him for money and position. What would Uncle Robert say if he knew how you were treating his brother's wife and child?'

Jane recoiled as if Alice had slapped her face.

'How dare you bring my sainted husband's name into this?'

'He was your husband, but he was also my uncle. He was a good, kind man, just like my papa, and I know that he wouldn't want to see my mother suffer unnecessarily.'

'You have brought this on yourselves,' Jane said bitterly. 'I'm sure that Beth backed you in your determination to flout my wishes, but for my husband's sake I'll give you a few days in which to find alternative accommodation.' She swept out of the room, almost knocking down Clara, who was standing outside the door, pale-faced and aghast. 'Go back to the servants' quarters, you stupid child. I don't know why I keep you on.'

Clara turned to flee but caught her foot in Jane's cloak and fell to the floor, uttering a howl of pain and fright. Jane marched off, heading for the stairs, and it was Alice who raised the sobbing child to her feet. 'Are you hurt?'

'Me bruises have got bruises,' Clara sobbed. 'I hurt me knee again and I think I'm crippled.'

'Let me take the cloak and bonnet and lean on me.'

With the garments safely stowed in the cupboard, Alice helped Clara to negotiate the back stairs. Mrs Jugg was seated in her usual position by the range, sipping a cup of cocoa. She jumped to her feet when she saw Clara leaning heavily on Alice's arm.

'Lawks, miss. What's happened to the silly girl now? She has more falls than a tumbler in the circus.'

150

'I thought I was going to be struck down,' Clara said, sniffing. 'Such a to-do above stairs, Mrs Jugg. You never heard the like.'

Alice guided her to a chair. 'Sit down and rest, Clara. I don't imagine you've broken any bones.'

'I never knew a girl to make such a fuss about nothing.' Mrs Jugg sighed and shook her head. 'But I'll see to her, Miss Alice. There's no need for you to worry your head about us below stairs.'

'The missis is throwing them out,' Clara said, stifling a sob. 'It ain't fair.'

Mrs Jugg shot a sideways glance in Alice's direction. 'It's none of our business, Clara. We don't gossip about our betters.'

'It's all right, Mrs Jugg.' Alice laid a comforting hand on Clara's shoulder. 'Clara only spoke the truth. I have to find somewhere to live and find it very soon.'

'I'm sorry to hear that, miss. Have you anywhere in mind?'

Alice shook her head. 'I don't know where we'll go, but something will turn up.'

With virtually no free time it was impossible for Alice to look for cheap accommodation, and their lack of funds made it even more difficult. They would have to live on the meagre wages paid by the Dearborns, and even then Alice's earnings would barely cover the rent. She kept the truth from her mother as long as possible but Jane decided that they must be out of the house by New Year's Eve, and Beth had to be told. She took the news with little show of surprise.

'I knew we would end up in the workhouse,' she said sadly. 'I suppose it was inevitable.'

Alice went down on her knees at her mother's bedside. 'That won't happen, Mama. I'll find a way, I promise.'

Help came from the most surprising source. Alice had just returned from work on Monday evening, and once again she was certain that she was being followed, but every time she stopped and looked over her shoulder there was no sign of anyone. She arrived home shaken and anxious, and was in no mood to find Horace waiting for her in the entrance hall.

'Haven't you done enough harm?' she said angrily. 'Have you come to gloat?'

He sidled towards her, clutching his top hat in his bony fingers. 'I was about to leave, Alice. I've just been talking to your mama. She'll give you the news.'

'What news? What are you talking about? I've had a very trying day and I'm not in the mood for games.' It was true. Flora had been fractious because the snow was melting and Alice had not allowed her to go out into the square.

Horace did not seem able to look her in the eye. He stared down at his boots. 'I should not have run to Aunt Jane like that. I know what happened afterwards and I'm sorry.'

'So am I, but I knew what the outcome would be if I refused your offer, Horace. You need not feel that you're to blame.'

He looked up, gazing at her in surprise. 'You're very generous to say so, Alice. But what I came to tell you is that my aunt has invited me to live here, with her.'

'How kind of her.'

A faint smile flitted across his face. 'Precisely, but that leaves my room vacant in Half Moon Passage. It's off Aldersgate Street and not too far from here so you could still walk to your place of employment. It's not what you've been used to, but I thought it might suit you and your mama, if only as a temporary measure.'

'It might, but I'm not sure I can't afford the rent, at least not until I get my wages from the Dearborns.'

'The rent is paid until the end of January. It would give you a roof over your heads and time to look round for something more suitable.'

'Why would you do this for me when I've lost you the chance of a house of your own?'

'I'm not a monster, Alice. I know you were being coerced into a marriage of convenience and it was unfair. I'm not the marrying kind. I'm a confirmed bachelor and to be honest I want to keep it that way. If I have to put up with Aunt Jane's foibles it's a small price to pay for living in a house like this. I hope she'll forget about the continuation of the Hubble name in time.'

Alice reached out to shake his hand. 'I don't know what else to say other than thank you, Horace.'

The year did not start well for Alice and her mother. Jane would not allow them to remain in Queen Square until Alice's only day off, which was Sunday. 'We'll have to take Flora with us today, Mama,' Alice said as she packed her mother's valise. 'I tried to ask Mrs Dearborn for time off but she wouldn't hear of it, and we'll need to take a cab. I know it's an extravagance but you can't walk that far.'

Beth tugged at her wedding ring and it slipped easily off her thin finger. She held it out to Alice. 'I've nothing left of value other than this, but it should fetch enough to pay for a cab and keep us in necessities for a few days.'

Horrified, Alice shook her head. 'I can't allow you to pawn your ring, Mama.'

'I carry the memory of your father in my heart. I don't need a band of gold to remind me of him. Take it, Alice. We can't exist on your meagre wages.'

Alice frowned but she took the ring and slipped it into her pocket. They would have barely enough to live on as it was. Much as she loved Flora and hated the thought of leaving her to the mercy of her uncaring adoptive mother, she knew she would have to find a position that paid better if they were to survive.

'I'll take it to the pawnshop, Mama, but I'll buy it back as soon as I'm able.'

'It's not important, my darling. We're together and that's all that matters. When I'm well again I'll find work, even if it's taking in sewing. I'm good with my needle.'

'Just concentrate on getting better. I'll look after you, Mama.' Alice put on her bonnet and tied the ribbons under her chin. 'I won't be long.' She reached for her mantle and shrugged it on as she hurried from the room. Suddenly the cold unfriendly house seemed more like home, and it felt as though they were plunging into a bottomless abyss. Alice braced her shoulders. She was young and strong and would find a way out of the difficulties that had been thrust upon them. Opening the front door she stepped outside in the bitter cold of a January day. Her first stop was the pawnbroker in Guildford Street, where she was forced to accept less than she had expected. She left with money in her purse, but it was not sufficient to keep them for more than a few days. As she made her way to Russell Square she tried to convince herself that all would be well, and that this was a new beginning and not a sad defeat.

To make matters worse, Mrs Upton greeted her with a lecture on the evils of unpunctuality, and a stern warning that if she was late again it would be brought to Mrs Dearborn's notice. Alice apologised humbly and hurried upstairs to the nursery where Flora was pacing the floor like a caged tiger.

'Where were you, Alice? I thought you weren't coming.'

'I'm sorry I'm late, Flora, but I had an errand to run.'

Flora's lips formed a sulky *moue*. 'The snow is melting and my snowman is disappearing so fast that soon there'll be nothing left but a puddle.'

'Well, I've got a surprise for you today,' Alice said with an attempt at cheeriness. 'We're going out on the little adventure.'

Flora's pout relaxed into a broad grin. 'Really? Where are we going?'

'You'll see when we get there,' Alice said mysteriously. Never having been to Half Moon Passage she was not in a position to describe it to Flora, but the name sounded romantic and exciting.

Needless to say, the reality was far different. As the hackney carriage made its slow progress through the crowded city streets of West Smithfield Alice realised that she had been deluding herself. After their experiences in Blossom Street she should have known better, but as always she lived in hope, though disappointment and disillusion were never far behind.

The cab drew to a halt in Aldersgate Street and Alice climbed out first. 'This isn't Half Moon Passage.'

The cabbie pointed his whip at a narrow opening between a pub and a taxidermist's shop. 'Can't drive down there, miss. It's too narrow.' He leaned down from the box, holding out his hand. 'That'll be one shilling, if you please.'

She paid him although it felt like an exorbitant amount to pay for a relatively short journey, but as she helped her mother from the cab she realised just how frail and delicate she had become.

Flora leaped to the ground, her golden curls bobbing as her bonnet slipped to the back of her head. 'What an exciting place,' she breathed, staring wide-eyed at the stuffed fox in the taxidermist's window. 'Is it real? Will it bite?'

'Not now,' Alice said, laughing. 'His biting days are well and truly over.'

Beth shuddered. 'Poor thing, to come to such an undignified end, and I can't bear to look at the poor little pussycat. Who would want a thing like that in their parlour?'

'The previous owner, maybe?' Alice suggested, picking up the cases. 'Although it's not something I would choose to have. Come along, Flora. This way.'

Half Moon Passage was narrow and dingy, lined on both sides with a hotchpotch of workmen's cottages, workshops and run-down lodging houses. The cobblestones were slippery with slush and ankle-deep in straw and all manner of detritus that had been carelessly tossed away or had blown in from Aldersgate Street. It appeared that none of the residents possessed a broom, and if they did they had no intention of putting it to good use. Alice consulted the slip of paper that Horace had given her, hoping desperately that the shabby four-storey building with cracked stucco and blistered paintwork was not their actual destination, but there was only one way to find out. She sent Flora up the steps to knock on the door and they waited. Beth was leaning tiredly against Alice while Flora danced up and down with excitement.

'It's like Blossom Street,' she said eagerly. 'Do you think your room will be in the cellar with lots of strange people?'

'I hope not,' Alice said with feeling. 'I'm sure that Horace wouldn't send us anywhere that was unsuitable.'

Beth sighed. 'I just need to sit down, dear.'

Alice was going to urge Flora to knock again when the door opened a crack and a beady eye glared at them.

'Who's there? I don't take kids in.'

'Mr Hubble sent us,' Alice said hastily. 'He said we can have his room until the end of the month.'

The door opened a fraction wider. 'Did he now? How do I know that you're telling the truth?'

Alice gave the slip of paper written in Horace's neat copperplate to Flora. 'Pass this to the lady, if you please.'

After the briefest scrutiny, the woman opened the door and stood aside. 'I suppose you'd better come in. Wipe your feet on the mat.'

It was hardly the warmest welcome in the world and Alice stepped inside with a feeling of foreboding. The narrow entrance hall smelled of carbolic and boiled cabbage, but at least it was spotlessly clean.

The floorboards had been scrubbed until they gleamed palely in the dim light and the landlady's gaze followed their steps as if waiting to pounce on the first sign of a muddy footprint.

'Follow me.' She picked up her black serge skirts and headed up the twisting staircase with surprising agility for someone of advancing years.

'Are you all right, Mama?' Alice asked anxiously. 'Can you manage the stairs?'

'She'll sleep in the coal hole if she can't.' The landlady's voice floated down from the first landing. 'Hurry up. I haven't got all day.'

'Lean on me, Mrs Radcliffe,' Flora said eagerly. 'I'm much stronger than I look.'

'Thank you, dear.' Beth accepted her offer with a smile. 'I'm fine, Alice. Flora is looking after me.'

By the time they reached the top floor Alice felt as if her arms were being dragged from their sockets by the weight of the two cases. It seemed unlikely that Horace would have rented an attic room, and she was beginning to think that they were being duped. 'Are you sure this was Mr Hubble's room, Mrs ... I'm afraid I didn't catch your name.'

'Mrs Leech. You didn't catch it because I didn't toss it to you. I'm choosy as to who I take into my establishment. This is a respectable house. No hanky-panky permitted.' She unlocked a door at the end of a dark passage. 'This is yours. Take it or leave it.'

# Chapter Nine

One look inside the room was enough to convince Alice that Mrs Leech was trying to cheat them. Horace, for all his shortcomings, seemed to be a fastidious man. She could not imagine him living in a cold, draughty attic with only a little roof window for light, and a fireplace so small that even when lit would barely relieve the chill.

'Mr Hubble's room was paid for until the end of January,' she said firmly. 'This can't be his.'

'How d'you know? You ain't been here afore so you ain't in a position to argue. If you don't want it there's plenty who do.'

A cry from Flora made Alice turn to see her mother collapse to her knees as she reached the top of the stairs. 'All right,' she said hastily. 'We'll take it, but as it's obviously a cheaper room I expect you to supply coal and kindling free of charge.'

'Just to show that I'm a fair woman I'll allow you a sample today, but after that you'll pay like the rest of my tenants.'

Alice did not stop to argue. She hurried to help Flora, who was struggling to get Beth to her feet. 'Come along, Mama. Almost there.'

Mrs Leech sidled past them, eyeing Beth with pursed lips. 'She don't look too good to me. If she's sick she'll have to go to hospital. St Bart's is just round the corner.'

'I'm not ill,' Beth said breathlessly.

'Ignore her.' Alice slipped her arm around her mother's waist. 'She's undoubtedly a crook, but at least we've got a roof over our heads and time to look around for something better.'

Beth bowed her head. 'I'm so sorry, darling girl. I'm holding you back, I know it.'

'Don't say that, Mrs Radcliffe.' Flora patted her on the shoulder. 'You're a nice lady. We'll take care of you.'

Between them Alice and Flora managed to get Beth into the room and onto the bed. Alice unlaced her mother's boots and pulled them off, covering her with one of the moth-eaten blankets that lay folded on the flock-filled mattress. 'At least we're used to Spartan living,' she said with a wry smile. 'A stay with Aunt Jane has taught us to be resilient.'

Beth managed a weary smile. 'It's not so bad.'

'There's not much furniture,' Flora said, moving

away to explore the dark corners beneath the sloping ceiling. 'I can see the sky in the gaps between the roof slates. I think it's snowing again.'

'I'll get a fire going and I'll see if Mrs Leech will let us have some more blankets.' Alice tried to sound positive. 'And we need candles and matches too. I'm going downstairs to face the Gorgon.'

'What's a Gorgon?' Flora asked innocently. 'Can I come, too? I've never seen one of those.'

'I think we should add Greek mythology to our curriculum,' Alice said, chuckling. 'The Gorgon was a mythical monster, Flora. I'm afraid I was being rather unkind about Mrs Leech, who is probably very nice when you get to know her.'

'I doubt that very much.' Beth lay back against the pillows with a sigh.

'I'll go downstairs and see what I can do.' Alice laid the second blanket over her mother, but it was impossible to ignore the smell of stale tobacco that clung to the material and she wrinkled her nose in distaste. 'I'd be grateful if you'd stay and keep my mother company, Flora. Mrs Leech obviously dislikes children so we don't want to get on the wrong side of her.' She hurried from the room without waiting for an answer.

Mrs Leech's parlour was warm to the point of stuffiness. With heavy velvet curtains half drawn and dark mahogany furniture that was too large for the size of the room, the atmosphere was claustrophobic and oppressive. Although partially illuminated by half a dozen expensive wax candles, Alice found it hard to accustom her eyes to the gloom, but she could see that every available surface was covered in bric-a-brac of one sort or another, mostly the type of fairings purchased from fairground stalls.

'I ain't your servant,' Mrs Leech said tersely when Alice enquired about the coal and kindling. 'If you want it you get the cellar key from me and you go down and fetch it yourself. One scuttle a day and a bundle of kindling will cost you threepence a week.'

'But that's too dear.'

'Take it or leave it.'

This seemed to be the answer to every question. Alice tried again. 'The attic room is very cold. Might we have some more blankets, please?'

'That'll be a penny a week for each extra piece of bedding.'

Alice opened her mouth to protest and thought better of it. 'If you say so. Where do I find them?'

Mrs Leech rose from her chair by the roaring fire and opened a wall cupboard from which she produced a large iron key. 'The cellar,' she said succinctly. 'I'll fetch the blankets and you can collect them on your way upstairs.' She reached in again and produced a book of Vestas. 'That'll be an extra farthing, and meals is extra.'

'But I assumed that was included in the rent.'

'I ain't a charity, miss. You pay for extras and food is definitely an extra.'

'I think we'll manage on our own.'

Alice managed to get a fire going and even if it did not provide much warmth it made the room seem a little more cheerful. Exhausted by her efforts, Beth was soon asleep and although Alice was reluctant to leave her mother she had to get Flora home before they were missed. She had hoped to return to Russell Square in time for luncheon, but everything had taken much longer than she had expected and now they would have to hurry.

As Flora had observed, it was snowing again and walking any distance was out of the question. Simply keeping their balance proved a challenge and the few hansom cabs and hackney carriages they saw passed them by without stopping. Alice had planned to walk in order to save money, but she was unfamiliar with this part of the city and soon they were lost. The swirling, whirling snowstorm was disorientating in itself, and only the foolhardy or those on an urgent mission were outdoors in such weather. People hurried by with their heads down and were reluctant to stop when Alice tried to ask the way.

'I'm afraid we're lost, Flora. I don't know which way to go.'

Flora grabbed her arm. 'I've been here before. My papa took me to his office in the city, and I think I recognise this street.'

'Do you remember which building it was? Perhaps we could shelter there until the snow eases off?'

'It's that one on the opposite side of the street. I'm sure of it because there was a green door.' She let go of Alice's hand and ran across the street, narrowly escaping being mown down by a brewer's dray. The driver shouted and swore, brandishing the horsewhip, but continued on his way. Alice had to wait until it was safe to cross and by this time Flora had disappeared into the building. When she caught up with her she found Flora in conversation with the desk clerk, chatting away as if she had known him all her life.

'This is Beasley,' Flora said eagerly. 'He remembers me from the last time I came to Papa's workplace.'

Beasley smiled indulgently. 'Indeed I do, Miss Flora. Although I don't know what your pa will say when he knows you've ventured out in this bad weather.'

'We don't need to trouble Mr Dearborn,' Alice said hastily. 'We were a bit lost, and I just need some directions to Russell Square and then we'll be on our way.'

'Uncle Rory.' Flora's cry of delight made Alice turn her head and to her dismay she saw Rory walking towards them.

'Floss, my love, this is a surprise.' Rory lifted her up and swung her round before setting her down on the marble-tiled floor. He glanced at Alice, eyebrows raised. 'This is hardly the weather for a day out, Miss Radcliffe.'

'I know, sir. We were on our way home, but I'm unfamiliar with the City streets and we lost our way.'

'I remembered where the office was situated,' Flora said, puffing out her chest. 'Papa brought me here when I was very young.'

Rory's lips twitched but he nodded in agreement. 'Well done, Floss.' He turned to the clerk with a persuasive smile. 'Beasley, would you arrange for some hot chocolate and a pot of tea to be sent to my office?'

'Certainly, sir.' Beasley lifted the hatch and scurried off towards a door marked 'Private'.

'We really should be getting back to Russell Square,' Alice said anxiously.

'You both look chilled to the bone.' Rory took Flora by the hand. 'I'll send for a cab to take you home, but first I suggest you come to my office and get warm; we don't want young Flora to take a chill. Come along, Miss Radcliffe. I'm afraid I won't take no for an answer.'

Half an hour later, seated round a roaring fire with a cup of tea clutched in both hands, Alice was just beginning to get the feeling back in her feet and her toes were tingling painfully. She had given Rory a brief explanation as to how she and Flora came to be lost in a snowstorm, but she had omitted the real reason why she had been compelled to leave her aunt's house.

'So you see,' she concluded, 'I had no choice other than to take the morning off to make sure that my mother was settled comfortably in our new lodgings.'

'It's not comfortable,' Flora said through a mouthful of cake, which Beasley had thoughtfully provided. 'It's an attic at the top of a house with a Gorgon of a landlady.'

'A Gorgon.' Rory nodded wisely. 'Your knowledge is expanding daily, Floss.'

She scowled at him. 'I don't know what that means, but Alice said she's one of those things. We're going to read about them when we get home.'

'I'm not sure if I'll still have a job,' Alice said, sighing. 'If Mrs Dearborn finds out where we've been I'll probably be dismissed without a character, and I suppose it will serve me right. I shouldn't have involved Flora, especially under the circumstances.'

'What circumstances?' Flora demanded curiously. 'Why do you grown-ups talk in riddles?'

Rory ruffled her damp curls, smiling. 'Never you mind, Floss. This is between Miss Radcliffe and me, so enjoy your cake and leave us to worry about things that don't concern you.'

'It's nice cake,' Flora conceded, eyeing the last slice. 'May I?'

'You may, but don't make yourself sick.' Rory turned to Alice, giving her a searching look. 'Wouldn't it have been better to have remained with your aunt in Queen Square, at least until the weather improved?'

'She imposed conditions that I couldn't accept,' Alice said evasively. 'But we will manage quite well.'

Rory sat back in his chair, eyeing her thoughtfully. 'Forgive me, but I doubt if my sister-in-law is over-generous when it comes to paying a living wage.'

'You must see that I'm in an awkward position. I can't afford to lose my job and I'd find it virtually impossible to find work elsewhere.'

He frowned thoughtfully. 'I seem to recall that you're a talented artist.'

'I can draw a little.'

'She's very good at it,' Flora said quickly. 'You could give her some work, Uncle Rory. You and Papa print all sorts of things with pretty pictures on them.'

'Perhaps you have something there, Floss.' Rory pushed his chair back and stood up. 'Would you like to see the office where our draughtsmen work, Alice? We have a printing works in Clerkenwell, but I want my brother to invest in chromolithography, which is a new system that will print in colour. We would take the lead in producing greetings cards and possibly Christmas cards, which I believe will become extremely popular, particularly if postage should become more affordable.'

Alice rose to her feet. 'I'd love to, but I really ought to get Flora home.'

'Don't worry about that.' He held his hand out to Flora. 'You'd like to look round the offices, wouldn't you, Floss? And then we'll see if your papa is free. With him on your side there'll be no question of Miss Radcliffe losing her job.'

Alice was not so sure, but Rory's enthusiasm was infectious. He took Flora by the hand and led the way to a room at the far end of a long corridor. Alice had been expecting to see a hive of activity, but it came as a surprise to find that there were only three people, working in total silence. 'We have visitors, gentlemen,' Rory announced grandly. 'Miss Flora Dearborn has asked if she might see you hard at work.'

Heads popped up above drawing boards as they stared at Flora and Alice, blinking like sleepy owls. Flora made her way between the desks, stopping at the side of the youngest of three, a youth who was on the green side of twenty. 'I remember you,' she said cheerfully. 'You're George.'

He nodded and his thin cheeks flushed scarlet. 'Yes, miss.'

She craned her neck to study his work. 'What are you doing?'

'He's busy, Floss. You can watch if George doesn't object, but don't hold up production.' Rory guided Alice to the desk of an older man. 'Mr Wall is our most senior designer. He is responsible for our best-selling line in playing cards.'

Rawlins Wall peered at Alice over the top of his spectacles, his pale eyes red-rimmed and watery. 'Good morning, miss.'

'Good morning, Mr Wall.' Alice gazed over his

shoulder at the design for a playing card. 'How lovely.'

He shot her a suspicious glance. 'I wouldn't exactly describe it as such.'

'Now, now, Rawlins,' Rory said mildly. 'Miss Radcliffe meant it as a compliment.'

'Yes, indeed I did.' Alice moved away quickly, sensing that she was an unwelcome intruder as far as Mr Wall was concerned.

The young man at the far desk was much more approachable. He leaped to his feet and bowed from the waist. 'How d'you do, Miss Radcliffe? It's a pleasure to meet you.'

'This bold fellow is Martin Collis.' Rory leaned over the drawing board. 'Not quite there yet, I see.'

Unabashed, Martin grinned broadly. 'It will be, sir. Just give me a bit more time. I'd be happy to show the lady how fast I can work.'

'I'm sure you would, but Miss Radcliffe is an accomplished artist in her own right.'

'Next thing we know we'll have women working with us,' Martin said, winking at Alice.

'It might come sooner than you think.' Rory made a move towards the door. 'We'll leave you to get on with your work, gentlemen.'

'Goodbye,' Flora said, blowing kisses to each one in turn. 'I'll come and see you again soon.' She danced on ahead, barging into the corridor and almost colliding with her father. 'Papa. I've come to give you a surprise.'

'Flora, my dear. I count myself very surprised indeed.' Frederick Dearborn's smile of welcome faded when he saw Alice. 'What's the meaning of this, Miss Radcliffe? Why have you brought my daughter out on a day like this?'

Alice opened her mouth to respond but Rory stepped in first. 'I'm afraid I'm to blame, Freddie. It was I who suggested it. I thought it would do Flora good to see how her papa made his living.'

Frederick did not look convinced. 'This is not the sort of weather for an outing. I would have thought you might have considered that before you embarked on such a trip, Miss Radcliffe.'

Once again Alice was prevented from answering. Rory slapped his brother on the back. 'A little adventure is good for the spirit, Freddie, and your daughter has come to no harm. I'll see them safely home.'

'Very well,' Frederick said grudgingly. 'But in future I expect you to check with me or my wife before you agree to any of my brother's hare-brained schemes. Do you understand, Miss Radcliffe?'

'Yes, sir.'

'Take them home by all means, Rory, but I want a word with you when you return.' Frederick's grim expression softened as he turned to Flora. 'It's time to go now, but I'll see you this evening.' He retreated into his office and closed the door.

Flora slipped her hand into Alice's. 'I'm sorry he was cross with you. I'll tell him it was my fault.'

'You'll do no such thing,' Alice said firmly. 'This

was entirely my own doing, and if you are blamed in any way I'll make sure that your parents know the truth.'

'There's no need for that,' Rory said. 'There'll be no repercussions, I promise.'

To Alice's surprise no one seemed to have noticed their absence, not even Nettie, who brought their luncheon to them full of apologies for being late. 'We're so busy below stairs,' she said breathlessly as she placed the tray on the table in the nursery. 'You never saw so much clearing up as we've had to do after all them guests. The rooms have had to be cleaned and the bedding changed, the chamber pots emptied and the washbasins scoured out. I've had to help the daily women with everything, so you might not get supper until bedtime. I'm run off me feet.'

Flora grabbed a spoon and began shovelling the soup into her mouth, receiving a warning look from Alice. 'Where are your manners, Miss Flora? And I think you should say thank you to Nettie. She's obviously had a very trying morning.'

Nettie's mouth gaped and her eyes widened. 'I'm just doing me job, miss, but ta all the same.' She whisked out of the room, leaving the door to swing shut of its own accord.

Alice took her place at the table. 'A kind word every now and then works wonders, Flora. Servants deserve to be treated like human beings. '

Flora broke a piece off a bread roll and stuffed

it in her mouth. 'I don't think Mama would agree with you.'

Alice smiled and said nothing. The soup smelled delicious and she was very hungry, but every mouthful made her feel guilty. She wished now that she had agreed to pay Mrs Leech for providing her mother with a midday meal. Outside the snow was still falling and that made her even more anxious. Walking home would prove a challenge.

When they had eaten their fill she returned their supper tray to the kitchen in order to save Nettie extra work, and was shocked and surprised to see the inordinate amount of food left over from the Christmas celebrations. Cook looked pale and tired, and was obviously at her wits' end.

'I suggested that we give it to the poor,' she said, brushing a stray lock of grey hair back from her forehead. 'But the mistress refused to consider it. "Cook," she says, "if we start that we will have all the beggars and miscreants in London coming to the door demanding to be fed."' She glanced round at the half-eaten pies and pastries. 'We won't be able to eat this up in a month of Sundays, and it will go off in a day or two.'

Alice thought of the soup kitchen where her aunt spent much of her time, no doubt lording it over the other volunteers, but it was a worthy cause. 'I could take some off your hands, Cook. I know a place where the poor and needy go to be fed. I'm sure they would be more than grateful.'

'Nettie.' Cook raised her voice to a shout. 'Fetch two baskets. Fill them with leftovers for Miss Radcliffe to take to them as is in need.'

Laden with food, some of which she intended to take home to her mother, Alice stepped outside into the bitter cold. The snow had ceased, and the temperature had dropped below freezing making each step more hazardous than the last. She reached the corner of the square without mishap, but she had to stop for a moment to catch her breath. The icy air stabbed at her lungs and made her eyes water, but it was not too far to the soup kitchen and she started off again, slipping and sliding in her efforts to keep from falling. By the time she reached her destination she was breathless and close to exhaustion. A gust of warm air greeted her as she entered the building and she found herself in the midst of a huddle of ragged bodies. Old and young alike had come in out of the cold, their faces ashen beneath the grime, and their skeletal appearance bearing witness to their desperate state. The children were too close to starvation to make a sound and too cold to cry, but almost immediately Alice was surrounded by those who had the strength to beg for food. Clutching hands delved into the baskets and she was in danger of being overwhelmed.

'Stop that at once.' A familiar figure cut a swathe through the crowd and for the first time Alice was glad to see Horace.

'I – I've brought food from the Dearborns'

kitchen.' Her lips were numb and it was difficult to form the words.

'A charitable act, Cousin.' Horace relieved her of the baskets. 'Come through to the kitchen. Make way there.' He marched towards the back of the room and the crowd parted to allow them to pass, but even as they bowed their heads Alice caught a glimpse of desperation etched on their faces by poverty and near starvation. She hurried after Horace and was glad when they reached the relative calm of the kitchen, although her relief was short-lived when she saw her aunt standing over a young volunteer who was stirring a large pot of soup on the range. Jane turned her head and her expression froze when she saw Alice.

'What do you want? I thought you'd abandoned us.'

'You sent us packing,' Alice retorted angrily. 'And you, Horace Hubble, you let me take my sick mother to that dreadful place with a devil woman in charge. You should be ashamed of yourself.'

'I don't know what you mean.' Horace stared at her, seeming genuinely shocked and astonished. 'My room was tolerable, if not luxurious.'

'We've been given the attic, which is freezing and barely furnished. She's charging extra for every single thing.'

'What do you expect?' Jane demanded, curling her lip. 'The woman has to make a living.'

'She is a bit penny-pinching,' Horace admitted

slowly. 'But the remedy is in your hands, Cousin. My offer of marriage still stands.'

'More fool you.' Jane turned on the woman who had stopped stirring the pot to listen avidly to their conversation. 'Get on with your work and mind your own business.'

The young woman's cheeks flamed scarlet and she bent her head over the pan, stirring the contents with a wooden spoon.

'Thank you, Horace, but the answer remains the same.' Alice made for the door, pausing for a moment with her hand on the latch. 'I'll collect the baskets tomorrow.'

'You've made your choice,' Jane said bitterly. 'Don't say I didn't give you every opportunity to better yourself, Alice. There are plenty of young women who would jump at the chance of marrying a man like Horace.'

The woman stirring the pot snorted, quickly turning it into a sneeze. Alice chose to ignore her aunt's caustic tongue and let herself out of a side door, which led into the street. She set off, walking as briskly as possible on the treacherous surface, and it was only when she was nearing her destination that she realised she had not saved any of the food for her mother. It was too late to find any of the vendors who plied the streets during the day, and she had little choice other than to try one of the taverns in Long Lane.

Inside the atmosphere was warm and fuggy, and

thick with tobacco smoke and the strong smell of ale and spirits. There were less pleasant odours, but no worse than those that had assailed her nostrils in the soup kitchen. After a little persuasion the landlord agreed to part with a jug of broth for twopence, plus a penny deposit on the enamel pitcher. It was overpriced watery soup, but at least it was hot, and if she hurried she could get it home to Half Moon Passage before it cooled completely.

As she was about to leave the taproom her attention was drawn to a small group of men and a couple of women who were seated in the corner. Through a haze of pipe smoke she realised that they were watching her, and a shiver ran down her spine. She left the pub, gasping as the cold air filled her lungs, and she set off as fast as she could go without spilling the soup. A sound like that of footsteps muffled by the packed snow made her stop and turn her head, but there was no one there. She hurried on.

# Chapter Ten

'Where have you been, Alice?' Beth demanded querulously. 'I thought something terrible must have befallen you.' She raised herself on her elbow, peering up at her daughter in the dim light of a single candle.

Alice placed the jug on the rickety table beneath the eaves. The fire had gone out long ago, judging by the chill in the room, and she could see starlight through the gap in the roof tiles.

'I'm sorry, Mama, but I had to take Flora home. I won't get paid if I don't do my job properly.'

'I know, but this place is awful. We were better off living with Jane.'

Alice moved to the bed and helped her mother to a sitting position. Having plumped up the pillows she reached for Beth's shawl and wrapped it around her shoulders. 'I've brought you some hot soup, but I'll have to go downstairs and ask for a bowl and some cutlery. Goodness knows how much the old dragon will charge for that.'

'I'm a burden to you, Alice. I wish I could be of more use.'

'Don't talk like that, Mama. We'll look after each other and this is only temporary. You'll feel better with some hot food inside you.' She left the room without waiting for a response. It was obvious that her mother's spirits were low, and it was little wonder considering the circumstances.

Alice went to find Mrs Leech, prepared to do battle, but there was no answer when she knocked on the parlour door, and no sound from within. She made her way below stairs to the basement kitchen and that too was deserted. Feeling like a thief, but driven by desperation, she helped herself to the items of crockery they might need and some cutlery. She found a crust of bread in the pantry and she spread it liberally with butter. Tomorrow she would pay the price that Mrs Leech would no doubt demand, but tonight her mother would have something nourishing to eat.

Despite all her attempts to make the attic room more comfortable Alice could not provide the warmth and good food that her mother needed to make a full recovery. Beth grew weaker by the day and, left alone for many hours in the dismal room, she became tearful and depressed. She was in constant pain and although she attempted to put a brave face on her suffering it was obvious that she could not survive in such straitened circumstances. By the end of the second week Alice knew that she must take drastic steps or her mother would become seriously ill, and might not recover. She had spent her last penny on coal and kindling, and she had already used up most of her weekly wage. Matters were desperate.

It was Sunday and Mrs Dearborn had given her the afternoon off. Flora was sulking at the prospect of spending time in the drawing room where her mother was entertaining her friends, but Alice was not in a position to argue with her employer, and she had an urgent personal matter to settle before she could return to Half Moon Passage. She hoped that she would catch her aunt between church services and she made her way to Queen Square.

Clara's face brightened when she opened the door and saw Alice standing on the step. 'Have you come home, miss?'

'I need to speak to my aunt. Will you ask her if she'll see me, please, Clara?'

'It ain't been the same since you upped and left, miss.' Clara stood aside to allow Alice into the entrance hall. It was chilly, as always, but compared to the intense cold in the attic room the temperature in her aunt's house seemed almost balmy. Alice waited while Clara scuttled off to announce her arrival. She reappeared moments later. 'She'll see you, miss.'

Alice entered the drawing room, moving one foot in front of the other like an automaton. She was about to take a step that would change the course of her life, but she had no choice if she were to save her mother from quietly fading away.

'So you've come grovelling,' Jane said with a triumphant smile. 'I didn't think you'd last very long in the real world.'

The temptation to walk away was almost too great, but Alice forced herself to remain calm. 'I've been thinking things over, Aunt. I'm ready to make a compromise.'

'Are you indeed?' Jane curled her lip. 'And what makes you think that you're in a position to dictate terms to me, young lady?'

Alice regarded her steadily. 'I know that you are desperate for an heir to the Hubble name. You've obviously tried to find a wife for Horace and failed.'

'You're impertinent, Alice. Horace is an eligible bachelor.'

'Then why did you want him to marry me?'

Jane's hand flew to the gold cross that she always wore. 'You are my dear Robert's niece. If you and Horace produce an heir to the Hubble name your child will be a blood relation to my late husband. Do you understand what I'm saying?'

Alice nodded slowly. 'I think so, Aunt.'

'I was unable to bear children, but your progeny will be part Radcliffe and part Hubble; a combination of which I could be proud.'

'I understand what you're saying, and I'm prepared to accept Horace's offer, but only if you will agree to give my mother a home and make her feel welcome. She is not a well woman and she needs medical attention, which you will pay for because we haven't a penny piece between us.'

'Is that your final word?'

'It is. I can't allow my mother to die of want.'

Jane rose to her feet and paced the floor, clasping her hands tightly behind her back. She came to a sudden halt. 'This doesn't alter the fact that I dislike you and your mother, but I will have a nephew of whom I can be proud. You are just a means to an end and that sickly mother of yours is just a cipher, but if she is part of the bargain, so be it. She can live here with me until you and Horace are married, when you will have your own home and can resume responsibility for her.'

'Thank you, Aunt.'

'Don't thank me. I'm doing this out of Christian duty and because you drive a hard bargain, but you will remain where you are until the wedding. I cannot have you and Horace living under the same roof. It wouldn't be proper.'

'Very well. I agree, but only if I can be certain that my mama is well cared for and gets the medical attention she needs.'

'You have my word on that. Ring the bell for Snippet. She will fetch Horace and we'll settle this now.'

Alice's feet felt like lead and each step towards the bell pull was like wading through water, but she knew what she must do. She rang the bell.

Horace stared from one to the other, his moustache drooping and his lips quivered as he took in the news. 'I – I don't know what to say,' he stammered.

'Get down on one knee, you fool,' Jane said crossly. 'Ask you girl to marry you.'

'But she's already refused me twice, Cousin.'

'Do I have to do it for you?'

He held up his hand. 'No, I can do this myself.' He moved closer to Alice, going down on one knee, which creaked ominously as it took his weight. He grimaced with pain and took a deep breath. 'Miss Radcliffe, would you do me the honour of becoming my wife?'

His gaze was fixed at a point somewhere above her right shoulder and his hand, as he took hers, felt cold and clammy. The thought of spending the rest of her life with such a feeble creature, let alone the physical side of marriage, of which she had only the very haziest knowledge, was so appalling that she was momentarily speechless. Then she remembered the dismal attic room and Mrs Leech, who was forever holding out her hand demanding money. She thought of her mother, rapidly fading away like the shadows of night at sunrise.

'Well, speak up, girl,' Jane said impatiently. 'Give him an answer.'

Alice turned her head, fixing her aunt with a hard stare. 'You will allow me to bring Mama here today, won't you?'

'I'll keep my part of the bargain if you'll keep yours. Are you going to accept his offer?'

'I'm not sure I agree with being part of a bargain.' Horace shifted uncomfortably, changing his weight to his other leg as he kneeled before Alice. 'This is between me and Alice, Cousin Jane.'

'If you believe that you're more of a fool than I took you for.' Jane waved her hand dismissively. 'Get it over with, girl.'

Alice licked her dry lips and swallowed hard. 'Yes, Horace. I will marry you.'

He clambered to his feet and opened his arms as if to embrace her, but she backed away. 'This is a business arrangement, Horace. I don't pretend to love you, but I will do my best to be a good wife.'

'I suppose it's all I deserve,' he said humbly. 'I know I'm not a great catch, Alice. I've never been one for the ladies, but—'

'Leave it at that, Horace,' Jane said dismissively. 'Alice has your measure, and you know what is required of you. Now I suggest you accompany her to your former lodgings and bring my ailing sister-in-law home.'

'She will need a fire in her room,' Alice said firmly. 'I can brave the cold, but poor Mama is suffering terribly.'

'I wouldn't mind a fire in my room too,' Horace

ventured nervously. 'It is rather chilly in this house, Cousin.'

'I can see that you'll bankrupt me if you go on like this.' Jane looked from one to the other, pursing her lips. 'However, it is a small price to pay for the continuation of the Hubble name. You may light fires as you wish, but you will purchase the coal, Horace. You're not paying rent for your room therefore you can afford luxuries for yourself, and your fiancée's mother.' She sailed out of the room with a triumphant twitch of her shoulders, head held high.

Alice tugged the bell pull. 'I'll ask Clara to light the fires and then I'll go to Half Moon Passage to fetch my mother.' She hesitated, eyeing Horace warily. 'Could you lend me the money for a cab? I've just paid the rent, which took most of my weekly wage.'

'I'll come with you, my dear.'

The mere thought of sharing a cab with Horace made her shudder. She managed a sickly smile. 'No, it's all right. I can manage on my own.' She could see that he was about to argue and she laid a tentative hand on his sleeve. 'It might be best if you stay here to make sure that the fires are lit. Clara does her best, but the poor child lives in terror of doing something wrong and being sent to the workhouse.'

He nodded. 'If you're certain.' A slow smile caused his moustache to twitch, moving as if it had a life of its own. 'Tomorrow I'll buy you an engagement ring.' He put his hand in his pocket and took out some coins, placing them in her outstretched hand.

'Jane promised to buy me the pretty little house I've had my eye on when I married. We can visit it together, my dear.'

Alice tucked the money into her reticule. 'I'll be off now, Horace. Please see that my mother's room is ready for her.' She hesitated. 'Will you make sure that she gets everything she needs? I wouldn't ask but I won't be here very much.'

He stared at her, clearly puzzled. 'I don't understand. Surely you'll give up your job now that we're engaged? I cannot have my future wife working as a servant.'

'Horace,' she said patiently, 'I don't think you quite understand the situation. My aunt is only willing to look after Mama because I've agreed to marry you. I have to remain in the lodging house, and I must continue to earn my own living until we're married.'

He grabbed her by the hand. 'Then we should get a special licence and be married as soon as possible.'

'Let's not be too hasty.' Alice drew away from him, suppressing a shudder. 'We don't want to upset Aunt Jane, so I suggest you do as I ask. I'm quite capable of looking after myself, but I need to know that Mama is well cared for. You will do that one thing for me, won't you?'

'To the best of my ability, but we do not want to wait too long before we marry. A house of my own, I mean a house of our own, is a very tempting thought.'

She eyed him suspiciously. Horace Hubble was

not as stupid as he seemed to be on first acquaintance. His ambition to own a property was obviously the force that drove him to agree to a marriage of convenience. Aunt Jane, she thought, was like a puppeteer, manipulating them both with a marked degree of skill in order to get what she wanted.

Alice moved towards the door just as it opened to admit Clara. 'Are you leaving already, miss?'

'I'm going to fetch my mother, Clara. I want you to light a fire in her room and make sure the bedding is properly aired.'

'You're coming home, miss?' Clara's cheeks flushed bright pink and her eyes shone. 'I'll tell Cook.'

'I'll be visiting more often, but I won't be living here. Mr Hubble will see that you have everything you need.' Alice turned to Horace with an enquiring look. 'You will, won't you?'

'Yes,' he said grudgingly. 'I suppose so. I want a fire in my room also, girl.'

'I have to go now, but I'll be back soon.' Alice stepped out into the hallway. 'What have I done?' she murmured as she made her way to the front entrance. She let herself out of the house and started walking, having decided to keep the cab fare in order to pay Mrs Leech for any further extras she might charge.

At first Beth complained that she was unhappy with the arrangement that left Alice to the mercies of an avaricious landlady, but as her health improved she began to see things in a more positive light. Alice visited her mother every day when she finished her duties in Russell Square, and she was pleased to see that Horace had kept his word. A fire was lit in Beth's room early each morning, and Mrs Jugg seemed to take personal pride in producing light but nourishing meals to tempt an invalid's appetite.

For the most part Horace kept to himself and with long hours working in the counting house he returned home late in the evening. Alice did her best be out of the house before he arrived. A notice of their engagement appeared in *The Times* and Horace bought her a diamond ring, although it would take a jeweller's eyeglass to find the tiny stone. Alice would have preferred to wear it on a ribbon round her neck rather than on her ring finger, but the announcement in the newspaper had precluded this.

To her chagrin, Rory was the first to congratulate her.

'You kept that a close secret, Alice,' he said, brandishing a copy of the newspaper.

Flora jumped up from the desk and ran to meet him. 'Is it true?'

Rory handed it to her. 'See for yourself. Miss Radcliffe is good at keeping things from us, it seems.'

'It was quite sudden,' Alice said, looking away. She could feel her cheeks burning and she wished that her aunt had consulted her before she made the announcement.

'Sudden indeed. Is the lucky gentleman the same person I saw you with previously? I thought he was a relation of yours.'

Even worse, Alice thought, clenching her fists so that her nails dug painfully into her palms. Having to admit that she was to marry a man like Horace was bad enough, but when the person asking was Rory that made it even more humiliating. Of course there was no question of there ever being anything between herself and the master's brother – their stations in life were too different to make such an alliance possible – but she valued his good opinion more than she cared to admit. 'Horace is my aunt's cousin,' she said slowly. 'We're related by marriage, that's all.'

Flora's bottom lip trembled ominously. 'But if you get married you'll leave me. You can't do that, Alice. You must not. I won't allow it.' She slid her arms around Rory's waist and buried her face in his waistcoat, sobbing loudly.

'Now, now, Floss.' He disengaged her clutching hands, holding them gently. 'Alice isn't going anywhere yet. People become engaged for all sorts of reasons and sometimes they have a change of heart.' He gave Alice a penetrating look. 'Isn't that so?'

'Yes, of course.' She held her hand out to Flora. 'One day you won't need me, but until then I'll stay.'

Flora walked slowly towards her. 'Do you promise?'

'Cross my heart and hope to die.' Alice gave her a hug. 'I don't abandon my friends, and I don't intend to get married for a long time yet.'

'How interesting.' Rory shot her an amused glance. 'You don't seem eager to tie the knot.'

'I don't think my private affairs are any concern of yours.' The words tumbled from her lips before she could stop herself and she regretted them instantly. 'I'm sorry,' she added hastily. 'I didn't mean to be rude, it's just that it's a private matter and I don't wish to discuss it.'

'When you do get married can I be bridesmaid?' Flora asked eagerly. 'You haven't any other little girls to ask, have you?'

Alice stroked a stray curl back off Flora's forehead. 'No, Flora. I have no other little girls to ask. If I need a bridesmaid I promise you will be the one I'll ask.'

Rory pulled up a chair and sat down. 'Enough of this talk of weddings. I came today with a specific purpose in mind.'

Flora abandoned Alice and hurried to his side. 'Tell me. Is it something exciting?'

'It's not about you, Floss.' He set her on his knee, but his attention was focused on Alice. 'Dearborns' have been printing playing cards, visiting cards and Valentine's Day cards for many years, but we've only recently considered producing Christmas cards.'

'Christmas is over,' Flora said, sighing. 'The snow has melted and my snowman is nothing but a soggy patch on the grass.'

'Christmas might be over, but that was last season and now we have to plan for next year. That is where you come in, Alice.'

She stared at him in surprise. 'Me? I don't understand.'

'I know what he's going to say,' Flora said eagerly. 'He wants you to draw mistletoe and holly. Isn't that right, Uncle Rory?'

He threw back his head and laughed. 'I couldn't have put it better, Floss.' His smile faded as he turned to Alice. 'I'm being serious for once. I think you're very talented, and what's more I think you might have ideas for cards that would be very popular with the public. The drawing you did of mistletoe was very clever.'

'I'm not a professional artist,' Alice said warily. 'It was just a sketch.'

'Even so, it had charm and I'd like to see your designs for cards with a seasonal theme. Fairies and spring flowers are in vogue at present, but in my opinion they are not the embodiment of Christmas.'

Alice nodded. 'Yes, I agree. I think that Mr Dickens has it exactly right in *A Christmas Carol*. I love that story. Papa used to read it to me on cold winter's nights, and I would sit by the fire lost in the magic of it all.'

Rory put his head on one side, regarding her steadily. 'You must have loved your father very much.'

'I did, and I still miss him.' Alice cleared her throat.

Tears filled her eyes every time she thought of Pa and how much she missed his kind, calm presence.

'I'm sure he would want you to put your talent to good use,' Rory said gently. 'Would you be interested in sketching out some ideas, Alice? You'll be remunerated for your efforts.'

'Do say yes,' Flora said eagerly. 'I could help you. I'm good at drawing, too.'

Alice thought quickly. It was a tempting offer and she had nothing to lose and maybe a lot to gain. She met Rory's questioning look with a smile. 'I can't promise anything, but I'd love to try.'

'Splendid.' He rose to his feet. 'It's a lovely sunny afternoon and I think I deserve some time away from the office, so why don't we take a cab to St James's Park and feed the ducks, and then go on for tea at Gunter's.'

Flora jumped up and down, clapping her hands. 'How lovely. Oh, do please say yes, Alice. May we?'

'It sounds perfect,' Alice said slowly. 'But what would Mrs Dearborn say? After our last outing she made it clear that I wasn't to take Alice out of the house unless she was consulted.'

'Don't worry about Lydia,' Rory said casually. 'Leave her to me. I'll wait for you in the entrance hall.' Blowing a kiss to Flora he left them to get ready.

The sun was shining but there were still small patches of snow left in the deep shade beneath the evergreen trees. A shimmer of ice remained at the edges of the lake and the ducks waddled across the grass, snatching up the crusts of bread that Flora had wheedled from Cook. The air was crisp and sweet far away from the stench of the city streets. Rory linked arms with Alice as they watched Flora darting about amongst the importuning wildlife. Sparrows and starlings vied with pigeons for the crumbs left by the ducks and moorhens, causing Flora to giggle helplessly. Her cheeks were flushed with cold and Alice felt a surge of pride to see her charge acting like a normal, happy nine-year-old.

'I know,' Rory said softly. 'The change in that child is miraculous and it's all down to you, Alice.'

She looked up, startled. 'No, I won't have that. You're the one who suggested the outing. You helped her to make the snowman. She loves you.' It was a simple statement of the truth but it felt as though something had changed between them and she turned away, confused and emotional. Suddenly she wanted to cry. She wanted to rail at the unfairness of the situation that had been thrust upon her by her father's bankruptcy and his early demise. The ring on her left hand seemed to burn into her flesh, reminding her of her promise to marry a man she did not love, but from that there was no escape. Her mother's health and happiness must come first, her own a poor second. She shot a sideways glance at Rory, who had remained silent, but his attention was fixed on Flora, who was testing the ice at the edge of the lake with one booted foot. He dashed forward just in time to catch her as the ice cracked and she was about to topple into the water.

'I think it's time for tea, Floss.' He planted her on the ground beside Alice. 'That was a near thing.'

Alice slipped her arm around Flora's shoulders. 'Are your feet wet? We'll have to go straight home if they are.'

'I was only trying the ice to see if I could stand on it,' Flora said apologetically. 'My feet are dry, and I would love some ice cream.'

'Then off we go.' Rory took her by the hand. 'Gunter's it is.' He winked at Alice. 'I think I'll do without the ice cream. A hot cup of tea would be just the thing.'

'And a cream cake,' Alice said, smiling.

Any awkwardness that Alice had felt has passed into nothingness by the time they reached Berkeley Square. It was impossible to remain aloof or withdrawn in the company of Flora, who was enjoying every precious moment of the rare outing. She demolished two bowls of ice cream and several pastries, which she washed down with a cup of chocolate. Alice drank tea and nibbled a cake, but all the time she was conscious of Rory's nearness as they sat side by side at the table in the window. She could feel the warmth of his body and the masculine scent of him filled her nostrils, making her feel dizzy. They had never been in such close proximity and it was hard to concentrate on Flora's incessant chatter, but she made an effort to look interested.

It was dark outside by the time they left and Flora insisted on walking home. Once again Rory tucked Alice's hand in the crook of his arm, and Flora danced on ahead. She stopped every now and again to peer into the shop windows in Oxford Street, beckoning frantically when she saw something that interested her before rushing on to the next.

'She is a completely different child now,' Rory said in a low voice. 'Your patience and kindness has brought about an amazing change in her behaviour.'

'No, I can't accept that. Flora just needed to be allowed to be herself.'

'Even so, I'm very fond of her and I'm grateful to you.'

'She's quite incredible. To have suffered such a bitter disappointment when the mother she'd been longing to meet was found to be less than perfect would have destroyed many children her age.'

'You've been more of a mother to her than my sister-in-law ever was. Lydia simply hasn't the ability to relate to a child. She's not a bad person, but she's the wrong woman to bring up a lively little girl like Flora.'

'Flora is more resilient than you give her credit for,' Alice said smiling. 'And she has you as well as your brother. He seems very fond of her.'

'Freddie is a good man, but he lives for the busi-ness, which is all very well but it doesn't give him

196

time for his family. When I marry I'll try not to make the same mistake.'

Alice felt her heart lurch against her ribs and she gasped as the air was sucked from her lung in a sigh. 'You're thinking of getting married?' She felt him shrug, although it was too dark to see him clearly.

'One day, I will. But only if the time is right.'

Alice came to a sudden halt. Something was wrong. Something terrible had happened. She slipped her arm free. 'I can't see Flora. Rory, I can't hear her. Where is she?'

# Chapter Eleven

There was no sign of Flora. They called her name and searched the surrounding area in case she had wandered on ahead and was lost, but without any success.

Breathless and close to panicking, Alice clutched Rory's arm. 'Molly Bishop,' she gasped. 'She threatened to take Flora by force if necessary.'

He covered her hand with his. 'If that's so they can't have got far.'

'That woman has been planning it from the start; she told me as much, Rory. Poor little Flora, she'll be so frightened.'

'It's possible that Flora has run home. I wouldn't put it past her. It's just the sort of mischievous thing she might do in order to give us a fright. We'll check at the house first.'

'And if she isn't there?'

'We'll take it one step at a time, but we'll find her. I promise you we'll find her whatever it takes.'

Flora had not come home and Lydia was waiting for Alice and Rory in the drawing room.

'How dare you take Flora out without first asking my permission? Didn't I make myself clear last time, Miss Radcliffe?' She turned to Rory, eyes blazing. 'Or should I blame you for undermining my authority in such a blatant manner?'

Rory held up his hand. 'I think you'd better sit down, Lydia. I have something to tell you.'

'Where is Flora?' Lydia demanded, sinking down on the nearest chair. 'What have you done with her?'

'It's my fault,' Alice said tearfully. 'I took my eyes off her for a split second and she was gone.'

'Gone?' The word echoed round the high ceilings of the drawing room as Lydia's voice rose to a screech. 'What do you mean – gone?'

'We'll find her,' Rory said hastily. 'But it's possible she might have been abducted by the woman who claims to be her mother.'

'Why would she do that?' Lydia stared at him, frowning. 'She was paid handsomely.'

'The woman lives in the most squalid conditions. She mixes with felons of all types and she threatened Alice at knife-point.'

Lydia uttered a shriek, pointing a shaking finger at Alice. 'I blame you entirely. I took you on out of charity and look how you've repaid me.'

'I'm the one to take responsibility for what's happened,' Rory said calmly. 'Alice was simply doing as I requested. We took Flora to feed the ducks in St James's Park and for tea at Gunter's. It was a rare treat for a child who spends most of her time locked away in a schoolroom.'

'And she has been abducted as a result of your actions. No doubt the wretched woman will demand a huge ransom, which we can ill afford to pay.'

Alice stifled a gasp of dismay. How could Lydia Dearborn think about money at a time like this? 'Molly Bishop has other plans for your daughter, Mrs Dearborn,' she said angrily. 'She plans to sell her favours to any man who will pay a high enough price.'

Lydia covered her ears with her hands. 'How can you say such things? How dare you bring the filthy talk of the streets into my drawing room? You are not fit to look after a child, Alice Radcliffe. You will leave my house now and you won't receive a penny piece from me.'

'Lydia, that's unfair,' Rory protested. 'This isn't Alice's fault.'

'I see how the land lies. You always were susceptible when it came to a pretty face and winning ways.' Lydia turned to Alice, her eyes narrowed and her lips drawn into a thin line. 'And you, Radcliffe, are dismissed without a character. Leave your uniform with Mrs Upton.'

Alice shook her head, saying nothing. Given the

circumstances there was little she could say in her own defence, but she could feel Rory's anger. She sent him a warning glance but he ignored her. 'That is cruel and unfair, Lydia. Alice is not to blame.'

'I know who is the more culpable, but unfortunately you are my brother-in-law and I can do nothing about that.' Lydia glared at him, and her fingers twitched. 'I have to put up with you for Frederick's sake.'

Alice edged closer to Rory, preparing to step between them if Lydia lost the last shred of self-control. If Lydia had claws, she thought warily, the angry woman would be sinking them into her brother-in-law's flesh like a feral cat.

'Surely the most important thing is to find Flora,' Alice said hastily. 'Nothing else matters at this moment.'

Lydia took a deep breath, fanning herself with her hand. 'You must send for a constable, Rory, and then you will go to the office and tell your brother what you've done.' She reached for her vinaigrette and waved it under her nose. 'Leave me now. I don't want to see either of your faces ever again.'

Rory ushered Alice out of the room. 'I'm sorry about that. You have borne the brunt of Lydia's anger, but I'll make my brother fully aware of the facts.'

'Never mind me. We must find poor little Flora. She'll be terrified.'

'I'm going to start at Blossom Street. I'm hoping that's where the woman has taken her.'

'I'm coming too.'

'No, Alice. It's a dreadful place. I'll do better on my own.'

'I'm coming even if I have to run after you.'

He met her determined look with a sigh of resignation. 'I believe you would.'

'Come along. We're wasting time.'

The building in Blossom Street was in total darkness when they arrived, and it appeared to be deserted. The door was barred and it was impossible to gain access.

'What now?' Alice demanded angrily. 'Where would they have gone from here?'

'I don't know. I'm afraid we'll have to involve the police. I didn't want to create a scandal, but there's no choice, and I'll have to tell Freddie what's happened.' Rory hit the door with his clenched fist and the sound echoed throughout the empty building. 'I'll take you back to your lodgings, Alice. There's nothing more we can do here.'

'I can't just give up. Flora is with that awful woman and she'll be so scared. We must find her quickly.'

'I know, but Bishop could have taken her anywhere. The police will know her and they might be familiar with her haunts. I doubt that she's far away, it's only a question of where.'

Struggling with disappointment and fear for Flora's safety, Alice had to accept his decision. If it were left to her she would have walked the streets all night, calling Flora's name in the vain hope that she might hear, but she knew in her heart that this would prove fruitless and she would be endangering her own life. After dark the East End streets were inhabited by the night people; criminals, vagrants, prostitutes and the dispossessed haunted the alleyways and courts. Opium dens, unlicensed pubs and gaming houses flourished, and blood flowed in the gutters as freely as the muddy waters of the River Thames.

Having reached Half Moon Passage, Rory hesitated outside the door of the lodging house. 'This isn't the sort of place you should live,' he said gravely. 'I'm surprised that your fiancé allows you to reside here.'

'It's all I can afford, and it suits me well enough.' Alice knocked and waited.

Eventually the door opened and Mrs Leech peered at them in the dim light of an oil lamp. 'No gentlemen callers. I told you that in the beginning, Miss Radcliffe.'

Rory doffed his hat. 'I applaud your caution, ma'am. I was just seeing the lady safely home.'

'You ain't a policeman, are you, cully? There's strange goings-on round here tonight, even though this is a respectable neighbourhood.'

'He isn't a policeman,' Alice said, stepping inside. 'He's just a friend.'

'Men is all the same. Give them a smile and they

think you're free with your favours. I knows it only too well. Come in and shut the door, miss. You can help me with this wild child what burst in not long ago. Says she knows you, but from the way she's been carrying on I think she's a halfwit. I'd have thrown her out on the street, but she bites and scratches.'

Alice turned to Rory. 'Flora,' she gasped. 'It must be.'

He tried to push past Mrs Leech but she barred his way. 'Here, you can't barge in like this. What did I just tell you? No gentlemen callers allowed.'

'Let me see the child, ma'am. If she's who I think she is then she's my niece.'

'Ho! A runaway, is she? I guessed as much.'

'You would know her,' Alice insisted. 'She came here once.'

'All kids look the same to me.'

'Let me see her.' Alice could hear wailing coming from the parlour. She pushed past Mrs Leech and hurried along the narrow passage. Flinging the door open, she stepped inside to see Flora standing by the fireplace with a poker clutched in her hand. She was tear-stained, dishevelled and close to hysteria.

'Darling, it's me,' Alice said gently.

Flora dropped the weapon and threw herself into Alice's open arms, sobbing and babbling incoherently.

'Who brought her here?' Rory turned on Mrs Leech, who had followed them into the room protesting loudly. 'She couldn't have come on her own.'

'I never saw no one.' Mrs Leech stood arms akimbo, glaring at them each in turn. 'This is a respectable house. Take the brat away and leave me in peace.'

Alice hugged Flora, smoothing her damp curls back from her forehead and rocking her gently. 'There, there, you're safe now. We've come to take you home.'

'Did they hurt you, Floss?' Rory asked anxiously. 'Are you all right?'

Flora raised her head from Alice's shoulder, hiccuping and sniffing. 'I'm not hurt. I bit that horrid woman and made her hand bleed and then I ran. I ran and ran, and then I remembered where Alice lived, but she wasn't here.' She subsided once again into a storm of sobbing.

'Don't ask her any more questions,' Alice said softly. 'Time enough for that later. We must take her home.'

'Of course.' Rory put his hand in his pocket and tossed a coin to Mrs Leech who caught it deftly. 'That's for your trouble, ma'am. We'll leave now.'

'Ta, guv. You're a real gent.' Mrs Leech tucked the money into her pocket. 'But I don't want this sort of thing happening again, Miss Radcliffe. I'll overlook it this once, but if I get any more trouble from you I'll have to ask you to pack your bag and leave.'

Alice nodded, more concerned for Flora's well-being than for her own. 'Come, my dear. You're quite safe now.'

Lights blazed in the windows in Russell Square, and the servants were scurrying about as if their lives depended upon being seen to be busy. Hoskins admitted them, his stony expression cracking into a genuine attempt at a smile. 'Miss Flora. Welcome home.'

Alice stared at him in surprise. Hoskins was normally a man of few words, and this was quite a speech. She gave Flora's hand a reassuring squeeze. 'Don't worry,' she whispered. 'You won't get into trouble.'

Rory handed his hat and coat to Hoskins. 'Is Mrs Dearborn in the drawing room?'

'Yes, sir.'

'There's no need to announce us.' Rory turned to Flora with an encouraging smile. 'Come on, Floss. Don't look so worried.'

'I want Alice to stay with me,' Flora said with a stubborn lift of her chin. 'I won't go without her.'

'Maybe I should say goodbye now.' Alice wrapped her arms around Flora, holding her close. 'Your mama doesn't want me to come here any more, and I don't blame her. I should have taken better care of you.'

'Nonsense,' Rory said angrily. 'You couldn't have cared more for Flora if she'd been your own flesh and blood.'

Flora opened her mouth and began to wail. 'Don't go. I won't let you go, Alice. I'll die if you leave me.' She sank to her knees, clutching Alice's skirt with both hands.

Her cries brought servants running and Frederick himself appeared at the top of the stairs. 'Flora, my dear, are you hurt?' He descended hurriedly, crossing the floor to lift his daughter to her feet, but Flora resisted, drumming her feet on the floor.

'I won't let her go. I love Alice.'

Frederick exchanged concerned looks with his brother. 'I need to know exactly what happened.'

'Flora is unharmed,' Rory said quickly. 'I think you ought to allow Miss Radcliffe to take her to her room.'

Flora raised a tear-stained face. 'If you send Alice away I'll go with her and live in that horrible attic room. I won't stay here without her, Papa.'

Alice pulled her to her feet. 'Now, Flora, you must listen to your papa and do whatever he says.'

'I'll hold my breath until I turn blue in the face. I'll make myself sick, but I won't let you go.'

'She's overwrought, sir,' Alice said simply. 'If I might settle her down for the night it would be for the best.'

'Very well.' Frederick gazed helplessly at Flora. 'Will you promise to be good if I allow Miss Radcliffe to put you to bed?'

'I want her to stay with me. I'll have nightmares if I'm left on my own.'

Frederick nodded. 'If that's all right with you, Miss Radcliffe, perhaps it would be for the best.'

'Yes, sir. Of course I'll stay if Flora needs me.'

He signalled to Nettie, who was hovering in the background. 'Take Miss Flora to her room. I want a private word with Miss Radcliffe.' He patted Flora on the head. 'Go with the maid. Miss Radcliffe will follow in a minute.'

Flora's eyes filled with tears and her bottom lip trembled. 'You will come, won't you?'

'Of course.' Alice bent down to kiss her on the cheek. 'Go with Nettie.'

Rory waited until they were out of earshot. He turned to his brother. 'Flora depends on Alice. You can't allow Lydia to dismiss her out of hand. None of this was Alice's fault.'

'Lydia is in a terrible state. She told me everything, but I'm as much to blame as anyone,' Frederick said, sighing heavily. 'I spend too much time at the office or at the factory and I fear that I've neglected my family, Flora in particular.' He turned to Alice, meeting her anxious gaze with an apologetic smile. 'You've done wonders with the child. I want you to know that I appreciate your good work.'

'Thank you, sir.' Alice waited, watching him carefully. There was something he was not telling her and she had a feeling it was not going to be what she wanted to hear.

'Miss Radcliffe,' Frederick said slowly, 'this business with Molly Bishop is unsettling and potentially dangerous. The woman is obviously unhinged and will stop at nothing to get what she wants. I think for her own sake that Flora should be sent away to boarding school as soon as possible.'

Alice stared at him, too shocked to speak. She could see the sense in what he was saying from a practical point of view, but Flora needed love and affection as well as a firm hand. It was hard to imagine how a sensitive child would cope with being far away from home.

Rory met her anxious gaze and she could see that he, too, was disturbed by the idea of sending Flora to live amongst strangers. 'I think we need to talk this over, Freddie.' He gave Alice an encouraging smile. 'Leave this to us, Alice, but at the moment Flora's needs are more important than anything. She loves and trusts you.'

'And I love her,' Alice said with a break in her voice.

Frederick had started towards his study, but he stopped, as if struck by a sudden thought. 'I'll speak to my wife, Miss Radcliffe,' he said, looking over his shoulder. 'Lydia told me that she had dismissed you, but I'll insist that you stay on until we find a suitable place for Flora at a school far enough away to be out of reach of Molly Bishop.'

'Thank you, sir.'

He acknowledged her response with an attempt at a smile. 'My study, Brother. Now, if you please.' He walked on.

Rory caught Alice by the sleeve as she was about to step away. 'I won't stand by and see you suffer for my failings. If Flora is sent away to school it means that you will lose your job.'

'I can't think about that now. Flora is all that matters.'

'If you have designs for the Christmas cards we talked about I'll show them to my brother. I can't guarantee anything, Alice, but I'm almost certain that Freddie will agree with me, and that we'll be able to offer you a position in the design department.'

She nodded dully. They had enjoyed a perfect afternoon in the winter sunshine and then darkness had fallen. The subsequent events had been a living nightmare and now she felt numb and emotionally exhausted. It was impossible to think, let alone make important decisions.

'I must go to Flora.' She walked towards the baize door and he made no further attempt to delay her. For a while she had forgotten that she was just a servant and could be replaced according to her employer's whim. Her place in the household hierarchy had been clearly redefined. She used the back stairs.

With amazing resilience Flora recovered from her ordeal more quickly than anyone could have hoped, but she was thrown into a fit of despair when her father told her that she was to be sent away to school. She tried every trick she knew to make him change his mind, but tears and tantrums proved to be futile and her father remained unmoved. Alice had to put up with Flora's sulks, but after a while even she began to lose patience.

A boarding school in Yorkshire was chosen and it was left to Alice to see that Flora was kitted out with her new uniform. This entailed several trips to the outfitters and they were always accompanied by Mrs Upton, although Alice doubted whether the housekeeper would be much use as a bodyguard should Molly make another attempt to abduct Flora. It was unlikely that she or her gang would try anything in broad daylight, but in the evenings when Alice walked back to her lodgings she made sure she varied her route and she kept as much as possible to the well-lit streets. Perhaps Molly had given up, but no matter how much Flora appealed against her father's decision he was adamant that Willoughby Hall Academy for Young Ladies was the answer. Nothing Alice could say would convince Flora had she might actually enjoy being in the company of girls her own age, and at the end of January, accompanied by her father, Flora left for Yorkshire.

Their goodbyes had been tearful and heart-rending, doubly so for Alice, whose employment was now terminated. She had been on excellent terms with Cook, Nettie and even Hoskins, who was very conscious of his senior position in the servants' hall.

As she left the house in Russell Square it felt like leaving home for a second time, and it was raining.

She made her way to Queen Square and was encouraged to find that her mother was out of bed, dressed and seated in a chair by the fire in her room, reading a copy of yesterday's *Times*.

'Horace saves it for me,' she said, smiling. 'He might be a little set in his ways, but he's a kind-hearted man, Alice. You know, my dear, you could do worse.'

Alice perched on the edge of the bed. 'You don't mean that, Mama. Horace is old enough to be my father and he picks his teeth at table.'

'Horace is a year older than me. He's just forty, which is a good age for a man to settle down. He's past his salad days, but a good heart is important in a husband, my love.'

'I only agreed to the engagement so that you had a roof over your head,' Alice protested. 'You know very well I have no intention of going through with the marriage.'

'But, darling girl, you have little choice now. You have no job and if Mrs Dearborn puts it about that you are unreliable you'll find it very hard to find employment elsewhere. I beg you to give Horace a chance, Alice. He's been telling me about a sweet little house for sale in Islington. It sounds delightful and all three of us could live there in perfect harmony. I've grown quite fond of him these past few weeks.'

Alice sprang to her feet. 'I'm sorry, but I can't go on with this conversation. Anyway, I have to go to Farringdon Street for an interview. I might have found myself a new job after all.'

'Oh, Alice, do be careful. You can be very wayward at times.'

Alice leaned over to drop a kiss on her mother's white lace cap. 'I'm glad to see you up and about, Mama. I'll come and see you again tomorrow.'

'Promise me that you'll give Horace's proposal some serious thought, my love.'

'I think about nothing else, Mama.' Alice hurried from the room. She had spoken the truth, but her thoughts were such that she could not share them with her mother. She would rather remain a spinster for the rest of her days than tie herself to a man she positively disliked. Their meetings in her aunt's house had been brief, as his job in the counting house meant that he worked long hours. He often arrived home just as she was about to leave, and sometimes she managed to miss him altogether. Evenings spent alone in the cold, cheerless attic room in Half Moon Passage were preferable to being in the company of Aunt Jane and Horace.

Despite everything that had happened, Alice had a spring in her step as she left Queen Square. It was cold and wet, but she was oblivious to the weather as she made her way to the Dearborns' office in Farringdon Street. Rory had promised her an interview, and she had a small portfolio of drawings and designs to show him. If she were taken on to work in the design office there would be compensations. She would have first-hand news of Flora's progress in her new school, and maybe she would get to meet her when she came home for the holidays. Having to part with her young charge had been painful, but Flora's wellbeing must come first. Molly Bishop would never find her in the wilds of Yorkshire, and Flora's education would be complete.

Alice entered the building with a feeling of renewed optimism, and was greeted by Beasley, who seemed genuinely pleased to see her.

'Mr Rory left instructions for me to take you to his office, miss. Follow me.'

Her feet hardly touched the floor as she walked behind him, and she felt as excited as a child on Christmas Eve as she entered Rory's office. He was seated behind a large kneehole desk, half-hidden behind overflowing filing trays, but he jumped to his feet, dismissed Beasley and hurried round the desk to pull up a chair for her.

'Welcome to the firm, Alice.'

Her knees were trembling and might give way beneath her if she did not sit down immediately. 'Thank you, Mr Dearborn.' She sank down on the hard wooden seat.

Rory moved to the fireplace and threw a shovelful of coal onto the already blazing fire. 'You're shivering,' he said cheerfully. 'It must be cold outside.'

'I stood outside the house in Russell Square to

wave goodbye to Flora. It started raining as they climbed into the cab. It was almost as if the clouds were crying too.'

He gave her a searching look as he resumed his place behind his desk. 'I'm sure you were as upset as poor little Floss. You'll miss her and she'll miss you.'

The ready tears sprang to Alice's eyes and she dashed them away with her gloved hand. 'I'm sorry. I know she'll be better off in the school, but it's such a long way away. I hope she settles in well.'

'She's young and she'll make friends. At least she's safe from that dreadful woman. The police haven't had any luck catching her. She gives them the slip each time they get close.'

'I'm sure they're doing their best.'

'I hope so.' Rory sat back in his chair, eyeing her speculatively. 'I see you've done what I ask. May I have a look?'

Alice opened her portfolio and took out her most prized possession. 'You once expressed interest in seeing this. I told you about it some time ago.' She laid the Christmas card on the desk in front of him. 'It's the first card to be printed commercially in 1843, the year I was born. My father gave it to me and I treasure it.'

Rory picked it up carefully. 'I've never seen one of these before, but as I recall you told me they were not a huge success.'

'Some people objected to the fact that all the

family, including the children, are drinking wine. Although I don't think that's important.'

'What does it say to you, Alice?'

'It shows a happy family together to celebrate Christmas. It shows people being generous to others in the season of goodwill.' Her eyes filled with tears and she could not go on. The card illustrated everything that she had lost.

'It's a fine sentiment, and I can see that it means a lot to you.' He laid his hand on hers for the briefest of moments, and then reached for the portfolio. 'But these are what I wanted to see, and it's your work I'll put before my brother.' He smiled and his dark eyes seemed to glow like warm honey in the firelight. 'Of course I know how excellent they are, but we have to be seen to do things properly. Freddie will take a look at them when he returns, but he's given me the authority to offer you a position should I consider you a suitable applicant.'

It was impossible to resist him in this mood and she smiled shyly. 'Am I suitable?'

'There are, of course, a dozen or so other candidates.' He chuckled. 'Don't look so worried, I'm teasing you. Of course you're the best person for the job or I wouldn't have encouraged you to apply. When can you start?'

She breathed a sigh of relief. 'I believed you for a second or two. That was mean, Rory.'

'I like that much better. Never call me Mr Dearborn unless my brother is present, when we'll observe the niceties.' He tempered his words with a disarming smile. 'Are you free to start immediately, or do you need to consult your fiancé about such matters?'

'I make my own decisions, and I can start right away.'

'Capital. You may consider yourself hired, Alice Radcliffe.' His eyes darkened. 'There is just one thing I have to tell you.'

His serious expression alarmed her. 'What is it?'

'I told you that I was trying to persuade Freddie to invest in chromolithography.'

'You did.'

'Well, he's taken to the idea but unfortunately it means that I will have to go to Ireland to learn the ins and outs of the business from the beginning. I'll be away for quite some time.'

# Chapter Twelve

The announcement hit Alice like a physical blow. 'How long?'

'A month or so, but Rawlins Wall will look after you. He's an experienced designer and he knows the business inside out. I'll make it clear that Martin and George must co-operate fully.' A wry smile curved his lips. 'They're not used to having a female colleague, but I'm sure that you're more than capable of dealing with them.'

Still reeling from the news that she would be joining the company without him there to support and guide her, she nodded. 'Yes, I suppose so.'

'You mustn't worry,' he said earnestly. 'George is little more than a boy. He's nineteen and lives at home with his parents and half a dozen younger siblings. As for Martin Collis, he's unmarried and thinks of himself as a lady-killer and man about town, but he's not a bad chap when you get to know him.'

'I'll be too busy working to pay much attention to anything else. I won't let you down.'

'I have absolute faith in you and your talent, Alice. When I return with the knowledge I've gained in Ireland we'll be able to produce Christmas cards by the thousand, and they'll be in colour. I've no doubt that your designs will make them irresistible.'

Late that evening, in the chilly solitude of her attic room, Alice sat by the fire, wrapped in a blanket with her stockinged feet resting on the wooden fender. Her toes were roasting, but the heat barely reached as far as her knees, and an icy draught pinched her cheeks and nose. She always tried to eke out her ration of coal in an attempt to make it last for two days or even more, but the temperatures at night rarely rose above freezing and the scuttle was almost empty. She was certain that Mrs Leech counted every nugget in the cellar, keeping a tally of how much each tenant took in order to extract more money from them.

It had been a long day and she was exhausted. Rory had put her to work immediately. Rawlins Wall had grudgingly made room for her in the design office, and had cleared a small corner by the window where she could work in daylight. George had tried to be helpful, showing her where the drawing materials were kept, but Martin had it clear that he was simply tolerating her presence. He was a young man who seemed very sure of his personal charm and good looks, but he was conceited and patronising. His casual style of dress added to the image he had chosen to create, clearly basing on his look on that of the Pre-Raphaelite Brotherhood. While working on a design he had a habit of loosening his cravat and then ripping it off with a dramatic expletive, as if overcome by artistic temperament. Alice thought him rather silly, but she kept her opinions to herself and ignored him as much as possible. Her main aim was to impress Frederick and to justify Rory's faith in her.

Rawlins Wall was another matter altogether. He was middle-aged and openly hostile. It was obvious from the start that he resented having a young woman foisted upon him, and she knew instinctively that he would watch her closely and any slight misdemeanour would be reported to Frederick. She had to be very careful when dealing with Rawlins.

She shivered and wrapped the blanket up to her neck. It smelled of cooking fat and wet dog, but it helped to combat the draughts that whistled around the room like angry spirits out to wreak their revenge on the living. At least it had stopped raining, and there was only a relatively small puddle beneath the gap in the roof tiles. Feeling slightly warmer Alice closed her eyes and allowed herself to relive the moment when she had said goodbye to Rory. He had come into the office and had spoken to each of them in turn, making her wait until last. He had held her hand and raised it to his lips; the warmth in his eyes had promised her much, but his words had been formal. He would return, but that did not fill the gap in her heart, which had opened like a knife wound the moment the door closed on him. She had been left alone with the three men with whom she must work in harmony. She had to prove herself capable of being creative in a male-dominated environment, and she suspected that given the choice all three of them would have preferred to share their office with another man. It would take time and effort on her part to win their approval and trust. The only thing that would help to make life bearable was the fact that Rory had doubled her wages. Even so, she could not afford to be extravagant, and while her mother was recovering her health and strength in Queen Square and dependent on Jane's charity, Alice knew she must keep up the fiction that she would marry Horace. If she could save enough money from her earnings she might be able to rent rooms in a respectable area where they could live in reasonable comfort.

She opened her eyes with a start at the sound of something scuffling across the bare boards, but the small creature had disappeared into the shadows and all she could hear was the sound of her heart beating. Wrapping the blanket around her, Alice rose stiffly from the uncomfortable chair and climbed into her equally uncomfortable bed. She was exhausted, but sleep evaded her and she found herself wondering how Flora was coping in her new environment. She closed her eyes, planning to write a long letter to Flora telling her about her experiences in the design office. She would keep the contents light and entertaining, with descriptions of her small corner of the office and the view she had of the inner well of the building. There would be descriptions of the pigeons that huddled from the cold on the windowsill, fluffing out their feathers in order to keep warm. She would tell Alice that she had begun to recognise individuals by their markings and had given them names. Having exhausted the supply of pigeon stories, she would describe her workmates, likening George to an engaging puppy, eager to please and make friends. Martin was a pet lapdog, spoiled and constantly demanding attention, and Rawlins was a terrier, snapping at her heels. She decided to add caricatures, which would be amusing rather than cruel, but she would have to keep her drawings out of sight, tucked away in the drawer where she kept her personal belongings. It would be a disaster if her colleagues were to find them. She drifted off to sleep, smiling.

At the end of her first week at Dearborns' Alice arrived early in the office, but to her surprise she found Martin was already at his desk.

He rose to his feet and sauntered over to her. 'Good morning, Miss Radcliffe.'

His wide grin put her in mind of the big bad wolf in the tale of *Little Red Riding-Hood*, but she returned his greeting with an attempt at a smile. 'Good morning, Mr Collis.'

He leaned against her desk with his arms folded. 'I think we should dispense with the formalities. My name is Martin, and from now on I will call you Alice.'

'I've no objection to that.' She took off her bonnet and hung it on a peg near her desk.

He moved a step closer. 'We should get to know each other better, Alice.'

'I'd like to get to know everyone,' she said tactfully. 'I know it must be difficult for you to have a woman working with you.'

He inched even closer, fingering the frogging on her mantle. 'You're little more than a slip of a girl, but I'd be happy to educate you into the ways of the world.' He winked and moved his hand to tickle her chin.

'Thank you, Martin, but I can manage very well on my own.' She backed away. Slipping off her jacket, she hung it beside her bonnet and took her seat at her desk. 'If you'll excuse me I must get on. I have work to do.'

'That's not very friendly, Alice.' He leaned over her. 'I was going to ask if you'd like to accompany me to the theatre this evening.'

'That's so kind of you, but I'm afraid my fiancé would be very unhappy if I accepted your invitation.'

Alice held up her left hand. She only wore the ring on days when she planned to visit her mother, and this was such a day.

Martin eyed her suspiciously. 'You weren't wearing that yesterday. I'm damned sure of that.'

She raised an eyebrow. 'Maybe you just didn't notice, Martin. It was very kind of you to ask me out, but you will understand why I have to refuse.'

Mumbling beneath his breath he made his way back to his desk, stamping his feet as if he were about to have a tantrum. Alice tried not to smile. She had seen Flora behave in such a way, but she would not have expected a grown man to act like a child.

She was saved from an awkward situation by George, who bounced into the office grinning from ear to ear. 'The boss has returned. I just saw Mr Frederick getting out of his carriage. We'll be back to normal now, and Rawlins will have his nose put out of joint.'

'Did I hear my name being taken in vain?' Rawlins Wall strode into the room, glaring at George, who flushed with embarrassment. 'What was it you were saying, Young?'

George hung his head. 'I was joking, Mr Wall. Sorry, sir.'

'Get to work, boy. You're very nearly late.'

Martin sprawled on his chair. 'I'd call that being bang on time, Rawlins old chap.'

'Less of the cheek, Collis. Being the most senior member of my staff doesn't give you the right to be rude to your superior.' Rawlins turned to Alice, frowning. 'You're to go to Mr Dearborn's office now. Toot sweet.'

'What have you done wrong, Miss Radcliffe?' Martin called out as she rose from her seat. 'You'll be taken down a peg or two, I hope.'

George faced him angrily. 'That's a bit rich, coming from you.'

Rawlins shrugged off his greatcoat. 'Get to work, gentlemen. The designs for the new sets of playing cards are due in the factory next week. I want to see your efforts by the end of the morning, and if they don't suit then you'll both be working tomorrow as well.'

'But tomorrow is Sunday,' Martin protested.

Alice slipped out of the office without waiting to hear more. Petty squabbles were common when Martin chose to challenge his superior's authority. Rawlins obviously considered that he was in charge, although everyone knew that the only real boss was Frederick Dearborn. She patted a stray hair into place and hurried along the corridor that led to his office. She knocked on the door and entered.

'You wanted to see me, sir?'

Frederick looked up from a pile of correspondence on the desk in front of him. His stern expression melted into a smile. 'Yes, Miss Radcliffe. Please take a seat.'

She sank down on the nearest chair. 'How is Flora, sir? I've been so worried about her.'

'She cried when I left.' He shook his head and sighed. 'But she will settle down in time, or so I hope, and it's only natural that she should feel home-sick at first.'

'Where is Willoughby Hall, sir? Is it very far away?'

'It's situated in the wilds of the Yorkshire Moors. She will be safe there, and I believe the discipline is strict, which is what Flora needs. I hope in time that she'll benefit from the education she'll receive and that she'll learn to be a young lady.'

Alice sensed that he was trying to convince himself that the far away school was the best thing for his daughter, but she experienced a sense of foreboding. In her mind's eye she could picture Willoughby Hall in a bleak moorland setting, and poor little Flora feeling lost and alone amongst strangers.

'I'd like to write to her if you have no objections, Mr Dearborn.'

His expression lightened. 'That would be a kind-ness, Miss Radcliffe. I'm sorry that your employment in my household was terminated so abruptly, and I know that you were doing your best for Flora. It's just a pity that my brother had to interfere. None of this would have happened if he hadn't told Flora about her mother.'

'With respect, sir, it was Smithson who told Flora that she was adopted.'

'So I believe, but we must put it all behind us.' He picked up a sheaf of papers. 'You're settling in well, I hope?'

Alice took her cue and rose to her feet. 'Yes, thank you, sir.'

'Good,' he said vaguely. 'I look forward to seeing your designs.'

'Yes, sir.' Alice hesitated. He was studying one of the documents and seemed to have forgotten her. 'May I have Flora's address, please?'

He looked up, blinking as if surprised to see her there. 'Yes, of course.' He reached for a pen and scribbled something on a scrap of paper. 'If you give the letter to Beasley he'll post it for you. Stamps are still quite dear, but we'll write it off as a business expense.' He handed her the paper and bent his head over his work.

Alice left the room and returned to her office.

Martin looked up as she entered. 'Got the sack, have you, love?'

'I expect she's been promoted,' George said quickly. 'She's probably your senior now, Collis, so you'd better watch out.'

'That's enough, gentlemen.' Rawlins popped his head up over the partition that separated his desk from theirs. 'Get on with your work or you'll make up the time on Sunday.' He glanced at Alice. 'I'll take a look at your drawings, Miss Radcliffe. Let's see how you're doing.'

'Yes, Mr Wall.' She went to her desk and fetched her latest design for a festive card.

He was impressed. She could tell by the way his eyes widened as he studied the sketches. He nodded with approval. 'They're not bad,' he said grudgingly. 'Obviously you need to work on them, but they're passable. I want to see the finished design by next Wednesday, and then I'll decide if they're good enough to present to Mr Dearborn.'

'You're lucky,' George whispered as Alice returned to her desk. 'He usually throws out the first dozen or so attempts.' His smile faded as he realised that Rawlins was glaring at him and he looked away quickly.

Alice resumed her seat with mixed feelings. Rawlins had not praised her efforts, but his reaction had been favourable, and at least George seemed to have accepted her presence with good grace. Martin would prove more difficult, but her main concern was Flora.

Rawlins always left the office at noon for his daily visit to the factory in Wapping, although everyone knew that he went first to the pub across the street for a pint of ale and a meat pie. Alice waited until he had gone and seized the opportunity to finish the letter to Flora. She sealed the envelope and was about to take it to Beasley when Martin called her back.

'Is that a billet-doux, sweetheart?'

She smiled sweetly. 'I'll leave that to your fertile imagination, Martin.'

'Answer that if you can,' George said, chuckling.

That evening Alice left the office and walked to Queen Square. Clara welcomed her with genuine pleasure, clucking like a small mother hen as she took Alice's rain-soaked mantle and bonnet.

'Lawks, miss, you'll catch your death of cold if you're not careful. You should have taken a cab.'

'I'm all right, thank you, Clara. How is my mother?'

'Much better, I think.' Clara hooked the wet garments over her arm. 'I'll take these to the kitchen where it's a bit warmer. Your ma is in the parlour with Mr Horace.'

'And my aunt?'

'On her knees in church, I suppose. I dunno, miss. She don't confide in the likes of us below stairs.' Clara sniffed and marched off with her head held high.

Smiling to herself Alice made her way to the parlour, but as she opened the door the sweet sound of her mother singing 'Come into the Garden, Maud' took her back to happier times. Beth was accompanying herself on the piano, and Horace sat listening with a beatific smile on his face. Alice clapped her hands as she entered the room and Horace leaped to his feet, looking so guilty that it was laughable.

Clutching her hand to her bosom, Beth rolled her eyes. 'Don't ever do that again, Alice. I thought Jane had returned early.'

'I'm not scared of Jane,' Horace said hastily. 'I just need to keep on the right side of her.'

Alice suppressed a giggle. 'You look like a pair of frightened rabbits.'

'That's no way to speak to your mama,' Horace protested, moving closer to Beth. 'We thought that Jane had gone out and you startled us.'

'Yes, dear,' Beth added gently. 'We weren't doing anything wrong.'

Alice went to sit by the fire, which to her surprise was blazing up the chimney. 'It's easy to see that you didn't expect her back soon.'

'I pay for the coal,' Horace said stiffly.

'I understand why Mama has to be careful,' Alice said, eyeing him curiously. 'But why do you allow Aunt Jane to bully you, Horace?'

He cleared his throat several times and his cheeks flushed. 'I'm living in her house and so I must abide by her rules. I have no choice.'

'But when you're married we will be free,' Beth said eagerly. 'Does it have to be a long engagement, Alice? I don't like the thought of you living in that dreadful attic room, and going to business every day isn't what a well-brought-up young lady should be doing. Your poor papa would turn in his grave if he knew.'

'If Papa had not left us in such a terrible plight none of this would have happened.' Alice spoke more sharply than she had intended, but she was tired after a long day at work, and chilled to the bone after the walk to Queen Square in the pouring rain. Her bodice was damp, as were her petticoats, and she was hungry.

'Your father did his best for us.' Beth's eyes filled

with tears. 'He loved us both dearly, but he was a scholar and not a businessman. Robert was very generous while he lived, but when he was taken so suddenly our income more than halved.'

Alice stared at her in surprise. 'I didn't know that. I wonder if Aunt Jane was aware that her husband was helping to support us.'

'I doubt it, but it's true. Robert was a kind man, and your father was devoted to him. Now they're both gone, and Viola too. I really do think we are cursed as a family.' She mopped her eyes with her hanky.

Horace laid his hand on her shoulder. 'There, there, my dear. Don't upset yourself. We are all the victims of misfortune and unfortunately Jane has the upper hand. I think she revels in the power it gives her.'

'I'm sure she does,' Alice said with a wry smile. She shook out her damp skirts, which were steaming in the heat from the fire. 'She takes great pleasure in our discomfort, but I hope to change that soon.'

Beth reached out to clutch her daughter's hand. 'Are you willing to name the day? The house I told you about is still on the market, isn't it, Horace?'

'So I believe, my dear.' Horace grinned nervously. 'Are you saying that we will be married soon, Alice?'

'No,' she said hastily. 'That's not what I meant at all. Mr Dearborn pays me double the wages I used to earn, and I was hoping to rent a room where Mama and I could live quite cheaply.'

Beth's hand flew to her mouth and her eyes widened. 'But, darling, you're promised to Horace. Surely you aren't going to break off your engagement?'

'Do you really want me to marry him, Mama?'

Beth looked from one to the other, shaking her head. 'Oh, I don't know. I'm so confused. All I want is to have a home of my own again.'

'Don't upset yourself, dear lady.' Horace took her hand in his. 'Of course you must have what you desire most in the world.' He turned to Alice, frowning. 'You've upset your mama.'

Alice leaped to her feet. 'I only agreed to our engagement to keep Aunt Jane from evicting us. If you're so fond of him, Mama, why don't you marry Horace instead of me?' She regretted her hasty words instantly, but Horace's reaction took her by surprise.

'Your mama is a wonderful woman, Alice,' he said angrily. 'You shouldn't speak to her in that manner. Any man would be fortunate to have such a lady for his wife.'

Beth's pale cheeks were tinged with pink as she stared up at him. 'What are you saying, Horace?'

He went down on one knee, raising her hand to his cheek. 'I would be honoured if you would consider me a suitable husband, Elizabeth.'

Alice stared at him in astonishment. 'You're proposing to my mother?'

'I realised from the start that you were forced into accepting me,' Horace said humbly. 'I've come to know and respect your mother, and I believe that true love will follow.'

'Mama, you're not taking this seriously, are you?' Alice stared at her mother, willing her to respond, but Beth was gazing into Horace's eyes like a love-struck schoolgirl.

'Do you really want to marry me, Horace?' she breathed, blushing rosily.

'I do,' he said simply. 'I really do.'

'But you're engaged to me,' Alice protested, stunned.

He shrugged, keeping his gaze fixed on Beth's flushed face. 'You never intended to go through with it, Alice. You were leading me on.'

'Maybe I was, but even so, Aunt Jane won't allow it.' Alice sat down suddenly as her legs gave way beneath her. 'She intended you to produce an heir, Horace. Have you forgotten that?'

Beth shot her a sideways glance. 'I'm only thirty-nine, Alice. It's not impossible.'

'You're delicate, Mama. You nearly died when you had me, or so I've always been told. This is madness.'

'Jane wishes to see me married.' Horace spoke with renewed confidence. 'If I choose to wed your mother it's none of her business. She promised me a home of my own and I'll hold her to that. The question of children is quite immaterial, as far as I'm concerned.' He kissed Beth's hand. 'Will you marry me, Elizabeth?'

Alice held up her left hand. 'You can't do this, Horace. I'm wearing your ring. Doesn't that mean anything to you?'

'You don't want me, Alice. You've made that abundantly clear.'

'It's true,' she said angrily. 'But we're still engaged and you are proposing to my mother. It's not the act of a gentleman.'

'You're being unreasonable, darling.' Beth met her daughter's furious gaze with a dreamy smile. 'Would you deny me this last chance for happiness?'

'Mama, are you out of your mind? If you wish to remarry why choose Horace? Do you really want to have Aunt Jane ordering you about for the rest of your life?'

Horace raised Beth's hand to his lips. 'I'll protect you from Jane. When we're married and have a house of our own she won't be able to interfere.'

'You are both deluding yourselves.' Alice pinched the soft flesh of her forearm to make sure she was not in the middle of a crazy dream. 'Ouch.' She rubbed the spot where it hurt. 'You can't do this, Mama.'

Beth turned her attention to Horace. She leaned forward and kissed him on the brow. 'Yes,' she said simply.

He blinked owlishly. 'You mean you'll marry me?'

'I will, Horace, and the sooner the better. Perhaps we could go and see that house in the morning.'

'And what about me?' Alice demanded. 'Am I

included in your plans, or would I be in the way of your two lovebirds?'

'There's no need to take that tone with me, young lady.' Beth helped Horace to his feet. 'I'm your mother and when we're married Horace will be your new papa. You will give him the respect due to him.'

'Of course you will come and live with us,' Horace said hastily. 'You will always be welcome in our home, Alice.'

'I'd rather live in Mrs Leech's attic for the rest of my life than play gooseberry to you two.' Alice tugged at the ring on her left hand and it slipped off her finger. She tossed it onto the floor at her mother's feet. 'There, Mama, it's yours now. I wish you well, but I think you're making a terrible mistake.'

She left the room, ignoring her mother's pleas for her to stop and talk things over. Her thoughts were chaotic as she ran downstairs to retrieve her outer garments from the kitchen, and she left the house by the tradesmen's entrance. Above all she wanted her mother to be happy and well cared for, but Horace was the last person she would have chosen to be her stepfather. She stopped to pull on her gloves and she paused, staring at the indentation on her ring finger. The realisation that she was a free woman washed over her in a feeling of relief. As she walked briskly towards home she had a sudden vision of Horace on bended knee in front of her mother, and she started to giggle as the ridiculousness of the situation occurred to her. But her laughter was cut short when she heard an all-too-familiar voice close to her ear.

'You won't find it so amusing if I has to cut you, dearie. Button your lip and keep walking.'

# Chapter Thirteen

'Leave me alone, Molly,' Alice said angrily. 'I know it's you.'

'Clever, ain't you? Keep moving.'

'Where are we going?'

Molly's answer was a sharp dig in the back with the tip of her knife. Alice muffled a yelp of pain as the blade pierced her skin. She stumbled and only just managed to save herself from falling, but Molly grabbed her by the arm. 'Don't try anything. Walk normal and keep your trap shut.'

There was nothing Alice could do other than obey her captor's command. The back streets were all but deserted, and those who were abroad after nightfall were not the sort of people who would be likely to come to her aid. It was almost pitch-dark in the alleyways and courts that Molly seemed to know so well, and after a while Alice had completely lost her bearings. Eventually they stopped outside a pub and Molly opened the door with her booted foot. She shoved Alice inside and marched her through the crowded, smoke-filled taproom to a private parlour at the back of the building. Seated on settles arranged around a desultory fire were two bearded brutes with scarred faces and ham-like fists curved around pint pots. They looked up as the door opened but their features remained stony, as if carved from granite.

'So you found her, then?' The elder of the two spoke in a gruff voice as if his throat was sore. He sported an eye-patch and his crooked nose must have been broken at some time in the past, which made him look even more villainous. His comrade looked quite meek and mild by comparison.

'She's going to help us find the brat.' Molly thrust Alice onto a chair. 'Sit there and don't move, unless you wants your throat slit, which I'd be more than happy to do.'

Alice sat bolt upright, not daring to speak.

Molly stood at her side, fingering the blade of her knife. 'It's sharp, Miss High and Mighty. It'll cut through your flesh like butter, so you'd better tell us where to find Flora.'

'I don't know exactly where she is,' Alice said truthfully. 'But it's a long way from London.'

Molly caught her a stinging blow across the cheek. 'That's not good enough. That kid is worth a fortune to me and I want her back.' She leaned closer so that Alice could smell her putrid breath and feel the heat of her body. 'Billhook enjoys pretty girls like you, don't you, Bill?'

The younger of the two men grinned and licked his lips. He was staring at Alice, although it was difficult to tell which eye was actually focusing on her, as they seemed to move independently and met occasionally over the bridge of his nose. A dribble of spittle ran down his chin and he licked it off. 'I could fancy her, Moll.'

'And you shall have her if she don't tell me what I want to know.' Molly held the knife close to Alice's cheek. 'I'll give you another chance, miss. Where is Flora?'

'I told you I don't know.' Alice was quaking inwardly, but she was determined not to let them see that she was terrified. She had no doubt that Molly would use the knife, and the man called Billhook made her skin crawl. The other fellow was no better.

With a quick swipe of her hand Molly snatched Alice's bonnet off her head and grabbed her by the hair. 'You're lying.' She pointed the knife at the big man. 'See him, Alice? Eric the Axe is a gentle chap until he's roused. He could wrench your arm from its socket with a flick of his fingers, and he's been known to crush a man's head between his hands like it was a walnut. He could trim your curls with one blow of his axe or sever your head from your body if you upset him. Couldn't you, Eric, love?'

241

'Just say the word, Molly,' Eric grinned, exposing a row of broken and blackened teeth. 'It'd be my pleasure.'

Alice was convinced and not about to argue. 'Flora has gone to Scotland.'

'Scotland?' Molly stepped back a pace, staring at her with narrowed eyes. 'You're lying.'

'They took her to Gretna Green,' Alice said firmly, it being the only Scottish place name she knew.

Billhook and Eric muttered together as if mulling it over, but Molly still looked suspicious. 'How do I know you're telling the truth?'

'If it's a choice between that or being viciously attacked by a madman with an axe what would you do?'

'You'd better not be lying.'

Alice shrugged, using her last scrap of courage. 'There's only one way to find out, but is she worth travelling all that way? Can't you find someone else to use for your vile trade?'

Another blow on the cheek almost unseated Alice and she clutched her hand to her face, but she fixed Molly with a hard stare. 'She's at a school for young ladies. I don't know its name but there can't be too many of those in a small place like Gretna Green.'

'Get out of here.' Molly tucked the knife in her belt. 'But if you're sending my men on a wild-goose chase you'll pay for it in blood, Alice Radcliffe. I know where you live and I also know where to find your ma. You wouldn't want Eric to carve his initials on her pretty face now, would you?'

Alice rose unsteadily to her feet. 'You're letting me go?'

'Why would I want to keep you here? Get out of my sight, but be warned. If I find out that you've tried to trick us you'll suffer for it. Now go.' She jerked her head in the direction of the doorway.

How she managed to make it as far as the street remained a blur in Alice's memory, but suddenly she found herself standing outside on the pavement with her bonnet clutched in her hand. A man lurched towards her. 'How much, my duck?'

She turned and ran, only stopping when she was certain that she was not being followed. Breathing heavily, she leaned against a wall and could have cried with relief when she heard the familiar sound of a steam engine. Unless she was very much mistaken she was close to the Metropolitan Rail terminus, and once there she was almost home. With a renewed spurt of energy she raced towards the rumbling, grinding sound of iron wheels on iron tracks. She could smell the smoke and hot oil and soon she was in familiar and well-lit streets. It was only a short distance to Half Moon Passage and the dingy attic room in Mrs Leech's boarding house.

Safely indoors, she collapsed on the bed still fully clothed. The feeling that she had just awakened from a nightmare persisted, but then the awful reality of what had occurred that evening began to dawn upon her.

It seemed unthinkable that her mother would actually want to marry Horace, although she had accepted his proposal with evident pleasure. Alice studied the ring finger on her left hand. A few hours ago she had been engaged to a man she actively disliked in order to provide a home for her ailing parent. Now, in a strange twist of fate, it seemed that her mother was going to marry Horace. One day she thought, she might find it funny, but she had never felt so alone or so completely abandoned. Her mother had allied herself to Horace and Jane, and would be lost to her. Flora had been sent miles away for her own safety, and Rory would be gone for weeks, which would seem like an eternity.

She reached under the bed and pulled out the valise in which she kept her possessions. Taking out the Christmas card, she held it close to the guttering candle, but instead of bringing her comfort the sight of the joyful family group brought tears to her eyes. 'We were like that once, Pa,' she whispered. 'The three of us were happy. Now it's all gone for ever.' She pulled the coverlet up to her chin and tucked the card under her pillow. She sighed heavily. 'I am all alone.'

There had been no word from either her mother or Horace, and after a week Alice decided to pay them a visit. It was not a success. Beth was bright-eyed

and full of plans for the house that had been promised to them. Jane herself blamed Alice entirely for
the change in her cousin's plans.

'You should have encouraged Horace,' she said
when they were alone in the parlour. 'Now he's going
to marry that silly milksop of a mother of yours,
who is extremely unlikely to produce a son and heir.
You've ruined everything, Alice Radcliffe. Your
father will be turning in his grave.'

'I don't think Papa would have forced me into a
marriage of convenience,' Alice said, making an
effort to remain calm and in control of her emotions.
'If Mama thinks she will be happy with Horace then
I'm glad he's asked her to marry him.'

'You had the ring, you silly girl.' Jane wagged her
finger at Alice, frowning ominously. 'You should
have kept the stupid fellow to his word. You could
have sued for breach of promise, or at least threatened him with the law. That usually works.'

Alice bit back a sharp retort. 'Well, it's done, and
Mama will have a home again. I can't argue with
that.'

'And what about you?' Jane curled her lip in a
sarcastic smile. 'Will you live with them like the
dutiful spinster daughter? You'll be on the shelf in
a couple of years.'

'I have my position at Dearborns', Aunt Jane. I
can support myself.'

'I can imagine the cheap lodgings in which you
find yourself. What a come-down for you.'

Alice glanced over Jane's shoulder as her mother burst into the room, pink-cheeked and beaming. 'Horace has just returned from the City and he's eager to see you, Alice. We don't want you to feel left out of things.'

Horace followed her into the room, smiling obsequiously. 'My dear Alice, I'm glad to see that you've come round to the idea of having me as your stepfather.'

'I wouldn't say that,' Alice said slowly. 'But I hope you two will be very happy.'

'Darling, you will be living with us.' Beth's eyes filled with tears. 'You will, won't you? The house isn't very large, but Horace says you can have the boxroom, and I'm sure it will be far more comfortable than the dreadful attic in Half Moon Passage.'

'I thought there were four bedchambers,' Jane said pointedly. 'Why consign your daughter to the smallest of them?'

Horace laid his finger on his lips as Beth was about to speak, and she hung her head. 'I'll deal with this, my dear.' He fixed Jane with a straight look. 'My wife and I will have the master bedroom, of course, but I need a dressing room, and we will have a cook/housekeeper who will have her own quarters. We can't expect a servant of any calibre to exist in a boxroom.'

'But that is good enough for your spinster daughter, is it, Beth?' Jane's tone dripped acid, and it was obvious that she was enjoying herself.

Alice held up her hands. 'Enough of this. It's immaterial because I won't be living with you, Mama. I am an independent working woman now, and I intend to remain so. I'm happy for you, but I won't be part of your ménage. It wouldn't do at all.'

'But, dearest, you can't wish to remain in that dreadful garret?' Beth clutched her fiancé's arm and her lips trembled ominously.

'Don't upset yourself, Mama,' Alice said hastily. 'I'll shortly be moving to a much nicer lodging house where I will be quite comfortable. You mustn't worry about me.'

'There, there, my dear. I'm sure Alice knows best.' Horace patted Beth's pale hand as it rested on his sleeve. 'She will be a welcome guest in our home whenever she chooses to pay us a visit.'

'The sooner you're all out of my house the better,' Jane said with a grim smile. 'The final reading of the banns is due to take place in a just over a fortnight, therefore I intend to book the church for your nuptials the following week. Have you any objection to that. Horace?'

His moustache quivered and his bushy eyebrows moved closer together, but then his frown was replaced by a confident smile. 'Anything you say, Cousin. Might we expect to move into the house immediately after the wedding?'

'Of course. That is my plan.'

Alice turned to her mother with a questioning look. 'Are you happy with that, Mama?'

'Yes, I think so. Everything is happening so quickly.' Beth glanced at Horace and he nodded emphatically.

'It can't come too soon, my love. I will be a proud man on the day we're wed.'

'You're a fool, Horace Hubble,' Jane said crossly. 'I suppose you realise that once you're married you'll be responsible for supporting your wife, and the running of the house? It's bought and paid for, but don't expect a penny more out of me.'

'I – I hadn't thought that far, Jane.' Horace paled beneath his whiskers, which bristled like the fur of an angry cat.

'But things might change if you should sire a boy child,' Jane cast a disparaging glance at Beth, who hung her head, blushing furiously, 'unlikely though it seems. But if you do produce a son and heir I will settle a considerable sum for his upkeep and education ...'

'That's most generous of you,' Horace said hastily. 'Most generous.'

'Let me finish.' Jane rose slowly from her chair. 'There is a condition, however, which must be met.'

'Anything, Cousin.' Horace's eyes sparkled with expectation. 'Whatever you wish, providing it's within my power.'

'You will consign the boy to my care, and I will see that he is brought up to fear the Lord. When he is old enough he will be sent to Oxford to study theology. I have it all planned.'

Alice stared at her in horror. 'You can't take a child from his parents. That would be cruel.'

'Who asked you?' Jane turned on her in a fury. 'What has it to do with you? Haven't you just said that you wanted nothing more to do with your mother?'

'No, that's not what I meant at all. Just because I choose not to live with them doesn't mean that I've cut myself off from my mother and her husband.'

'It does sound a bit harsh,' Horace ventured nervously. 'I mean, taking a child from its mother is not a very Christian act, Jane.'

Beth slid silently to the floor in a dead faint.

Alice pushed past Jane and went down on her knees beside her mother. 'Smelling salts,' she said tersely. 'Have you any sal volatile, Aunt Jane?'

Jane threw up her hands. 'You expect that feeble creature to bear a child, Horace?' She moved to the bell pull and tugged at it. 'But I meant what I said. You won't get a penny piece more out of me unless I can be sure that there is a male heir to continue the family name.' She swept out of the room, passing Clara in the doorway. 'Help Mrs Radcliffe to her room. She's having a fit of the vapours again.'

Horace made a move towards Beth but Alice held up her hand. 'She's all right, leave me to deal with it. I'm used to looking after Mama when she is unwell.' She beckoned to Clara. 'Where does my aunt keep the smelling salts?'

Clara delved into her pocket and pulled out a small

bottle. 'I keep them to hand, miss. Your ma quite often feels a bit faint and a whiff of this works a treat.'

'What shall I do?' Horace said faintly. 'Should I lift her onto the sofa?'

Alice uncorked the bottle and wafted it under her mother's nose. Beth shuddered and opened her eyes. 'What happened?'

'You're all right now, Mama. You just need to rest.' With Clara's help she managed to get her mother onto a chair.

'Should I send for the doctor?' Horace asked anxiously.

Alice straightened up. 'That won't be necessary, but what you need to do is to stand up to Aunt Jane. You have to tell her that what she demands is out of the question.'

Horace paled visibly. 'I depend on Jane for everything.'

'What sort of man are you?' Alice laid a comforting hand on her weeping mother's shoulder. 'More importantly, are you sure you want to marry him, Mama? I'm earning more now and I could find somewhere better for us to live. You don't have to give your life to this man and his hateful cousin.'

Beth mopped her eyes on her hanky. 'Horace is a good man, and when we are in our own home we will be free of Jane.'

'You heard what she said, Mama. If you should have a son she'll take him from you. Is that what you want?'

Beth smiled feebly. 'But if I'm blessed with a child it might be another girl, just like you. You're a woman now, Alice, and you don't need me any more. I want to be needed, it's as simple as that. I will have Horace to protect me, and a baby to love. One day you will marry and you'll have a child of your own. You'll understand then.'

Alice shook her head. 'I don't think I'll ever fully understand you.' She turned to Clara. 'I'm leaving now. Will you fetch my bonnet and mantle, please?'

Clara's pursed lips resembled a pink prune, but she merely nodded and hurried from the room.

'Don't go like this,' Beth pleaded, holding out her hand. 'I want you to be happy for me, Alice.'

'If you're happy then so am I, but I won't stand by and watch you being ruled by a termagant like Aunt Jane.' Alice leaned over and dropped a kiss on her mother's forehead. 'I have to go. It's a long walk to West Smithfield.'

She did not add that yet again she thought she was being followed, and it was not hard to imagine who was trailing her to and from her place of employment. The person melted into the shadows whenever she stopped and turned her head, but she was certain that it was Molly. How long it would be before Miss Bishop discovered that she had lied about Flora's whereabouts was a matter of conjecture, but it could not be long now. Billhook and Eric the Axe would soon return from their fruitless trip to Gretna Green, and then there would be trouble: of that she had no doubt.

She made a move to the door but hesitated, holding it open. 'Are you absolutely certain that you want to go ahead with this marriage, Mama? It's not too late to change your mind.'

Beth gave her a wan smile. 'I will marry Horace. I just wish that you would come and live with us.'

Alice shook her head. 'Thank you, but my mind is made up. I'll attend your wedding, but I don't want to share your home.' She left the room without giving her mother a chance to protest.

Outside the cobblestones glistened damp in the gaslight. The rain had ceased, leaving a pale mist clinging to the treetops in the square garden, and the roofs of the tall buildings were blotted out by low-hanging cloud, giving them a weird decapitated appearance. Alice glanced round anxiously, but the passers-by looked innocent enough and there did not seem to be anyone sinister following in her wake. She kept to the main streets for as long as possible, but as she left Duke Street and entered Bartholomew Close she realised that she was no longer alone. She quickened her pace and broke into a run, but the footsteps grew closer and she could hear noisy breathing. Whoever was pursuing her it was not a woman. Judging by the heavy tread it might even be Eric, and he was catching up with her. As she neared Half Moon Passage she was afraid she might not make it as far as the boarding house, but as she hurtled into the dark alleyway she collided with someone coming from the opposite direction.

'Alice, is that you?'

Her cry of fright froze in her throat as he wrapped his arms around her, preventing her from falling. 'George?'

He stiffened, holding her close. 'Who's there?' The answer was a clatter of hobnail boots on the cobbles as Alice's pursuer ran away. George peered at her in the dim light of a streetlamp on one of the houses opposite. 'Someone was chasing you.'

She regained her balance and straightened her bonnet with a shaking hand. 'Yes. I don't know why, it should be obvious I've nothing worth stealing.'

'It's not always about theft,' George said darkly. 'You shouldn't be wandering about the streets on your own.'

'I have to get back to my lodgings every evening after work, George.'

He frowned, taking her by the hand. 'I wouldn't like any of my sisters to live alone in a place like this. Come on, I'll see you safely home.'

Alice led the way into the gloomy depths of Half Moon Passage. 'Why are you here anyway?' She came to a halt outside the lodging house. 'How did you know this was where I live?'

'Beasley gave me your address, but only because I was sent by Mr Frederick.' He put his hand in his pocket and took out an envelope. 'The boss came looking for you, but you'd just left the office. He gave this to me, and said if I was passing to drop it in to you as tomorrow is Sunday and he knew that you'd been anxious about Flora. Does that make sense?'

Despite everything Alice felt her spirits rise as she took the crumpled envelope from him. 'Yes, it does. I'm so grateful, George. I've been sick with worry about the poor child.'

'My brothers and sisters drive me mad at times, but I'd miss them if I had to leave home.'

Alice stood on tiptoe to plant a kiss on his cheek. 'Thank you for taking the trouble to find me, George. And thank you for turning up at exactly the right moment.'

'You need to be more careful.' George glanced up at the shabby exterior. 'This isn't a good place to be.'

'I'm looking for a room elsewhere, but I don't get much free time.'

'I could help you,' George said eagerly. 'We live in Five Foot Lane. It's between Old Fish Street and Upper Thames Street, quite handy for the office. Ma lets a room every now and again, when things get tight moneywise. It's noisy and chaotic, but you'd never feel lonely. You can't miss our house – it's got a blue door and there's always washing hanging out.'

She smiled up into his earnest face. 'Thank you, George. I'll give it some thought.'

'That would be splendid. You'd love my sister, Carrie. She's the eldest and the best, but the other girls are fine as long as you keep them in their place, and the boys are little imps, but they mean well, most of the time.'

'I really will think about it, George. But if you don't mind I'd better ring the bell. Mrs Leech doesn't allow gentlemen callers, so I can't ask you in.'

He backed away. 'I wouldn't dream of it anyway. Ma is very strict about manners and how to treat a lady with respect. I'll see you in the office on Monday.'

'Thank you, George.' Alice tugged at the chain and the bell clanged sonorously inside the building.

The door opened a fraction and Mrs Leech peered out. 'You're too late for supper; I fed it to the dog.' She stood aside, glowering, but Alice did not choose to stop and argue.

She hurried upstairs to her room and lit a candle. In its flickering light she pored over Flora's childish handwriting, which was smudged and covered in blots. All her worst fears were realised before she had read the first paragraph. Flora was utterly miserable and if only half of what she described were true then the establishment sounded more like a penal colony than a school for young ladies. Alice slumped down on her bed, staring at the single sheet of paper with tears running down her cheeks. Flora's last words stood out on the page as if written in flames – 'Save me, Alice. Save me, please.'

# Chapter Fourteen

Alice barely slept that night, and when she did drift off in the cold small hours her dreams were haunted by Flora's plea for help. Next morning she rose early. It was clear that Mr Dearborn knew nothing of his daughter's plight and must be made aware of it as quickly as possible. She could not wait until Monday morning when he would be occupied with business matters, and so she set off for Russell Square with the letter in her reticule.

Hoskins let her in although he seemed doubtful as to whether the master would be willing to see her. 'The mistress left instructions that you weren't to be admitted under any circumstances, Miss Alice,' he said in a low voice. 'But she's still abed and unlikely to rise before noon.'

'It's about Miss Flora. I must speak to Mr Dearborn; it can't wait.'

Hoskins glanced over his shoulder. 'I suggest you go to the kitchen, miss. Cook will take care of you until the master comes down for his breakfast, and then I'll ask him if he'll see you.'

The prospect of a warm fire and perhaps a hot cup of tea was too tempting to resist. As she went down the back stairs and the aroma of cooking assailed her nostrils Alice realised that she was very hungry. She had missed supper and had left the house too early for breakfast, which in any case was usually tea and toast with the merest a scrape of butter.

Cook was busy preparing the joint to roast for Sunday luncheon, and Nettie was the first to spot Alice. She hurried round the table to give her a hug. 'I know as how I shouldn't say it, miss, but I'm so pleased to see you.'

'Get back to work, Nettie,' Cook said, frowning. 'What can I do for you, Miss Radcliffe?'

'If I might sit for a while I'd be very grateful, Cook. I came to see Mr Frederick on an urgent matter.'

'Miss Flora, is it?' Cook reached for the teapot. 'Nettie, fetch a cup and saucer and bring the fruit-cake from the pantry. Miss Radcliffe looks perished and half-starved.'

'It is about Flora,' Alice said, mystified. 'How did you know?'

'She'd be the only reason you would enter this house again, miss.' Cook poured the tea and cut a generous slice of cake. 'Pass this to Miss Radcliffe, Nettie. Then get on with peeling those vegetables. We haven't got all day.'

'It does concern Flora,' Alice said carefully. 'But I need to discuss it with her father.'

'I understand.' Cook attacked the leg of lamb, stabbing sprigs of rosemary into the flesh. 'The sort of school she's been sent to is just for rich folk to get rid of the children they can't be bothered with, if you ask me. It was bound to end badly.'

Alice sipped her tea, saying nothing. The cake was rich, fruity and delicious, and she ate hungrily, all the while keeping an eye on the clock above the mantelshelf. She looked up with a start as one of the bells on the wall board jangled impatiently.

Cook gave it a cursory glance. 'Dining room, Nettie. You'll have to go because Dora has the day off to visit her mother.' She waited until Nettie had disappeared up the stairs carrying a pot of coffee and a jug of cream. 'Bring Miss Flora home, if you can. She was a naughty child until you came along, but we've all seen a different side of her since you took her in hand.'

Hoskins appeared on the staircase. 'The master will see you in the dining room, Miss Alice.'

Frederick was seated alone at the vast table with a plate of bacon, devilled kidneys and buttered eggs in front of him. He glanced at Alice, eyebrows raised. 'What is so urgent that it could not wait until business hours tomorrow, Miss Radcliffe?'

Alice took the letter from her reticule and laid it on his side plate. 'This will explain everything, sir. I'm very worried about Flora.'

Frederick studied the sheet of paper. 'I've had something similar, but we must allow for exaggeration and Flora's gift for the dramatic. I hope that in time she will settle down.'

'It's not just that, sir.' Alice realised that she would get nowhere unless she told Flora's father the real reason for her state of near panic. She clasped her hands tightly in front of her, choosing her words carefully. 'There are others involved, Mr Dearborn. You need to know the whole truth.'

'I can see that you're not going to let this rest.' He pushed his plate away. 'Sit down and tell me everything.'

When she had finished telling him about Molly and the threat she posed to Flora she sat back in the chair, hoping that she had done the right thing.

Frederick was silent for a moment and his expression gave nothing away. 'This is more serious than I had thought,' he said gravely. 'The police must be informed.'

'Do you think that's wise, sir? Molly has a whole gang under her command, or so I believe. The police might catch a couple of them but she's determined to get Flora, and if she is her real mother there's very little that the law can do to stop her.'

He frowned thoughtfully. 'I've never met Molly Bishop, but I doubt if a woman from the criminal class could produce a child like Flora. Even if she has a birth certificate in her possession it would probably be a forgery. However, that is immaterial at the moment. She must be stopped somehow and the law is our only recourse.'

'Wouldn't it be better to move Flora to another school in a different part of the country? She might be happier in a different establishment.'

'First things first, Alice. I have friends in the constabulary and I will contact someone today, if possible. There's no point taking Flora away from Willoughby Hall until the felons are under arrest.'

Alice gazed down at her hands, which had clenched into fists in her lap. She knew better than to argue with her employer, especially when he had seemingly made up his mind. She rose from the chair. 'Thank you for seeing me, sir. I'll have to leave the matter in your hands.'

He smiled and his features relaxed. 'I'm glad you've seen sense.' He picked up his knife and fork. 'And by the way, I'm very impressed with the designs you've put before me. Rawlins tried to take the credit for some of the ideas, but I know his work too well, and I could tell that the drawings were yours and yours alone. Well done, Alice. Rory has convinced me that there is a growing market for Christmas cards and I'm beginning to think he's right, especially if we can adopt the new chromo-lithography technique. Now go home and enjoy what is left of your day of rest.'

Alice left the house feeling let down by Frederick's casual acceptance of his daughter's unhappiness. There was a sense of desperation in Flora's untidy scrawl that did not bode well for her future at Willoughby Hall, and Alice feared that it was only a matter of time before Molly discovered her whereabouts. There was little enough for the police to go on, and she doubted whether they would instigate a search on the basis of threats alone. Molly had so far managed to evade the law and would probably continue to do so, but she seemed unlikely to give up her quest to find Flora. Alice glanced nervously over her shoulder, but the only people she could see were families on their way to church. She experienced a sudden pang of regret. Perhaps she ought to have been more sympathetic to her mother's desire for home and security. If Horace was the man to fulfil such a desperate need then she would have to accept their union with good grace, but of one thing she was certain: living with them was not an option.

She arrived back at her lodgings to find Mrs Leech quite literally hopping up and down with rage.

'I don't like the company you keep, Miss Radcliffe.'

'I beg your pardon?' Alice stood in the entrance hall, staring at her in surprise. 'I don't understand.'

'You've fallen in with a bad lot,' Mrs Leech continued angrily. 'I don't want people like that knocking on my door. Next thing you know it'll be the coppers with a warrant to search my house, and

I ain't having any of it, so you can sling your hook, miss.'

Baffled, Alice continued to gaze at her. 'But I haven't had any visitors, not that I know of.'

'Don't act innocent with me. A great hulking brute came looking for you. He said you was stepping out together. Well, I took one look at his dial and I slammed the door. I can spot a villain a mile off, and I thought you was a respectable young person.'

'I am,' Alice protested. 'He's lying.' From Mrs Leech's brief description the man in question could only be Eric the Axe.

'Well, he knew where to find you, miss. So like I said, I want you out of here.'

Alice could see that Mrs Leech had made up her mind. 'All right. Give me time to pack my bag and I'll be gone.'

It did not take long to throw her belongings into the valise she had stowed beneath her bed, nor did she feel any qualms about leaving the miserable garret, and she walked away from Half Moon Passage without looking back. To remain there would be courting danger now that Molly knew she had lied about Flora's whereabouts. It was only as she reached the main road that she realised what she had done. She was once again homeless, but to return to Queen Square was unthinkable. Aunt Jane would doubtless enjoy her humiliation and would take her in, but she would never let her forget that she was living on charity. Residing with her mother and Horace would be even worse, and anyway they would not be in their new home for another two weeks. There was a real possibility that she might end up sleeping rough beneath the railway arches. Alice set her shoulders and headed in the direction of Upper Thames Street. George had made her a vague offer of accommodation and he was her last hope.

The house in Five Foot Lane boasted a bright blue front door, as George had said, and was situated between a ship's chandler and a pub. All four storeys looked as though they had been squashed into a small space as a last thought by a builder who was in a desperate hurry, and the result was slapdash and slightly eccentric. The brickwork was interspersed with bands of coloured tiles, set in geometric patterns, and the dormer windows frowned sleepily at the busy street below. Even though it was Sunday, washing hung from poles sticking out of the building like the prickles on a hedgehog. Tiny nightgowns and larger articles of underwear twisted and turned as if in a mad dance as the wind whistled up the side streets that led to the river.

Alice raised the knocker and let it fall once, twice and a third time. The racket going on inside the house must make all within deaf to such a small sound, she thought, stamping her cold feet on the frosty pavement. She was about to knock again when the door was opened by a tall, fair-haired young woman who bore a striking likeness to George.

She greeted her with a smile. 'You must be Alice.'

'I am, but how did you know?'

'My brother talks about you all the time.' She held out her hand. 'Do come in. I'm Carrie, by the way.'

Alice stepped over the threshold. 'George told me that you might have a room to let.'

'Who is it, Carrie?' A plump woman carrying a baby in her arms with a toddler clinging to her skirts came hurrying towards them.

'It's George's friend, Ma. He told her we'd got a spare room.'

Mrs Young came to a halt. 'Oh, my dear, I am so sorry. I let the room to one of my husband's work-mates last evening.' She raised her voice to make herself heard above the din emanating from the front room. 'Be quiet, children. We have a visitor.'

The smell of cooking wafted from the basement kitchen and the sound of childish chatter and gales of laughter filled her ears. Alice closed her eyes as the narrow hallway seemed to close in on her.

'Watch out, Carrie. She's going …' the words barely registered in Alice's brain as darkness swirled around her.

The next thing she knew she was lying on a sofa in the front room surrounded by curious faces. She struggled to raise herself. 'I'm sorry. I don't know what came over me.'

'You're all right now,' Carrie said kindly. 'Move away, you little monkeys. Give Miss Radcliffe some air.'

'When did you last eat, dear?' Mrs Young peered at her over the baby's fuzzy head.

'I – I had some cake,' Alice said dazedly.

'Off you go, children.' Mrs Young shooed the youngsters out of the door. 'Carrie, make a pot of tea. You'll stay for Sunday dinner, of course, but it won't be ready for another two hours. We have to wait until my husband finishes work. Mr Young always insists on a proper Sunday roast, even if we exist on bread and dripping for the rest of the week.'

'How you do go on, Ma,' Carrie said, laughing. She leaned over Alice, feeling her forehead with a cool hand. 'You don't seem to have a fever so that's something. I'll go and make the tea.' She glanced at the sleeping baby. 'Shall I put little Jackie in his cot, Ma?'

Mrs Young handed the baby to her. 'Thank you, dear.' She rubbed at a milky stain on her bodice. 'A mother can never be completely tidy when there are babes to care for, Miss Radcliffe.' She bent down to pick up the toddler, who was demanding attention. 'There, there, Annie, there's no need to snivel, dear.'

'I'm better now.' Alice swung her legs over the side of the sofa, but her head swam and she leaned back against the cushions. 'Well, almost. I'll be gone directly, Mrs Young. I'm sorry to have troubled you on a Sunday.'

'Rest a while longer, my dear. You look all in.' Mrs Young took a seat in a worn and threadbare armchair by the fire, dandling the toddler on her knee. 'George has often spoken of you, but if I might ask, what has brought you to this sorry pass?'

'I just need a place to sleep, Mrs Young. It's purely temporary.'

'I know nothing of your background, Alice, but it's obvious that you're used to better things.'

'It's a sorry tale, ma'am. I do find myself in straitened circumstances, but I'll manage very well, so you mustn't worry about me.'

'But I'm right in thinking that you have nowhere else to go?'

'I'm sure I can find lodgings somewhere.'

'I won't pry into your affairs, but you can stay here if you don't mind sharing a room with Carrie. It won't be what you're used to, but I simply can't allow you to wander these streets looking for accommodation.'

'I can pay you, Mrs Young. I earn a good wage at Dearborns'.'

'You can give me something towards your keep, but we won't worry about that now.' With Annie still clinging to her she rose from the chair. 'I have to go and check on the dinner, but you stay here and I'll see that the young ones don't disturb you.' She hitched Annie over her shoulder as she made for the door. 'My name is Rose. We don't stand on ceremony in this house.' She was gone before Alice had a chance to thank her, and the door had barely closed when it was thrust open and Carrie entered carrying a cup of tea. She placed it on a small table within Alice's reach.

'There you are. Be careful because it's piping hot.'

'You're very kind.' Alice sipped the sweet tea. 'This is wonderful, thank you.'

'George had told me a little about you,' Carrie said, smiling. 'He said you're an extremely talented artist.'

Alice managed a self-deprecating smile. 'I'm just learning.'

'No, really, he's very impressed by what you've achieved in such a short time. He went out earlier, but he should be home soon and I'm sure he'll be delighted to see you.' Carrie hovered by the doorway. 'I'd love to stay and chat, but I have to help Ma with the dinner. The girls try but they're not much use when it comes to cooking. You'll meet them all when we sit down to eat.'

Alice gulped and swallowed. 'I don't want to put you out. Your mama said I could share your room, but it seems like an imposition.'

'You talk like a toff,' Carrie said, chuckling. 'I don't mean to be rude, but it's obvious you're a young lady, and I dare say you'll find us a bit rowdy.'

'I think you're the kindest people I've ever met, and I'm truly grateful to you.' Alice turned away as her eyes brimmed with tears. It was easier to deal with the harsh treatment she had received from Mrs Leech than the overwhelming generosity of the Young family.

'You might not say that when you've met the young 'uns.' Carrie opened the door. 'I'll be back in a while. Put your feet up and rest while you can. Life in our house is anything but peaceful, as you'll soon discover.'

Carrie had spoken the truth. When she came to meet the rest of the children Alice found it almost impossible to remember their names, as they never seemed to be still for more than a few seconds at a time. There were three younger girls, apart from Annie who was barely toddling. Winnie, Nellie and Lizzie were incredibly alike, with mops of red, curly hair and blue eyes, and so close in age that they seemed to be interchangeable. The boys were slightly easier to tell apart. Charlie was fourteen, shy and fair-haired like his eldest brother and sister, and Bill was a lively ten-year-old who chattered non-stop, and Ned, aged sixteen, was the image of his father, whose booming presence filled the house from the moment he walked through the door.

Harold Young shrugged off his pea-jacket and tossed it to Ned. 'Hang it up, old chap.' He greeted his children with a casual grin and ruffled the hair of those nearest to him before enveloping his wife in a great bear hug. Annie released her mother's skirt and clung to her father's leg, begging to be picked up. He reached down and swung her up in the curve of his arm. 'And how's my little flower?'

Annie smiled and sucked her thumb.

'My dear, we have a visitor.' Rose turned to Alice

with an encouraging smile. 'Miss Radcliffe is going to stay for a few days while she looks for more suitable accommodation.'

Harold gave Alice a cursory glance. 'Do you have another name, miss? We don't choose to be formal in the Young household.'

Alice bobbed a curtsey. 'It's Alice, sir.'

He guffawed loudly. 'Ho, I see we have a young lady in our midst. Best mind your manners, children.' He set Annie down on a stool next to Winnie. 'Look after your sister, Nellie.'

'I'm Winnie, Pa. You're always getting us muddled up.'

He ruffled her copper curls. 'Well, you shouldn't look so alike. It's a natural mistake.' He moved to his seat at the head of the table. 'Serve up, Mother. I'm so hungry I could eat a horse.'

'This might well be such an animal,' Rose said as she opened the oven door. 'The butcher promised me it was prime beef, but from the price I think it might have been an old nag from the knacker's yard. What it might lack in flavour will be made up with plenty of mustard or horseradish sauce. Stir the gravy, Winnie, if you please, and, Nellie, you can slice up the Yorkshire pudding. Pa will carve as always.' She lifted the joint from the roasting tin and placed it on a china platter. 'Here you are, Father. There's plenty to go round.' She glared at the boys, who were already seated, clutching their knives and forks with eager expressions on their faces. 'Did you wash your hands?'

They nodded, but Alice saw the sly grins they exchanged when their mother's back was turned. She hesitated, not knowing where to sit, but Lizzie tugged at her skirt. 'You can sit next to me, miss.'

'Take a seat, do,' Harold said grandly. 'All are welcome in this establishment.' He stood up to receive the platter of meat. 'It's a fine joint, my dear. It's no matter what animal it came from, I'm sure it will be magnificent. What a pity that Chapman is missing this feast, but he's visiting his aunt who lives in Wapping. She's very religious and doesn't believe that anyone should work or do anything other than go to church on Sundays.'

Alice smiled at Lizzie and sat down beside her. It occurred to her that Chapman's aunt would have a lot in common with Aunt Jane, but she kept her thoughts to herself. Any remark she might have made would have been lost in the general chatter as the children took their places at the table.

'Well, she wouldn't approve of you working then, Harold,' Rose said, ladling gravy into a large jug.

'I have a family to feed,' he said piously. 'I think the Good Lord would rather I put food on the table for my young 'uns than spend Sunday on my knees in church. Someone has to keep an eye on everything at work or there'd be pilfering and goodness knows what else going on under our noses.' He proceeded to carve the meat, laying a slice on each plate as it was passed to him. He glanced at the empty place at the end of the table. 'Where's that boy? If George can't be punctual for meals he will have to go without.'

Almost as the words left his mouth the door opened and George breezed in, pink-cheeked and breathless. 'Sorry I'm late, Ma. I got into a conversation with Bert and forgot the time.' His eyes swept round the table and his mouth fell open when he spotted Alice. 'You came. Alice, that's wonderful.'

'Sit down, boy.' Harold scowled at him beneath lowered eyebrows, but his tone was jovial. 'Your mother's cooking deserves our full attention and our grateful thanks for all her efforts.'

This remark was greeted by an enthusiastic murmur of appreciation and at last the children fell silent as they bent their heads over their plates. George took his seat, grinning broadly as he picked up his knife and fork. 'Welcome to our home, Alice.'

She smiled and nodded as she tucked in with the rest of them. It was the best meal she had had since she left the Dearborns' establishment.

Later, when the last scrap of suet pudding and custard had been consumed, Alice helped the girls clear the table while the boys fetched water from the pump at the end of the street, and Carrie rolled up her sleeves to begin the washing up. Mrs Young was consigned to the parlour to put her feet up and feed the baby, while Harold sat in his usual seat by the fire and smoked his pipe. George directed the efforts of his younger brothers like a maestro conducting an orchestra, which amused Alice greatly.

'It wouldn't hurt you to take a turn at the sink,' she said, smiling.

'That's woman's work,' he replied casually. 'But you're a guest. You shouldn't be helping.'

'Indeed I should. Your mother was kind enough to take me in,' Alice said in a low voice, 'and Carrie is willing to share her room with me. I'm overwhelmed by their kindness to a complete stranger.'

Carrie glanced over her shoulder, half hidden by the steam rising from the hot water that Winnie was pouring into the sink. 'You might change your mind when you've been here for a few days, Alice. If living in a madhouse with kids chattering like monkeys is your idea of heaven then welcome to paradise.'

Alice shrugged and continued to wipe the dishes, handing them to Lizzie, who put them away in the oak dresser. Even as she worked Alice could not help smiling. The noise, the constant babel of young voices, the warmth and the genuine affection that enveloped the family members like a warm hug was touching and something to which she had always aspired. But even in the midst of the rough and tumble of the cheerful household she could not forget Flora's plight. It had been possible to put the worry from her mind for a short while, but now it all came back to her threefold. She could empathise entirely with the fear and loneliness that Flora must be feeling far away from the only family she had ever known, and her heart ached for the unhappy child.

'What's the matter, Alice?' George asked anxiously. 'Have I said something to upset you?'

'No, George. I was thinking of Flora having to remain in the place she hates so much.'

He laid his hand on her shoulder. 'At least she's safe from those who wish to harm her.'

'I'm not so sure. I think Molly has found out that I sent them on a wild-goose chase. I know her men are following me, although I think I gave them the slip this morning after I went to see Mr Dearborn.'

'You went to the boss's house? Why?'

'I went to warn him that Flora is in danger, but he seems to think that the police are the best people to handle things.'

'Maybe he's right. There's little enough you can do, so you'd best leave it to Mr Dearborn. He is Flora's legal guardian, even if he isn't her father. You must leave it to them, Alice. Don't put yourself in danger and don't think you can stand up to the sort of people who join these criminal gangs, because you can't. You'll come off the worst.'

Alice folded the drying cloth and laid it on the table. 'I suppose you're right,' she said reluctantly, although in her heart she did not agree.

That night, Carrie sat by the simple pine dressing table in her room vigorously brushing her blonde curly hair. She glanced at Alice's reflection in the mirror and sighed. 'I do envy you having such lovely straight hair. I spend hours trying to brush out my wretched curls but they insist on returning, especially when it's damp or raining.'

Alice was already in bed, propped up on pillows as she watched her new friend complete her toilette. Her hand flew automatically to her own hair, which hung straight and loose around her shoulders. 'I hadn't given it much thought lately,' she confessed. 'But you have lovely hair. It's the colour of a golden guinea – not that I've seen too many of those recently.'

Carrie twisted round on the stool. 'I'd like to hear all about you, Alice. My life is so dull compared to yours.'

'I don't think you'd want to know all the details,' Alice said evasively. 'She had not even told George the full extent of her trials, and she did not want to burden Carrie with her problems. She put her head on one side. 'You say your life is dull, but I saw you blush when George talked of his friend Bert. Is he someone special?'

Carrie's cheeks flushed bright pink and her eyes shone. 'He is rather a splendid person.' She leaned forward, lowering her voice. 'I'll tell you a secret, but you must promise not to tell anyone, least of all George.'

Alice made the sign of the cross on her bosom. 'I promise. Do go on.'

# Chapter Fifteen

'Well, Bertie is George's friend really, but I could tell by the way he looked at me that he thought I was rather special. Anyway, he asked me to go for a walk with him one Sunday after supper. That was back in the summer when the evenings were light, and we walked and talked and found that we had a lot in common.'

'And you fell in love?' Alice asked eagerly.

'Yes, to tell the truth we did, but it's difficult.'

'I don't understand. He sounds like a nice young man.'

'His family own a rival printing firm to Dearborns'. They make beautiful greeting cards with such lovely sentiments and pretty pictures. They're very well off and have a nice house overlooking the river in Chelsea.'

'I don't see the problem. Does George object to you seeing him?'

'He doesn't know about us. Nobody does except Ma, but I've sworn her to secrecy. The trouble is that Bertie is engaged to be married.' Carrie tugged at a particularly stubborn tangle and her eyes filled with tears.

'I'm sorry,' Alice said hastily. 'I can see that makes things difficult.'

Carrie wiped her eyes on the back of her hand. 'They'd known each other since they were children, and their fathers were close friends as well as business partners. Bertie said it was always assumed that they would make a match and he went along with it to please his parents.'

'Has he spoken to his fiancée about you?'

'Yes, of course he has, but she won't release him. His family wouldn't approve of me anyway.'

'I don't see why. You're lovely and you're nice. Bertie would be a lucky man to marry someone like you.'

'Thank you, but we're not the sort of people that Bertie's parents would think suitable. The girl they want him to marry has been brought up to be a lady; a bit like you, Alice. She talks proper and she knows how to conduct herself in society. I'm afraid I'm just a common girl and not good enough for a man like Bertie Challoner.'

'Stuff and nonsense,' Alice said angrily. 'I've only known you and your family for half a day – apart from George, of course – but I've never met such fine folk.' She frowned thoughtfully. 'But a previous engagement is a problem, I admit.'

Carrie abandoned the hairbrush and swivelled round on the stool to face Alice. 'I've told you my sorry story, now tell me yours.' She rose to her feet and moved to the bed, pulling back the patchwork coverlet. 'I hope you don't mind sharing with me. I don't think I snore.'

Alice pulled the quilt up to her chin. A fire burned in the grate and the room was pleasantly warm. In the adjacent room she could hear the subdued chatter and giggles of the younger girls as they settled down for the night. From the room above there was the sound of heavy footsteps as the lodger made ready for bed, and there was the occasional dull thud followed by a stern warning from George as the boys larked around in the attic when they should be in bed fast asleep. All was quiet from the ground floor, where their parents shared the back room with the two youngest children. Alice was a stranger in their home and yet she felt more comfortable and relaxed than she had since the terrible day of the eviction from Doughty Street.

The bedsprings creaked as Carrie climbed in beside her and snuggled down. 'Come on, Alice, don't be a spoilsport. I've told you my secret, now you must tell me yours.'

'It's a long story.'

'I love long stories.' Carrie yawned and pulled the covers up to her chin. 'Go on, please.'

Once again Alice was compelled to relive the difficulties she had faced since her father's death.

'... So you see,' she said in conclusion. 'I don't know what to do for the best. Mr Dearborn says that Flora is safe and must be left to settle into her new life, but I can't accept that.'

Carrie raised herself on one elbow. 'What a time you've had, Alice. It's hard to believe – not that I doubt you,' she added hastily. 'But I know what I'd do.'

'Really?' Wide awake suddenly, Alice peered at her in the soft glow emitted by the dying embers of the fire. 'Tell me, Carrie. I need to know.'

'I'd go to Yorkshire and visit Flora at the school. Then you'd know for certain how she was placed.'

'But what if I was followed? Molly Bishop seems desperate to get her hands on Flora.'

'You'd have to make sure you weren't seen.'

'You make it sound so easy.'

'There must be a way, Alice.' Carrie curled on her side. 'Perhaps if we sleep on it we'll come up with a solution.'

Next morning there was barely time to think, as Alice discovered the moment she opened her eyes. Carrie was already dressed and doing her best to tame her wildly curling hair into a snood at the nape of her neck. The sound of footsteps thundering down the stairs was a sign that the boys were also up and about, and George's voice was raised to make himself heard above their protests as he marshalled them into a semblance of order. The more subdued tones of the new lodger could be heard as he passed their door, followed by the shrill voices of the girls as they tumbled out of their bedroom and made their way downstairs.

'I'm late,' Carrie said, pulling a face. 'I'm usually first to rise. It's my job to see to the fire in the range and then I light one beneath the copper in the wash-house.'

Alice sat up and swung her legs over the side of the bed. 'I suppose you must have a lot of washing with such a large family.'

Carrie fastened the last pin in her hair. 'Ma takes in laundry as well as doing our own. She says it's the only way to make ends meet, Alice. Pa works hard but money is always short, even though George and I contribute what we can, and the older boys have jobs too.'

'I didn't realise,' Alice said humbly. 'I was brought up to think that we were poor, but now I can see that wasn't the case at all. I'm afraid I've got a lot to learn.'

'We've all got our place in the scheme of things. That's what I was trying to say last night when I told you about Bertie. We're not desperately poor because we all work hard, but that doesn't make me Bertie's equal, or that's what his parents would think if they knew he wanted me for his wife instead of the rich and beautiful Margery.' Carrie opened the door. 'I've got things to do, but you can take your time.'

Alice was already out of bed, pulling on her clothes. 'I'll be down in a minute and I'll help all I can.'

If supper had been chaotic then breakfast was pure bedlam. Rose had gone outside to the wash-house, leaving Winnie to see to the two youngest children, while Carrie served dollops of porridge to Charlie and Bill, Ned having already left for work on the docks with his father. Alice found herself in charge of the large Brown Betty teapot and she filled cups, dealing out small lumps of sugar, which Carrie explained had to be carefully rationed or the boys would fill their pockets and munch it like sweets on their way to work in Billingsgate Market. Nellie and Lizzie had to be cleaned up and made ready for school, and finally George put in an appearance, looking dapper as ever in his city suit.

'Are you ready to go to the office, Miss Radcliffe?'

She put the teapot on the table and brushed a stray lock of hair back from her forehead. 'Yes, George. Just give me a minute to put on my bonnet and cape.'

'But you haven't eaten,' Carrie protested.

'I'll see that she gets something at dinnertime,' George said cheerfully. 'I'll look after her, so don't fuss, Mother Hen.'

Carrie flicked the wooden spoon catching her brother on the cheek with a splodge of porridge. He wiped it off with the tip of his forefinger and licked it clean. 'Excellent shot. Remind me to get you back for that one, Carrie.' He headed for the doorway, almost tripping over Annie, who was holding up her arms for a cuddle. He ruffled her hair. 'Not now, poppet. George has to go to work or the nasty man will tell him off and keep some of his money on pay day.' He picked her up and handed her to Carrie. 'This one is as slippery as an eel. She tried to follow me out of the house yesterday.'

Carrie took the protesting toddler in her arms. 'Did you have a nice time with Bertie?'

George shrugged and opened the door. 'What sort of question is that? We talked shop mostly and had couple of pints in the pub. Come along, Alice. We'll be late if you don't hurry.'

As they walked briskly along the street Alice had to quicken her pace in order to keep up with George's long strides.

'I love your family,' she said breathlessly, 'but I can't impose on them like this.'

He shot her a sideways glance, eyebrows raised. 'I don't understand. You're more than welcome to stay with us. Ma and Pa both said so.'

'And they're the kindest people I've ever met, but I need to find somewhere more permanent.'

'What's the matter? Aren't we good enough for you, Miss Radcliffe?' George strode across the street, ignoring the shouts of the cabbies and draymen whose paths he crossed regardless of the danger. Alice followed more slowly, catching up with him as he reached Ludgate Hill.

'That's not fair and it's certainly not true. But I've seen how hard you all work to keep a roof over your heads, and if I overstay my welcome you'll come to resent me. You all will, and I don't want that to happen.'

'I can't see it myself,' he said sulkily. 'Why are you women so difficult to comprehend? There's Carrie moping because my friend Bert is engaged to an heiress. She thinks I don't know, but anyone can see that they're both moonstruck, and then there's young Annie constantly demanding attention and she's not yet three. Why can't you be more like the boys?'

A gurgle of laughter escaped from Alice's lips. 'Would you really like girls to be the same as boys? If I were like you I might punch you on the jaw if you said something that offended me.'

'I suppose that's true. But you must admit that you complicate our lives and your own.' He came to a halt outside the door of Dearborns' establishment and held it open. 'After you, Miss Radcliffe.'

She stepped inside, coming face to face with Martin. He looked from one to the other with a smile twisting his lips. 'So that's how the wind blows, is it? You two are getting very friendly.'

'Stow it, Collis,' Alice said gruffly.

His jaw dropped. 'Well, I'll be damned.'

Martin's shocked expression was exactly what she had expected; young ladies were not supposed to answer back, let alone use common parlance. She winked at George, who seemed equally startled, and holding her head high she sashayed off towards the office, greeting Beasley with a friendly smile as she passed his desk.

As she opened the door she could hear Martin speaking in a hushed tone and George's loud response. 'Well, what do you expect, old man? You always treat her like one of your brainless popsies. Alice is a colleague and you'd better get used to the fact.'

'Thank you, George,' Alice whispered as he caught up with her.

'You made your point,' he said sheepishly. 'I don't think Collis will make that mistake again.'

'What's all this? You two are late.' Rawlins erupted from behind his partition, glaring at the clock on the wall.

'One minute, sir,' George said pointedly. 'I'll take care to work one minute past my time tonight, Mr Wall.'

'And so will I,' Alice added boldly. Standing up to Martin had made her feel that she was their equal, although she doubted whether men would ever acknowledge the fact. She had the satisfaction of seeing Rawlins at a loss for words as she went to her desk. There were decisions to be made that would affect her future as well as Flora's, and there was no time to lose. She bent her head over her work and began to draw.

Perhaps Mr Dearborn was right and Flora simply

needed more time to settle into the school routine. She was a bright child and if she put her mind to it she could do very well. Maybe all she needed was discipline and guidance, but it was not that simple: Molly Bishop still posed a threat and the school needed to be informed of a possible attempt to kidnap one of their pupils. If only Rory were here, she thought, chewing the end of her pen. He would know how to persuade his brother that some action was needed. It was not her place to interfere in Mr Dearborn's arrangements, and yet she felt in some way responsible for Flora, and it was clear from her letter that the poor child was utterly miserable.

Alice went to the office next day, trying hard to concentrate on the work in hand, but Flora's plight was never far from her thoughts. At the first opportunity she raised the subject once again with her boss, but Mr Dearborn brushed her fears aside.

'Miss Radcliffe,' he said, smiling, 'it's to your credit that you worry about my daughter, but I can assure you that Willoughby Hall is as secure as any of Her Majesty's prisons. It's situated in the middle of inhospitable moorland at least five miles from Ryby, which is the nearest village, and then it is little more than a hamlet. Flora is safer there than she would be in the Tower of London. I suggest you concentrate on your work, which is excellent. I can't wait to show it to my brother when he returns from Ireland.'

Alice felt her heart flip against her ribcage at the

mention of Rory's name, and Flora was momentarily forgotten. 'Will he return soon, sir?' The words tumbled from her lips before she had time to think and she felt the blood rush to her cheeks. 'I mean, it will be so exciting to see the new machinery in action. Printing cards in colour will be an amazing achievement.'

Frederick's eyes lit up and he nodded vigorously. 'I agree entirely, and that is why I need you to come up with designs that will thrill the public and encourage them to buy. You must stop worrying about Flora and concentrate on your work, Alice. You know that as well as I.'

That evening Alice repeated his words to Carrie as they made ready for bed.

'It makes sense,' Carrie said after some thought. 'But I can see that you're not convinced.'

Alice sank down on the flock-filled mattress. 'My head tells me that he's right but my heart won't agree. I know that Flora is in danger and that she's unhappy. I can't explain it, but that's how I feel.'

'Is she more important to you than your work?'

'I didn't think so, but she's just a child, Carrie. She's nine years old, and she's far away from home. If Molly gets her hands on Flora she'll make her life hell, or even worse. The woman has no conscience and no morals. She scares me, so what would she do to Flora?'

Carrie finished plaiting her hair and fastened the braid off with a ribbon. 'I think you've answered your own question. You must follow your instincts, Alice.' She rose from the dressing stool and went to sit beside her. 'What would Rory do in similar circumstances?'

'Rory?' Alice stared at her in surprise. 'What has he got to do with anything?'

Carrie threw back her head and laughed. 'I've kept my feelings for Bertie hidden for a long time and I can recognise a fellow sufferer. You blush whenever his name crops up in conversation, and when you told me about the Christmas tree and the snowballs in the square there was a dreamy look on your face.'

'It's not like that. We're just friends.'

'How often have I said that? Come along, Alice, this is me you're talking to. We've come to know each other quite well over the last few days. It's more what you don't say about Rory Dearborn that gives you away.'

'I do like him a lot,' Alice admitted grudgingly. 'But you and I are in a similar situation, Carrie. Rory is kind and he's fun to be with, but he'll marry someone from his own class, not a humble working girl like me.'

Carrie slipped her arms around Alice and gave her a hug. 'He'd be lucky to have someone like you.'

'Yes,' Alice said, chuckling. 'He would, but if I were ever to marry I would prefer a husband who was a bit more reliable than Rory Dearborn. My parents married for love, but Pa was a dreamer and lived for his books and his intellectual friends. My mother was always delicate and had no idea how to manage a household. I hardly saw her while I was growing up as she took to her bed with the slightest ailment, leaving the servants to do as they pleased. I don't want to live like that.'

'You'll have to take a chance sometime,' Carrie said softly. 'Maybe Rory is the one, or perhaps you need someone more like George?'

Alice stared at her in surprise. 'George? Goodness me, I've never thought of your brother in that way. I like him enormously, but he's just a boy.'

'He's the same age as you and he's growing older each day.' Carrie stood up and took off her wrap. 'Anyway, I'm tired and I need to sleep.'

Alice moved over to her side of the bed and slid beneath the covers. 'You don't think that George fancies me, do you? I mean I'd hate to lead him on.'

'Don't worry about him. He'll have his heart broken a few times before he finds the right girl, and in case you're worried, I don't think that it's you. You're too bright and too ambitious to want to tie yourself to someone who doesn't match up to you. I love my brother, but he'll always be happy to plod along in a nice safe job. He'll be a wonderful family man, but I don't suppose he would provide the excitement you crave.'

Alice turned her head to gaze at Carrie's profile outlined against the starched white pillowcase. 'Heavens above, what a strange opinion you have of me.'

'Do I?' Carrie met her startled look with a smile. 'I don't think you know yourself very well, Alice Radcliffe.'

Alice was silent for a moment, watching the flickering shadows on the ceiling above the fireplace as tiny flames licked around the coals. 'I'd always led such a quiet life until Pa died,' she said thoughtfully. 'Then everything turned upside down and now I have nothing.'

'Nonsense,' Carrie said severely. 'You have friends, and you have talent, which landed you a job in the workplace. That is beyond the reach of most women. You're thinking of travelling to the wilds of Yorkshire to see a little girl you care about, and quite obviously she has a strong attachment to you.'

'Yes, you're right. I can't desert Flora and I won't rest until I know that she's safe and happy, but Mr Dearborn won't allow me time off to go and see her.'

'So what will you do?'

'I'll get a train to York and make my way to the school. I have to find out if it's as bad as Flora says it is. I can't just leave the poor little thing to suffer.'

'At least you'll know how matters lie,' Carrie said sleepily. 'Seeing Flora again should put your mind at rest.'

'I'll have to tell George, but I'm not going to mention it to anyone else. He can tell Rawlins that I'm unwell, and that I'll be back in the office as soon as I'm better.'

'I hope you know what you're doing.' Carrie turned on her side. 'Good night, Alice.' Within minutes she was snoring gently.

Alice lay awake for some time. There was one thing she must do before she embarked on such a journey, and that was to visit Queen Square and make sure that all was well with her mother. She closed her eyes.

Beth greeted her daughter with a bright smile. 'I'm so glad you came, darling. I've been worried about you. It was all a silly misunderstanding.'

Alice kissed her mother's flushed cheek. 'It's all right, Mama. I do understand, I really do.'

'No, dear, you don't. You can't know what it's like to lose the man you've loved for most of your life, and be at the mercy of someone who actually despises you.'

'I don't think Aunt Jane despises you, Mama,' Alice said hastily.

'She can't wait to get me out of her house, but I don't mind now because I'll soon have a home of my own again.' Beth looked away, and her hands shook as she twisted her handkerchief around her fingers. 'Can you forgive me for stealing your fiancé? I know it was an unforgiveable thing to do, but I was desperate and Horace is a kind man. I think we'll do well together.'

Alice seized her mother's hands, holding them in a firm clasp. 'Mama, I'm grateful to you. I couldn't have gone through with it, but I hope you'll both be very happy.'

'Do you mean that, Alice?'

'With all my heart.'

Beth's lips trembled and she moved away to stand by the window, staring out as if mesmerised by the view. 'I'm sorry about the boxroom. I did suggest that you ought to have the larger bedchamber, but Horace pointed out that you would probably marry some day and move out, and that we were in desperate need of a superior type of cook-housekeeper, one who would not be satisfied with a such a tiny room.'

'Don't upset yourself, Mama. There's no need to feel bad about it because I wouldn't want to live with you and Horace anyway. I have a good position at Dearborns'. At the moment I'm staying with friends, but I'll be looking for more suitable accommodation very soon.'

Beth turned to her with a sigh. 'You are so clever and brave, my darling. You are much more like your papa than me, thank goodness. I am a poor weak thing compared to you, but I want you to know that I'm very proud of you.'

'Thank you, Mama. That means a lot to me.' Alice glanced at the clock on the mantelshelf. Horace would be returning from his job in the counting house very soon, and there was always the chance that Aunt Jane would walk into the room. 'I really should be going. I just wanted to make sure that you were all right.'

Beth hurried towards her, arms outstretched. 'Don't go, Alice. Won't you stay until Horace returns? I know he'd like to see you.'

'I doubt it,' Alice said with feeling. 'I'm sorry, but Horace and I will never get on well together. I'll tolerate him because he'll be your husband, but please don't expect me to like him.'

'If only things were different.'

'Well they're not. If you're happy then I'll be happy too. I can't say fairer than that, but Jane and Horace will never be my favourite people.' Alice gave her mother a quick hug. 'I'll see you in the church.'

Beth nodded emphatically. 'I was hoping you'd be my bridesmaid.'

'I'll be there to wish you well, but I wouldn't feel comfortable taking part in any other way. You don't need me. You have Horace to care for you from now on.'

'Yes, dear, I know.' Beth did not sound convinced. 'Are you sure you won't stay for supper?'

'I'm expected back at my friend's house.' Alice squeezed her mother's hands. 'I love you and always will. Goodbye, Mama.'

As she left the house she thought she saw a shadow slip behind one of the trees in the square gardens. There had been no sign of anyone following her for the last few days, and she realised that she had been lulled into a false sense of security since she left Half Moon Passage. Molly knew of her deception and was not the sort of person to forgive or forget that her plans to abduct Flora had been thwarted. The mere thought of what Flora might suffer at Molly's hands sent a chill down Alice's spine and, forgetting her own safety, she ran to the railings, peering into the gloom. 'Leave me alone,' she shouted angrily. 'If you come within twenty paces of me I'll fetch a constable and have you arrested.'

A couple of roosting pigeons rustled the bare twigs and they fluttered from a branch overhead, making her jump, but otherwise there was no response.

'I know you're there,' Alice said shakily. 'Keep away from me.'

She turned and fled, running as fast as she could until she was too breathless to keep up the pace, and a painful stitch in her side caused her to stop and bend double until the spasm passed. Walking on more slowly, she was conscious of footsteps behind her but every time she turned round there seemed to be just ordinary folk going about their daily business. Convincing herself that it was her imagination playing tricks, Alice hurried homeward, arriving outside the now familiar blue door at the same time as Carrie.

'What's the matter?' Carrie demanded anxiously. 'You look as though you've seen a ghost.'

'It's nothing. I thought I was being followed but I must have been imagining things.'

Carrie raised the knocker and rapped on the door. 'I thought that had stopped.'

'So did I,' Alice said, glancing over her shoulder. She uttered a gasp of fear as she spotted the large man, leaning against the lamppost at the corner of the street. 'Oh no,' she breathed. 'It can't be! I thought I'd given him the slip.'

# Chapter Sixteen

The sight of Eric the Axe was enough to convince Alice that the time had come for action and not words. The next day after work, with her wages tucked safely in her reticule and a few things stowed in her valise, she arrived at King's Cross station and bought a return ticket to York.

It was late at night by the time the train pulled into the station at the end of her journey and Alice was close to exhaustion. She found a porter and asked him where she might find a room for the night. He looked her up and down, pushing his cap to the back of his head and scratching his bald pate. 'There's the Royal Station Hotel, miss, but thee doesn't look as if thee could afford such a place.'

His forthright attitude was embarrassing, but came as something of a relief. At least she would not have to explain her straitened circumstances. 'Somewhere a little less expensive would be better.'

'Come with me, lass. I'm just going off duty and I'll put thee on the right road. There's a respectable woman who takes in commercial travellers not far from here. She might be able to give thee a bed for the night.'

Alice could have kissed his whiskery cheek, but she simply smiled and thanked him. He took her valise and led her through the ticket office to the station forecourt. It was too dark to see very much and she was in a strange town, but she was glad of his company as he walked her to the house in a side street.

The landlady gave her a calculating look as if assessing the cost of her outfit and the value of her belongings. 'What's a young woman like you doing travelling all alone, I might ask?'

'I'm planning to visit a young friend at her school,' Alice answered truthfully.

'Take her in, Mrs Updyke. You can't leave the poor lass to wander the streets.' The porter dumped Alice's valise on the holystoned doorstep. 'I'm off home.' He turned on his heel and trudged off into the darkness.

A cold wind whipped at Alice's bonnet and tugged at her skirts. She shivered, waiting for an answer.

'Very well.' Mrs Updyke stood aside to let Alice into the narrow hallway. 'Come in. Luckily for you I've got a room vacant, but only for the one night, mind you.'

'That's all I want. Thank you, ma'am.' Alice picked up her case and entered the house. The smell of lye soap and carbolic assailed her nostrils as she followed the landlady upstairs to a small bedroom at the back of the house.

Mrs Updyke put the oil lamp down while she lit a candle, placing it on a deal chest of drawers, which was the only furniture in the room apart from an iron bedstead. Alice's breath formed a halo around her head in the chilly air, but at least she had a roof over her head and a bed for the night.

'That will be one shilling in advance. Breakfast is extra. It's served between seven thirty and eight thirty, not a minute later. I expect you out of the house by nine sharp.'

Alice took a coin from her purse and placed it in Mrs Updyke's open hand. 'Thank you.'

Mrs Updyke pocketed the money. 'I don't usually take in single young women,' she said, sniffing. 'But I've made an exception this time.' She picked up the lamp, hesitating in the doorway and her stern expression was softened by a hint of a smile. 'I expect a nice hot cup of tea wouldn't go amiss.'

Alice sank down on the edge of the bed. 'That would be lovely, ma'am. Thank you.'

'You may be a southerner, but you have nice manners.' Mrs Updyke left the room, closing the door behind her.

Alice had just unpacked her nightgown when Mrs Updyke reappeared bringing a cup of tea and a slice of ginger cake. 'Parkin,' she said tersely. 'I made it this morning. You look famished, lass.' She put the cup and plate on the chest and whisked out of the room without waiting for Alice to respond.

Revived by the tea and cake, Alice undressed hastily and jumped into bed, curling up in a ball in an attempt to keep warm. The room was even colder than those in Aunt Jane's house, and she wished she had brought warmer clothes with her, but eventually she drifted off to sleep.

When she awakened next morning she thought for a moment she was in Carrie's room in Five Foot Lane, but then she realised that she was on her own. She sat up, wrapping the coverlet around her. It was still dark but the intensity of the cold and a pale glimmer of light through the thin cotton curtains suggested snow, and a quick peek outside confirmed her suspicions. The rooftops were white all over, as was the street below. Footsteps were barely audible and the sound of horses' hoofs and cartwheels was muted by the snowfall, which must be several inches deep. It did not bode well for a visit to the wild moorland, but Alice had come this far and she was not going to be put off now.

Despite her desire to save money she decided to take breakfast in the parlour where several gentlemen were already seated at table. They glanced at her without any sign of interest and went back to their bowls of porridge or munched on thick slices of buttered toast. Mrs Updyke clattered into the room with a tea tray and did not seem surprised to see Alice. 'You won't get far on an empty belly in this weather,' she said tersely. 'That will be another three-pence – fourpence if you want jam.'

Alice shook her head. 'Tea and toast will be fine.'

'Porridge is included. I'll bring some in a minute.' Mrs Updyke glared at one of her clients. 'Mr Liversedge, how many times have I told you not to wipe your mouth on the tablecloth. Do you behave like that at home?'

The man flushed to the roots of his hair, peering at her through the thick lenses of his spectacles. 'Apologies, ma'am. I thought it were me table napkin.' He rose from the table with the cloth still tucked into the neck of his shirt, and it was only through the quick action of the man sitting next to him that a disaster was prevented.

'I should see an eye doctor, old chap,' he said cheerfully. 'Maybe your spectacles need changing.'

Liversedge nodded. 'Aye, happen you're right.' He left the room mumbling apologies.

'You'll be setting off soon then?' Mrs Updyke placed a cup of tea in front of Alice. 'The snow will make travelling by road difficult in any event. Where are you bound, lass?'

Alice was uncomfortably aware that heads were raised and she was suddenly the focus of atten-tion. 'Willoughby Hall. It's near Ryby, so I've been told.'

'That's a fair stretch from here,' Mrs Updyke said,

nodding her head as if agreeing with her own statement. 'You'll need to find someone who can transport you there. You can't do it on foot, not at this time of year.'

'I'm going that way.'

Mrs Updyke turned to the man who had spoken. 'How are you getting there, Mr Jones? Could you take the lass with you?'

'I've arranged to go on the carrier's cart, missis. Dunno if he's got room for another, but he's travelling through Ryby village. I know that for certain.'

'There you are then,' Mrs Updyke said triumphantly. 'Get some food down you, lass, and maybe you can go with Mr Jones. He's one of my regulars so you can trust him.'

'You hear that, lads? I'm a respectable traveller.' He guffawed with laughter amidst ribald comments from the three other gentlemen at the table.

Mrs Updyke tossed her head. 'Don't prove me wrong, Joe Jones. If I hear you've let me down you won't find me so accommodating next time you're in this area.' She stomped out of the room.

'Only joking, girl,' Joe said with an apologetic smile. 'We have to have a laugh every now and again or we'd die of melancholy. I'll be leaving in twenty minutes. Join me if you want to.' He stood up, flipping his hand across the head of the man seated next to him. 'And no more sly comments from you, Bill. You'll put the young lady off.' He strolled out of the room, winking at Alice as he passed her chair.

His friend leaned towards Alice. 'You'll be all right with Joe,' he said in a whisper. 'He's a married man with ten little tykes to feed.'

Alice smiled in response. She was desperate to visit the school and find out how Flora was faring, and she had already decided to risk travelling with Joe Jones. She could not afford to delay in York a minute longer than was necessary.

The journey on the carrier's cart was less than comfortable. She had to lodge herself between a wooden tea chest and a crate filled with squawking hens, while Joe perched on top of a brassbound trunk, which according to the label was being transported to Willoughby Hall. Alice had paid the carter a shilling to be jolted over rutted roads without so much as an umbrella to shelter her from the elements, despite the sudden snow flurries. Joe himself seemed to be used to such modes of transport and he huddled in his old-fashioned caped greatcoat, keeping up a one-sided conversation largely concerning his brood of children and his ever-patient wife, who was bringing them up seemingly single-handedly as he was almost permanently on the road. After a while the cold had seeped into Alice's bones, numbing her fingers and toes. Breathing the icy air was painful in itself and she could see the tip of her nose glowing pink like a beacon.

'H-how far n-now?' she asked after what seemed like hours on the road.

Joe shrugged his shoulders. 'I dunno, miss. What is your name, lass?'

'Alice Radcliffe.'

'Nice,' he said approvingly. 'My youngest is called Alice. Did I mention her?'

Several times, Alice thought wearily, but she managed a smile despite the fact that her lips were cracked with the cold. 'Yes, you did.'

'How far now, mister?' Joe called to the carter, who had been silent, sitting on the box, smoking a foul-smelling pipe. 'How long will it take to reach the village?'

'Can't say in this weather. Wheels keep slipping on the ice. Might end up with a broken axle at this rate.' With his pipe clenched between his teeth the carter puffed a cloud of blue smoke into the grey sky where it joined the bank of pot-bellied clouds. 'Willoughby Hall first. Got a trunk for Miss Cotton, the new teacher.' He glanced over his shoulder. 'If you're after the job it's already gone. She's sent her things on in advance.'

'I'm not,' Alice said quickly. 'I'm just visiting.'

He shook his head. 'They don't allow visitors unless it's a school holiday. Very strict, they are. I know that for a fact because my youngest lass used to work there. Gave it up, though. Couldn't stand seeing them poor little mites treated so bad.'

Alice experienced a sudden shiver running down her spine that was not due to the bitter cold. 'What do you mean?'

He took the pipe from his mouth and spat onto the snow. 'Forget I said anything, miss. It ain't my place to say what goes on in that place.'

Joe leaned over to pat Alice on the arm. 'Don't worry, lass. Little tykes need a bit of discipline now and again.'

'But I must see Flora.' Alice stared at the trunk, an idea forming in her head. 'You say this trunk belongs to Miss Cotton, the new teacher.'

'Aye, so it says on the label.' The driver flicked the reins as the horse skidded on a particularly icy patch. 'We'll be lucky to get as far as Ryby at this rate.'

Alice sat in silence, studying the label written in neat copperplate. *Miss A. Cotton, Willoughby Hall, near Ryby, Yorkshire.* She looked up with a start when Joe tapped her on the shoulder.

'You'd best return to York with the carter, miss.' He glanced up into the gunmetal sky. The bleached moorland seemed to melt into the clouds as the snow began to fall in earnest. 'There's no accommodation to be had in the village, and it doesn't sound as if they'll make you very welcome at the school.'

'I think I'll take my chances,' Alice said slowly. 'Surely they wouldn't turn away a traveller on a day like this?'

'I wouldn't bet on it, lass.' He cupped his hands over his lips and blew on them. 'Sometimes I wish I were travelling in leather goods. I could do with a new pair of gloves. I lost mine a couple of days ago.'

'There's the school yonder.' The carter pointed with his whip and in the distance Alice could just make out the dark grey shape of a large building. As they drew nearer she could see the crenellated roof, giving the impression of a fortress, and this was emphasised by the high stone walls that surrounded the school. As they drew up in front of tall wrought-iron gates Alice was struck by the lack of trees or bushes that might soften the stark lines of the edifice. The flat, snow-covered expanse within its walls suggested an unrelieved sweep of gravel or grass. Willoughby Hall did not look welcoming and Alice was immediately certain that Flora's description of life at school had been accurate. She knew that she must gain admittance, and she knew now exactly how she was going to do it.

'I wouldn't fancy leaving any of my daughters here,' Joe said grimly. 'Best do as I suggested, Alice. You won't get in there. I've seen prisons that look more accessible.'

She clambered down from the cart. 'I have to try. Thank you for the lift.' She stood ankle-deep in snow while the carter hefted the trunk onto his back.

'Ring the bell for me, miss,' he said breathlessly. 'I think the young lady has filled this with bricks. It weighs a ton.'

'It's all right,' Alice said confidently. 'Leave it by the gate and go on your way while you can.'

'We can't just leave you here, lass,' Joe protested. 'What will you do if they refuse to let you in?'

'It would be a hard-hearted person who would condemn me to certain death in a snowstorm,' Alice said with more confidence than she was feeling. 'Go quickly and I'll ring the bell. They'll have to admit me.'

Reluctantly the carter climbed up on the driver's seat and urged the horse on. 'Good luck, miss,' he called over his shoulder.

Alice tugged at the bell pull. The snow was falling faster than ever and the light was fading even though it was midday. She yanked at the chain, and the sound echoed eerily. A thin stream of light shone on the icy particles as the heavy oak door opened and a cloaked figure made its way towards her. 'What do you want?' The female voice was as cold and hard as the ice beneath Alice's feet.

'I'm the new teacher,' she said boldly.

'But you're supposed to be ill. We heard that you would not be able to start for a week or two.'

'I made a rapid recovery, but I'll surely die of lung fever if you keep me standing here much longer.'

The woman produced a bunch of keys, selected the largest and unlocked the gate. 'Come in.'

'I'll need someone to bring my trunk.' Alice tried to keep the note of relief from her voice. She was acting a part and she must remember that at all times.

'I'll send the caretaker to fetch it. Follow me.'

Making her way carefully across the smooth surface of the hard-packed snow, Alice followed the woman into the house. It was marginally warmer inside than out, but the severity of the architecture was repeated in the uncompromising lines of the entrance hall. The stone walls were unadorned and the flagstone floor was bare of any kind of rug or carpet. A wide oak staircase led to a galleried landing, and icy draughts whistled through the dimly lit corridors.

'You should have sent word that you were coming.' The woman threw back her hood to reveal a fine-boned face with pale skin and hooded eyes that seemed to bore into Alice's soul. 'I am Miss Millington, the principal, and you are …?'

'Alice Cotton.'

Miss Millington's tightly drawn skin formed a semblance of a frown. 'I have you down as Agnes.'

'I never liked the name. I choose to be known as Alice.'

'That sounds like pure vanity to me, Miss Cotton. We don't encourage our girls to be vain or to think too highly of themselves. Humility, modesty and obedience are the attributes we encourage in our pupils. Discipline is strict here and rebellion quickly crushed. We are educating the future mothers of our glorious Empire, who will do their duty and obey their husbands in all things. Wayward spirits have to be humbled. Do you understand what I'm saying?'

'I most certainly do,' Alice said, biting back angry words.

'Follow me.' Miss Millington headed towards the stairs, but the sudden clanging of a bell shattered the silence and she came to a halt, turning her head to glance at Alice. 'The noon bell summons the girls to the refectory. Their lives are governed by that sound, as you will soon discover.'

Alice waited at her side, listening to the sound of approaching footsteps, which grew louder until the thunder of marching feet was almost deafening. Lines of children appeared from all directions, walking two by two like an army of small soldiers. Their heads were bent as they moved, neither looking to the left nor the right, and the youngest came first. They're little more than babies, Alice thought with a stirring of emotion. They looked too young and defenceless to be away from the nursery, let alone sent to survive in this inhospitable place. The older girls followed in total silence, and what struck Alice the most was the fact that they seemed to have been stripped of their identities. Their plain grey cotton frocks were worn with starched white pinafores and their hair confined to goffered mobcaps. With their hands clasped tightly in front of them they reminded Alice of the cut-out paper dolls she had made as a child, each one identical to its neighbour. She searched in vain for Flora but it was impossible to tell one from another, and her heart ached for the lively, spirited little girl who had come to mean so much to her, but had seemingly been swallowed up in this amorphous mass of downtrodden children.

Miss Millington stood to attention as they passed, like a general reviewing his troops, and when the last pupil disappeared from sight she ascended the stairs, motioning Alice to follow.

'You will take dining-room duty at mealtimes,' she said curtly. 'But you may begin with supper this evening. Until then you will familiarise yourself with the layout of the school and study the set of rules, which you will find pinned to your door.'

'Yes, Miss Millington.' Alice had the distinct impression that the discipline for the teachers was just as strict as that suffered by the pupils. She quickened her pace in an attempt to keep up with Miss Millington's long strides, and at the end of a long corridor they came to the room that had been allocated to the unfortunate Miss Cotton.

'This is where you will reside,' Miss Millington said, thrusting the door open. 'Your trunk will be sent up directly. My office is on the ground floor; anyone will direct you there. You'll find a timetable on the chest of drawers.'

Alice glanced round the room, which would have delighted Aunt Jane in its austerity. The chill in the air made her shiver. 'Might I have coal and kindling?' she asked boldly. 'It's rather cold in here.'

'There is a fire in the staff common room. You'll find that on the ground floor next to the refectory, but that doesn't mean you can idle away your time there. I expect teachers to work hard, Miss Cotton. The students work even harder.'

Miss Millington strode away and Alice found herself alone in a cell-like room. Snow had obliterated most of the view from the window, frosting the small panes and leaving just a small clear space in the centre of each. She tested the bed, and found, as expected, that it was not designed for comfort. The mattress was hard and sagged in the middle as if the previous occupant was a much larger and heavier person than she. The chest of drawers was placed beneath the window and on it stood a single brass candlestick. The stub of the candle would not last long but she struck a match and lit it anyway. At least she could see to read the timetable, although the list of school rules pinned to the inside of the door would take much longer to absorb. She took off her gloves and laid her mantle on the back of the wooden chair together with her bonnet. There was no sign of Miss Cotton's trunk and when it arrived at last Alice realised that she did not have the key. Frustrated but more interested in finding Flora than investigating Miss Cotton's belongings, Alice left her room and headed downstairs in search of the refectory.

Faced with a maze of passages leading off the entrance hall, Alice tried to remember which way the children had been heading; she instinctively turned one way and was rewarded by the smell of food. It was not particularly appetising and the uppermost odour was that of boiled cabbage, but she was hungry and she quite literally followed her nose. She had hoped to hear the sound of childish voices as the students enjoyed their meal, but the chilling silence persisted, broken only by the echoing pitter-patter of her feet on the hard stone floor. It came as something of a shock to hear muffled sobs and she came to a sudden halt outside a door that had been left ajar. Pushing it open, she could see a small girl standing on a stool in the corner of a deserted classroom. On her head she wore a conical dunce's cap, and she was swaying on her feet.

Alice rushed towards the child in time to catch her as she collapsed. 'You poor little thing,' she said, holding her close. She sat on the stool rocking the little girl in her arms. 'There, there, you're all right now.'

'Miss Cotton, what is the meaning of this?' Miss Millington burst into the room, standing arms akimbo, her eyes blazing. 'How dare you interfere? This has nothing to do with you.'

Alice hugged the child closer. 'The poor little mite was about to faint, ma'am. What has she done to merit such cruel treatment?'

'Mary Morgan is disruptive in class. She is idle and refuses to learn.'

'She can't be more than five or six years of age, Miss Millington. She's little more than a babe.'

'Children her age still work in the cotton mills, but Mary is lazy and needs to be punished. Put her down, Miss Cotton. I will deal with her now.'

'I think she has suffered enough,' Alice said slowly.

'I believe she will remember this always.' She set Mary on her feet and stood up, resting her hands on the child's shoulders. 'Perhaps I could give her some extra tuition this afternoon. She could show me round the school in return.'

Miss Millington hesitated, visibly bristling like an irate hedgehog. 'Very well, but you will both miss luncheon. Perhaps an empty stomach will make Mary more receptive to learning.' She pointed a long thin finger at the trembling child. 'You have Miss Cotton to thank for your reprieve, but misbehave in class again and you will be caned. Do you understand?'

Mary gulped and nodded. 'Yes, miss.'

'Remember what I said, you stupid child.' Miss Millington left the room as abruptly as she had entered.

'Well, then,' Alice said, bending down to wipe Mary's tears away with her own handkerchief, 'you're going to spend the afternoon with me, my dear.'

Mary eyed her warily. 'Yes, miss.'

Alice raised her hand to pat Mary on the shoulder and the child flinched. 'There's no need to be afraid. I won't hurt you.' Alice gazed at the small upturned face with a feeling of dismay. There was no call for gratuitous physical violence against a child of this age, even though she knew that corporal punishment was commonly used in schools all over the country. Perhaps wayward young boys benefited from the strap, although she doubted it, but tiny undernourished little girls like Mary needed to be treated with kindness and patience in order to flourish. She could only hope that Flora had fared better.

'I'm hungry, miss,' Mary whispered.

'Well, so am I. Let's see if we can find something to eat.'

'I'm not allowed in the dining room, miss. I've been bad.'

'Miss Millington said you were to show me round the school. Let's start with the kitchen, shall we?' Alice plucked the dunce's cap from Mary's head and tossed it into the wastepaper basket, and as she did so she spotted the cane hanging from the wall above the blackboard. She was even more certain that this was not the place for Flora, or any child, if it came to that. She took Mary by the hand and led her from the classroom. Her priority now was to see that the small girl was fed and comforted after her ordeal, but then she must look for Flora and work out a way to escape from their snowbound prison. It was not going to be easy.

# Chapter Seventeen

Mary was not very articulate but she managed to take Alice to the kitchen, where a surprised cook was persuaded to give them two bowls of thin soup and a couple of slices of bread, thinly spread with butter. Judging by the looks given them by the other two women who worked there it was the first time anyone had had the temerity to make such a request, but Alice did not care. Her main aim was to feed poor half-starved Mary and to keep her from Miss Millington's gaze for the rest of the day.

With a full belly Mary was much more cheerful and able to show Alice round the ground floor where most of the classrooms were situated, but the tour came to an abrupt end at the sound of a bell, which summoned the children back to lessons. Alice took Mary to the staff common room where she introduced herself as Miss Cotton. There were only two teachers present, a tall angular woman who introduced herself as Miss Stamp, teacher of mathematics and divinity, and the other woman was Miss Oglethorpe, whose subjects were history and geography.

Miss Stamp eyed Alice curiously. 'So you're the new English teacher. I hope you're good at art and sewing as well. We haven't had anyone who specialises in those subjects for years.'

'No,' Miss Oglethorpe added in a low voice. 'They don't last long here on the moor. No one does.'

'Except for us.' Miss Stamp put her arm around her colleague's shoulders and gave her a hug. 'We've got nowhere else to go, have we, Oggy?'

'Be careful, Stamp,' Miss Oglethorpe said, glancing nervously at Alice. 'We don't know the enemy yet.'

'The real enemy are disgusting little creatures like that one there,' Miss Stamp said, pointing at Mary, who cowered against Alice, clutching her skirt as if afraid they might be forcibly parted.

'Yes, indeed,' Miss Oglethorpe agreed. 'They make our lives a misery. Add that to the cold and bleakness of the moors in winter and the appalling diet – this place is not fit for anyone.'

'So why are you here?' Alice asked curiously. 'It does seem an inhospitable place.'

'Can't get jobs elsewhere,' Miss Stamp said, adjusting her tie. 'Come on, Oggy. Back to the battlefield. I've got your class for mathematics; might as well try to teach cats to fly. Good luck to you,

Cotton. You'll need it.' She glowered at Mary. 'And you should think yourself lucky, Morgan. If it were up to me you'd wear the dunce's cap day in and day out.'

Alice opened her mouth to protest but Miss Oglethorpe propelled her forthright friend out of the room, allowing the door to swing shut behind them. Mary was sobbing quietly and Alice sat down on the nearest chair, taking the little girl onto her lap. 'Don't cry, dear. I myself am very bad at mathematics, but we're all good at something. You'll find out what you're good at as time goes by.' She could tell that Mary had not really understood a word, but she laid her head on Alice's shoulder and within minutes was fast asleep. When she was certain that Mary would not awaken easily Alice laid her on the sofa and moved silently to the window. It was snowing in earnest and the world outside was a whirling white wilderness. She had initially planned to leave as soon as she had satisfied herself that Flora had settled into life at the school, but judging by the treatment Mary had received and her first impression of the staff at Willoughby Hall, Alice had already decided that this was most definitely not the place for Flora. She would worry about Mr Dearborn's reaction later. She spun round at the sound of the door being thrust open.

A small girl flew into the common room. 'What have you done with my friend?' she cried angrily.

'Flora.' Alice moved out of the shadows. 'It's me, Alice.'

'Alice is in London,' Flora said suspiciously. 'You look a bit like her, but it's a trick.'

Shocked to see Flora looking so pale and thin, Alice held out her arms. 'It is me, Flora. I've come to take you away from this dreadful place.' She staggered backwards as Flora threw herself at her.

'It really is you, Alice? I'm not dreaming?'

'No, dear. I'm here to take you home.'

'I knew you would,' Flora said, wrapping her arms around Alice's neck. 'I was certain you'd come.' She glanced over her shoulder. 'What did they do to Mary? Did they beat her?'

'No, Flora. I came across her in time to prevent any further punishment. She's been with me all afternoon.'

Mary stirred and opened her eyes. 'Flora?'

'I came to find you, Mary. I won't let them hurt you.' Flora disengaged herself from Alice's arms and went to sit beside her friend. 'Are you all right?'

'I am now.' Mary tucked her small hand into Flora's, looking up at her with adoring eyes.

'You'll have to take both of us,' Flora said, raising her chin with the stubborn look that Alice knew of old. 'I'm not leaving her here with these bullies. She's got no one, Alice. She's an orphan and her guardian put her here because he can't be bothered with her.'

'That's terrible, but I can't kidnap her. The police would come after us.'

Mary began to weep silently and Flora rose to her feet. She seized Alice by the hand, gripping her fingers with surprising strength for someone so small. 'You don't understand. I listen to the big girls talking at night in the dormitory. This is a place where rich people send the children they don't want. Some of them haven't been home since they got here, and they know they won't have anywhere to go when they leave. They'll be sent out as governesses or teachers in missionary schools as soon as they're old enough.'

'I can't believe that,' Alice said stoutly. 'It's certainly not what your pa had in mind for you.'

'I know that, but it's what will happen to Mary if we leave her here.' Flora's eyes filled with tears. 'You'll have to go without me if you won't take her with us.'

Alice stroked Flora's flushed cheek, wiping away a teardrop. 'I'll give it some thought, but getting away from here is going to be difficult. Travelling on the moor must be almost impossible by now, and I'm masquerading as Miss Cotton, the new English mistress. I'll have to keep it up for a day or two while I try to think of a way out of this.'

Flora wiped her eyes on the back of her hand. 'You're wonderful, Alice. You'll work out a way to save us.'

A sound outside the door made Alice turn with a start. 'Someone's coming. Go along with what I say and do, Flora. They mustn't find out that we know each other.' She grabbed her by the ear as the door opened to admit Miss Millington.

'What is going on here?'

'I found this child wandering about, ma'am,' Alice said curtly. 'I'll take her back to her classroom.' She beckoned to Mary. 'Come along, Morgan. We have work to do this afternoon. Follow me.'

Flora yelped and protested loudly as Alice dragged her out into the corridor. 'All right,' Alice whispered. 'Don't overdo it, Flora.' She smiled down at Mary, whose lips trembled ominously. 'We're only play-acting. I'm pretending to be cross with Flora.'

Flora rubbed her ear, grinning ruefully. 'That hurt.'

Alice shooed them along the wide passage away from the common room. 'It had to look real. Where are you supposed to be, Flora?'

'Miss Oglethorpe's class,' she replied, hanging her head. 'Can't we go now, Alice? I'd rather brave the snow than stay here another day.'

'We'll leave as soon as possible, but till then you must keep up the act. Now lead on. I'll tell your teacher that you've been severely reprimanded.'

'I could get locked in the cellar all night for what I just did.'

'That won't happen, I promise you.' Alice said firmly. She took Mary by the hand. 'Don't be afraid.'

Life in Willoughby Hall was just as bad as depicted by Flora. The discipline was harsh, and meted out with such relish by those in charge that Alice was beginning to think they took a sadistic pleasure in treating children in such a barbaric fashion. It was heartrending to see young girls cowed into submission, their personalities suppressed and crushed to the extent that they became virtual automatons. The strongest characters would survive, but the more timid girls were afraid of their own shadows. Alice longed to throw the doors open and release them all like caged birds, although she doubted if those who had been there longest would be able to fly. She could foresee a bleak future for the meekest and most biddable children, especially those bullied from an early age, knowing nothing else. They would be the browbeaten wives and mothers of years to come, or pale spinsters left to care for elderly parents, or put-upon companions to the lonely rich.

A week went by and there was no sign of a thaw and no danger of the real Miss Cotton making a sudden appearance as the roads were virtually impassable. At the end of the second week Miss Millington announced to the staff that supplies were running low and food would be rationed. Alice thought privately that it would make little difference. Their diet was frugal enough at the best of times, and the children were painfully thin as a result. She had seen better fed street arabs than the daughters of parents wealthy enough to afford the fees at Willoughby Hall.

After a fortnight, when it had seemed that winter was never going to loosen its hold, there came a spectacular thaw. Looking out of her window one morning Alice could see tufts of heather rising out of the snow and patches of green grass. The real Miss Cotton would inevitably put in an appearance and the time had come to make a move, but Flora was adamant that they must take Mary with them and had refused to leave without her. Alice could tell how much Mary meant to Flora, and she herself had grown fond of Mary. To abandon her to her fate in such an institution was unthinkable.

Late that evening, when all the lights were out and everyone had gone to bed, Alice lit a candle and made her way to Miss Millington's study. On an occasion when she had been summoned to the headmistress's office, she had taken the opportunity to inspect the shelves while she waited for Miss Millington to make an appearance. She had noted where the admissions book was kept and it was this she selected now, placing it on the desk and leafing through until she found the entry that marked the arrival of two-year-old Mary Morgan. Alice discovered to her relief that Flora had been correct in saying that Mary was an orphan. Her guardian appeared to be an elderly maiden aunt residing in Kent. There was a note in the margin stating that Mary was to stay at school during the holiday periods, and that any future correspondence was to be addressed to Miss Morgan's solicitor, a Mr Doolittle with an office in Chislehurst. She made a hasty note of both names and addresses before replacing the book and hurried from the office, undiscovered. Armed with this information, Alice decided that she would take Mary, even though their progress would be slower. The little girl's aunt must surely take pity on the child if the facts were put before her, or maybe Mr Doolittle, despite his name, might be persuaded to help. In any event, Mary was not going to be left to face the rigours of life at Willoughby Hall.

Alice returned to her room and sat down to pen a letter to Frederick, explaining why she had been absent from work for so long and revealing the truth about the school that he had thought would be a place of sanctuary. Her plan for the next day was to walk as far as the village, where she hoped she might find transport to York. From there it was a simple matter to get the London train and they would return home. Surely Frederick must relent when he was in full possession of the facts: she was pinning her hopes on gaining his support, and she could not believe that Lydia would turn Flora out when she knew how the poor child had suffered. At the very least they might find a better school, closer to home, where Flora would be safe and happy. As to Mary – Alice was certain that one more mouth to feed would not bother kind-hearted Rose Young. Who could fail to be touched by the fate of a small orphan? Perhaps she was being naïve, but if all else failed she could afford to rent rooms in a better neighbourhood and have Mary live with her. Flora could visit during the school holidays and they would have a lovely time together. Alice sighed; she knew she was being over-optimistic, but she had to cling to hope or she would have given in long ago. She folded her letter and sealed it with wax melted in the candle flame.

Next morning she was up before dawn and made her way to the dormitory where Flora and Mary slept. She awakened them without disturbing the other girls and led them to her room, where she helped them to dress in their warmest clothes.

'We must travel light,' she said softly. 'We're going on a big adventure, Mary. Flora will hold your hand and I want you to creep like little mice.'

'We're going home.' Flora's voice broke with excitement. 'We're leaving here for ever, Mary, and you're coming with me.'

Alice stiffened at the sound of a horse-drawn vehicle pulling up outside the gates. She ran to the window and peered out. Dawn was breaking with faint green and silver streaks piercing the darkness in the east, and there was just enough light to see the silhouette of a man who had alighted from the carrier's cart. His battered top hat and bulky over-coat made him look sinister and threatening. There was something disturbingly familiar about him as he tugged at the bell pull, and the metallic clanging sound echoed around the deserted courtyard like a clarion call. Alice held her breath and her pulse was racing, but it was fear and not excitement that caused the blood to drum in her ears. A male visiting this entirely female domain was unheard of in term time.

'No!' she gasped. 'It can't be. He can't have discovered us.' But she knew that he had. Unless she was very much mistaken it was Eric the Axe who demanded admittance, and as a woman alighted from the cart, shaking out her skirts the hood of her cape slipped off her head and Alice knew without a doubt that it was Molly Bishop.

'Quick,' she said, grabbing her valise into which she had crammed a few necessities for the girls. 'Follow me. Be very quiet because no one must hear us.'

Flora clutched at her sleeve. 'Is it the woman who says she's my mother?'

'Yes, Flora, it is and she's a bad woman. No mother would treat her child in the way she wants to use you, but I won't let her get you. I'd die first.'

'Don't die.' Mary's brown eyes widened and her lips trembled. 'You can't die.'

'Of course not,' Alice said hastily. 'It was a figure of speech. Come, we have to hurry.'

She led the way down the back stairs and out into the stable yard. It was a three-mile walk to the village across open moorland, and she had planned to go on foot when the weather improved, but the arrival of Molly and Eric had put paid to that and now she was risking everything in a dash for safety. Having successfully negotiated the open yard, Alice unbolted the wicket gate and ushered the children outside into the chill of the early morning.

'Wait here a moment and don't move,' she said softly. 'Hold Mary's hand, Flora. Be brave girls and soon we'll be away from here.'

It was a desperate gamble but Alice was banking on the fact that the carter would have pressing business in the village, and that Molly would insist on gaining admittance. She could hear her arguing with Miss Millington as she rounded the corner of the building.

'But I'm the child's mother,' Molly said loudly. 'You will let me in. I want to see her.'

'We don't allow visitors in term time, as you must know, madam.' Miss Millington's voice was as cold as the ground beneath Alice's feet. She held her breath, hoping for a miracle.

'You'll let us in or I'll break the bloody door down.'

Alice could not see their faces but she could imagine the shock on the headmistress's face on being spoken to by a lout like Eric the Axe. She waited, praying silently that the carter would not lose patience and drive off. Miss Millington seemed to be losing the war of words and Alice did not hear her response, but the rasp of the key in the lock was followed by the grating of the hinges as the gate opened. Alice poked her head out in time to see Molly surge into the school yard followed by Eric. They headed for the front entrance and Alice waited until she heard the door closed before making a dash for the wagon. 'Can you take me and two little ones to the village?' she asked breath-lessly.

The carter turned his head, shifting the pipe from one side of his mouth to the other with a puff of smoke. 'I remember you, miss.'

'That's right. You brought me here a couple of weeks ago.' Alice delved into her reticule and took out a florin. 'We're going on a visit.'

He took the money and stuffed it into his pocket. 'Running away, are we?'

'The children are my charges, I'm taking them home.'

'Can't say I blame you, miss. I wouldn't want to leave any of my bairns in this place.'

Alice hesitated. 'The man and woman you dropped off – are you waiting for them?'

'Picking them up on me way back – that was what we agreed.' Taking the pipe from his mouth, he spat onto the ground. 'I'd like as not leave them to make their own way to York. Can't stand Southerners, present company excepted, of course.'

'I'll fetch the children.' Alice turned to see Flora's pale face peeping round the corner of the building and she beckoned frantically. At any moment Molly or Eric might suddenly reappear and her plans would be ruined. Flora needed no further encouragement and holding Mary by the hand she raced towards them. Alice helped them onto the cart and leaped up after them. They were barely settled when the driver urged his horse to walk on and Alice could have cried with relief, but she managed a smile as she slipped her arms around the girls' shoulders. 'We're off on a big adventure.'

'That's the first time I've heard anyone say that about yon village.' The carter chuckled deep in his belly. 'You won't find much there apart from a few cottages and the church.'

'I was hoping to find transport to take us to the railway station in York.'

He took the pipe from his mouth and tapped out the ash on the side of the cart. 'Why didn't you say so in the first place, miss? I've got a delivery at Fox Farm and then I'm on me way back to town.'

'But you've got to pick up those people at the school.'

He held the reins in one hand while he refilled his pipe with the other. 'What people? They haggled over the price and beat me down to the bare bone. I don't hold with folk like that. Let 'em walk, I say.'

'I can pay extra,' Alice said, doing a quick calculation in her head. Miss Millington had given her two weeks' wages, informing her with grim satisfaction that she would have to wait until the end of the quarter to be paid in full. It was not much but at least she had just about enough money to get them to London.

'It's going to rain.' The carter licked his finger and held it up to the chill wind that had sprung up. 'Can't guarantee a comfy ride.'

'That doesn't matter,' Alice said, breathing a sigh

of relief. 'Just get us to the station and I'll be grateful for the rest of my life.'

The carter had been right on both counts. It was not a comfortable journey and it did rain, starting with a light shower, which rapidly turned into a downpour. Alice did her best to keep the girls' spirits up, but they were wet, cold and hungry by the time they reached York station. It was mid-afternoon and Alice was stiff and sore from being bumped about on the hard seat.

She paid the carter. 'Thank you for bringing us here. I'm truly grateful to you.'

He tipped his cap. 'Glad to help a young lady like you, miss.'

She opened her reticule and took out the letter to Frederick. 'Would you do me a favour and post this for me?'

'Be glad to, miss.' He took it from her and put it in his pocket.

She gave him the penny for postage and, with a strange feeling of being alone and unprotected, watched him drive away. It seemed silly to send the letter when they would be arriving back in London later in the day, but she planned to go straight to Five Foot Lane, and Frederick should receive the letter by first post next day. It was important for him to know exactly why she had been absent from work, and that Flora was safe and sound, and he needed to be apprised of the terrible conditions at Willoughby Hall.

329

She ushered the children into the booking office where she purchased tickets for London. It was hard to believe that they were on their way home at last, but there was an hour to wait before the train arrived and Alice bought tea and cake from a stall on the platform. There was a fire in the ladies' waiting room and they made themselves comfortable, sipping the hot beverage and munching cake. Flora soon regained her spirits, but Mary curled up on the wooden bench and closed her eyes.

'She's only little,' Flora said, seriously. 'But I'm glad we're taking her home with us. Do you think Mama will like her better than me? I know I wasn't always a good girl, but little Mary never does anything wrong.'

Alice put her cup on the table, wondering how best to answer the question that had been worrying her. 'I'm not sure that Mrs Dearborn will want to take her in. Mary might have to stay with me in Five Foot Lane, at least for the time being. You know your mama, she doesn't take easily to strangers, and Mary has an aunt in Chislehurst who might decide to give her a home.'

Flora's bottom lip protruded ominously. 'Mary is my friend. I won't go anywhere without her.'

'And that feeling does you credit, but you have to be practical, and you must behave yourself if you're to get on well with your mama.'

'We could both live with you, Alice,' Flora said eagerly. 'I love you and we'd be very good, both of us, I promise.'

'And I would love to look after you, but I haven't got a home of my own, and there's still Molly Bishop to contend with. She almost caught up with us today, and she's not likely to give up now.'

'I hope the train comes soon,' Flora said nervously. 'I want to go home.'

Alice rose to her feet. 'I'll go out onto the platform and take a look at the clock.' She went outside and saw to her relief that the train was due at any moment. In fact she could hear the distant whistle announcing its approach. She returned to the waiting room and awakened Mary.

'Come along, sweetheart. The train is about to arrive and we'll be on our way.'

Flora grabbed the valise and hefted it out onto the platform with Alice and Mary following on her heels. 'It's coming,' Flora cried excitedly. 'I can see it now.'

Clutching Mary's small hand, Alice drew Flora back from the edge. 'Be careful, we don't want any accidents.'

'No indeed.' Molly's voice rang out loud and clear above the roar of the steam engine as it thundered into the station.

Alice spun round. 'How did you get here so quickly?'

'You thought you'd got us beat, didn't you?' Molly moved closer with Eric at her side. 'You took our place on the cart, you bitch. We might have been stranded in that godforsaken place for days, but luckily some prim old maid arrived and caused a stir. You've been a bad girl, Alice Radcliffe. The old hag who runs the school is after your blood.'

'We took a ride back to town in her hired carriage,' Eric said smugly. 'We had a more comfortable journey than you did.'

Alice drew the girls closer to her as the train came to a halt. 'We're leaving and you can't stop us.'

Molly threw back her head and laughed. 'See that constable at the end of the platform? Well, I just told him that you was taking my daughter from me.' She seized Flora by the arm. 'One word from me and you'll be arrested.'

'The old bitch gave the carriage driver money to send a telegram from York to Flora's father. Soon they'll know what you've done.' Eric moved forward and gave Alice a shove. 'And when the coppers discover that you passed yourself off as a teacher and took payment what was due to another, you'll be up before the beak and thrown in clink. What will your boss think of you then? That's if you still have a job, which I doubt.'

'Don't let them take me, Alice.' Flora's face paled to ashen. She looked up at Molly with tears pouring down her cheeks. 'Please let me go. You aren't my mother. I want to go with Alice.'

'Please,' Alice cried, holding out her hands. 'Don't do this, Molly. I'm sure Mr Dearborn will give you money if that's what you want. Let her come with me. I beg you.'

# Chapter Eighteen

'It's all right, mate,' Eric said gruffly as the police constable headed towards them. 'The young person has seen sense. We've got our little girl back.' He lifted Flora bodily and threw her over his shoulder. 'She's a bit simple, is this one. But my old woman will see to her needs.'

Molly laid a warning finger on her lips. 'Say one word and you'll end up in the mill, or worse.' She marched off after Eric, and Flora's screams were drowned by a burst of steam from the engine.

'Best get on the train, miss.' The young policeman eyed her warily. 'Lucky for you they didn't press charges.'

Alice stood for a moment, speechless and at a loss as to what to do for the best. Mary was clinging to her, sobbing as if her heart would break. Molly had enmeshed her in a web of lies from which there was no escape. If she wanted to keep her freedom she had no choice other than to board the train and return to London. She would have to tell Mr Dearborn that her attempt to help Flora had ended in disaster and now she had a small child wholly dependent upon her.

'I'll help you, miss.' The constable opened the carriage door. 'You take the little lass and I'll see to your case.'

Alice lifted Mary onto the train and climbed in after her.

It was late afternoon when they arrived at King's Cross station. Mary had slept most of the way, but Alice had spent the journey in a daze. She had tried so hard to keep Flora safe, but all her efforts had been in vain and the Dearborns would almost certainly blame her for what had occurred. The thought of Flora suffering at the hands of Molly and her companion was too terrible to contemplate, and she wished that she had told the policeman that they were lying, but it was their word against hers. If approached by the police Miss Millington would be only too pleased to give evidence, and it would not be in Alice's favour. She knew that she must speak to Frederick and explain as best she could, after which the matter would be out of her hands. She led Mary to the cab rank and hailed a passing cab. 'Russell Square, please, cabby.'

*

Hoskins admitted them and Alice knew instantly that the news must have preceded their arrival.

'It's a bad day, miss. I doubt if the master or mistress will wish to see you.'

'But I must see Mr Dearborn,' Alice insisted. 'It's very urgent.'

'What is it, Hoskins?' Frederick leaned over the balustrade on the first-floor landing. 'Is that Miss Radcliffe? I was expecting her.'

Alice stepped forward. 'It is, sir. I must speak to you.'

'And I want words with you. Come up.' He disappeared in the direction of the drawing room.

'Best do as the master says.' Hoskins stood aside.

'Come with me, Mary,' Alice said, controlling the tremor in her voice with an effort. 'Don't be scared.' She took her by the hand, giving the small fingers a gentle squeeze. 'You're going to meet Flora's mother and father.' With an outward display of confidence she negotiated the wide staircase and entered the drawing room.

Frederick stood with his back to the fire. His grim expression was not encouraging. 'Where is Flora?'

Lydia rose slowly from her seat, fixing Alice with a hard stare. 'I don't know how you have the nerve to walk in here as if nothing had happened, Radcliffe.'

'You must hear me out,' Alice said hastily. 'I don't know what you've been told, but I acted with the best of intentions.'

'We received a telegram from Millington to say that you had abducted Flora and another child. I see that one is with you, but where is our daughter?' Frederick's hands clenched and unclenched at his sides, and his voice shook with emotion. 'What have you done with our little girl?'

Alice slipped her arm around Mary's shoulders as the child began to sob uncontrollably. 'You have no idea what a terrible place that is, Mr Dearborn. Flora begged to be brought home and this little one was being bullied by the teachers and the pupils alike. Flora refused to leave without her.'

Lydia rose slowly to her feet and to Alice's surprise her face softened as she held her hand out to Mary. 'Come here, dear. Come and sit with me.'

'Lydia, you can't make a fuss of the child,' Frederick said crossly. 'She has a family somewhere who will be anxious about her.'

Mary settled herself beside Lydia on the sofa. 'The bad man took Flora away.' She laid her head on Lydia's shoulder and fresh tears spurted from her eyes.

'What is she talking about?' Frederick demanded angrily. 'Where is Flora? You took her from the place of safety and you turn up here without her.'

'Miss Millington obviously didn't tell you that Molly Bishop and her man came to the school with the intention of abducting Flora. I knew they'd try something, which is why I went to Willoughby Hall in the first place. Flora was desperately unhappy there and with good reason, as I found out.'

'You had no right to interfere,' Frederick snapped. 'You should have warned me about Bishop and I would have informed the local police.'

'I would have done so, but we were snowed in and I had to wait until the roads were passable before I could do anything. We were waiting for the train to arrive when they took Flora by force.'

'This is your fault,' Lydia cried angrily. 'I blame you entirely for what's happened.'

'You betrayed my trust, Miss Radcliffe. You were supposed to be working for me and yet you decided to travel to Yorkshire without so much as a by-your-leave.' Frederick moved away from the fire and paced the floor. 'I gave you a chance to prove yourself in the workplace, and all you've done is to show me that women are unreliable and untrustworthy.'

'If what you say is true,' Lydia said slowly, 'why didn't you go to the police and tell them that Flora had been taken against her will?' She turned to her husband. 'Stop that silly pacing, Frederick, and sit down. You're making my head spin. You should be cross-examining this trollop, who is probably telling us a pack of lies.'

'That's unfair,' Alice protested. 'I've only ever done my best for Flora. I care for her as if she were my own flesh and blood, which is more than you've ever done, Mrs Dearborn. You made it quite clear that you didn't really like her, let alone love her as a mother should.'

'That's enough.' Frederick came to a halt in front

of Alice. 'You're coming to the police station with me, Miss Radcliffe. You'll give a full statement and we'll let the authorities take it from there. Flora must be found and brought home.'

'I couldn't agree more,' Alice said with feeling. 'I'm more than willing to do anything I can to save her from that dreadful creature.' She glanced anxiously at Mary. 'I'll come and collect you as soon as I can, dear.'

Lydia placed her arms around Mary and hugged her. 'This child stays here. She will be looked after until we can return her to her rightful family.' She stroked Mary's straight hair back from her flushed face. 'I'll take care of you, sweetheart. You can have Flora's bed tonight and Nettie will tend to your needs just as she has done all these years for your friend.'

Alice stared at her in astonishment. Lydia Dearborn had never, to her knowledge, shown a maternal streak where Flora was concerned, but now she was fussing over Mary like a mother hen. She glanced up at Frederick and realised that he was having similar thoughts; their eyes met in a moment of mutual understanding and then he looked away.

'Come,' he said brusquely. 'There's no time to waste. Those people could have taken Flora anywhere. They might even try to leave the country.'

Alice rose to her feet. 'I doubt that, sir. I think Molly has someone in mind for Flora, and that person is willing to pay a great deal of money for her trouble. There's no other way to explain why she has gone to so much effort to kidnap her.'

'You can tell all that to the police,' Frederick said grimly. He turned to his wife. 'I may be gone for quite a while, Lydia.'

'Mary stays here.' Lydia met Alice's anxious gaze with a determined lift of her chin. 'Don't come here again, Radcliffe. The servants will have instructions to throw you out if you try to put a foot over the threshold.'

'But I have the address of Mary's aunt and also her solicitor,' Alice protested as Frederick hurried her from the room. 'I was going to contact the lady as soon as I was able.'

'You must give it to me. I'll see that it's done.' Frederick hesitated, giving her a steady look. 'I believe you had my daughter's best interests at heart, but you were misguided.'

'I'd do anything for Flora. I am truly sorry that it all went wrong, but it wasn't my fault.'

'You do realise that your employment with my company is terminated, Miss Radcliffe? Under the circumstances I cannot have someone I can't trust working for me. I see now that women are a prey to their emotions and unstable. You are a bad influence and as far as I'm concerned it was an experiment that failed. You will collect your things in the morning and Mr Wall will pay you what is due to you and not a penny more.'

Alice bowed her head. She would challenge his

decision in the morning, but for now her mind was on Flora and nothing else seemed to matter.

It was late evening when Alice arrived in Five Foot Lane. Carrie let her in and enveloped her in an affectionate hug.

'Where have you been? We've all be out of our minds with worry. Did you find Flora?'

'It's complicated and I'm exhausted,' Alice said tiredly. 'Do you think I might have something to eat?'

Rose came hurrying towards them, wiping her hands on her apron. 'Good gracious, girl, you look as if you're about to collapse. Come through to the kitchen and get warm. I've just made a pot of tea and there's some stew left from supper. You'll feel better when you've got something inside your belly.'

Their kindness was more affecting than the harsh treatment Alice had received that day. The police sergeant who took her statement had been brusque and treated her like a criminal, and her reception at the Dearborns' house had been upsetting, although it was little more than she had expected. She wiped her streaming eyes on the back of her hand. 'Th-thank you.'

'Don't cry, Alice,' Carrie said softly. 'You're home now. George will be pleased to see you. He's in the kitchen cleaning his shoes ready for work tomorrow.'

Alice gulped and sniffed. Even in the midst of such genuine kindness she could not help feeling like an outsider. She followed Carrie and her mother into the kitchen and found George, as his sister had said, polishing his black shoes until they shone. He looked up and grinned.

'So you've come home. It's good to see you, Alice. Where've you been all this time?'

'Food first, questions later.' Rose pulled up a chair. 'Take off your bonnet and mantle, and sit down, dear.' She turned to her son, frowning. 'Leave her be until she's got some vittles inside her, George.'

'It's all right, Mrs Young,' Alice said tiredly. 'George might as well know now that Mr Dearborn has given me the sack. I've lost my job because I tried to help Flora and it all went wrong. Molly Bishop has kidnapped her and it's all my fault.'

Carrie took Alice's bonnet from her limp fingers and helped her off with her mantle. 'I'm sure it's not as bad as you think. They must know you were doing what you thought was right.'

'They can't kick you out,' George said angrily. 'You're a better designer than Collis and he knows it. I reckon he's put a bad word in because you didn't fall for his sweet talk. He's a conceited ass if ever there was one, and I never trusted him.'

Rose placed a bowl of soup on the table in front of Alice. 'Eat up and then you can tell us what happened. Carrie, love, pour the tea, will you? And George, take the boot black off the table and put the brushes away. You should do that in the scullery, not in my nice clean kitchen.'

'You mustn't worry about work,' Carrie said

earnestly. 'I'm sure that Bertie could help in that direction. His pa is one of Dearborns' biggest competitors. Isn't that right, George?'

'It is, but that would be like going over to the enemy. They're business rivals, Carrie. But you're just a girl so you wouldn't understand.' George ducked as his sister threw a crust of bread at him. It fell to the floor and was immediately gobbled up by Skipper, Harold's bull terrier.

'Stop that,' Rose said severely. 'You're supposed to be grown-ups.' She tempered her words with a smile. 'Ignore them, Alice. At least you're home in time for your ma's wedding. It's tomorrow, isn't it?'

Alice choked on a mouthful of stew. 'Oh my goodness – I'd forgotten it completely. I barely know what day it is.'

'You will go, won't you?' Carrie asked anxiously. 'I know how you feel about Horace, but your ma will be very hurt if you stay away.'

Alice nodded. 'Of course I'll go. After all, I haven't got a job now, so there's no excuse. Anyway, I hope she's happy and that Horace treats her well.' She glanced down at the dog as he nuzzled her hand, looking up at her with what seemed like sympathy in his big brown eyes. She patted his head. 'Why can't people be as nice as dogs?' she said with an attempt at a smile.

Rose chuckled. 'Skipper can be fierce when he needs to be. Harry relies on him when he's on the night watch.'

'Did I hear my name taken in vain?' Harold Young breezed into the kitchen. He was muffled up in his outdoor clothes. 'Come on, boy. It's time for work.'

Skipper bounded over to him and Harold clipped a leash onto the dog's collar. 'I'll see you in the morning. Let's hope it's a quiet night.'

'Be careful, dear.' Rose smiled tiredly. 'Don't take unnecessary risks. Your life is worth more than a few barrels of brandy or a bolt of silk.'

He grinned and tipped his hat as he left the room.

'Tomorrow I'll speak to Bertie,' Carrie said firmly. She shot a sideways glance at her brother. 'I might just happen to bump into him on my way to work.'

'You're getting a bit too friendly with that young man,' Rose said, frowning. 'I don't want to see you hurt, love. His family are stuck-up toffs and they wouldn't want anything to do with the likes of us.'

Carrie flinched visibly. 'Bertie doesn't think like that, Ma.'

'Well, I don't want you seeing him, Carrie. He's already engaged, unless you've forgotten that fact. It will end in tears.' Rose patted Alice on the shoulder. 'I'll say good night, but just remember that you're home now, my dear. I'm sure things will work out for the best.'

'Thank you,' Alice murmured. 'You're very kind, Mrs Young.'

'It's Rose, as I said before. You're one of us, dear.'

George waited until his mother had left the room.

He leaned across the table. 'That goes for all of us, Alice.'

'Yes,' Carrie said, nodding. 'And I will tell Bertie about you.'

'No you won't,' George said firmly. 'I heard that Rory is back. He'll have something to say about Alice being dismissed out of hand.'

Alice put her spoon down, her appetite suddenly deserting her. 'You say that Rory has returned from Ireland? He was supposed to be gone for longer.'

'That's as maybe, but I overheard Rawlins telling Collis that he'll be back in the office on Monday. Things will improve when he's around. He's a good chap.'

Alice was suddenly overwhelmed with a feeling of exhaustion and she yawned. 'Would you mind if I go to bed now? I should get up early and go to Queen Square. I really must be there to help Ma get ready for her big day.'

'My darling girl, I knew you wouldn't let me down.' Beth's eyes were bright with tears as she hugged her daughter. 'Why have you kept away for so long? I was afraid that you were angry with me.'

Alice returned the embrace, kissing her mother on the cheek. 'Of course not, Mama. I'll tell you all about it while I help you get ready.' She glanced at the ivory silk wedding dress, which was laid out on the bed. 'It's lovely and you'll look beautiful in it.'

'I wish you'd allowed me to buy you a new gown, Alice. You should have been my bridesmaid.'

'I'm quite all right as I am.' Alice slipped the creation in silk and lace over her mother's head, and spent the next few minutes fastening the tiny fabric-covered buttons down the back of the frock. She stood back, surveying the result with a critical eye. 'You look wonderful, Mama, but what about your hair? Would you like me to put it up for you?'

'I suppose it would look strange if I walked down the aisle with my hair still in rags. Yes, please, Alice. You were always very clever with your hands.' Beth took a seat, peering at her reflection in the scrap of mirror on the chest of drawers. 'I do miss having a dressing table.'

'I know where there is one, and as this is a special day I don't think Aunt Jane will disapprove.' Alice rang the bell and filled in the time by untying the rags.

Clara bounded into the room without stopping to knock. 'Yes, miss.' She came to a halt, staring at Beth. 'Oh, lawks, you look a picture, ma'am, if you don't mind me saying so.'

Beth met Clara's admiring gaze with a smile. 'I don't mind at all. Thank you.'

'What can I do for you, miss?' Clara turned to Alice with a broad grin. 'It's good to have you home, although I know I should keep me trap shut. Cook is always telling me off for talking too much.'

'That's quite all right, Clara. But there is something I'd like you to do.'

'Anything, miss. Anything at all.'

'Will you fetch the key to the locked room? The bride ought to have special treatment on her wedding day, and I cannot do her coiffure justice without a proper mirror and a dressing table.'

Clara leaped to the doorway. 'I'll be back in two shakes of a lamb's tail, miss. I never thought to enjoy such excitement in this house, not never. Cook's made a cake and we're to have a roast capon for luncheon. It's better than Christmas.' She left the room and Alice could hear her chattering to herself as she headed towards the staircase. 'Well, there's someone who is very happy for you, Mama.'

'But what about you, Alice? I know how you feel about Horace, but he is a good man in spite of his awkwardness and fussy little ways, and I think we will do tolerably well together.'

'I do hope so,' Alice said with feeling.

'I will always love your father, nothing can change that, but I know I'm doing the right thing. I'll have my own home again and a place in society. A penniless widow has little more standing in the world than a woman who is well and truly on the shelf. I want you to bear that in mind, Alice.'

Alice patted her mother on the cheek. 'I hear what you're saying, Mama. You mustn't worry about me. I can make my own way, I promise you.'

'That's what worries me. You are too independent for your own good, and you're stubborn just like your dear papa.' Beth reached up to clutch her daughter's hand. 'Now tell me what kept you away from us these past weeks, although I'm afraid I won't like what I hear.'

Alice stifled a sigh of relief as Clara reappeared brandishing the key. 'Her majesty says it's all right to use Miss Viola's room. She said it's time her ghost was laid to rest, whatever that means. I'll open it up for you.' She raced off with the boundless energy of an eleven-year-old buoyed up with excitement.

Alice and her mother followed more slowly and by the time they reached the room Clara had flung back the curtains and opened the windows. A stream of cold air disturbed the thick layer of dust, sending up small eddies that settled once again on every surface. 'It'll take a month of Sundays to get this room clean,' she said, shaking her head. 'Is there anything else, miss? I have to go downstairs and help Cook. She's in a bit of a state.'

'It's quite all right, Clara. Off you go.' Beth took a seat at the dressing table. 'You said this was Viola's room. I can't believe that Jane has kept it as it was all those years ago.'

'I don't remember seeing Aunt Viola very often,' Alice said thoughtfully. 'I do recall that she was very pretty and always laughing.'

'She wasn't much older than you when she died,' Beth said sadly. 'Viola was spoiled and selfish and cared for no one but herself, but it was tragic to die so young.'

'Aunt Jane said that it was consumption.'

'That was the story put about to save face.' Beth

sighed, shaking her head. 'You might as well know the truth, Alice. Your father had a visit from a woman called Smithson, the midwife who attended Viola's confinement. She told him that his half-sister had died in childbirth and that the baby was still-born.'

'Smithson?' Alice stared at her mother's reflection in the mirror. 'She was Flora's nursemaid who was sacked for mistreating her and drinking on duty.'

'I know nothing of that, dear. All I know is that a woman named Smithson came to us with the sad news. She said it was Viola's last wish that the family knew of her fate.'

Alice continued to brush her mother's hair. 'Go on,' she said gently. 'What else did Smithson say?'

'Just that Viola's lover had deserted her and she had been left in straitened circumstances. Your father was very upset and Robert was heartbroken. He adored Viola.' Beth turned her head to look Alice in the eye. 'I was afraid that history was repeating itself and that some man had persuaded you to run away with him.'

Alice recoiled, staring at her mother in surprise. 'Where did you get that idea, Mama? I've more sense than to do something so foolish.'

'I could see that you were very taken with that young man you met at the Dearborns' establishment.'

'If you mean Rory Dearborn, then yes, I like him very much, and he was good to me, but that's as far as it went. He's been away in Ireland and I haven't seen him for weeks.'

'I'm so relieved, my love. One tragedy in the family is quite enough to bear.'

'Don't think about it, Mama. I'm sorry about Aunt Viola, but it all happened a long time ago and today you should be happy and think of the future. I'll finish putting up your hair and then you'll be ready. Horace is a very lucky man.'

Jane was waiting for them in the entrance hall when Beth and Alice finally arrived downstairs.

'You took your time,' she said icily. 'Hurry up or we'll be late arriving at the church.'

Cook and Clara stood at a respectful distance, waiting to see the bride. Mrs Jugg clutched her hands to her generous bosom and her eyes misted. 'Oh, ma'am, you look a picture, you really do.'

'Yes, indeed.' Clara clapped her hands, but subsided when she realised that Jane was glaring at her.

'Get back to work,' Jane snapped. 'You've seen what you wanted to see. I expect luncheon to be on the table when we return.'

Mrs Jugg scuttled off in the direction of the servants' staircase, dragging Clara by the hand.

'Give them an inch and they'll take advantage of it,' Jane said grimly. She opened the front door. 'We're walking. It's not far to the church and it's not raining so I saw no point in taking a cab.'

'Let me help you with your cape.' Alice slipped the cloak around her mother's shoulders with a feeling of pride. Her mother might be in her late thirties but she had the figure of a young girl and her pretty face was surprisingly unlined.

Jane appeared to be unimpressed by the wedding dress, which was daringly low cut, fitted to the waist and the skirts draped at the front, ending in a small bustle and a hint of a train. 'It's barely decent,' she said, shaking her head. 'But you always were a flirt, Beth Dearborn. I just hope that you're still able to bear a child, or this marriage will be a sham.'

Beth's cheeks flushed bright pink. 'You are entitled to your opinion, Jane, but I suggest you keep your thoughts to yourself. Horace loves me and I intend to make him a good wife.'

Jane's mouth opened and then closed like a trap door. Alice tucked her mother's hand through the crook of her arm. 'Well said,' she whispered, adding loudly. 'Lead on, Aunt Jane. We don't want to keep the groom waiting in the cold. You know how delicate he is.'

'Less of your cheek, young lady.' Jane descended the steps and marched on ahead of them.

'Take no notice of her,' Alice said softly. 'She's just jealous, Mama.'

'I don't care.' Beth tossed her head and the white ostrich feathers in her perky little hat waved in the breeze. 'This is my last day in Queen Square. I shan't be sad to leave.'

They walked arm in arm to the church and found Horace was waiting there with the vicar at his side. He had dispensed with the formality of a best man, and as Beth had no one to give her away she walked up the aisle on her own. Alice sat in the front pew next to Jane and watched with mixed feelings as her mother and Horace intoned their vows. They signed the register, witnessed by Jane and the verger, and the happy couple walked down the aisle without the accompaniment of the organist. Alice suspected that this was one of Jane's economies, but Beth and Horace were beaming at each other and she could not begrudge them their moment of happiness.

A fitful sun had edged its way between the clouds as the small procession emerged from the church. There were a few curious onlookers but one in particular caught Alice's eye and she came to sudden halt. Her heart was beating a tattoo against her ribs and she was finding it hard to draw breath.

# Chapter Nineteen

'Rory.' His name escaped her lips on a sigh and she moved towards him, but he was not smiling. 'Rory?' she repeated his name in a nervous whisper. 'What are you doing here?'

'Where is Flora?' he demanded angrily. 'I want you to tell me exactly what happened yesterday.'

Alice glanced anxiously at her mother and Horace, but they had already walked on with Jane as usual in the lead. 'This isn't a good time,' Alice said hastily. 'It's my mother's wedding day.'

'This is far more important. A child's life depends on your account of events.'

'I told your brother everything.' Hurt and defensive, Alice was about to walk away when he caught her by the wrist.

'This can't wait. I must hear it from you.'

'The police took a statement from me. I can't tell you any more than that.'

He gave her a searching look and she was quick to note the dark smudges under his eyes and the indentations of a frown on his forehead. Anger tugged at the corners of his generous lips and she felt his pain, which was even greater than her own. 'Please,' he said, lowering his voice. 'I need to talk to you now. I love that child and I want her found before they destroy her.'

'I love her too, and I was trying to save her from that dreadful place.'

'Tell me what happened yesterday.'

'Not here. Come with me to my aunt's house. I can't leave without wishing my mother and her husband well. We'll stay only as long as necessary and then I'll give you as much time as you need, but I doubt if there's any more I can add to what I've already said.'

Rory tucked her hand in the crook of his arm. 'Very well. Have it your way.' He stared straight ahead as they walked briskly towards Queen Square. 'The groom looks familiar,' he said as Horace assisted his bride up the steps and over the threshold. Rory came to a sudden halt. 'Isn't that the fellow you were going to marry?'

'My mother sacrificed herself on the altar of matrimony instead of me,' Alice said drily. 'If you're coming in with me please say nothing, just go along with everything and I promise I'll get away as soon as possible. I want to find Flora just as much as you do.'

Rory nodded. 'All right, I'll play along with this charade, but for heaven's sake make it quick. Every minute that Flora is with that woman puts her in even greater danger.' He followed Alice into the house, receiving an open-mouthed stare from Clara.

'Who is this?' Jane demanded, looking Rory up and down. 'You weren't invited, sir. Kindly leave.'

Beth hurried towards them, holding her hand out to Rory. 'You must be Mr Dearborn. I've heard so much about you.'

Rory shot a sideways glance at Alice, who shrugged. 'I am indeed, ma'am.' He raised her hand to his lips. 'May I be one of the first to offer my felicitations to the happy couple?'

'How charming,' Beth breathed, smiling happily. 'Alice has always spoken most highly of you, Mr Dearborn.'

Horace moved swiftly to her side, grabbing her hand as if he were afraid that Rory might make off with his bride. 'Won't you introduce us, Alice?'

'Yes, of course.' Alice went through the motions as if she were acting a part in a play, but Rory behaved impeccably and even Jane unbent a little.

'You will join us for the wedding breakfast?' Jane said in a tone that was more a command than a request.

Rory acknowledged her invitation with a nod of his head. 'You're very kind.'

'Snippet, serve luncheon now.' Jane strode into the cheerless dining room, leaving everyone to follow and find their place at table.

Rory sat next to Alice, providing the polite small talk, and Beth did her best to respond but the atmosphere was strained and Alice said little. Horace ate his food glowering at the interloper, and Jane sat in her usual place at the head of the table with a pained expression on her face, as if she wished that the whole uncomfortable business would come to a speedy conclusion. The only person who seemed to be enjoying herself was Clara, who bounded about clearing the table in between courses, eavesdropping shamelessly on the stilted conversation. Alice could only guess at the chitchat below stairs when Clara collected the next course, but at least the food was edible and the portions reasonably generous. Jane's expression hardened as she watched her guests consume the feast she had provided.

There was no wine to drink to the health and future happiness of the bride and groom, but Rory took it upon himself to propose the toast. Taking her cue, Alice rose to her feet. 'Mama and Horace,' she said, raising her glass of water.

'I'm your stepfather now,' Horace said stiffly. 'It's improper to call me by my Christian name.'

Alice put her glass down with a thud. 'I was prepared to be civil to you for Mama's sake, and I thought we might even be friends. I see now that I was mistaken.'

'Alice, please,' Beth whispered. 'Not now.'

'You have married a pompous fool, Mama. I would as soon call the milkman's horse papa. My father is dead and buried.' Alice swept out of the room with angry tears coursing down her cheeks.

She turned with a start as Rory laid his hand on her shoulder. He produced a clean hanky from his breast pocket. 'You certainly know how to make an exit.' His lips twitched and his eyes twinkled. 'Sarah Siddons would have been proud of you.'

'I wasn't acting,' Alice said, blowing her nose in the softness of a fine cotton handkerchief with a lingering aroma of laundry dried in frosty air and the individual scent that was Rory's own. She would have recognised it anywhere and it made her smile. 'Thank you.'

'That's quite all right.' He held up his hand, shaking his head as she offered to return his hanky. 'Keep it. I've plenty more. Lydia gives me a dozen every Christmas and another twelve on my birthday.'

'We can't talk here,' Alice said as Clara walked slowly past them, and it was obvious that she was listening to every word they said.

'Come with me. We'll find somewhere more private.' Rory beckoned to Clara. 'We're leaving now. Would you be kind enough to fetch our outdoor garments?'

'Yes, sir. Certainly, sir.' Clara smiled up at him, blushing furiously as she scampered off to do his bidding.

'You've made a conquest there.' Alice tucked the hanky into her reticule. 'Did you steal hearts in Ireland too?' She had not meant to blurt out her innermost thoughts and she could have bitten off her tongue. Rory's good opinion was important to her but such childish remarks were unlikely to endear her to him. She shot him a sideways glance and realised that his smile had widened into a look of amusement.

'Of course,' he said lightly. 'On a clear day the sound of weeping can be heard from Dublin to Liverpool.'

'Then it's lucky that I'm not one of them.' Alice took her mantle and bonnet from Clara. 'Thank you.'

'You will return, won't you, miss? You'll come back and see us every now and then?'

Alice patted her on the shoulder. 'Of course. Take care of yourself, Clara, and thank Mrs Jugg for a lovely meal.'

'I will, miss.'

Clara was still watching them from the top step when Alice turned her head to wave. 'The poor child has a miserable time in that household,' she said softly. 'If I had my own home I'd take her in and see that she was properly trained. As it is she'll be stuck with my aunt until that miserable woman gets tired of her.'

'I'm more worried about Flora at this moment in time.' Rory proffered his arm. 'We'll go to Russell Square.'

'No, that's not a good idea. I'm not welcome there.'

'Lydia is visiting friends and Freddie is at the office. We won't be disturbed and I'm not going to sit on a bench in the square in this weather. It's going to rain at any moment.'

Hoskins blinked like a startled owl when Rory ushered Alice into the entrance hall. 'Really, sir. I was given orders—'

'And I'm countermanding them,' Rory said without giving him time to finish the sentence. 'We'll be in the drawing room, Hoskins. See that we're not disturbed.'

'Very good, sir.' Hoskins' face was a study in self-control, betrayed only by a muscle twitching at the side of his mouth and the stiffness of his movements as he closed the front door.

'Come, Alice.' Rory walked on ahead and she followed him up the stairs to the drawing room, which held so many memories, most of them discomforting.

Alice hesitated in the doorway. 'Do you think this is a good idea? Your brother and his wife made it abundantly clear that I wasn't to come here again. They blame me entirely.'

Rory motioned her to take a seat. 'You shouldn't have acted alone. Freddie chose the school and he was satisfied that Flora would have settled down eventually. She was sent there for her own safety, but you had to interfere.'

She remained standing, clutching her gloved hands in front of her. 'Flora sent me a letter begging me to take her away from that place. I was there for over a fortnight and I can tell you that it was little better than a prison. The children were beaten or locked in the cellar for the slightest misdemeanour. They had only to make the smallest error and they were caned on the hands or forced to wear a dunce's cap and stand in the corner for hours on end. They were underfed and humiliated by the teachers, and as far as I could see their education was minimal.'

His shoulders drooped and he shook his head. 'You make it sound grim indeed.'

'I went there with the best of intentions. I would have persuaded Flora to stay had I thought that she would benefit from being there, but that wasn't the case. When Molly and her rough turned up I had no choice but to flee with the girls.'

'I suppose by that you mean Flora and Mary. What were you thinking of? You could be arrested for kidnapping young Mary.'

'I have the address of her aunt who lives in Chislehurst, and the lady's solicitor. I intended to contact them and tell them how the poor little soul was being treated. Besides which, Flora refused to leave without her small friend. What would you have done in similar circumstances?'

A reluctant smile flitted across Rory's stern features. 'I'm hardly likely to find myself in such a position.'

'But you do understand what I'm saying?'

'Yes, I do. I don't agree with what you've done, but the main thing now is to find Flora and bring her home.'

'I couldn't agree more, but I don't know where to start.'

'I'm going to Blossom Street,' Rory said firmly. 'I doubt if Molly would be fool enough to return there, but maybe one of the creatures in the cellar might be able to give me a clue as to where she's gone.'

'I'm coming with you.'

'It's not safe; beside which you have your work.'

'Your brother dismissed me. You must know that.'

'And I want you reinstated. I've seen your designs, Alice. They're brilliant and beautiful. We'd be fools to lose such a talent.'

She eyed him doubtfully. 'The others in the office resent working with a woman. Martin and Rawlins have made that very clear. The only people who tolerate me are Beasley and George. In fact, I wouldn't have a roof over my head if it weren't for George. His family were kind enough to take me in even though their house is overcrowded.'

'George is just a boy,' Rory said dismissively. 'He's little more than an apprentice, but the others will do as I—' Rory broke off as the door burst open and Frederick marched into the room.

'What do you think you're doing?' he demanded angrily. 'Hoskins told me that you'd brought that woman into my home. I thought I made it plain that she wasn't to come anywhere near here in future.'

'Just a minute, Freddie. If you give the matter your due consideration you'll realise that the real culprit is Molly Bishop. Alice was doing what she thought was best for Flora.'

'I'd better go.' Alice made a move towards the door but she hesitated, turning to Frederick. 'You can't make me feel worse than I do already, and I know that an apology is useless, but I am terribly sorry. I would do anything to help find Flora and bring her safely home.'

'You'll leave at once. I can't bear to look at you.'

'Freddie, have a heart,' Rory protested. 'You can see that she's sincere. Alice is as devoted to Flora as you or I. We should all be working together to find the child.'

Frederick sat down suddenly, bowing his head. 'This is a nightmare. I keep thinking I'll wake up and see that impish little face grinning up at me, and then I realise that she's gone. I daren't even try to imagine what must have befallen her.'

'I'm going to find her, Freddie. What's more, I've told Alice that she has her job back.'

'You can't do that.' Frederick looked up, his face drained of colour and expression. 'I don't want her working for me.'

'I'm part of the business too, and I say she stays.'

Alice held up her hands. 'Stop it,' she cried angrily.

'I don't need your job. I can find work elsewhere and I won't stay somewhere I'm not wanted.' She hurried from the room, fighting back tears of frustration as she descended the stairs and crossed the wide entrance hall. Hoskins opened the door for her.

'You did your best for Miss Flora,' he said in a low voice. 'We all know it below stairs.'

Alice paused, looking up into his lined face. 'Thank you, Hoskins. I just wish I could help.'

'Might I make a suggestion, miss?'

'Of course.'

'Miss Flora was looked after by a woman called Smithson, who was sacked for being drunk on duty.'

'Yes, I heard something like that, Hoskins. What has Smithson to do with Alice's disappearance?'

'Probably nothing, miss. But there's talk in the servants' hall, and Mrs Upton remembered that Smithson was the person who brought little Flora to us when she was just a babe, only then the woman went by another name.'

'Thank you, Hoskins, but I'm not sure how that might help us to find Flora.'

He tapped the side of his nose. 'Smithson knows the identity of Flora's real mother. Find Smithson and you might find Miss Flora.'

'Flora's mother is the one who abducted her.' Alice stared at him, frowning. 'But I suppose this woman Smithson might be able to help find Molly. Anything is worth a try. Did Mrs Upton have an address for this person?'

'I doubt it, miss. But she was known to frequent the Museum Tavern in Great Russell Street. You might start there.'

Alice considered her options. She was loath to involve herself further with either of the Dearborn brothers, but Flora's future was at stake. 'Hoskins, would you be kind enough to ask Mr Rory to come downstairs and speak to me before I leave?'

'Certainly, miss.' Hoskins hobbled across the marble-tiled floor, moving as swiftly as a rheumaticky tortoise, ascending the stairs painfully and slowly.

Alice waited, pacing the floor. Smithson might still frequent her old haunt or she might have moved on, but unaccompanied young ladies did not visit taverns. This time she intended to seek help, and Rory was the person to ask.

Alice stood in the street while Rory made enquiries in the saloon bar. He emerged from the tavern shaking his head. 'She's not known there, but the potman suggested I try the public bar.'

Alice glanced over her shoulder at a man loitering beneath a lamppost who had been ogling her and making suggestive remarks. 'I'm not staying out here. I'll come in with you.'

They entered the taproom and were engulfed in a wave of sound and a gust of warm air laced with tobacco smoke and the smell of stale beer and damp sawdust. Rory edged his way towards the bar, and Alice kept as close to him as possible, although she found herself jostled by the male drinkers and slyly propositioned. She ignored them, keeping an eye on a group of women seated round a table in the corner. Their general appearance was slatternly and their raucous laughter was pitched higher than the deeper guffaws of the men, and they were extremely drunk.

Alice moved closer to Rory and tugged at his sleeve. 'Over there,' she whispered. 'Maybe one of them will know her.'

He glanced over his shoulder and nodded. 'Barman, four pints of porter, if you please.' He placed some coins on the counter and was served without a second glance. He handed two tankards to Alice. 'Take these and I'll bring the other two. It might loosen their tongues.'

Alice made her way between the tables and the women stopped talking, but it was Rory who had their full attention. They looked him up and down, nudging each other and whispering. Alice received no such recognition as she set the drinks on the table. The boldest and brassiest of the women ogled Rory shamelessly. 'What have us done to deserve this, mister?' She fluttered her sandy eyelashes, licking her lips as if to devour him in one greedy mouthful.

'Are you looking for a good time, dearie?' One of her companions clasped Rory's hand, pressing it to her generous bosom. 'I'm Mattie. I do special rates for handsome toffs.'

Rory smiled, withdrawing his hand and patting her on her rouged cheek. 'No, thank you, Mattie, but I'm hoping that you might be able to help us in another way.'

'Do any of you know a woman who goes by the name of Smithson?' Alice moved closer.

Their smiles froze. 'Who's asking?' Mattie demanded suspiciously.

'It's a business matter,' Alice said uneasily.

'We need a bit more information, dearie.' The brassy woman slapped her tankard down on the table. 'Is it laying out or lying in you want?' She stared at Alice's belly with a suggestive smirk. 'Or is it a young lady's problem that needs my expert attention? I'm more skilful than Jessie Smithson when it comes to intimate matters.' She nudged Alice in the ribs and winked. Her companions nodded and rocked with laughter.

Rory opened his mouth to speak but Alice silence him with a glance. 'It's none of those things,' she said firmly. 'If you know where I can find her it will be to her advantage.'

'For the love of God tell her what she wants to know, Mattie,' the brassy woman urged, apparently bored with the subject. 'But it should be worth a few more drinks.'

Mattie gave Rory a sly look. 'What's it worth, mister?'

He threw a handful of small change on the table. 'That's all you're getting. Do you know where we can find this woman or not?'

There was a scramble for the coins, Mattie grabbing the most. She gave him a toothless grin. 'Try the pop-shop down the road. Jessie does business with old Quint.' She rose unsteadily to her feet. 'I'm getting them in. Who's for a refill?'

Rory grabbed Alice by the arm. 'Come on. We're not going to get any sense out of them now.'

'Going so soon, dearie?' The brassy woman attempted to stand up, but collapsed onto her chair with a throaty chuckle. 'Come again, love, but next time leave the dollymop at home.'

Outside in the street Alice drew deep breaths of the cold night air. The daytime stench of the city was diluted by the frosty chill, but it was preferable to the stink of unwashed humanity in the pub.

'Are you all right?' Rory asked anxiously. 'You're not going to faint, are you?'

She shook her head. 'No, I'm perfectly all right. It's just that a woman called Smithson was involved in a tragedy that occurred in my own family some years ago.'

'Smithson is a fairly common name,' Rory said dismissively. 'I wouldn't put too much importance on it if I were you.'

'You're right, of course. Let's find the pawnbroker's shop and see if he knows Smithson. That woman could have been lying.'

Rory proffered his arm. 'There's only one way to find out. Are you sure you're up to it, Alice?'

'I'm quite all right.'

Quint appeared from the depths of the gloomy shop in answer to the jangling of the bell. He unlocked the door and blocked the entrance but Rory pushed past him and Alice followed him into the dingy premises. In the light of Quint's oil lamp she could see possessions that had been pawned spilling from shelves onto the floor. There was a mad jumble of objects of every shape and size, from walking canes to top hats, and fob watches to spades and hoes. Coats, capes and ladies' frocks hung from rails, and boxes were filled to the brim with gloves, scarves and underwear. A musty smell pervaded the darkness.

Quint faced them, pale as a ghost. 'What d'you want?' he demanded querulously. 'You can't barge in here at this time of night and expect to be served. Ain't an honest shopkeeper allowed to have his supper in peace?'

'I'm sorry to disturb you, Mr Quint,' Rory said calmly. 'We just require some information.'

'Information?' Quint's voice rose to a squeak. 'You took me away from a tasty pig's trotter to ask for information. Is it the price of something in the shop, or do you want to know how much you can get for that handsome fob watch, mister?'

'We're looking for Jessie Smithson,' Alice said with

a persuasive smile. 'We've been told that she comes here quite often.'

Quint backed away. 'If you ain't here to pawn your valuables or to make a purchase you can push off. I dunno what you want this person for, but it's none of my business.' He picked up a battered police truncheon, brandishing it in his hand. 'Now get out of me shop. I don't want nothing to do with you.' He took a menacing step forward. 'Don't think I won't use this. I ain't a patient man, so get out of me shop now afore I does something I ain't proud of.'

# Chapter Twenty

'All right,' Rory said hastily. 'We're leaving.' He hurried Alice outside onto the street. 'I'm sorry,' he said apologetically. 'I shouldn't have brought you to a rough place like this.'

'I don't know where you think I've been living since my employment in Russell Square was terminated, but I can assure you I've had to cope with worse than this.'

He bowed his head. 'I'm sorry you became involved in our affairs. You weren't to blame for introducing Flora to her real mother. I was the one who started all this and yet you've paid the price for my interference.'

'That's not strictly true,' Alice said hastily. 'Flora already knew that she had been adopted because Smithson blurted it out in a fit of pique. You were just trying to help a disturbed child.'

'They say that the road to hell is paved with good intentions, and that certainly seems to be the case here,' he said with a wry smile. 'I'll see you home, Alice. It's the least I can do.'

'I can hail a cab. I'll be fine.'

'You are too independent for your own good, Alice Radcliffe. You must allow a mere male to feel that he's of some use.'

'I'm sure it's out of your way. The Youngs live in a modest house in an unfashionable area.'

'I know where they live.' He raised his hand to hail a passing hansom cab. 'Don't look so surprised. I know quite a lot about our employees, and I'm not such a snoot that I look down on those who are less well off or those who have fallen on hard times. As a matter of fact I rent rooms not far from there.' He handed her into the cab. 'Five Foot Lane, please, cabby.'

'What can we do now?' Alice asked as he took his seat beside her. 'I think that Quint knows something. Perhaps I could do better if I visited him alone.'

Rory laid his hand on hers. 'Don't do anything rash. You mustn't place yourself in danger on our account. This is Dearborn business and you shouldn't get involved.'

'But I am already,' she protested. 'Flora means a lot to me and I need to find her as much as you do. If I hadn't taken her from Willoughby Hall none of this would have happened.'

'Molly would have found her anyway and the result would have been the same. It's Molly we have to trace and then we'll find Flora, but you must keep out of it, for her sake and yours.'

Alice was acutely conscious of the warmth of his touch. She knew she ought to snatch her hand away, but in the dark streets it was easy to ignore the rules of propriety that had been drummed into her since childhood. 'I have little else to do,' she said softly. 'Although I must find work. I can't expect the Youngs to support me.'

'I'll speak to Frederick first thing in the morning. I'll make him see sense.'

'I might be better off working for the Challoners,' Alice said thoughtfully.

'What do you know of them? They're our biggest rival.'

The sharp edge in Rory's voice made her turn to look him in the eye. 'Carrie said she would introduce me to her friend Bertie Challoner. She was sure he would take me on or at least give me work that I could do at home.'

'Don't even think about it,' Rory said urgently. 'You mustn't waste your talents in a firm like theirs. They produce greetings cards by the thousand and they're not too fussy about the quality. They're sickly and sentimental, and they'd make sure your designs for Christmas cards were the same. I can't allow you to be exploited in that way, Alice.'

She sat back against the squabs. 'I don't think it's

up to you, Rory. Your brother has dismissed me twice from his employ, and I am not going to beg for my job. I know I'm good and I want to work for someone who appreciates me.' She looked away. 'As for Flora, nothing will prevent me from looking for her. I'm not scared of Molly Bishop, nor am I frightened of your brother. I'll do as I think fit and no one will stop me.' She tapped on the roof of the cab and the small window flipped open. 'Drop me off on the corner of Five Foot Lane, please. I'll walk from there.'

Rory tightened his grip on her hand. 'Don't do anything rash. If you leave it to me I'll sort matters out with my brother. I don't want to lose you, Alice.'

As she lay in bed that night Rory's words echoed in her brain. He had sounded sincere but she had avoided meeting his gaze. He had a way with him that could make the depths of winter seem like summer, and a smile that could soften the hardest heart. But he was well aware of his charms and she had seen him use them to his advantage. She did not want to fall a victim to a man who was interested in using her artistic talents only to further his business.

'Are you still awake, Alice?' Carrie whispered.

'I'm sorry. Did I disturb you?'

'No. I've been lying here trying to think of a solution to your problems.'

'So have I, but I don't know what to do for the best. Rory wants me to leave it to him, but I have a nagging feeling that the pawnbroker knows more than he was telling us.'

Carrie raised herself on her elbow, her face a pale translucent oval in the semi-darkness. 'I think you ought to follow your instincts. You won't rest until you know that young Flora is safe, so you must do as you think best and never mind what Rory or his brother say. Men think they're always in the right, but we know better.'

Alice snuggled down beneath the coverlet. 'I'll go and see Quint in the morning. Maybe I'll find him in a better mood, and perhaps he'll be more forthcoming without Rory breathing down his neck.'

'I'd come with you but I have to go to work,' Carrie said, sighing. 'We'd best not mention any of this to George. He's worried about you as it is, and he's angry because you've lost your job when you were only trying to help.'

'He's a good friend.'

'I think he'd like to be more than that.'

Alice was suddenly wide awake. 'What are you saying, Carrie?'

'Just that I know my brother, and I think he's fallen in love with you.'

'I didn't realise,' Alice said softly. 'If it's true then I'm very sorry. I'm very fond of George, but I've never thought about him in that way.'

'I was afraid of that.' Carrie subsided onto her pillow. 'He's a good man, Alice. I know what I said before, but I think you could do worse.'

Alice had no answer to this. She knew what Carrie said was true, but it was a shock to learn that George's feeling for her went deeper than friendship. Why, she thought, is life so complicated? She fell asleep with Carrie's words repeating over and over again in her brain, but the face she saw in her mind's eye was Rory's.

'I'm going to speak up for you at work this morning, Alice.' George rose from the breakfast table, taking his empty bowl and spoon through to the scullery. He returned moments later. 'I'm going to tell Mr Frederick that we can't manage without you. Rawlins is good at geometrical patterns for playing cards, and Martin is a capable draughtsman, but neither of them can put heart and sentiment into their work. I've seen your designs and they're lovely.'

'Please don't say anything.' Alice stared down at the rapidly cooling porridge in front of her. 'I'd rather do this my way, George. But I am very grateful to you for wanting to help me.'

'I'd do anything for you,' he said in a low voice, ignoring his younger sisters, who were giggling and nudging each other. 'You know I would.'

'You'll be late for work, George,' his mother said quietly. 'Best go now, dear. You don't want to give that Rawlins fellow a reason to pick on you.'

'He don't need a reason, Ma.' George snatched his jacket from its peg on the wall. 'I'll wait and see if they reconsider, Alice, but if nothing happens I am going to say something.'

She rose to her feet, her food untouched. 'Please don't, George. You're a wonderful friend and I'm truly grateful for everything you've done for me, but this is my battle. If I can't stand up for myself in the workplace it doesn't bode well for my future employment, or for any other young woman who wishes to work alongside male colleagues.'

'Off you go, George,' Rose said, rocking baby Jackie in her arms as he had begun to whimper. 'You can chat to Alice this evening, but if you don't go now you might find yourself looking for another job. Carrie and your brothers left a good half-hour since.'

George crammed his bowler hat on his head. 'I'm going, but we'll discuss this later, Alice.'

His mother waited until he had left the room. 'Winnie, Nellie, Lizzie – off to school or you'll be late too. Coats on, please. It may be sunny outside but it's still winter and I don't want anyone going down with a chill.' She shooed them out of the room. 'My son is very fond of you, Alice,' she said, taking a seat with the baby cradled in one arm and two-year-old Annie making an attempt to climb onto her lap. 'George is a tender-hearted boy.'

'I really had no idea how he felt about me,' Alice said, choosing her words with care. 'Carrie told me last night and I was shocked to think that I'd been so wrapped up in my own affairs that I hadn't noticed. I'm flattered, of course, but I don't feel the same and it hurts me to know that I'm going to cause him pain. I am very sorry, Rose.'

'My dear, you can't help how you feel. You can't make yourself love someone if the feeling isn't there, so you mustn't blame yourself. I know I can trust you to do the right thing by my boy.'

'I'll speak to him this evening.'

Rose gazed at her soulfully. 'You'll let him down gently?'

'Of course I will. I care a lot for George and you've been like a mother to me. I can't bear to think that I've caused you distress.'

'My dear girl, I've lived a lot longer than you and I've had my fair share of ups and downs. Having you here has been a pleasure and we're all very fond of you, but you must make your own way in the world. George will have his heart broken a few times before he finds the right person for him. He'll be upset, but he'll recover.'

Alice moved swiftly to her side and kissed her on the cheek. 'I'll look for accommodation elsewhere, but there's something I must do first.'

'I understand, and it's probably for the best, but I'll be sorry to see you go. You'll always be a welcome guest in our house, Alice. Always.'

Despite her urgent need to find work and a new place to live, Alice had only one thing on her mind as she made her way to the pawnshop in Great

Russell Street. It was cold and sunny, with frost particles sparkling on the pavements, and she walked briskly, her mind filled with the questions she would ask Quint. She had hoped to find him in a better mood than the previous evening, but his general demeanour was less than welcoming when she entered the shop. 'What's your business, young woman?'

'I seek information, Mr Quint.'

He peered at her short-sightedly. 'Was you here last evening?'

'I was, and you were less than helpful when I enquired about Jessie Smithson.'

'I told you last night I got nothing to say. Never heard of her.'

'I was told that she often visits you here.'

'They was mistook.'

Alice could see that he was not going to co-operate and she decided to try another tactic. 'That's a pity because I might have some information which would be of value to her.' She shrugged and turned to look at a case containing items of jewellery. Fragmented rays of sunlight filtered through the grimy window-panes and her attention was caught by a silver fili-gree brooch. 'Might I take a closer look at this?' she asked.

He lumbered over to the case and produced a key ring from his pocket. After trying several he managed to find the right one. His bare fingers protruded from woollen mittens like gnarled twigs as he unhooked the small silver butterfly. 'Thought you wasn't buying.'

Alice examined it closely. 'Where did you get this?'

'That ain't none of your business. Pay me half a crown and it's yours.'

'This brooch is stolen property,' Alice said boldly. 'I shan't pay you a penny piece and if you don't tell me who brought it in I'll go straight to the police.'

'You little bitch.' Quint moved nearer, thrusting his face so close that she could see the dirt engrained in his pores and the remains of his breakfast sticking to his greying beard and moustache. 'You'll get out of here now, or do I have to throw you out?'

'Do as you please but I'll go to the police and I'm sure they'll be very interested to inspect your stock. All I want to know is who pawned this brooch. I've reason to believe that Smithson might be part of the Bishop gang. Was it her?'

Quint was clearly baffled by her boldness and his dirty fingers plucked nervously at his beard. 'What if it was?'

'I need to contact her, Mr Quint. It's very urgent.'

His scowl was answer enough, but she was desperate. She took her purse from her reticule and produced a half-crown. 'I'll buy the brooch but only if you tell me where I can find Smithson.'

'And you'll leave me alone? You won't go to the police?'

'I give you my word.'

He held out his hand. 'Brownlow Buildings, Clare Market, but don't tell her that I let on.'

'I won't.' Alice handed him the money, closing her fingers around the precious silver butterfly. Memories of last Christmas came flooding back: she had refused the pearl ring that Rory had wanted to give her, and sacrificed the silver butterfly in order to make Flora happy. It must have been taken by force, she thought angrily. Flora would never have given it away willingly, but good might come of it after all. If she could find Smithson she would be on her way to rescuing Flora.

Clare Market was situated in the midst of the worst rookeries in London, and Brownlow Buildings was a dilapidated Elizabethan town house that had escaped the Great Fire of London only to crumble into disrepair. Alice knew that the area was the haunt of thieves and the worst sort of villains, but she was determined to find Smithson. Ignoring the taunts of the slatternly women who hung around the doorways of shops and pubs, soliciting trade, she edged away from men who offered her money for her services. Ragged children accosted her, begging for coins and old women huddled on the pavement held their hands out in silent entreaty. It was Alice's idea of hell and it was a relief to escape into the dark interior of Brownlow Buildings.

She hesitated, waiting until her eyes grew accustomed to the gloom and found herself in a narrow passageway that opened into an oak-panelled entrance hall. What had once been the home of a prosperous London merchant was now reduced to a cheap lodging house. A man was slumped at the foot of the stairs, and at first she thought he was dead, but then a loud snore shook his skinny frame and he groaned. The sound of raised voices, shrieks and screams, raucous laughter and infants wailing echoed off the walls, but doors were firmly closed. Alice was beginning to wish that she had listened to Rory. The thought of making enquiries and disturbing the occupants was daunting and she was about to retreat when the body on the floor snapped into a sitting position. He opened his eyes, focusing his bloodshot gaze on her with difficulty.

'Who are you?'

She took a step backwards, prepared to run if need be. 'I'm looking for Jessie Smithson.'

'The bitch took all me money,' he groaned. 'Drank me under the table and left me to crawl home.' He closed his eyes, swaying as if about to collapse.

Alice would have shaken him, but his clothes were filthy and the smell emanating from him was enough to make her retch. She prodded him with the toe of her boot. 'Where might I find Mrs Smithson?'

He opened one eye. 'I need a drink. Got a tanner, lady? Is it worth sixpence to find me old lady?'

'You're Mr Smithson?'

'For me sins.' He held his head in his hands. 'Give

me a tanner or leave me alone to die here. She don't care, the hard-hearted besom.'

Once again Alice was forced to take out her purse and hand over some of her hard-earned money. He grabbed the small silver coin and staggered to his feet. 'Never let it be said that Nat Smithson ain't a man of his word.' He gesticulated in the direction of the upper floor. 'It's the door facing you on the first landing.' He lurched past Alice and headed for the street.

She made her way up the stairs, pausing and holding her breath at the sound of a door opening, followed by shouted abuse and hysterical screams, and then silence. She knocked on the door, and to her surprise and relief it opened. A large, red-faced woman glared at her through a mop of tousled grey hair.

'What d'you want?'

'Are you Mrs Jessie Smithson?'

'Who wants to know?'

'May I come in?' Alice asked, glancing nervously over her shoulder at the sound of footsteps on the stairs. For a moment she thought the angry woman was going to slam the door in her face but then an arm shot out and dragged her into the room.

'Who are you?' Jessie peered at Alice.

'My name is Alice Radcliffe. You don't know me.'

'So what d'you want?' Jessie narrowed her eyes, glancing suggestively at Alice's belly. 'In a bit of trouble, are you, dearie?'

'No. Nothing like that.'

'Then what d'you want with the likes of me?'

'I've come about Flora Dearborn.'

Jessie recoiled, staring at her in disbelief. 'How do you know Flora?'

'I found something of hers in Quint's pawnshop. He gave me to believe that it was you who popped it.' It was a lie but Alice was prepared to go to almost any lengths in her search for Flora. She produced the silver brooch from her reticule. 'She wouldn't have parted with this willingly.'

'I don't know nothing about it.'

'Quint said you pawned it, Jessie. I don't care how you got it, all I want is to find Flora and bring her home.'

'What is the kid to you?'

'I was her tutor for a short while. I think you know the rest. It was you who told her about Molly Bishop, although why you made up such a lie I can't imagine. I don't believe that Molly is Flora's mother, but she took her by force and I want to know the reason why.'

Jessie drew her wrap around her ample person and went to sit on a chair by the window. She picked up a clay pipe and filled it with tobacco. 'I dunno nothing about it.' She struck a match and lit it, puffing smoke with obvious satisfaction. 'You come to the wrong place, little Alice.'

'You're lying. I want to know the truth or I'll go to the police and report you for theft of this brooch.'

'You can't prove nothing against me.'

'Quint will back me up,' Alice said, hoping it was

true. 'He'll do anything to save his own skin. Tell me where Flora is and I'll leave you in peace.'

'She's with her real mother and that's where she belongs.'

'I know she's with Molly.'

'Molly is just a go-between, like me.'

'So who is Flora's mother? You know, don't you?'

'Of course I knows her. Wasn't it me who helped her give birth to the brat? Wasn't it me who had to find a home for the fatherless infant? Wasn't it me who was sent to keep an eye on the kid while she was growing up?' Jessie gripped the stem of the pipe between blackened teeth, her lips curved in a derisive sneer. 'You don't know nothing, you stuck-up little cow. You're just like your silly ma, who reckoned she was too good to speak to the likes of me.'

Alice stared at her in disbelief. 'You knew Flora's mother all along, and yet you kept it a secret. Who is this woman and where is Flora? I'm not leaving here until you tell me.'

Jessie looked her up and down. Taking the pipe from her mouth she tapped the ash into a saucer. 'I think it's time Jessie Smithson took charge again. I want to see her ladyship's face when I tell all.'

'Does that mean you'll take me to Flora?'

'Give me a minute or two to get dressed. I wouldn't miss this, not at any price.'

Outside the crowds parted as Jessie charged through them, and Alice did her best to keep up with her long strides. It was, she thought, like following in the wake of Britannia or Boadicea, and no one dared accost her while she was with the formidable Jessie Smithson. They stopped when Jessie reached the Strand and she turned to Alice with a questioning look. 'Got the money for a cab?'

'How far are we going?'

'A bob should do it. We're within the four-mile limit.'

Alice did a quick calculation. 'Yes, I've got a shilling for the fare.' But Jessie had already hailed a cab and was about to climb in.

'Hertford Street, cabby.' Jessie sank back on the seat. 'You might wish you hadn't pried when you find out the truth, Miss High and Mighty.'

Alice climbed in after her. She was trembling with anticipation and yet assailed by doubts. It all seemed too easy. She had put her trust in Smithson, but the woman seated next to her had admitted to past deeds that had affected two families, and probably many more. The cab weaved its way through heavy traffic in Trafalgar Square and made its way at a painfully slow pace along Cockspur Street, picking up speed in Regent Street and slowing down again in Piccadilly. Alice could hardly breathe as her excitement mounted. She had to believe Smithson; after all why would the woman accompany her on a fruitless mission? She shot her a sideways glance but Smithson was staring straight ahead with her clay pipe wedged between her teeth.

'Nearly there,' Smithson said gruffly as the cab pulled up outside an elegant four-storey house in Hertford Street. 'Pay the man, Alice. I ain't got that sort of money to spare.'

Alice stepped down to the pavement and handed the cabby what was almost the last of her money, but as the vehicle disappeared into Curzon Street she experienced a sudden wave of panic. She turned to Smithson. 'Are you sure this is the right place?'

# Chapter Twenty-One

Smithson marched up the steps and knocked on the front door. 'We'll soon find out,' she said tersely.

Alice looked up and down the street with a feeling of awe. She had once thought that Aunt Jane's house in Queen Square was the epitome of elegance, although that building had been eclipsed by the Dearborns' establishment in Russell Square, but she realised now that Mayfair was worlds apart from Bloomsbury. These houses belonged to the rich and fashionable, and she felt suddenly dowdy and out of place. Smithson looked confident, but it seemed unlikely that the people who lived in such an exclusive area would associate with the likes of Jessie Smithson or Molly Bishop.

Alice laid her hand on Smithson's sleeve. 'I think you must be mistaken. This can't be right.'

The door opened before Smithson had a chance

to reply and she stepped forward, towering over the trim parlourmaid, who blanched visibly. 'We've come to see Mrs Considine.'

'I'm afraid she's out of town, ma'am.' The maid was about to close the door when Smithson placed her large foot over the threshold. 'In that case we'd like to see Miss Flora.'

'Miss Flora went with Mrs Considine.'

Smithson barged into the entrance hall. 'Now listen to me, dearie. We've come all the way across town to see your mistress, and we ain't leaving until we've spoken to someone who can give us some information.'

Alice pushed past Smithson. She could see that the maid was intimidated by the large woman and was likely to call for help if she felt threatened. 'Is there someone who could help us?' she asked, smiling. 'It would be a great kindness if there were.'

The maid shot a wary look in Smithson's direction. 'Mrs Considine's solicitor is here, miss. He's in the study.'

'Then we'll see him,' Smithson said firmly. 'Mrs Considine is an old friend of mine so point us in the right direction, dearie.'

The maid looked doubtful. 'I'll ask him if he'll see you. What name shall I say?'

'Miss Radcliffe,' Alice said without giving Smithson a chance to answer. 'Miss Alice Radcliffe.'

'Wait here, if you please.' The maid darted off.

'You don't want to let them put you off,' Smithson

said. 'I could set the pavements of London on fire if I was to tell all I know about Mrs Considine's past, and she's well aware of the fact.'

'What would a wealthy woman want with someone else's child? And why is she keeping Flora here against her will?' Alice put her head on one side. 'What is it that you're not telling me, Jessie? I'm at a definite disadvantage.'

Smithson backed towards the front door. 'You'll find out soon enough, but I ain't too fond of solicitors and the like. You're on your own from now on, dearie. I've done me bit. Never let it be said that Jessie Smithson is a bad woman.' She let herself out, closing the door behind her and Alice was tempted to follow her but the maid reappeared.

'This way, miss.'

Alice followed her along a wide corridor where crystal wall sconces sparkled in the flickering light of expensive candles, and the scent of melting wax mingled with the perfume of the hothouse flowers that spilled from urns and vases set on pedestals and side tables. Everything around her spoke of money and good taste. The contrast between this elegant abode and the dosshouse in Clare Market was shocking, and yet in a strange way it filled her with hope. There was life outside the poverty-stricken areas of the East End, and if it was attainable for some then it must be possible for others to better themselves.

The maid ushered her into a book-lined study.

'Miss Radcliffe, sir.' She bobbed a curtsey and left the room.

Alice faced the man who was seated behind a large desk. She judged him to be in his mid-forties, and despite the smile pasted on his classic features she felt a shudder run down her spine. His appearance was business-like with a touch of flamboyance. The points of a scarlet silk handkerchief protruded from his breast pocket, and a diamond stick pin secured his cravat. His greying hair was slicked back with pomade, and a neatly trimmed moustache seemed to float above his top lip. He rose to his feet. 'I'm Philip Hart, Mrs Considine's solicitor and business advisor. What can I do for you, Miss Radcliffe?'

She was about to answer when she noticed the large portrait in oils that hung on the wall behind him. Something inside her stirred as she struggled to recapture an elusive memory from long ago. It was connected in some mysterious way with the beautiful golden-haired woman who looked out at the world with a mischievous twinkle in her blue eyes.

'The lady in the painting, sir. Who is she?'

He followed her gaze. 'That is Mrs Considine, my employer and the owner of this fine house. It is a very good likeness.' Moving swiftly round the desk he pulled up a chair. 'Take a seat, Miss Radcliffe.'

'She looks familiar, but I can't quite place her.'

'Mrs Considine is a well-known personage, Miss Radcliffe. Perhaps you've seen her at a social function, or even the theatre. Mrs Considine is a great patron of the arts and renowned for her charitable works. What is your business with her?'

Alice dragged her thoughts back to the present. 'I'm looking for a little girl called Flora. I've been told that she's here.'

Mr Hart resumed his seat. 'Why do you seek this child, Miss Radcliffe? And what makes you think she resides here?'

'Does the name Molly Bishop mean anything to you, sir?'

'Answering a question with another question isn't going to get us very far, Miss Radcliffe, but I will say that I have no acquaintanceship with a person of that name.'

'Molly Bishop abducted Flora from York station and, according to Jessie Smithson, Flora was brought here. Where is she, sir? Her family are desperate for news of her.'

He leaned back in his chair, resting his hands on the desk. 'I think the person of whom you speak was mistaken. The only child who resides in this establishment is Mrs Considine's daughter, but both she and her mother are out of town at present.'

His blank expression gave nothing away and yet Alice did not believe him. She was certain that Smithson had told her the truth, and she was not going to give up without a fight. 'Might I have her address, Mr Hart? I would very much like to meet Mrs Considine.'

'She is a very busy woman, Miss Radcliffe. Her business interests are wide and varied and she rarely allows herself the luxury of relaxing in the country.'

Alice rose to her feet. She could see that she was not going to elicit any useful information from him. 'Thank you for seeing me, sir. I won't take up any more of your valuable time.'

'I'll ring for the maid to see you out. I'm sorry I can't be of more help.' He reached for the bell pull.

'How old is Mrs Considine's daughter, sir?'

'Nine or ten, I think, but I can't be certain. Why do you ask?'

'She is the same age as Flora. I'm sure that Mrs Considine would have sympathy for the family of a lost child. She would only have to look at her own daughter to understand how they must feel at this moment.'

'I'm sure she would be very sympathetic.' Mr Hart picked up a sheaf of papers. 'Good day, Miss Radcliffe.'

There was something in his manner that made her suspicious. It was not that she trusted Jessie Smithson, but more the fact that she did not trust this man. She was about to enquire if he had a family of his own, and if so how he would feel if one of his children were abducted and had disappeared seemingly without trace, when there was a soft tap on the door and the maidservant entered.

'Show Miss Radcliffe out, Lipton.'

'This way, miss.'

Alice had little choice other than to follow the maid. She waited until Lipton opened the front door, turning to her with a rueful smile. 'I am a silly thing. Mr Hart has just this minute told me the name of Mrs Considine's country house and I've forgotten it already.'

'It's Hazelwood House, miss.'

'Of course it is, and it's near ...' Alice threw up her hands. 'I have such a poor memory, Lipton. Where is it situated?'

'Near Hatfield, miss.' Lipton gave her a pitying look. 'And I thought I had a memory like a sieve, or at least that's what Mrs Johnson, the housekeeper, says.'

'You've been very helpful, and I shall tell Mrs Considine so when I see her.'

'If you're thinking of travelling there today I might be able to help,' Lipton said eagerly. 'Mrs Considine's coachman returned yesterday with a list of things that madam requested. You might just catch Briggs before he leaves and if he's agreeable you could travel with him.'

It seemed too good an opportunity to miss. Alice grasped her by the hand. 'Would you take me to him? If he thought that Mr Hart had sanctioned it, he could hardly refuse.'

Lipton frowned, biting her lip. 'I dunno, miss. Mr Hart never said nothing to me.'

'My business is with Mrs Considine. You won't get into trouble for helping me, I promise.'

'I suppose it'll be all right then. Best hurry or he'll have left.'

Briggs had been reluctant at first, but it seemed that he and Lipton were more than just friends, and with a little persuasion he agreed to take Alice to Hazelwood House. She would have been travelling in style and comfort if there had not been quite so much luggage piled up on the seats, but she resigned herself to being squashed in a corner, half buried beneath hat boxes and garments wrapped in calico. At the end of the three-hour journey she was cramped and aching. When they came to a halt Briggs climbed down from the box to open the door. 'Are you front entrance or servants' entrance, miss?'

'I'm a guest,' she said, crossing her fingers.

He regarded her steadily. 'If you say so, miss. Front entrance it is then; you'd best alight here.' He proffered his arm and she slid out from beneath the weighty pile of fabric. She knew that he did not believe her, but she was not about to admit that she was uninvited and probably unwelcome.

'Thank you,' she said with all the dignity she could muster. 'I'm much obliged to you, Mr Briggs.' She crossed the gravel carriage sweep, forcing her cramped limbs to move although each step caused her pain and her feet were tingling with pins and needles. She paused, gazing up at the imposing frontage of the Jacobean mansion with its mullioned windows and ornate brickwork. Ivy clambered up the walls, softening the somewhat austere outlines of the building, and white doves perched on the guttering, peering down at her with bright beady eyes. Alice raised the heavy iron ring and knocked on the metal-studded oak door. She glanced over her shoulder as the carriage disappeared in what she assumed must be the direction of the stables, and it was only then she realised that the house was miles from its nearest neighbour. The large expanse of lawn was punctuated by ancient oaks and surrounded by a brick wall over six feet in height.

She was about to knock again when she heard approaching footsteps and the door opened on well-oiled hinges. The male servant looked her up and down, his shaggy eyebrows raised in an unspoken question.

She cleared her throat. 'I've come to see Mrs Considine.'

'Is she expecting you, miss?'

'No, not exactly, but if you tell her that I've come about Miss Flora I think she'll see me.'

'Best step inside.' He stood back to allow her to enter. 'What name shall I say, miss?'

'She does not know me but I'm Alice Radcliffe and it is very important.'

'Wait here.' He strode off across the wide entrance hall, leaving Alice to look round at her leisure. Hazelwood House could not have changed much since it was built in the seventeenth century, and she felt as though she had stepped into a bygone era.

The wainscoting and highly polished floorboards glowed with the patina of age and the energetic application of beeswax and lavender polish. The furniture was equally old, heavily carved and solid. A log fire blazed up the chimney, emitting sparks that fell harmlessly onto the stone hearth. The scent of burning apple wood filled the air, and the house felt warm and surprisingly welcoming. Alice suppressed the urge to call out to Flora. She had a feeling that she was near and her stomach churned with excitement mixed with anxiety as she waited for the servant to return.

A cry from the top of the stairs made her turn with a start and she uttered a gasp of delight. 'Flora.' She rushed to the foot of the staircase in time to catch a flying bundle of lace-trimmed petticoats as Flora slid down the balustrade, toppling off before she collided with the newel post. They collapsed onto the bottom step, arms around each other, laughing and crying. 'I can't believe I've found you,' Alice whispered into Flora's golden curls.

'Hawkins said a lady had called and I knew at once it was you. I told Mama that you'd be here as soon as you could.'

'Mama?' Alice held her at arm's length.

'It's true. Flora is my daughter.' The voice was vaguely familiar, conjuring up long-forgotten memories.

Alice scrambled to her feet, looking up at the woman who might have stepped out of the portrait in Hertford Street. 'I know who you are,' she said slowly.

'She's my mama,' Flora said happily. 'I've found my mummy at last. Isn't she beautiful?'

Viola Considine seemed to glide as she descended the stairs. A shaft of sunlight slanting through an oriel window turned her golden coronet of curls into a halo. In her simple white muslin gown she looked like an angel.

'You're supposed to be dead,' Alice said dazedly.

Viola threw back her head and laughed, dispelling the angelic image she had created. 'So that's what they told you, little Alice.' She came to stand at her side, looking at her closely. 'But you're not so little now, my dear. You're a grown woman and you've been the saviour of my child. Even were we not related by blood I would love you for that alone.' Viola enveloped Alice in a perfumed embrace.

Alice was the first to break away. She stared at her in disbelief. 'You are my Aunt Viola, and you are Flora's mother. I can't believe it.'

Flora grasped Alice's hand. 'Come into the parlour. My mummy will tell you everything. She's explained it all to me and I love her, but I love you too, Alice,' she added hastily. 'You were the first person to be my friend, apart from Rory, and I'm still very fond of him. Does he know you've come here?'

'No, he doesn't. Nobody knows, apart from Lipton and Briggs. I doubt if Lipton will have told Mr Hart that she helped me to find you.'

'Come,' Viola said softly. 'We'll continue this conversation in the morning parlour and I'll send for some coffee and cake. You must be hungry, Alice.'

'I am rather,' Alice admitted. She had forgotten about food, but now it was mentioned her stomach rumbled expectantly.

Still holding her hand, Flora danced across the hall. 'When I awakened this morning I had no idea that this would turn out to be such a perfect day. I've missed you so much, Alice.'

'And I've missed you more than you could possibly know, and now I understand why. We're cousins, Flora. We're related by blood – we're family, and I think it's wonderful.' Confused, but happy, Alice allowed herself to be led to the parlour, which despite the stone mullions and the small windowpanes was surprisingly bright and sunny. The furnishings were old-fashioned and some of the upholstery was well worn but the atmosphere was cosy and welcoming.

Hawkins appeared in answer to Viola's summons and brought a tray of coffee and a large chocolate cake, which Flora hacked into overly large slices, much to her mother's amusement. She pressed a plate into Alice's hand.

'Tell my mummy your story, Alice. Tell her how you travelled all the way to Yorkshire to save me.'

Viola lit a cigarillo with a spill from the fire. She exhaled with a sigh of pleasure and took a seat close to the hearth. 'Well,' she said when Alice had told her everything from the time the bailiffs entered the house in Doughty Street to the moment Molly erupted onto the platform at York, 'that makes my story seem almost tame.'

'I was told you had died,' Alice said simply. 'Why did they lie to me?'

'Mummy has had such an exciting life.' Flora licked chocolate cake off each finger in turn. 'You won't believe half the stories she has to tell.'

'I'm sure I won't,' Alice replied, smiling. 'You've heard all about me, Aunt Viola. Now it's definitely your turn.'

Viola cast her eyes heavenward. 'Oh, please. Don't call me "aunt"; it reminds me of Jane. She always hated me.'

'That's not what she says,' Alice protested. 'She's kept your room exactly as it was when you left home.'

'That's balderdash,' Viola said dismissively. 'Jane was jealous because Uncle Robert was fond of me.' She lowered her voice. 'A little too fond, if you know what I mean, Alice.'

'No! Really?' Alice stared at her in astonishment.

'It's all in the past, but I can tell you that I was desperate to escape from the mausoleum and my uncle's clutching hands. Then I met Edmond. I was just seventeen and he was young and exciting. We fell in love, but Uncle Robert forbade me to have anything to do with Eddie, so we ran away together.'

'And you never returned to Queen Square?'

'Oh, yes, just the once.' Viola smoked in silence,

a frown puckering her brow. 'It was a few months later that I realised I was in the family way. I was unmarried and Edmond, as I had discovered, was a gambler. If he won at the tables we could eat, if he lost we went hungry.'

Flora reached up to hold her mother's hand. 'Poor Mummy,' she said softly.

'Poor and foolish.' Viola exhaled a stream of blue smoke, watching it dissipate into the atmosphere with a wry chuckle. 'You know Aunt Jane only too well, I'm sure, Alice. You can imagine how she reacted when she saw me. I was promptly ejected from the house and told never on any account to return.'

'I'm shocked,' Alice said angrily. 'She said that you'd died of consumption, and my mother told me that you'd died in childbirth, and that the baby was stillborn.'

'As you can see I'm very much alive and so is Flora. The tragedy was that Eddie made me choose between him and my baby, and after a difficult birth I was too ill to fight him. Then the midwife he'd hired to deliver Flora said she knew of a wealthy couple who longed for a child. Jessie Smithson told me that the family were prepared to pay handsomely, and they would give my little girl everything that I could not provide.'

'So it's true,' Alice said slowly. 'You sold Flora to the Dearborns.'

'I was young and desperate, and besotted with

Edmond. He said that the money would secure our future, and when we were rich we would take Flora away from her adoptive parents. I believed him.' Viola's large blue eyes misted with tears. 'I had no choice.'

Flora moved closer to her mother. 'Don't cry, my mummy. We're together now.'

'The Dearborns took Flora,' Alice said thoughtfully. 'And I take it that Jessie was the same Smithson who was hired to look after Flora in Russell Square.'

Flora nodded emphatically. 'Smithson used to drink and hide the empty bottles in the book cupboard.'

Alice turned to her aunt, eyebrows raised. 'Why would Smithson want to look after Flora?'

'I have a feeling that Molly put her up to it. Maybe she viewed my baby as an investment for the future. I don't know.' Viola flicked ash into the grate. 'Anyway, Eddie hired Smithson to attend me at the birth and she was well paid for her services. He'd had a run of good luck at the time, although needless to say it didn't last long.'

'What happened then?' Alice asked eagerly. 'Where is Edmond now?'

'It's not a happy ending,' Viola said, sighing. 'He bet the money we had from the Dearborns on a certainty, so he said, and I was beside myself with rage. I'd been forced to give up my baby and he was risking everything on a horse.'

'I'm so sorry.'

'The animal came in at 100 to 1. Would you believe it? Suddenly we were in possession of a small fortune, and I begged him to use his winnings wisely. I urged him to go to Russell Square and repay the Dearborns every last penny so that they would have to let Flora come back to us, but he made me put on my best gown and insisted that I accompany him to the gaming club in Piccadilly. I tried my best to persuade him otherwise, as I was convinced that he would lose all our money, but once again he seemed to be on a lucky streak and he won every hand of cards.'

'But you didn't come for me, Mummy,' Flora said with a break in her voice.

'It was my intention to do so, my darling. We left the club with more money than I had ever dreamed of possessing, but we were followed and held up at gunpoint.'

Flora's hands flew to her mouth and her eyes widened in horror. 'Oh, no!'

'What happened then?' Alice laid a comforting hand on Flora's shoulder, but she could see from Viola's bleak expression that the outcome was not good.

'Eddie thrust the money bag into my hands and told me to run. I did just that. I ran and ran, in and out of the back alleys like a feral cat until I reached the rookery where we rented our room. I waited for him to come home. I waited up all night and early next morning I went to look for him. I found him lying in a pool of blood where his attacker had left him.'

'He was dead?' Alice murmured, but she already knew the answer.

'Murdered,' Viola said, shuddering. 'I was distraught. I didn't know what to do and panicked. I just left him there, cold and lifeless and all alone. I walked and walked until I found myself in Doughty Street.'

'You came to our house? Didn't my pa offer to help?'

'The maidservant told me that the family were attending a church service in memory of Miss Viola who had died young. The girl was new and obviously had no idea who I was.'

'But didn't you put her right?' Alice demanded.

'I was still suffering from shock, and I couldn't believe that Jane would have told everyone that I was dead. I think at that moment I wished that I'd been shot to death, too. I'd lost my child and the man I adored. The next thing I remember I was standing on Waterloo Bridge, staring down into the swirling water. I don't know if I would have jumped, but as I stretched out my arms I think I just wanted to fly away like a bird.'

Flora buried her face in Alice's shoulder. 'Don't, Mummy. I don't want to hear any more.'

Viola tossed what remained of her cigarillo into the fire. 'It's all right, poppet. I'm still here, as you see, and all thanks to Mr Considine, who had guessed my intention and dragged me away from the brink of destruction.'

'So that's where you got your name,' Alice said slowly. 'Who is this man who saved your life?'

'Aidan Considine was my saviour in more ways than one. It was he who set me on the path to make my fortune. I owe him everything. He took me to his house in Hertford Street and he looked after me. I don't remember much about those first days; it's all a blur in my mind, but I had youth on my side and he was kind and very patient.'

Alice leaned forward, eager to hear more. 'You married him?'

'We lived together as man and wife.'

'Did you love him, Mummy?' Flora put her head on one side, eyeing her mother like a bright-eyed robin. 'Did you fall in love with him because he saved you from a watery grave?'

Viola laughed and pinched Flora's cheek. 'You are a true romantic, child. No, I didn't love him as I loved Eddie, but I was fond of Aidan, and I respected him. He had a brilliant brain and a talent for making money, even if it was sometimes on the shady side of the law.'

'You talk about him in the past,' Alice said thoughtfully. 'Is he no longer with us?'

'He's not dead, if that's what you mean.' Viola selected another cigarillo from a silver box on the table at her side. 'He's in prison, serving a long sentence for fraud and misappropriation of funds.

I was left to run the businesses that were not sold off to pay the fines set by the court, but I discovered that I have a good head on my shoulders.' She lit the cigarillo and smiled through a haze of smoke. 'We women are raised to think we are subservient to men, and that we have few brains in our pretty little heads, but I've proved that to be wrong. I'm very successful in my own right and my daughter will benefit from my labours, as will you, Alice. We might be the family outcasts, but we will eclipse them all. One day I will have Jane grovelling at my feet and I'll take great pleasure in her humiliation.'

A shiver ran down Alice's spine and the sunbeams that filtered through the small windowpanes were suddenly obscured by a bank of clouds. 'Why bother?' she said in an attempt to lighten the mood. 'You seem to have everything you could possibly wish for.'

'Respectability,' Viola said briefly. 'I'm lauded and fêted for my charitable acts, but people have long memories. The father of my child was a rake and a gambler, and my common-law husband is branded a cheat and a fraudster, both of which make me *persona non grata.*'

'My mummy, don't talk like that,' Flora pleaded. 'It makes me sad. You are kind and beautiful and I love you.' She scrambled to her feet, flinging her arms around her mother.

Viola abandoned her cigarillo and wrapped her arms around her daughter. She smiled at Alice over the top of Flora's curly head. 'Forgive me. I shouldn't burden you with my woes. Now that I have my child restored to me I'm a very happy woman, and you are my brother's child, Alice. I was fond of Clement, even though he always had his head in the clouds. Anyway, you must remain here with us and we'll be a family again.'

'But I have to return to London, Viola. My life is there and I hope to get my job back at Dearborns'. Besides which, I can't let Rory down.'

Viola's expression hardened. 'Your life is worth nothing to the Bishop gang. They want to bleed me dry and if they can't get their hands on Flora again they'll happily turn their attention to you. Molly knows my weak spots – I've already paid her a ransom for Flora, but I know she won't want it to end there – and now we're reunited you are my Achilles heel. You have to remain here where you are safe. I can't allow you to leave.'

# Chapter Twenty-Two

'I'll be missed,' Alice said hastily. 'I'm not afraid of Molly Bishop or her gang. I must return to London. My friends will be looking for me.'

Flora jumped to her feet. 'I want to see Rory. I want him to know that I've found my real mama at last. He would love to meet you too.' She shot her mother a cheeky sidelong glance. 'He's very handsome – you'd like him a lot.'

'I'm afraid that won't be possible, poppet.' Viola's smile faded. 'You are safe here, but I can't let you to return to London, or you, Alice. Hawkins will protect you and I'll see to it that you girls have everything you could ever want, but you have to remain here indefinitely.'

Alice stared at her in amazement. 'You can't mean that, Viola.'

'Oh, but I do. I'm sorry, Alice, but by coming here

you've inadvertently alerted my enemies to Flora's whereabouts. Smithson will tell Bishop that she took you to my home in Hertford Street, and then it's only a matter of time before they trace you here. I only recently bought this house and it's supposed to be my secret hideaway, but they have ways of finding things out.'

'This is ridiculous,' Alice protested. 'Molly Bishop received the ransom for Flora and she has nothing against me. I have to return to London, but I promise to visit you often.'

Viola rose to her feet. 'I'm afraid you don't quite understand my position, Alice. Smithson and Molly Bishop work together. If I were a betting woman I'd wager that Smithson has gone straight to Frederick Dearborn, who is still Flora's legal guardian, and told him that I was behind his ward's abduction. She will then try to extort money in return for information as to Flora's whereabouts.' She paced the floor, wringing her hands.

'But she doesn't know about Hazelwood House.' Alice watched her with a growing feeling of unease. 'Why would Molly be a danger to me now?'

'You don't know her,' Viola said urgently. 'She will do anything and use anyone in order to get what she wants.'

'Even if my pa found out that I'm with you, I know he wouldn't do anything to hurt me,' Flora said stoutly. 'Mama Lydia didn't like me, but he was always kind. He'd be happy that I'd found my real mummy.'

Viola wrapped her arms around her daughter, fixing Alice with a pleading look. 'I cannot let you leave this house, both for your own safety and that of my child. I'll explain fully later, but I'm begging you to remain here with us.'

'I don't know,' Alice said doubtfully. 'I'll have to think it through.'

Viola seized her by the wrist, her fingers cutting into Alice's flesh. 'Give me your word that you won't try to leave. Please, Alice, I'm in deadly earnest.'

That evening, when Flora was safely tucked up in bed, Alice and Viola were seated by the fire in the drawing room. The tapestry curtains were drawn, shutting out a blustery February evening, and the light of many candles added a warm glow to the oak-panelling. They had enjoyed an excellent meal accompanied by a fine claret, and Alice was beginning to feel sleepy, but she was still wrestling with the problem Viola had set her. She sipped her after-dinner coffee, regarding her aunt with a puzzled frown.

'How did Aidan make his money, Viola? Was he a gambler too?'

Viola relaxed in the wing-back chair, a cut-crystal glass of brandy cupped in her hands. 'In property, mainly, and yes, he was a gambler but not at the gaming tables or the racecourse. He played the stock market and for the most part he came out on top, which was how he managed to purchase run-down properties in the East End. He had them refurbished as cheaply as possible and then let them out at extortionate rents.'

Alice stared at her in horror. 'I've heard of landlords like that. In fact, I've been a victim of sorts, and I've seen whole families condemned to sharing dank basements with dozens of others. Is that what keeps you in luxury, Viola?'

'It was,' Viola said casually. 'I admit it freely, but I've been doing my best to make amends. I want you to believe that, Alice. I've spent a fortune improving the properties and making them habitable. I've had the worst cases razed to the ground and constructed new buildings to replace them, but it takes time and eats into my capital. I don't want Aidan to be released from prison only to find that we're bankrupt.'

'I think you're better off without him.' Alice gazed into the flames as they licked round the glowing coals.

'Maybe, maybe not.' Viola sipped her drink. 'I do love him, in my way. It's not like the passion I felt for Eddie, but Aidan saved my life and he was good to me. I think you understand how I feel. I saw the look in your eye when you mentioned Rory Dearborn. I don't know him, but he's obviously made a great impression on you.'

'He's just a friend,' Alice said quickly. 'It was he

who persuaded his brother to give me a job. I owe him a lot.'

'And he's very handsome. Flora said so.'

'Yes, he's good-looking and funny too, although he can be very annoying at times, but I don't want him to think that I'm ungrateful.'

'He'll get over it,' Viola said with a cynical curve of her lips. 'Forget him, Alice. We could build a good life here. You were Flora's tutor, you could see that she continues her studies and I'll show her how to run a profitable business.' She angled her head, eyeing Alice with a knowing smile. 'I might consider going into the printing business – greetings cards and Christmas cards, designed by you. We could make a fortune.'

'That sounds very tempting, but that doesn't alter the fact that my friends will be anxious. They might even go to the police and report me as missing.'

'I think the Metropolitan Police have better things to do than to search for one of the hundreds who disappear daily in the capital.' Viola held out her hand. 'Please, consider what I've proposed. I don't want to keep you against your will, but there is real danger for you if you return to London.'

Alice did not reply immediately: she was certain that Viola was keeping something from her. 'Tell me one thing,' she said slowly. 'Why is Molly Bishop so intent on destroying you and your daughter?'

Viola blinked and recoiled as if she had been slapped across the face. She tossed back the last of her drink. 'Edmond's surname was Bishop. Molly is his sister and she blames me for his downfall and sudden death.'

'She's Flora's aunt?' Alice stared at her in horror. 'But that makes it even worse.'

'The Bishop family head one of the toughest gangs in the East End and after their father was killed in a fight Molly became their leader. Edmond wanted nothing to do with their criminal activities.'

'I still don't understand why she would want to harm Flora. Surely she would want the best for her brother's child?'

'When Flora was born Molly wanted to take her and bring her up as her own, but Eddie wouldn't have any of it. He wanted Flora to be brought up to be a lady.'

'That explains a lot, but how did Smithson become involved?'

'Jessie Smithson is Molly's cousin, but they were always at loggerheads, or so I believed. Eddie was fond of Jessie, which is why he called on her to help me at the birth.'

'So how did she know that the Dearborns wanted a child?'

'I found out later that she was employed by them, working in the sewing room as and when they needed her services. She knew that they were desperate for a child and I think she saw an easy way to make money for herself, even though she knew that Molly wanted to take my baby from me.

Perhaps they had had a falling-out – that's something I'll never know – but Smithson took Flora while I was too ill to do anything to stop her.'

'Why didn't you try to get her back? You married a rich man.'

Viola's eyes misted with tears. 'Aidan wouldn't hear of it. He didn't want children and he certainly didn't want to raise another man's child. I had to accept that I would never see my baby again.' Her voice broke on a sob. 'It wasn't easy. I might appear to be a hard-headed businesswoman, but inside my heart was breaking.'

'I'm beginning to understand, but what I can't work out is why Molly returned Flora to you, and it seems that Jessie is now on her side. Do you know why things are changed so dramatically?'

'Money, Alice. It's always down to money. Molly must have been desperate for funds and she wanted revenge.'

'That's terrible, Viola. What you say makes sense, but where does Jessie Smithson fit in to this now?'

'I imagine that Molly bought Jessie's loyalty, such as it is. Jessie always had a fondness for strong drink and she'll do anything providing the price is right. Taking you to Hertford Street was a deliberate ploy, and if you return to London now they won't stop until they've dragged the information as to our whereabouts from you. Molly knows how to make people talk.'

'I'm so sorry. By coming here I've put Flora in danger, and that's the last thing I'd want.'

'It wasn't your fault. Jessie would have found out about Hazelwood House eventually. I paid the ransom without question, but I know very well that Molly won't give up. She has no affection for Flora, and I think it amuses her to allow me to get to know and love my child, and then she will strike again. She will bleed me dry and get her revenge for Eddie's death by ruining me and breaking my heart all over again. Flora is just a pawn.' She reached out once more and this time Alice held her hand in a firm grasp.

'I'm not afraid of Molly and her roughs, but Flora is my flesh and blood too. As to my remaining here, I've brought nothing with me. I have only the clothes I stand up in.'

'You may have the pick of the garments you brought with you from my London home. We're about the same height and size, so take what you want.'

'That very generous of you, Viola. I'll remain here for a while on one condition.'

'You're learning, my dear. We all have to fight for what we want. What is it you require?'

'I need to write to Carrie and let her know that I'm all right and will return soon. The Youngs will be worried about me.'

'What about your mother, Alice? Won't she be concerned?'

'I'll ask Carrie to call on her and put her mind at rest, but I think Mama will be too busy trying to cope with her new husband to give any thought to me,' Alice said, chuckling. 'Did you ever meet Horace?'

Viola pulled a face. 'My dear, I spent most of my time avoiding him. Whenever he came to the house I hid in my room until he had gone, which was a test of will in the depths of winter. Aunt Jane refused to allow fires in bedrooms and the ones in the main reception rooms were not lit until midday. I think your mother is either very brave or extremely foolish to take such a creature on for life.'

'My feelings exactly,' Alice laughed and some of the tension leached from her. 'But I must send word to my friends.'

'Very well. Write your letter and give it to me. I have to return to London tomorrow and I'll post it in town.'

'You're going back to Hertford Street?'

'I would far rather stay here with you and Flora, but I have businesses to run and I can't leave matters entirely to Philip. Eddie's sister won't try to harm me physically; she's too clever for that. I must act as if nothing has happened and continue as I would normally, but I will return at every possible opportunity.' She reached for the decanter and poured two tots of brandy, handing one to Alice. 'Here's to us, the Radcliffe girls, and to hell with the Bishop gang.'

Later in her own room, seated at the burr walnut

escritoire beneath one of the tall windows, Alice penned a letter to Carrie, explaining her absence. She was not to worry, Alice wrote in bold capitals, adding a postscript asking Carrie to visit Beth in Islington. In the morning she would ask Viola to seal the envelope, but now it was time for bed. It was not until she sank into the depths of the feather mattress that exhaustion overcame her, and despite the worries that lingered in her mind she slipped into a deep and dreamless sleep.

Hazelwood House, as Alice soon discovered, was run by a small staff. Hawkins was in overall charge and a much-trusted servant, having been with Viola for many years. He was a dour soul, not over given to conversation, but Alice knew that she could rely on him as Viola had done. His large stature and lantern jaw would deter all but the most desperate intruders, and he patrolled the grounds with his bullmastiff, Duke, at his heels. In the kitchen Mrs Abbott was queen and ruled over two kitchen maids and a daily woman who came in to do the cleaning. Viola had deliberately kept the staffing to a minimum in order to avoid the risk of gossip being passed on in the village, but the house was not overly large and therefore easy to maintain.

In Viola's absence Alice and Flora settled down to a daily routine. The book-lined study was transformed into a schoolroom, where Alice tutored Flora in English, mathematics and geography, with a nod to history. While Flora pored over her books, Alice used the time to work on her designs for Christmas cards. They worked in amicable silence, with Duke wandering in to sit at Flora's feet, resting his great head on her lap.

Walks in the grounds on frosty mornings supplied Alice with fresh ideas for her artwork. There was a particularly magnificent holly bush in the shrubbery, together with laurel and a fine old yew tree. Milky white snowdrops carpeted the ground at the edge of woods, interspersed with starry golden celandines, and beneath the hedgerow pools of yellow primroses opened their sunny petals in a salute to spring. Alice never went out without her drawing materials, and while Flora played with Duke, who had taken it into his furry head to protect her from everything including squirrels and bold pigeons, Alice would perch on a fallen tree trunk and sketch.

In some ways it was an idyllic existence, free from fear and worry, but Alice could not forget the friends she had left in London. She wondered how George was getting on in the office, and if Frederick had found a replacement for her. Was a stranger seated at her desk beneath the window, taking over the job that had been hers? There was nothing she could do about it, but she worked compulsively, spending her evenings refining her drawings and painting them in delicate watercolours. Viola, at her request, had purchased everything that she needed from Cornelissen's art supplies shop in Great Russell

Street. In the past Alice had often gazed at their window displays, but had never had enough money to indulge her passion, but her aunt was more than generous and Alice wanted for nothing in the way of materials.

Viola returned as often as possible and she was extravagant in her praise for Alice's designs. 'These are too good to be hidden away,' she said, holding up a watercolour that had caught her eye. 'I love this one, Alice. You must have drawn this from life. I feel I could step into the picture and gather an armful of snowdrops.' She put it down and picked up another. 'And this fat little robin redbreast is so cheeky. I love the twinkle in his beady eye.'

Alice brushed a stray lock of hair back from her forehead. 'There is so much inspiration in the country, Viola. I miss London, but it's lovely here.'

Viola perched on the edge of the desk, swinging her booted foot. 'I'm seriously thinking of going into the printing business, but I know nothing about the process or what would be needed to start up.'

'Rory spent some time in Ireland studying the new process of chromolithography, but I haven't seen him since his return.'

Viola stared at her, frowning. 'You'd like to see him again, wouldn't you?'

'I expect he's forgotten all about me.'

'It's springtime, Alice. You've been here six weeks without a word of complaint; although I know you miss your life in London. I really appreciate what you've done for Flora. She's changed into a happy, normal child. Just look at her.' Viola stood up and walked over to the window. 'She's racing around with that huge dog and she's a picture of health. I can't begin to express what that means to me.'

'I do miss my friends.' Alice abandoned her work to stand beside Viola. She smiled. 'You're right, Flora looks wonderful, and she's a bright child and so eager to learn. It's a pleasure to teach her, but I'm afraid she'll soon outstrip me. What she needs is proper schooling amongst girls of her own age.'

'I know,' Viola agreed. 'I've already thought of that and it worries me. I don't want to send her away to boarding school, but a day school is out of the question.'

Alice gave her a searching look. 'Have you been approached by Molly?'

'No, but I find their silence more worrying than overt threats.'

'Perhaps she's given up. Maybe the ransom was all that she really wanted.'

'She'll be back as soon as the money runs out, which is why Flora must remain here until I can find a better way. But I'm afraid I'm being unfair to you, Alice. I can't keep you here.' She returned to the desk and picked up another painting. She studied it, shaking her head. 'Talent like this mustn't go to waste.'

'What are you saying?'

'I'm going to stay here for a few days. I want to spend more time with my daughter, and you need to see your friends. That's what I came to tell you. Pack your bag, Alice. Briggs is in the kitchen enjoying some of Mrs Abbott's cooking, but I've given him instructions to drive you to Five Foot Lane, or wherever you want to go. He'll be back to pick you up at the end of the week.'

'I – I don't know what to say,' Alice said breathlessly. 'Do you think it's safe? I'm not afraid for myself, but if Molly finds out I'm in London she might have me followed and eventually that must lead her here.'

'It's as safe as it's ever going to be. You need this time to yourself, and if you see Rory you can find out more about this chromolithography process, and maybe get him on our side. I've plans for us, Alice. You and I are going to start our own greetings card business. I'll supply the funding and you'll provide the knowledge and expertise.'

Viola's words were still fresh in Alice's mind when she alighted from the carriage outside the Youngs' home in Five Foot Lane. She glanced round with a wry smile. Nothing had changed: the fat tabby cat sunning himself on a nearby doorstep replete after gorging fish heads in Billingsgate Market was in the same position he had been when she last saw him. The ragged boys bunking off school were playing tag, their unshod feet barely touching the cold

422

cobblestones as they raced around, shouting at the tops of their voices. An angry mother came into view, shaking her fist and shouting at her errant son, who immediately fled together with his fellow truants.

Alice realised with a rueful smile that despite the sweet fresh air in the country and the beauty of nature, she had missed the hurly-burly of city life. The noxious odours emanating from the manufactories along the river and the polluted waters of the Thames mingled with the stench of the night soil, as yet uncollected, and the piles of horse dung that carpeted the roads. Even so, it was good to be home for this was where her heart truly resided. She raised her hand and knocked on the door. Jackie's high-pitched wailing was accompanied by the patter of footsteps and Rose opened the door. Her momentary shocked expression was quickly replaced by one of delight.

'Alice, my dear, you've come home.'

Alice stepped over the threshold and hugged mother and child. 'I've missed you all, Rose. It's so good to see you.'

'I was just about to feed this troublesome infant.' Rose scuttled along the passage heading for the kitchen. 'The family are all at work or school, and Harry is in bed asleep, with Skipper at his side, so it's only us and little Annie. Put the kettle on, Alice, and we'll have a nice cup of tea.'

Having satisfied Rose's curiosity with a long and

detailed account of how she had discovered that Aunt Viola was alive and well and that Flora was her long-lost child, Alice was quite exhausted. Rose was suitably enthralled with the tale and bombarded her with questions, which she did her best to answer. Finally, after drinking several cups of tea and eating a slice of bread and scrape, Alice made her excuses and left the house, promising to return later in the day.

A chilly March wind was whistling up the river and the sun was shining as Alice left the house, but there was a hint of spring in the city air and she had a sudden urge to visit the Dearborns' offices in Farringdon Street. Of course, she told herself firmly, it was George she wanted to see, but she had matters to discuss with Rory. She might not be employed there but Frederick had her designs and she was entitled to know whether or not they intended to use them. It would simply be a business meeting; nothing more.

She was almost there when she came to a halt. To walk into Dearborns' as if nothing had happened might be a mistake. She had left under a cloud, and if Rory had wanted to see her he would have made an effort to discover her whereabouts. Rose would have been sure to mention his name had he made enquiries about her, but she had simply rambled on about George, and how much he missed her. She knew instinctively that Rose would be delighted to welcome her into the family as George's wife, but if there was one thing she had learned about herself during her sojourn in the country, it was that George could never be more to her than a dear friend. She hailed a cab and gave the driver her mother's address in Islington. Family must come first, and Ma was entitled to know where she had been and why she had left London so suddenly. Everyone else must wait, even Rory.

Beth greeted her with a cry of delight and a warm embrace. 'You naughty girl,' she said, halfway between tears and laughter. 'You disappeared without trace and it was almost a fortnight before Carrie came to tell me that you were staying with friends in the country.'

She ushered Alice into the front room of the terraced house, and Alice recognised at once the oddments of furniture that had come from the house in Queen Square. Beth, however, had put her touch of magic on the shabby old-fashioned sofa and chairs with sparkling white antimacassars, and the faded mahogany had been polished until it glowed like horse chestnuts fresh from their spiny carapaces. Glass vases filled with daffodils were placed strategically around the room and a coal fire burned brightly in the grate.

'What do you think of my front parlour?' Beth asked, smiling happily. 'It's small, but it's home.'

'It's very cosy, Mama.' Alice took off her mantle and draped it over the back of a chair. 'Are you happy? Is Horace treating you well?'

Beth tugged the bell pull before arranging herself daintily in an armchair by the fire. She folded her hands in her lap and a smile curved her pretty lips. 'He is an ideal husband, which may surprise you, Alice.'

'Ideal? Yes, that does come as something of a shock.'

'You're too hard on him, my dear. In fact, I don't think you gave poor Horace a chance to prove himself. He's kind and gentle beneath that bumbling manner of his. He's very thoughtful and undemanding, besides which he's out at work all day and often remains at the office until late in the evening. We meet over the supper table and he tells me what has happened during the day, and then he reads the newspaper until it's time to retire.' She blushed delicately. 'I am more than content with my lot, dearest, so you mustn't worry about me.' She looked up as the door opened and a small, plump woman bustled into the room.

'You want something, missis?'

'Tea for two, please, Mrs Hoddinot, and some biscuits if my husband hasn't demolished them all.' Beth turned to Alice with a wry smile. 'Horace has a sweet tooth, and Mrs Hoddinot makes the most delicious cake and biscuits.'

'I'll take a peek in the pantry, missis, but the master has an appetite like a gannet, if you'll excuse me for saying so.' Mrs Hoddinot backed out of the room, staring at Alice as if committing every feature to memory.

'She's a treasure really,' Beth said apologetically. 'But she used to be a cook in a local public house, so she is something of a rough diamond. She makes poor little Snippet seem well-trained and quite a treasure. Mrs Hoddinot's manners leave something to be desired, and her language is rather colourful, but she is an excellent plain cook.'

'And she works for next to nothing,' Alice suggested mischievously. 'I'm sorry, Mama,' she added hastily, noting her mother's pained expression. 'I was joking, of course. Horace isn't mean like Aunt Jane.'

'No, indeed. I have had enough of Jane to last a lifetime. It was the happiest day of my life when I walked out of that mausoleum for the last time.' Beth sighed. 'Your poor papa would have turned in his grave had he seen the way Jane treated me. Now, tell me everything, my love. Who are the mysterious friends with whom you were residing in the country?'

'It's as well you're sitting down, Mama. This will come as rather a shock, but Aunt Viola didn't die in childbirth. She is very much alive and young Flora is her natural daughter.'

Beth fanned herself with her hand. 'My goodness, this is a surprise. Are you sure?'

'I've been staying with Viola and Flora for the last few weeks, Mama. Not only is she alive and well but Aunt Viola is a very successful business-woman, and extremely wealthy.'

Beth's mouth turned down at the corners. 'She

always was a bit of a madam. I knew she would come to no good in the end. I doubt she's done an honest day's work in her life.'

Torn between laughter and exasperation, Alice shook her head. 'That's so unfair. You know nothing of her life after Aunt Jane threw her out.'

Beth opened her mouth to reply but was cut short by Mrs Hoddinot, who burst into the room, bristling with indignation. 'There's a gent at the front door what says he wants to see her.' She pointed her finger at Alice. 'I give him a mouthful and told him to sling his hook, but he stepped inside bold as brass. Shall I call a copper?'

Beth turned to Alice in alarm. 'What shall we do? We're three helpless women, and it might be that libertine who ran away with Viola.'

'That's impossible, Mama. Edmond Bishop is dead.'

'Bishop?' Mrs Hoddinot's voice rose to a shriek. 'If he's one of the Bishop gang I'm off.'

Alice leaped to her feet. 'Don't worry, Mama. I'm not afraid. I'll soon sort this out.'

# Chapter Twenty-Three

Alice stepped into the narrow hall, fearing the worst, but even though he was standing with his back to the light she could see that the intruder was not Eric the Axe. 'What's the meaning of this? Who are you, sir?'

He took off his hat. 'What sort of welcome is that?'

'Rory.' There was no mistaking his voice and as he stepped out of the shadows she could see that he was smiling. Flustered and taken off guard, she resorted to sarcasm as a means of defence. 'Answering a question with another question is futile,' she said, repeating Philip Hart's words.

'Is that all you have to say to me?' His smile faded. 'I've spent the last few weeks chasing round London in an attempt to find you.'

Her heart was thudding against her ribs but she

was determined to remain calm. 'Well, now you have. I suppose you still blame me for Flora's abduction, but I want you to know that she is safe.'

'I know that already,' he said, moderating his tone. 'My search took me to Hertfordshire. I've seen her and spoken to her mother.'

Mrs Hoddinot poked her head round the door before Alice had a chance to respond. 'Shall I send for a constable, miss?'

'No, it's all right, thank you. I know this gentleman.'

'Huh!' Mrs Hoddinot emerged from the parlour, standing arms akimbo as she looked Rory up and down. 'Gentlemen don't force their way into respectable persons' homes.' She marched off towards the back of the house.

'Is everything all right, Alice?' Beth's querulous voice was almost drowned by the slamming of the kitchen door.

'You'd better come into the parlour,' Alice said hastily. 'Please don't say anything that will alarm my mother.'

Rory followed her into the room where Beth was seated on the edge of her chair. Her frightened expression dissolved into a smile and she rose to her feet, holding out her hand. 'Mr Dearborn, you startled us.'

'I'm sorry, Mrs Hubble. It wasn't my intention, but I needed to speak to Alice.'

'I understand, and anyway I have to see Cook

about dinner. Please excuse me.' Beth fluttered from the room with a swish of starched petticoats.

Alice faced Rory, regarding him with a steady gaze. She had regained her self-control, but her pulse was still racing. 'How did you know where to find me?'

'I was growing desperate. I'd just returned from Hertfordshire, having missed you by a few hours, and I went straight to the office. George didn't know where you were, but I decided to visit Five Foot Lane on the off chance of finding you there.'

'And Rose told you where I'd gone.'

'Exactly. Once again I'd missed you by a whisker.'

Alice threw back her head and laughed. 'That's really funny because I almost called in at the office in Farringdon Street, but I thought I might not be welcome, so I changed my mind and came here. I could have saved you the bother of coming all this way to find me.'

His expression lightened. 'I've come to apologise.'

She sank down on the sofa. 'For what exactly?'

'For everything.' He pulled up a chair. 'I blamed you for your actions that led to Flora being kidnapped, when in truth you were trying to help her.'

'I was only doing what I thought best.'

'I realise that now, and it's partly my fault that you had a hard time in the office. I should have done more to make life easier for you because you are a talented artist in your own right, and your drawings are unique and incomparable. George told me how you've been treated while I was away and it's just not on. If we employ more women I'll see to it that they are given the respect due to them.'

'That's quite a speech. I don't know what to say.'

'Flora is safe now and for that I'm truly grateful. She showed me the designs you've been creating and they're marvellous. I want you to come back to work.'

The surge of joy that had almost overwhelmed her when he apologised dissipated like morning mist. 'So that's what this is all about? You want me to return to Dearborns'.'

'That wasn't my main reason for coming here today, Alice. Surely you must know how I feel about you?'

'If you'd said that at the start I might have fallen for your flattery, but you were speaking as my employer, not my friend.'

He grasped her hands in his. 'I want to be more than a friend, Alice. I've been a fool and I should have listened to my heart and not my head.'

'If you'd had any genuine fondness for me you wouldn't have behaved as you did. You didn't trust me to do the right thing by Flora, and I can't forgive that so easily.' She snatched her hands away and stood up. Her knees were shaking but the emotion that threatened to overcome her was anger. 'Your only real love is your printworks.'

He stared at her, frowning. 'That's not true. Of course I want you to return to us, but ...'

'Did George tell you that his sister was going to introduce me to Bertie Challoner, your arch rival? Is that why you've taken all this trouble to find me?'

'He might have mentioned it in passing, but that's not the reason I came here today. You're deliberately misunderstanding my motives.'

'Really?' She faced him coolly. 'As it happens I am going to work for another company, but this time it will be my own, or at least I'll have half shares. My aunt is going to put up the capital and I'm going to design greetings cards, and in particular cards for the festive season. I don't need your forgiveness or that of your brother. Flora is my cousin – we're family – and families look after each other. I had every right to take her away from that dreadful school, which should be closed down for mistreating children.'

'Aren't you forgetting one thing?' Rory stood up, meeting her angry gaze with a questioning look. 'Molly Bishop is out for revenge. Viola told me the whole story and she's worried for your safety. The Bishop gang are notorious and ruthless, as we know. And I want to protect you. Is that so wrong?'

'Do you want to protect me or is it your business interests that make you care about so passionately?'

'What do you want me to say, Alice? How can I convince you that my feelings for you are genuine?'

'Are they? You haven't once mentioned the word

love. You like to make a joke of everything, and I never know when you're being serious. I wonder if you have it in you to care for another person more than you care for yourself, or your wretched business.'

'Is that what this is all about? Do you want me to write poetry in your honour? Do you need me to shower you with jewels and red roses? Have I got to serenade you like some lovesick troubadour to prove how I feel?'

'How you feel,' she repeated slowly. 'It's all about you, isn't it? Your brother is the same, so no wonder Lydia behaves as she does. I only hope she can find it in her heart to be good to Mary, and not treat her like a china doll to be set apart and admired but never cuddled or told she was loved.'

'You might find this hard to believe, but Lydia dotes on the child. They both want to adopt Mary, and Frederick is in contact with her aunt.'

'That's good news,' Alice said stiffly. 'I'm glad for Mary's sake, and Flora will be delighted. I just hope Lydia doesn't tire of her new toy.'

'I'm sorry you think so little of me and my family. I'd better go now and leave you to make matters right with your mother. At least she seems happy.' He made a move towards the door and then came to a halt. He turned and strode towards her, taking her in his arms before she had a chance to resist. His lips found hers in a kiss that was almost brutal in its intensity, and just as suddenly he released her.

'If you change your mind or if you need anything, you know where to find me.'

And then he was gone, leaving a faint scent of bay rum and printer's ink in his wake. Shocked, stunned and struggling with unfamiliar emotions, Alice moved swiftly to the window and drew back the net curtain. She heard the front door open and then close and watched him walk away, suppressing the desperate urge to race after him.

'What's the matter with you, Alice?' Beth's angry voice made her turn with a start. Her mother stood in the doorway, her pale cheeks flushed and her blue eyes flashing. 'What were you thinking of, sending him away like that? Are you mad? Can't you see that the man is head over heels in love with you?'

Carrie repeated the same sentiment that evening when she and Alice were alone in the kitchen, washing up the supper dishes. Alice had been careful not to mention Rory's name when she was explaining her absence to Rose and Carrie over supper, but somehow it kept cropping up in conversation.

'You can't keep ignoring him, Alice,' Carrie said, handing her a wet plate. 'He came here looking for you a couple of days ago, and he was clearly distraught because you'd disappeared without a word. George knew where you were, of course, but I'd sworn him to secrecy. He tried to calm Rory's fears but he was failing miserably.'

Alice almost dropped the china plate. 'Did you tell Rory where I was? Is that how he found Hazelwood House?'

'I couldn't lie to him, Alice. He'd been trying to find Smithson and he would have discovered your whereabouts sooner or later.'

'You're right, of course, and Jessie would have gone straight to her cousin Molly and the whole miserable business would have started up again.' Alice put the plate on the table and picked up another.

Carrie flicked greasy water at her. 'Now you're beginning to see sense.'

'I'll get you for that, Carrie Young.' Alice dipped her hand in the rapidly cooling water, but she allowed it to trickle through her fingers. 'You've just told me what I need to do next.'

'I have?' Carrie said nervously. 'You're not going to tip the bowlful over my head, are you? It was only a joke.'

Alice smiled and shook her head. 'You're safe for now but I'll get you next time. It was what you said about Smithson going straight to Molly that's given me an idea as to how to put an end to all this nonsense once and for all.'

'No!' Carrie said, shaking her head. 'You wouldn't.'

'Oh yes I would. I'm going to see Molly Bishop. It's time someone did some straight talking.'

'Alice, no. It's too dangerous.'

'Don't tell anyone, least of all George. I'm going to

find Jessie in the morning while she's still reasonably sober, and she'll take me to Molly. This has to stop.'

The taproom in the Museum Tavern was relatively quiet, but as Alice had suspected, Jessie Smithson was seated in the corner with two of the women Alice had seen on her previous visit. One of them spotted her and nudged Jessie.

'Look who's come to see you. It's the hoity-toity bitch who come with the good-looking toff.'

Jessie rose somewhat unsteadily to her feet and came to meet Alice with a questioning look. 'What are you doing here?' she hissed. 'I thought I'd seen the last of you.'

'I want to see Molly. Where can I find her?'

'You what?'

'I need to talk to her, Jessie. This vendetta can't continue.'

'Dunno what that is, but take my advice and steer clear of Molly Bishop. She's a wrong 'un, even if I says so meself; she being me cousin and all that.'

'Is she still living in Blossom Street?'

'You're nuts. She'll have your guts for garters.'

'It's a risk I'm prepared to take.'

'All right, be it on your own head then, but don't blame me if you come off worst.'

'Never mind that now,' Alice said impatiently. 'I know that being related to both Molly and Flora makes this difficult for you, but I want to make things right.'

Jessie glanced nervously over her shoulder. 'White Lion Street,' she said in a low voice. 'The house with the blue shutters and lion's head doorknocker. Molly bought the place with the ransom money, but unless I'm very much mistaken the cash will have run out by now and she'll be after more, so you'd better watch your step or you'll be the next one locked up in the cellar.'

Alice put her hand in her pocket and took out a florin, which she pressed into Jessie's hand. 'Buy yourself a decent meal. I can't say it's been a pleasure knowing you, but I hope we can put all that in the past.'

'I'm not doing Moll's dirty work any longer. Me and Nat have made it up, and I got plenty of work laying out the dead. They don't give me no trouble and they don't talk back.'

Alice was still chuckling as she left the pub and hailed a cab. 'White Lion Street, please, cabby. The house with the blue shutters and the lion's head doorknocker.'

Eric the Axe opened the front door and his jaw dropped. 'You!' He leaned past Alice to look up and down the street. 'You never come here on your own, did you?'

'I need to see Molly,' Alice said, hoping that Eric had not heard the slight tremor in her voice. She was quaking inwardly but she looked him in the eye with a determined lift of her chin. 'Is she at home?'

'Who is it? Shut the bloody door – there's a draught.'

The sound of Molly's voice was invitation enough and Alice slipped past Eric, who was still peering out into the street. She entered the front parlour without knocking and found Molly sitting by the fire with her bare feet in a mustard bath. Her nose was red and her eyes were bloodshot and streaming.

'What the hell are you doing here?' she demanded thickly.

Seeing the leader of the infamous Bishop gang brought down by the common cold made Alice want to laugh, but she managed to keep a straight face. 'You're unwell,' she said, making an effort to sound sympathetic. 'I'm sorry to intrude, but I had to speak to you.'

Eric barged into the room, red-faced and angry. 'She pushed past me, the little bitch. Shall I throw her out, or shall I give her a good pasting and then throw her out?'

'Go away, Eric,' Molly said, wiping her nose on a crumpled and none too clean hanky.

'Yes'm.' He backed out of the door, glaring at Alice as if he had been cheated out of a pleasurable pursuit.

Without waiting to be asked, Alice took a seat in a chair opposite Molly. 'Have you tried blackcurrant tea? Cook used to make it for me when I had a cold.'

'Blackcurrant tea? Are you mad? What are you doing here?'

'It's very soothing,' Alice said firmly. 'Honey will help if your throat is sore, especially if mixed with lemon juice and hot water.'

'Maybe I'll just let Eric beat you up and toss you out onto the street.'

'You won't do that, Molly. We need to talk sensibly for once; woman to woman.'

'Gawd give me strength!' Molly lifted her feet from the bowl of hot water and mustard seed, and wiped them on a towel. 'Say what you have to say and get out.'

'All right, I'll get straight to the point. I want you to stop your vendetta against Flora and her mother.'

'That woman was the cause of my brother's death. I can't forgive that, and she kept Edmond's child from me. That was cruel.'

'Viola is my aunt,' Alice said slowly. 'She was just seventeen when she ran away with your brother. My family blamed him for seducing a young girl.' She held up her hands. 'I'm not saying that's what I think because I've come to know her and she has a mind of her own. I'm sure she went willingly and that she loved Edmond, as he loved her.'

'She turned him against me.'

'You're not giving your brother much credit, are you? It seems that he chose not to be involved in your criminal activities. You can't hold that against him, or Viola for that matter, and he paid for it with his life. Was it you who sent the villain to rob and murder him?'

'No. I never did such a thing. I loved Eddie, but he turned his back on me, and he sold my niece to that stupid rich cow. If he'd come to me with his problems I'd have taken Flora in and brought her up as me own.'

'You would have condemned her to a life in the underworld, but Edmond wanted her to be brought up as a lady.'

'Eddie was weak and foolish. He would have faced ruin sooner or later. I've seen it happen to gamblers – they never win in the end, and then they resort to drink, or drug themselves on opium or chloral. Viola would have lost her looks and ended up on the streets, selling her body to keep them from starvation, and Flora would have been lost to us all. I want her and I'm going to get her.'

'I thought you were going to sell her to the highest bidder.'

Molly blew her nose loudly. 'That's what I told you, but I never meant a word of it. She's family and we look after our own.'

'Maybe that's true, but Flora is an innocent child and Viola has the means to raise her as Edmond wished. She'll be a well-educated young woman, free to choose her own path in life. Do you really want to drag her down to your level?'

'Her ma abandoned her,' Molly said sulkily. 'I wouldn't have done that.'

Alice met her angry gaze with a straight look. 'I believe you, Molly. I think you have a lot of love to give Flora, but this isn't the way to go about it.'

'Oh, yes, and what do you suggest I do, Miss Know-all.'

'Make your peace with Viola. She's a reasonable woman and she wants what's best for her child. You are Flora's flesh and blood and she's all you have left of Edmond. Why would you want to harm her?'

Molly sneezed and blew her nose. 'You've caught me at a disadvantage. I wouldn't have heard you out if I'd been meself.'

'I think you are being the real Molly Bishop now,' Alice insisted. 'The cruel brutal woman you show the world is not what you are underneath. I believe you when you say you never meant to harm Flora. It was all talk and bluster to make people scared of you.'

'I grew up knowing nothing but life with the gang. Eddie was supposed to take over from Pa, but he wouldn't have none of it. I had to be tough or I wouldn't have survived out there.' Molly lay back in her chair, closing her eyes. 'I'm very unwell. I want you to go.'

'I'll leave when you've given me your word that you won't try to take Flora away from her mother.'

'The kid is scared of me. She'll never forget what I did.'

'Flora has been through a great deal in her short

life, but she's a bright child and she understands more than you think.'

Molly's eyes watered and she buried her face in her hanky. 'It's too late for me to change.'

'That's nonsense,' Alice said stoutly. 'Flora has a birthday coming up soon. Perhaps a party might be a good time for you to see her again and prove that you mean her no harm. If I can persuade my aunt to agree to such a meeting will you promise to come alone and with Flora's best interests at heart?'

'You're a bloody witch.' Molly sniffed and shrugged. 'I ain't promising nothing, but I'll think about it. Now sling your hook. I ain't in the mood for social chitchat.'

As promised, Briggs returned at the end of the week to take Alice back to Hazelwood House. She had said her goodbyes to everyone, Carrie in particular, but her parting with George had been fraught with emotion. He had made broad hints as to his feelings, and Alice had had to make it clear that there could never be anything more than friendship between them. Carrie and Rose sympathised with both of them, but Alice knew that returning to live with the family in Five Foot Lane was out of the question. If she were to set up business in London she would need to find alternative accommodation.

She brought this up over dinner on the evening of her return to Hazelwood House.

'Yes, I see the problem,' Viola said thoughtfully.

'But there's no reason why you can't live in Hertford Street. There's plenty of room.'

'Please say yes,' Flora added excitedly. 'I'd like to return to London, although of course I love it here, Mummy,' she added hastily. 'But I do miss things like feeding the ducks in the park and ice cream at Gunter's.'

'I don't know about that.' Viola sipped her wine, eyeing Alice over the rim of the glass. 'I applaud your courage for bearding the lioness in her den, but do you think she meant what she said, or was she having you on?'

'You saw a lioness?' Flora cried excitedly. 'Did you go to the zoo, Alice?'

'In a manner of speaking I suppose I did.' Alice was quick to see the warning look in Viola's eyes, and she reached for her reticule. 'I have something for you, Flora,' she said, changing the subject.

'Is it a present from London?'

'You might call it that.' Alice brought out the silver filigree butterfly and placed it on the table in front of Flora. 'I don't know where you lost it, but I spotted it in a pawnbroker's shop close to the British Museum.'

Flora snatched it up and kissed the tiny wings. 'How wonderful.' She turned to her mother. 'Rory gave it to me last Christmas. That nasty woman took it from me and I thought it was gone for ever.'

'How clever of you to spot it, Alice,' Viola said, smiling. 'When we return to London we must invite

444

Rory to dine with us. You'd like that, wouldn't you, Flora?'

'More than anything.' Flora pinned the brooch to her bodice. 'I've never had a birthday party, but I heard some of the girls in school talking about the parties they had before they were sent away. Perhaps we could invite Rory to tea and I could have a cake and ice cream.'

'Why not?' Viola said casually. 'It would be advantageous to know someone with so much experience in the printing business. Don't you think so, Alice?'

Alice gulped a mouthful of wine. 'Yes, I suppose so, although I was thinking of asking Bertie Challoner for advice. He and Carrie are very close, and I'm sure he would be only too pleased to help.'

'They'll be our fiercest competitors,' Viola protested. 'It would be madness to believe anything he said. You're good friends with Rory, aren't you? And they're only dabbling in the greetings card business. I'm sure you could use your charm to elicit valuable information, especially about this new mode of printing in colour.'

'Uncle Rory has a soft spot for Alice,' Flora said knowingly. 'I heard my other mama say so, and I love him. We had a snowball fight in the square gardens, and we built a snowman, too. It was such fun.'

'Then you shall ask him to your birthday celebration and we will have a party in Hertford Street.'

Flora clapped her hands, eyes shining. 'Can Mary come too?'

Viola refilled her glass with wine and took a sip. 'Why not? I've no idea how to organise a children's party but I'm sure Alice will help. You could include the Young children too, and perhaps your friend Carrie would like to give a hand, Alice.'

'I'm sure she would,' Alice said, dazed by her aunt's overt enthusiasm.

'Then that's settled. We'll invite the person to whom we were referring earlier, Alice, and Flora will help you make a list of anyone else she would like to attend.'

'I'm so excited.' Flora jumped up from her seat. 'May I go to my room and do it now, my mummy?'

'Of course, dear. Off you go.' Viola waited until the door closed behind Flora. 'Well,' she said, raising her glass. 'Here's to freedom, Alice. If Molly finds it in her heart to forgive Eddie and me, then you will be officially a miracle maker.'

Alice drank the toast. 'Freedom from fear,' she said fervently.

'And let's drink to our new project. I've been working hard on plans while you were in London. In the morning we'll go over them together, and then I intend to return to town and tell Philip to make up the necessary arrangements for a lease on the building I have in mind.'

'Where is it?' Alice asked curiously.

'I own a property in Wheat Sheaf Yard that will be eminently suitable.'

'I'm not sure where that is.'

'It's off Farringdon Street, quite close to the Dearborns' establishment, as it happens. It's very central and a good place to start up a new business.' Viola stared at her over the rim of her glass. 'What's the matter, Alice? I thought you would be more enthusiastic?'

'I am very excited, of course, but I'm rather tired. Would you mind very much if we talked this over tomorrow? I'd like to get a good night's sleep so that I'm fresh in the morning.'

'Of course, darling. I'm afraid I'm like the nightingale – at my best late in the evening and in the small hours. But I'll endeavour to rise early so that we can get a good start.' Viola twirled the stem of her glass between her fingers. 'Before you retire for the night I just want to say that your ideas for Christmas cards are truly lovely. Rory thought so too,' she added slyly. 'Perhaps when you're rested you'd like to tell me what passed between you two in London? I sense a change in you whenever his name is mentioned.'

'There's nothing to tell. Good night, Viola.'

'I'm glad to hear it because we need his expertise. Without you I don't think they'll go ahead with the greetings card plan, for a while at least, so we need to step in as soon as we can. It's tough in the business world, Alice. That's something you'll have to learn very quickly if you're to compete with the male of the species.'

Alice went to her room. She was tired and the feather bed looked welcoming, but she knew that she would not sleep. She undressed slowly and stood naked in front of the tall cheval mirror, seeing her whole reflection for the first time. The house in Doughty Street was too small to allow such a luxury, and Aunt Jane had room enough for dozens of such items, but the mirrors in Queen Square had been tiny, no doubt to discourage the sin of vanity. She cupped her breasts in her hands, closing her eyes as desire ran through her veins like a flame, and the memory of that kiss brought a blush to her cheeks. She would surely go to hell for the wicked thoughts that turned her into a wanton. She reached for her nightgown.

# Chapter Twenty-Four

Alice and Viola returned to Hertford Street, leaving Flora in the care of Mrs Abbott and Hawkins. Flora had protested, but had had eventually accepted her mother's decision with the promise that it was only a temporary measure, and she would be allowed to travel up to London in time for her birthday party.

Alice was delighted with the room that Viola had allocated her. The hand-painted wallpaper depicted dainty birds perching on the stems of climbing roses, and the colours were picked out in the curtains and thick-piled Aubusson rugs. Everything had been done with good taste and regardless of expense, but she was rarely there long enough during waking hours to fully appreciate her luxurious surroundings. Her days were filled with appointments of one sort or another. Viola's dressmaker came to the house to measure her for new gowns suitable for a woman in commerce. She also had meetings with Philip Hart and Viola to discuss the business side of starting a printing works. She accompanied her aunt to the premises in Wheat Sheaf Yard, which had been owned by a printer of catalogues for auction houses and political pamphlets. He had died suddenly, and his widow needed the cash from the sale. Then there were trips to the various warehouses to order the supplies they would need to begin production.

Alice had little chance to brood over her personal life, although in the odd moments when she had time to reflect she tried hard to put Rory out of her mind. His pride had been hurt by her rejection of his advances, but she convinced herself that he would soon recover. He was, she decided, both selfish and shallow, and had only pursued her due to a fit of pique because his charm and good looks had failed to make a conquest. As far as she could see the only genuine affection he felt was for young Flora, and for that reason alone she sent him an invitation to Flora's birthday party.

Having done her utmost to banish him from her heart and mind Alice put all her efforts into her work. High on her list of things to do was to visit Dearborns' offices, simply as a courtesy call. Wearing her new grey worsted gown with a white lace collar and cuffs, and a blue velvet mantle and matching bonnet, Alice knew that she was looking her best, although inside she was quaking at the thought of having to face Rory. It had to happen sooner or later as their paths were bound to cross, and she had rather it was on her own terms than his.

The cab set her down outside the office in Farringdon Street. Having paid the cabby she took a deep breath, squared her shoulders and marched into the building. She walked up to the desk, greeting Beasley with a smile. 'Good morning, Mr Beasley.'

He jumped to his feet, beaming at her with genuine pleasure. 'It's so nice to see you again, Miss Radcliffe. Dare I hope that you are returning to us?'

'I'm afraid not. I've come in the hope of seeing Mr Frederick.'

'I'm sorry, miss. Both Mr Frederick and Mr Rory are at the printing works today, and not expected to return until late this afternoon.'

'Might I have a pen and some paper, Mr Beasley? I'd like to write a note for Mr Frederick.'

'Of course, miss. If you'd care to go into the office you could use your old desk. I'm sure that your former colleagues would be pleased to see you.'

Alice had her doubts, but it seemed churlish to refuse, and in any case she wanted to have a few words with George.

'Of course,' she said, nodding. 'That would be splendid.' She followed Beasley along the familiar corridor and he ushered her in as if she were an honoured guest.

'Miss Radcliffe has come to see you, gents.'

Rawlins popped out from behind his partition

like a jack-in-a-box. His face was a study in surprise. 'Miss Radcliffe? You haven't …'

'No, Mr Wall, I'm not coming back to work here. Mr Beasley said I could use my desk to write a note to Mr Frederick.'

Martin looked up and grinned. 'You can't keep away, can you, Alice? You miss me after all.'

She acknowledged him with a frosty smile as she crossed the floor. 'I miss you as much as you miss me, Martin. You were glad to see the back of me, I'm sure.'

'Harsh words, both uncalled for and unkind.' He held his hand to his heart with a pained expression. 'George, old man, look who has graced us with her presence.'

George had just entered the room, staggering beneath the weight of a large cardboard box, which he hastily dumped on his desk. 'Alice, this is a surprise.' His voice shook with emotion and spots of colour appeared on his cheeks.

'Did she turn you down, old chap?' Martin said in a mocking tone. 'Poor George. You broke his heart, Alice.'

'That's enough, Mr Collis,' Rawlins said sharply. 'Leave the boy alone and get on with your work. Mr Frederick wants that design finished by the time he returns.' Glaring at them, he returned to his desk.

Alice ignored Martin, who continued to aim sly remarks at George, and took her seat. Her note to Frederick was brief, assuring him that Flora was safe and well and happily reunited with her real mother. It would have been better to see him in person, but at least she could set his mind at rest as far as Flora was concerned. She stood up and, ignoring Martin's attempts to attract her attention, beckoned to George. 'Might I have a word in private?'

He flushed scarlet, glancing nervously at Rawlins, but he was seated at his desk, apparently engrossed in his work. 'Of course,' George said in a low voice. 'I'll follow you out.' He sent a meaningful glance in Martin's direction.

'I'll say goodbye then,' Alice said loudly. 'I doubt if we'll meet again, Martin, so I wish you well.' She walked past him with her head held high. He was one person she would not miss, and Rawlins was another.

George caught her up as she reached the vestibule. 'You look very fine, Alice,' he said shyly. 'What is it you wanted to say?'

'I'll get straight to the point, George. I'm starting up a business with my cousin, Mrs Considine.' Alice spoke softly just in case Rawlins had his ear to the keyhole. 'We're going to print greetings cards and Christmas cards. I'm offering you a job.'

His mouth opened and shut soundlessly. He gulped and swallowed. 'Is this a joke? It's not very funny if it is.'

She laid her hand on his sleeve. 'It's not a joke. I'm in deadly earnest. We'll need a man with your experience, and I can't think of anyone I'd rather have to manage the office. You're not appreciated here, I know that. Martin and Rawlins don't give you credit for what you do, but without you they'll be struggling.'

'I – I don't know what to say,' he stammered. 'I don't suppose you've changed your mind about ...'

'No, George, but I do value you as a dear friend. I owe you and your family a huge debt of gratitude for taking me in when I had no home, and quite apart from that I think you will be an asset to our company. What do you say?'

'I say yes.' He clutched her hands, grinning boyishly. 'How could I refuse such an offer? I'll give in my notice now, this minute.' He glanced over his shoulder, following Alice's startled gaze. 'He's back early. Come with me, Alice; we can tell Mr Rory my good news.'

Alice hesitated, wondering if she could somehow slip past Rory, but it was too late. He had spotted them and he came striding along the corridor, a broad smile on his face. 'Alice, this is a nice surprise. Don't tell me you're looking for a job.'

'No, that's not my reason for being here.' She tucked her hand in the crook of George's arm. 'As a matter of fact I came to see Frederick to tell him that Flora is well and happy, but you've probably told him that already.'

He regarded her with a puzzled frown. 'Yes, of course I did. Freddie was beside himself with worry about the child.'

'I realise that and I hope that he and your sister-in-law will accompany Mary to Flora's birthday party in a fortnight's time. You should receive your invitation in the next post.'

'Really? I thought I was last person you wanted to see.'

George cleared his throat and made as if to move away but Alice tightened her hold on his sleeve. 'There's no reason why we can't be friends, if only for Flora's sake. She's very fond of you and she misses you.'

'I'm glad that someone has fond feelings for me.'

George gave an embarrassed cough. 'I really should return to the office, Alice.'

'No,' she said firmly. 'This is as good a time as any to tell Mr Dearborn that I'm poaching his staff.'

'What's this?' Rory looked from one to the other, eyebrows raised.

Alice nudged George in the ribs. 'Go on, George. Tell Mr Dearborn what we've agreed.'

'I – I have to give notice that I'll be leaving at the end of the week, sir. Alice – I mean Miss Radcliffe – has offered me a position in her office.'

'Now I know this must be a poorly timed jest. What are you up to, Alice?'

'I really need to get back to work,' George said urgently.

Alice released her hold on his arm. 'Of course you must. I'll call in to see you on Sunday and we can discuss matters then.'

He nodded, casting a wary look in Rory's direction before hurrying off. Alice folded her hands in front of her. 'I suppose you're wondering what this is all about.'

'You could say that.' He proffered his arm. 'Shall we go to the coffee house across the street and you can tell me all about it?'

She hesitated, trying desperately to control the familiar tug of attraction that had always drawn her to him. 'I'm rather busy, as it happens.'

'Not too busy to take a little refreshment, surely?' His smile would have melted an iceberg and her instinct to flee was overtaken by the desire to spend some time with him.

'All right,' she said reluctantly. 'But I have a meeting to attend in Wheat Sheaf Yard.'

His smile broadened. 'Then it's fortunate that the coffee house is on the corner of that street. I'm eager to hear your plans, Alice. You won't deny me that pleasure, will you?'

'You might not be so pleased when you find out what they are.' She took his arm, steeling herself to remain aloof. It was all a game to him, she told herself as they left the building and crossed the street, but it was impossible to ignore the envious glances of the female passers-by. Women of all ages seemed to fall under Rory's spell. He had only to look their way and smile and they fluttered their eyelashes, blushing rosily as they went on their way.

Safely installed in the dark confines of the coffee

house, Alice concentrated on stirring her cup as she outlined the plans for her business venture with Viola. Rory sipped his drink and listened in silence until she came to an end. She looked up and met his intense gaze. For a moment she thought he was going to upbraid her, but to her surprise he threw back his head and laughed, causing some of the patrons to turn their heads and stare.

'What's so funny?' she demanded angrily. 'Do you think it's ridiculous for two women to enter the business world?'

He shook his head, his biting back a chuckle. 'Of course not.'

'Then why are you laughing?'

'What does amuse me is the image of you and your aunt setting out to conquer a world that has been dominated by men for centuries, and the funny thing is that I know you can do it. I've seen that determined glint in your beautiful eyes before, and I know what it means.'

Alice stiffened, trying hard to ignore the compliment. 'But you still think it hilarious.'

'No, I don't.' He was suddenly serious and he reached across the table to cover her hand with his. 'I wish it were otherwise because I've seen your designs and I know what you can do. I also know that Mrs Considine is an excellent businesswoman, and hard-headed as any man, but what happens when her husband is released from prison? Have you thought of that?'

Alice choked on a mouthful of hot coffee. 'I under-stood that he had a few years to serve as yet, and anyway, what difference would that make?'

'As a married woman your cousin's assets belong to her husband. Aiden Considine was well-known in the City, but his reputation was tarnished by sharp practice, which is what landed him in jail in the first instance. Should he secure an early release he might decide that printing greetings cards is not profitable enough and withdraw the funds that his wife had invested.'

'I understand what you're saying, but Viola wouldn't allow him to do such a thing.'

'There's the rub, Alice. The law in that case is on his side. He can do what he likes with his wife's money.'

Alice bowed her head. 'That seems as good a reason as any for a woman to remain a spinster.'

'In your case that would be a terrible waste.' He leaned forward, lowering his voice. 'Did I ever tell you that your eyes are like moonstones? They change colour with your mood.' He withdrew his hand. 'And at the moment they're flashing fiery warning signs, so I'll say no more. If it were up to me I'd invest every last penny I had in your talent, and for what it's worth, I think Christmas cards are the coming thing. Do you still have the copy of Horsley's card that your father gave you?'

Still reeling from his suggestion that Aidan could put an end to her hopes and dreams, Alice nodded dully. 'I keep it in a safe place.' She downed the remainder of the coffee. 'My pa wouldn't want me to give up now. You're right to remind me of his gift. He wasn't a practical man but he stuck to his beliefs and he was true to himself.' She rose from the table. 'But I appreciate your candour, Rory. I know you mean well.'

He stood up. 'But you're still going ahead.'

'Of course I am. Now, if you'll excuse me I have a meeting with Viola and Philip Hart in Wheat Sheaf Yard.' She swept out of the coffee shop with her pride intact and her heart in ribbons.

The printing shop was fully operational and Philip had invited the former staff to attend an interview together with two experienced lithographers. The formalities were over by the time Alice joined them and she was just in time to meet the men in question. She had no fault to find with any of them and after a brief discussion with Viola and Philip it was agreed to take them on for a trial period. Philip was left to make the offers, which were accepted without question. It remained for Alice to explain why she had taken it on herself to offer George the job of managing the office, and neither Viola nor Philip put forward any objection.

When everyone had gone their separate ways, Alice and Viola were left alone in the somewhat dingy rooms with the smell of printer's ink and turpentine still lingering in the stale air. Rory's warning about Aiden Considine's reaction on finding that his wife had used some of his money to start up another business had been buzzing around in Alice's head like a swarm of angry wasps. She repeated what he had said in detail.

Viola took a small silver case from her reticule and selected a cigarillo. She struck a match on the bare brick wall, and lit the cigarillo, exhaling a thin plume of smoke into the beamed ceiling. A spider hanging in the middle of its web took exception to the tobacco smoke and disappeared into a crack in the wooden beam.

'I wouldn't worry about that, darling,' Viola said casually. 'It's not something you should worry about.'

'But it's true, isn't it? A woman's property falls into her husband's hands when they marry.'

'It's absolutely true and the law should be changed,' Viola held up her left hand, which unusually for her was bare of rings. 'We never made it official, Alice.'

'But you said that you and Aiden were married.'

'I say a lot of things, sweetheart, and some of them are true, but if it suits me to lie I will do so without a qualm.'

'Oh.' Alice stared at her in surprise. 'I see.'

Viola raised the cigarillo to her lips and drew on it. 'I've lived by my wits since Eddie died,' she said, allowing the smoke to trickle from her pursed lips. 'It pleases me to allow the world in general to view me as a matron. Aiden did propose marriage, but I refused and he accepted it with good grace. I think he enjoys the fact that we're not shackled to each other like prisoners being transported to the colonies. He is a free spirit, as am I. Does that shock you, Alice?'

'No, as a matter of fact I'm beginning to think that we're more alike than I would have thought possible for mere cousins.'

'Half-cousins, darling. Don't forget I'm a child of your grandpa's second marriage, not that it made any difference to dear Clement, but Robert hated his stepmother and I think it gave him pleasure to treat me like a whore.'

'You told me that before,' Alice said, shuddering. 'But it still shocks me.'

'Don't worry about it. It's all past history, but the future is what matters now. You and I are going to make a fortune with this business.'

'I agree, but perhaps we ought to call ourselves Radcliffe and Radcliffe, or simply Radcliffes' – keeping it in the family, so to speak.'

Viola nodded enthusiastically. 'I like Radcliffes' because one day Flora will inherit my business interests, and as Eddie and I were unmarried her birth certificate is registered in my name.'

'It's probably best if Molly doesn't find that out. I hope I did the right thing by inviting her to Flora's birthday party.'

'It's going to be quite a gathering,' Viola said with a wry smile. 'I've decided to hire Gunter's for the whole afternoon. Flora seems to have taken a fancy to the place.'

'Gunter's ice cream and snowmen,' Alice said thoughtfully. 'I think that will always mean Christmas to Flora.' The memory of tea at Gunter's with Rory and Flora came flooding back, tugging at Alice's heartstrings. She might not have realised it then but she had been halfway to falling in love with him that day, and when he had taken Flora into the snowy square and helped her to make a snowman her heart had gone out to him. It had belonged to him ever since, even though she was loath to admit it to herself.

Viola dropped the butt end of her cigarillo onto the floor and ground it in with the heel of her boot. 'Come along, Alice. We've finished here for the day. We've hired professionals to do the work for us, and now it's up to you to provide the brilliant designs that will sell by the thousand. I'm not in this to peddle a few hundred cards or just enough to break even – we're going to make a fortune in our own right.'

'But what will Aiden say when he comes home?'

'I hadn't given it a thought for years, but I realise now that I can barely remember what he looks like. He stopped corresponding a long time ago, and I don't have time to write more than once or twice a year. I imagine Mr Considine will take what is his and retire to Ireland, where he was born.'

'Doesn't that make you sad, Viola?'

'Me, sad?' Viola laughed and patted her on the cheek. 'You dear, sweet innocent girl – my affair with Aiden ended the moment he was dragged from the court to the cells beneath. I'm fickle, Alice. I fear that I'm flighty like my late mother. I'm a silver butterfly like the one you gave my girl. I don't think I've got the capacity for true love.'

'You're wrong,' Alice said slowly. 'You adore Flora and you'd do anything for her. If that's not true love I don't know what is.'

'Of course, but then Flora is part of me. You'll understand that when you have children. Family is what really matters. You taught me that, Alice, but I only realise the truth of it now. She picked up her reticule. 'Come on, let's find a chop house. I'm starving.'

In the weeks that followed, Alice went to work every day, preferring to use the small office in Wheat Sheaf Yard even though Viola had suggested that she do her designs in the comfort of the study in Hertford Street. Alice had thanked her, explaining that she needed to work closely with George, who was well versed in the technical side of printing. It transpired that he was also something of a poet, and when it came to greetings cards he had a talent for creating the sentiments that were to be conveyed. Alice was able to utilise many of her previous designs and sketches for Christmas cards, and it was decided that they would produce New Year greetings cards as well as Valentine cards, which had proved extremely popular. There were already beautiful embroidered silk cards available for those with the money to purchase them, but it was Alice's ambition to produce equally attractive cards at a price that could be afforded by all. Her head was filled with a kaleidoscope of ideas, all jostling to be transposed onto paper. She thought of little else and spent long hours at her desk, arriving home at night red-eyed and exhausted, with ink-stained fingers and a feeling of fulfilment.

'You're working too hard,' Viola said one evening over dinner.

'There is so much to do, and colouring each card by hand is very time-consuming.' Alice stared at the food on her plate; it looked and smelled delicious but she had little appetite.

'Then we must invest in the most modern equipment.' Viola placed her knife and fork at right angles on her plate. 'I can't have my partner falling into a decline from overwork. It's ridiculous.'

'It would be wonderful to see the prints coming off the press in colour,' Alice admitted, stifling a yawn.

'Then that is how it shall be. We have to keep ahead of our competitors or we might as well give up now. You said that Rory had been to Ireland to study the new process.'

'Yes, he did.'

'He's accepted my invitation to Flora's party, which is tomorrow, in case you'd forgotten. I suggest you tackle him on the subject. Find out what he thinks of chromolithography and if it's worth the investment.'

Alice pushed her plate away. 'It's not really appropriate to talk business at a party. Beside which, there'll be so many people there ...'

'What are you afraid of, Alice?' Viola snapped her fingers at Lipton, indicating that her wineglass was empty. She lowered her voice. 'You know that the man is besotted with you so use it to your advantage. How do you think I'd have got on in business all these years if I hadn't used every weapon I have in order to get what I want?'

Lipton refilled Viola's glass and returned to her position, hovering tactfully in the background.

Alice rose from her seat. 'I'm sure you did what you thought was right, but you must allow me the same freedom of choice. If you don't mind I'll go to my room now.'

'I do mind,' Viola said sharply. 'Sit down and wait for dessert. You shouldn't go to bed on an empty stomach.'

Alice was too tired to argue and she slumped back onto her chair. 'If you insist, but I doubt if I can eat another morsel.'

Viola was silent while Lipton cleared the table. She waited until the maid had left the room. 'You have to stop moping about Rory Dearborn, Alice. You told me that he'd declared his feelings for you, so stop behaving like a prim little puritan and admit that you're in love with the fellow.'

'I can't put my trust in a man who treats everything as a joke. I think he just sees me as a challenge because I didn't fall at his feet.'

'For heaven's sake give him a chance to put things right. Men are clumsy creatures at the best of times. They find it hard to put their feelings into words.'

'Why do you care?' Alice demanded angrily. 'You keep telling me to use men for my own ends, and yet you want me to act like a silly schoolgirl when it comes to Rory Dearborn. You can't blame me if I'm confused, Viola.'

'Use him or marry him, I don't care which, but please make up your mind which it's to be.' Viola drained her glass. 'You'll have a chance to speak to him tomorrow.'

Alice was struggling to think of a response when Lipton entered carrying a silver salver, but instead of giving the contents to her mistress she approached Alice.

'A messenger left this for you, miss. He didn't wait for a reply.'

'Is it a love letter, Alice?' Viola asked, chuckling.

Alice broke the seal and unfolded the paper. The bold handwriting danced before her eyes. 'It's from Rory,' she said breathlessly. 'He's enclosed a leaflet giving details about the process we were just speaking about, and he's returned the designs I did for Dearborns'. He's given them back to me to use as I see fit.'

Viola reached for the decanter and topped up her

glass. She raised it in a toast. 'Here's to a true gentleman, and if that doesn't prove that he loves you I don't know what will. Marry him, Alice. That's an order.'

# Chapter Twenty-Five

Gunter's was packed with guests and Flora was surrounded by children. Rose and Carrie had brought the younger girls, but Alice was quick to notice that Ned, Charlie and Bill were absent.

'They think they're too grown-up to attend a children's party,' Carrie whispered. 'But I think they'll regret it when they hear of the delicious treats they've missed.' She glanced at the tables set with dainty cakes, sparkling jellies and creamy blancmange. Glass dishes filled with ice cream rested on bowls of crushed ice and the centrepiece was a birthday cake covered in snowy white icing.

'Flora seems to be enjoying herself,' Alice said, smiling. 'She's been looking forward to this day. I hope nothing happens to spoil it for her.'

'What could go wrong?' Carrie glanced round the

crowded tea shop. 'Everyone seems to be having a wonderful time.'

'I invited Molly,' Alice said in a low voice, 'but I'm not sure if she'll come.'

Carrie stared at her open-mouthed. 'Why did you do such a thing? What happens if she brings her thugs with her?'

'She won't. At least, I don't think she will. She's Flora's blood relation, Carrie. I believe she was misguided in her actions, but I know she's sorry for what she put Flora through, and deep down I think she cares for her.'

'I hope you're right.' Carrie smiled dreamily. 'I have some news for you, Alice.'

Alice dragged her gaze back from Flora's excited face. 'You don't mean ...?'

Carrie held up her left hand. 'Bertie proposed and I accepted.'

Alice enveloped her in a hug. 'I'm so happy for you.' She released her, eyeing her with a worried frown. 'But what do your ma and pa think?'

'They're resigned to the fact that I'll be marrying into a wealthy family,' Carrie said with a gurgle of laughter. 'They've got used to the idea, and I met Bertie's parents while you were away. They were very kind and didn't seem to mind at all that I'm not from their class.'

'You're every bit as good as them, so don't let anyone tell you otherwise.' Alice squeezed Carrie's hand. 'You deserve to be happy.'

'And what about you?' Carrie's attention wandered and she nudged Alice in the ribs. 'I think the Dearborns have arrived, and Rory is with them.'

Alice turned to see Frederick, who was his usual smiling self, but Lydia was obviously uncomfortable. She glanced round nervously as if she had just entered a den of iniquity, and she tightened her hold on Mary's hand. Despite her reservations, Alice felt her heart lurch when she spotted Rory and, as if drawn together by some mysterious magnetic force, their eyes met. She hurried to greet the Dearborns.

'How kind of you to come,' she said, addressing herself to Lydia, who met her smile with a frosty stare.

'It's for Mary's sake only. She's been asking for Flora.' Lydia looked Alice up and down as if assessing the cost of her magenta-silk afternoon gown. 'We won't stay long.'

'Come now, my dear,' Frederick said easily. 'It's a party and Mary is Flora's guest.' He leaned over, placing a small packet tied with a blue satin bow in Mary's small hands. 'That is for Flora. Go and give it to her, my love.'

Mary looked up at Alice and smiled. 'You're the lady who saved us.'

'She is indeed.' Rory stepped forward. 'We have a lot to thank her for, haven't we, Lydia?' He turned to his sister-in-law, waiting for her response.

'Yes, of course.' Lydia's expression softened from chilly to lukewarm. 'Mary is a delight and we're now her legal guardians. Her aunt was more than happy to allow us to adopt the child, so some good has come out of your interfering ways. We already love her as if she were our flesh and blood.'

Frederick took his wife by the arm. 'Come, my dear. I want to introduce you to our hostess, Mrs Considine.'

'I didn't realise you were acquainted with that woman,' Lydia said in a loud whisper as her husband hurried her away.

Rory grinned in answer to Alice's unspoken question. 'Mrs Considine is well known in the City, but I doubt if that will satisfy Lydia. Poor Freddie will be put through a thorough interrogation when they are on their own.'

'I'm glad that Mary has found a good home,' Alice said, changing the subject. 'She's a dear little thing and your sister-in-law seems genuinely fond of her.' She kept her gaze focused on Flora and Mary, who were dancing up and down and hugging each other. 'I'm so pleased that she allowed Mary to come today.'

'She could hardly refuse. Mary is always asking about Flora and it's obvious they formed a special bond while they were in that dreadful school.'

Alice nodded. 'That's true.' She struggled to find the right words; it was difficult to concentrate on anything other than the fact he was standing so close she could feel his breath on her cheek. Despite the crowded room she felt as though they were set apart from the rest of the guests. The achingly familiar scent of him brought back memories of his kiss, and the warmth of his body wrapped around her like a hug. Moving away was not an option in the press of people, but she had to restrain herself from edging even closer. She took a deep breath in an attempt to bring some sense back to her scattered thoughts. 'Thank you for returning my drawings. It was very kind of you.'

'Morally they're yours, Alice. In any case we've decided not to go further with greetings cards. We've enough business to keep us going for now, although we might decide to review our options in the future.'

She shot him a curious glance. 'Is it because of me? I wouldn't want you to lose business on my account.'

'You have such a tender conscience. If you're to make a fortune you need to have a ruthless streak, like your aunt.' He held up his hands. 'Don't look at me like that. I admire her dedication and her determination to win at all costs.'

'I'm not sure that's a compliment,' Alice said, frowning. 'Viola has had to struggle to survive, and she's overcome everything to come out on top. You can't hold that against her just because she's a woman—' She broke off, realising that his attention was elsewhere. 'What's the matter?'

'I think another obstacle has just walked in,' he said softly.

473

Alice spun round and, following his gaze, she saw Molly standing in the doorway. For once Molly Bishop did not seem threatening, or perhaps it was because she had seen her at her worst, laid low and suffering from a cold like any ordinary mortal. Even more surprising, perhaps, Molly had dressed for the occasion in a fashionable scarlet cashmere Garibaldi jacket trimmed with black braid, worn over an embroidered chemisette and a dark blue wool merino skirt. Her wild curls had been tamed into a sleek chignon and her hat was a replica of an officer's shako. She stood at the edge of the crowd and for the first time Alice realised that Molly Bishop was not as bold as she liked to make out. Without the backing of Eric the Axe she appeared to be smaller and quite defenceless. Alice left Rory and made her way through the press of people.

'Molly, I'm so glad you came.'

'I ain't so sure I done the right thing,' Molly said doubtfully. 'This ain't the sort of place I'm accustomed to.'

'Then it's high time you came out of the shadows.' Alice took her by the hand and guided her to where Viola was standing a little apart from everyone else, watching her daughter with a fond smile as Flora tucked into jelly and blancmange. 'Viola, look who's come to wish Flora well on her special day.'

Viola turned her head and her smile froze. 'So you decided to come?'

'I ain't come to create no fuss.' Molly glanced

round nervously. 'Me and Flora are blood kin and I don't mean her no harm.'

Viola took a step towards her, eyeing the knife that lay in readiness to cut the birthday cake. Alice snatched it up and hid it behind her back. 'Molly means what she says. She wants to get to know Flora and she's promised to reform.' She nodded to Molly. 'You're going to leave the gang, aren't you?'

Molly recoiled, frowning. 'I don't remember saying that.'

'But you inferred it,' Alice insisted. 'You want the best for Flora and you can't achieve that if you're in prison, can you?'

'I'm too fly to get caught.'

'And you're too clever to waste your life running away from the law,' Alice said firmly. She turned to Viola. 'She means it. You have to give her a chance. After all, you loved her brother – you both loved Edmond, and you both love Flora. It's stupid to fight.'

Viola fumbled in her reticule and brought out a silver cigarillo case. She flicked it open and offered it to Molly. 'My head tells me that this is madness, but I did love Eddie, and I know you loved him too. Maybe we can be civil to each other.'

Molly took a cigarillo and waited while Viola struck a match and lit it for her. She blew smoke into the air above their heads and a grim smile curved her rouged lips. 'Well, never let it be said that Molly Bishop ain't able to change for the better.

If you'll let me see the kid sometimes I'll try to be a better person.'

'There, you can't ask more of anyone than that, can you, Viola?' Alice replaced the knife, satisfied that it was not going to be used in anger.

'I'll believe it when I see it happen.' Viola drew on her cigarillo, squinting at Molly through a thin veil of smoke. 'Swear it on Eddie's grave and I'll think about it.'

Molly crossed herself. 'If it makes you happy I swear on my brother's grave that I will never do anything to harm his child.' She flicked ash onto the floor. 'I only wanted to get close to her in the first place, you silly cow. I never intended to do the things I said. I'd cut me right hand off afore I'd harm the nipper.'

'I paid you a king's ransom to get my child back. You owe me, Molly Bishop.'

'Took it and spent it. Bought meself a house in Spitalfields and I lives there amongst respectable folks. You wouldn't want Flora to visit her auntie in Blossom Street, now would you?'

'And what about Eric?' Alice asked nervously. 'Are you still living with an axe murderer?'

'He never chopped no one up with an axe, dearie. He got his name because he used to cut wood for a charcoal burner out Essex way. Eric's got a heart of gold beneath his tattoos. I might even go all the way and marry him, if that makes a difference.'

Realising that she could do no more and that

Viola and Molly would sort out their differences without her help, Alice made her way across the floor to where Rory was chatting with her mother and Horace.

'Thank you for coming, Ma.' Alice kissed her mother's pink cheek. 'You're looking well.'

Beth smiled happily. 'Married life suits me, darling, but you're looking peaky. Are you working too hard?'

'You need to be careful, Alice,' Horace said, nodding. 'Overwork for a lady can lead to debilitation and overwrought nerves.'

'I think Alice looks a picture of health,' Rory said stoutly. 'I don't see Mrs Hubble here today?' he added innocently. 'Is she unwell? Or perhaps suffering from the strain of contributing to her many charities?'

Horace coughed and cleared his throat, a dull flush rising above his stiff white collar to stain his cheeks. His moustache bristled and Alice stifled a giggle. 'My cousin is a righteous woman, sir,' he said angrily. 'She lives by strict rules, which we must all respect.'

Beth laid her hand on his arm. 'Come now, my dear. We all know that Jane is a sanctimonious, penny-pinching bore.'

'I think you're forgetting that it was Jane who purchased our house for us,' Horace said stiffly. 'We owe her a lot.'

'And we're never allowed to forget it.' Beth tossed her head. 'I see cake and ice cream. Do you think I might be allowed to join the children at tea?' She grasped Alice's arm. 'But first I must greet Viola. I'm afraid I treated her rather badly all those years ago when she came to us for help. I could have done so much more for her. I hope she'll forgive me.'

'I'm sure she will, Mama,' Alice said earnestly. She watched her mother and Horace as they made their way to the table where Viola was supervising the distribution of the cake.

'Your mother looks well,' Rory said softly.

'It's hard to believe, but I think she's really happy with Horace.'

'Are you sorry that you didn't go through with it?'

She glanced up at him and to her surprise she realised that he was being serious. 'Of course not. I only agreed to it under duress, and even then I had no real intention of marrying him.'

'And what about George?'

'George?' She followed his gaze and saw that George had arrived and was talking to Carrie and his mother. 'I was never interested in George. He's just a friend.'

'But you want him to work for you, and that means you'll see him almost every day.'

'He wasn't appreciated at Dearborns'. Martin and Rawlins made his life a misery.'

'I would have done something about it had I known.'

'I'm fond of George, but not in the way you're

hinting at.' Alice glanced at the children, who were crowding round Viola as she handed out plates of iced cake. 'I really ought to go and help my aunt. She's outnumbered.' She was about to head for the top table when Rory barred her way.

'Wait a moment, Alice.'

'I think we've said all there is to say.'

A slow smile lit his dark eyes and he held her hand, raising it to his lips. 'Not quite, my love.'

'I – I don't understand.'

'You will.' He released her abruptly and moved forward, clapping his hands together. 'Ladies and gentlemen and children, may I have your attention, please?'

A sudden hush fell upon the gathering. The children stopped eating, gazing at him with faces smeared with chocolate and dribbles of ice cream. Viola extricated herself from the crowd of small people, pushing her way to a gap between the startled partygoers.

'What's this all about, Rory? Is there a fire or a riot outside? I demand to have a good reason for this interruption.'

'The best of reasons,' he said, pointing to the red velvet curtains at the back of the tearoom. 'There is something that is very close to the heart of the woman I love, and I want to share this tribute to her with everyone here.'

At a signal from him the waiter who had moved unnoticed to the back of the room tugged on the gold ropes. The heavy curtains slid back to reveal a life-sized tableau representing the Christmas card that Alice's father had purchased to celebrate her birth.

A gasp of surprise and appreciation rippled through the onlookers and Alice's hands flew to cover her mouth. She gazed at the festive scene, which was faithful to the last detail.

'You did this for me?' She looked Rory in the eyes and saw the reflection of herself surrounded by a halo of light.

'I wanted to show you how much I love you, Alice. You once accused me of taking things too lightly and never being serious. Well, I'm serious now.'

A collective intake of breath was followed by silence and Alice felt rather than heard the fluttering of hearts as she glanced around at the expectant faces of friends and family. The small child on the tableau seemed in danger of toppling off the dais as she forgot herself and leaned over the edge, only to be yanked back by her stage mother. The waiters hastily drew the curtains and the tableau disappeared from sight.

Rory went down on one knee, clutching her hand to his heart. 'I've loved you from the start, my darling Alice. Will you do me the honour of becoming my wife?'

Alice caught sight of Flora, who was jumping up and down and waving her arms. 'Say yes, Alice. Please say yes,' she shouted.

Halfway between tears and laughter, Alice nodded her head. 'Yes, Rory. I will marry you.'

He leaped to his feet and pulled her into his arms, kissing her enthusiastically to a roar of approval from everyone present. Releasing her gently, he put his hand in his breast pocket and took out a small shagreen box. He flicked it open to reveal the pearl ring. 'I bought this for you as a Christmas gift, Alice, but it will have to do until you choose a more suitable diamond engagement ring.'

She gazed at the pearl ring with tears in her eyes. 'I love it. I don't want diamonds, Rory.' She held out her left hand. 'This ring means more to me than any precious jewel because you chose it for me.'

He slipped it onto her finger and drew her once again into his arms to a tumult of cheers and clapping.

Beth was the first to reach them and she wrapped her arms around them both. 'I'm so happy for you,' she said, misty-eyed. 'Welcome to the family, Rory.'

He kissed her on the cheek. 'Thank you. I promise to take great care of your beautiful daughter.'

'Congratulations,' Horace said, slapping him on the shoulder. 'But I'm not sure what Jane will say when she hears about this.'

Beth tapped him gently on the wrist. 'It has nothing to do with Jane, my dear. Alice's future happiness is all that concerns me.'

'I'm glad you've learned how to stand up to Jane Hubble at last. She's a prig and a bully.' Viola elbowed Beth out of the way. 'I wish you all the happiness in the world, Alice, my love.' She spun round to face Rory and poked him in the ribs with the tip of her finger. 'You will have to deal with me if you fail to make my niece happy, Rory Dearborn.'

'There's no danger of that,' he assured her, but was caught off balance and almost bowled over by Flora, who flung herself at him.

'I'm so glad,' she cried, hugging him. 'You really will be my uncle now.' She let him go, only to throw her arms around Alice. 'This is the best day of my life.'

Alice kissed her fondly. 'And there'll be many more to come, darling Flora.'

Molly pushed George and Carrie out of the way as they attempted to add their congratulations. 'As I'm young Flora's aunt I suppose I'm part of this family too.' Her tone was harsh, but she was smiling. 'Where's the champagne?'

Flora put her head on one side, eyeing her aunt with a knowing look. 'You'll have to behave yourself then, Aunt Molly. You're not going to spoil things for Alice. This is a happy ending like they have in storybooks.'

Rory slipped his arm around Alice's waist. 'This isn't the end – this is just the beginning.'

# My First Christmas Book

I've always loved Christmas – I start looking forward to it in September when the evenings draw in and there's a touch of winter in the air. I think my fascination with the festive season must have started when I was very young as I could recite the whole of ''Twas the Night Before Christmas' when I was two years old – although I had to take my late mother's word for that – and I can still reel off most of it. I love Christmas films, especially *It's a Wonderful Life* and my favourite story, of course, is *A Christmas Carol* by my all-time favourite, Charles Dickens. I have several copies of the book and I think I've watched every movie version ever made. I always have tears in my eyes at the end of both *Home Alone* films when Macaulay Culkin is finally reunited with his mother, and I still love pantomime. I was in one aged twelve, dancing in the chorus and understudying the cat in *Dick Whittington*. The girl who played the cat was a real trouper and so I didn't get to wear the furry cat suit, but we did get paid five shillings for each performance. We toured church halls in north east London and once ventured south of the river. I remember that it snowed on the way home – very Christmassy.

All that aside, I'm a pushover when it comes to buying Christmas decorations for the home and the tree. Tinsel, glass baubles, Lametta . . . they bring out the magpie in me and I have a cupboard under the eaves filled with treasures waiting to be brought out once a year.

I'm quite traditional in my preparations too. I make the Christmas cake in October and douse it in brandy before wrapping it up in a blanket of cling film and foil for all the lovely flavours to mature. I used to make the Christmas puddings, but to be honest the shop-bought ones are so good these days, it's easier to buy them. I start buying presents and put them away – but that sometimes backfires and I can't find them – and above all I love choosing Christmas cards. It was this that first inspired me to write my first Christmas book.

I researched the history of Christmas cards and discovered that the first card was commissioned by Sir Henry Cole (the first director of the Victoria and Albert Museum) and illustrated by his friend, John Callcott Horsley, in 1843. Only one thousand were printed in the first run and hand-coloured, but the cards cost a shilling each, which was roughly equivalent to five pounds today. The central illustration of three generations of a family, including children, raising a toast did not go down too well with the Temperance League, despite the scenes on either side depicting the poor being given food and clothes. Even so, the idea caught on, aided by the Penny Post and the introduction of lithographic printing in 1873, which enabled cards to be mass produced in colour. The Christmas card as we know it today was born and I, for one, love them.

If all this sounds very materialistic and worldly, I haven't forgotten the real message of Christmas – Peace on Earth and Goodwill to All Men – and in the immortal words of Tiny Tim, 'God Bless Us, Everyone.'

Dilly

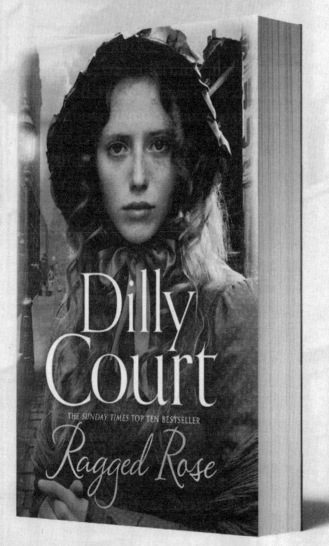

Will Lottie Lane ever
live the life she dreams of?

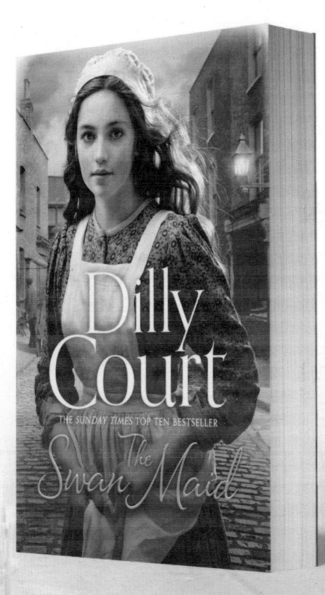

'As always Dilly keeps
you absorbed right to the end'
*Choice*

Look out for news online
about Dilly's brand
new novel,

The
Button Box

coming early 2017

f /DillyCourtAuthor
www.dillycourt.com